Books of Merit

National Library of Canada Cataloguing in Publication Data

Clarke, Austin, 1934–
    Choosing his coffin : the best stories of Austin Clarke.

ISBN 0-88762-117-1

I. Title.

PS8505.L38C48   2003   C813'.54   C2003-900120-2
PR9199.3.C526C48   2003

Cover and text design: Gordon Robertson
Editors: Patrick Crean / Sarah Williams
Front cover photograph: David Middleton / *January Magazine*

Published by Thomas Allen Publishers,
a division of Thomas Allen & Son Limited,
145 Front Street East, Suite 209,
Toronto, Ontario M5A 1E3 Canada

www.thomas-allen.com

At Thomas Allen Publishers we are working with suppliers and
printers to reduce our use of paper produced from ancient forests.
This book is one step towards that goal. It has been printed on 100%
ancient forest–free paper (100% post-consumer recycled), processed
chlorine- and acid-free and supplied by New Leaf Paper; it has been
printed with vegetable-based inks by Transcontinental Printing.

ONTARIO ARTS COUNCIL
CONSEIL DES ARTS DE L'ONTARIO

The publisher gratefully acknowledges the support of
the Ontario Arts Council for its publishing program

We acknowledge the Government of Ontario through the
Ontario Media Development Corporation's Ontario Book Initiative

07 06 05 04 03   1 2 3 4 5

Printed and bound in Canada

Native ancestors warned the day that the tar washed in
like a fierce lava and filled the grooves of natural artistry,
    Clear tar as it comes
    It shall hover over you, like lead
    Make your insides morose
    Until you can no longer hear the beating of the drum.

· · ·

For now I vow to lift my pencil, grind it to its short end
Strengthen my muscles until I pry open the shell
Scrape the tar, polish the bark
Smash it violently, and purge it from the memory
Prepared to live under a delicate tapestry that
Allows me to breathe completely.

— GINA SILVESTRI, "Desert Island Song"

CONTENTS

THE
DISCIPLINE

. . . and I remember, from the time I could remember, seeing my grandmother go behind the velour curtain that separated her "room" from the rest of the house in which we all lived, father, mother, brother, and me, punctually at eight o'clock each Saturday evening. The moment she closed the blind, the BBC overseas news came on. She disappeared from us for the rest of that night; and from behind the black curtain her words would join us as she mumbled verses from the Bible: ". . . in the dark they dig through houses, which they had marked for themselves in the daytime." It seemed as if her voice was meant to discipline the rest of us. I grew up with this discipline.

And I remember her leaving the house at twenty-nine minutes to eleven each Sunday morning, in rain and in sunshine, dressed in a black sharkskin dress down to her ankles, her arms manacled by the white ruffs, her neck ruffled also, and starched and ironed; black, worn Bible in her right hand, a walking cane in her left, she'd go to matins at St. Barnabas Anglican Church.

And I remember her returning to the house at one, to the house now filled with the smells of Sunday dinner. I walked with her many times: as a boy, and even as a man. It took her a longer time to walk back. And on the way back, she would walk and stop, and talk and inquire about children and chickens and women in the family way, and men in hospital or overseas. She urged all the women, even those who were not mothers, to attend the Mothers' Union meeting at the church on Monday evenings. She would hold my hand during these Sunday journeys, for support, and then for love . . .

The office in which I am sitting now with this woman is in Toronto, on Bay Street, on the fourteenth floor, in a building whose insides and offices have been renovated to make them look old and English, and financial. This office is stiff and panelled. The woman wears black, and she's as stiff as the ruffs on my grandmother's dress. She has just told me that her services will cost me one thousand dollars, "two hundred now, the rest in four equal instalments," to get me off the charge—"as a favour," she adds, using the same voice I had heard my grandmother use when she gave me a Kit-Kat chocolate bar. But unlike my grandmother, she said it like a curse. "I have to charge you this amount because the charge is a serious one."

Everything in this city is a charge. I am charged when I park my car in front of my house. I am charged to get permission from the city to park my car. I am charged if I do not get permission from the city. I am charged and I am charged.

The car suddenly stopped working the day after I was last charged . . .

"I don't understand why you're telling me all this about the way your grandmother brought you up. We all had mothers and grandmothers." She says that as if it was a shame.

She lights a cigarette, swings her chair without making any noise. This office is so silent! It could be in Barbados in the small house at eight o'clock on any Saturday evening. She faces the buildings that look through the window at us, that show us the backs of women sitting at typewriters and moving behind screens; and all I have to talk to now is the silk of her black waistcoat. She is dressed like a man in a three-piece suit. The back of her head and the sweep of her hair make me feel her strength and her force, and I think of her as a man. Her muscles jerk each time I tell her something I remember. I'm giving her the evidence.

Without turning to face me, she says, "You're charged with assaulting your son."

"Assaulting my son?"

"You beat him up."

"I slapped him."

"You struck him with your fist. You smashed his ribs."

"I disciplined him."

"You didn't discipline him. You assaulted him."

"I disciplined him."

"You brutalized the boy. The Crown will say you brutally assaulted him."

Her back is still turned to me.

. . . and I remember that I came home one day, the end of the month, with my salary from the Civil Service, inflated as my ego. And my grandmother made me sit down, and she counted the money and gave me my share. One-fifth. She handed my mother her share—she didn't mention my father!—and then she told me, "Because you're drawing a paycheque, it don't mean you is a man. You hear me?" And each payday she did the same thing, with the same regularity as her ritual of going to church. She met me at the door the next morning as I was leaving for work, and she told me, "You are still a child in this house. You will always be a child, no matter how old you get."

I remember I came home after twelve-thirty one night, and even though I was twenty-eight years old, she said, while my mother remained silent in her approval, "You is not the man in this house! You hear me? Your father, wherever the hell he is, is the *only* man here." She never gave me a key. The door was locked after that at eight o'clock each night.

I remember that when I passed the Cambridge school-leaving certificate which qualified me to enter the Civil Service, I decided to leave her, to escape her discipline, to emigrate, to have a better life in Canada. The moment I entered the front door, my grandmother came up to me, and I thought she had come to congratulate me. But in her hand was an old shoe. It belonged to my father. She held the shoe, tapping it nervously against her long dress, not smiling, with my mother sombre beside her; she said, "Once a child, always a child." And then, with no warning of her change of attitude from anger to resignation, she broke into the hymn, one of her favourites, "O God, Our Help in Ages Past!" And when she could not remember the words, she improvised with "always a child, always a child . . ."

"Really! I don't understand why you're telling me all this," the woman lawyer said.

The large chair wheeled around and I was facing her neck, with a long linked gold chain around it and an oval watch attached. I thought I could hear it ticking. It was soft and appeasing and soothing, that magnificent small oval piece of ticking and tocking workmanship. It hung between her breasts. On the outside. And it rested in the softness of her white silk blouse that had long sleeves with ruffles at the wrist. I imagined the muscles beneath the soft silk. She held the golden oval, grabbed it really, and immediately became tense. I could see the time. "Twelve-thirty," she said as if she didn't want it to be so late. "You're living in the past. We need to know the present."

I was trying to make her see that the defence of my present predicament and the future was to be found in my ability to remember the past.

"Everybody has a past." She ran her hands through the thick files on her desk and gave them importance. She touched the bundles the way men riffle through huge sums of money. There were only three files on the desk. All the other briefs and opinions of jurisprudence she had already committed and kept in her head. I looked at her head. It was a large, prominent head.

"Forget your past. In the present circumstances, talking about your *case*, I would suggest that you forget everything about your past . . ."

And I remember thinking of those days in Barbados, secure because I knew where I would end up when I crossed the threshold of a door and ventured into the bright mornings or the sensual evenings; and I knew whom I would meet at the end of each street on each journey; I knew whom to call a friend and whom to ignore as enemy, and whom to love. I remember how bold and caution-less I was, for there was no need for pretences; and I knew that when I died I would be protected on all sides in the brown pol-ished box, in the warm, thick welcome of dust and ashes.

"Oh, by the way," she said, "please wear something dark, a con-servative suit." I knew I was dismissed, although she did not say so.

I missed my stop after that. On the way from her office to Millicent Street, where I live, where there was a bus stop beside the traffic lights two blocks before the street, I missed my stop.

In all the time I've lived in this neighbourhood of Italians, Portuguese, Indians from Pakistan, and Canadians who leave for work before the sun rises, I have never been sure which stop is mine.

In the summer and the warm weather, when I can see better, when the afternoons are not cold, bare, and white, and the road is not hazy as if covered by cigarette smoke and every house in the row looks alike, I can see for blocks and blocks in the almost West Indian road. And at six o'clock, behind the thick curtain like my grandmother's "room," I imagine I'm not in this cold, cramped, cruel country.

When I reach home, the lock on the front door is frozen. My hand is as frozen as the slit of the brass-coloured key. And when I put the key into the slit, I still have another key to put into the door. Two keys for one door. For this is a neighbourhood and a fortress of night latches and double locks, deadbolts and suspicion.

The children of this neighbourhood come out as numerous as Dutch bulbs in the summer; as thick as weeds after a rainfall in Barbados. And none of these children have ever said good morn-ing in a language I could understand. Some of them, boys mainly, I would find sitting on my new couch with their shoes melting, run-ning on my new carpet, bought on time from the Italian store where I paid more because I did not understand his English after he asked me if I had a language black people spoke. And my own son would be in their midst, eating popcorn and potato chips, speaking English like an Italian, and Italian too; and leaving the crumbs and destroying the pattern on the carpet.

My son is their age and equal in their language and customs. He can no longer understand the way I speak. And my discipline to him is the same as their language to me. With a new anger strange to me, and a new resentment each time I tell him the couch costs money, each time I tell him about my grandmother, he says, "I was born here."

My wife leaves at ten in the evening for the Toronto General Hospital, to work as a nurse's aide until seven or eight the next morning. Our lives overlap and crisscross and barely touch except for one day on weekends.

My son has again brought his friends into the empty house. He has his key. He's a man. He cannot get into the house without his own key, for I get home from my cleaning job at five. Until four in the afternoon I run messages for the large firm on Bay Street where my woman lawyer works; and from nine at night and before they arrive the next morning, I clean their offices. My immediate boss, the manager, is a woman. Her boss is a woman, and the head of the firm is a woman. The only worker under me is another man, from Jamaica.

I'm a man with a wife and a son thirteen years old and a house with two locks on the front door. And still I have to justify and explain to a woman who does not know me, and scarcely knows my ability to pay one thousand dollars in fees, that I have the right, as my grandmother had the right, to chastise a child; and that biblical blessing drove me to discipline him.

Yes, as a man I drove my hand across his face when he continued to disobey me. And the blow blew this profanity from his lips: "You're a damn old-fashioned West Indian. I was born here, man! I am a Canadian." He said that to me. The words flew from his lips, and the uncontrolled venom and spit struck me in the face, cold as I was always cold when I stood for minutes on the exposed front step, trying to open the two locks.

I was still cold when I recovered from the words of his new allegiance. *I am a Canadian* repeated itself like an echo, like a bad dream that you have more than twice in one night. In the dream he said, *You are dead and I am alive. I am alive but you are dead.* My right hand was driven to the nearest object. We were standing in the kitchen, feet apart, for when he said it, spit from his mouth touched me, we were so close. My hand lifted the chair, and I felt the impact of wood on flesh and the disintegration of the chair in the rage and disappointment . . .

I did not sleep that night. I lay on my back in thought; and when the thoughts weakened, I heard the breathing beside me and the murmuring of speculation and hope. My wife had just come to bed. "That would teach him. Canadian children don't have any damn discipline." She pronounced the word *dis-cip-pline.* "I see some o' them where I works talking back to their mothers in front o' strangers, making the poor mothers shame-shame-shame, and even I myself have to turn my head aside, I does be so shame too!"

The boy had said nothing. He didn't say another word about being a Canadian. I had made dinner for the two of us, which I did on Mondays, Tuesdays, Wednesdays, Thursdays, and Fridays. And he sat on the same couch that had caused the problem, and I on the other chesterfield, and together we watched television in silent disinterest until ten o'clock, when he got up and left the room.

"I pay the 'lectric'ty and the taxes, as you ask me," she said, making an inventory of her own thoughts. "I wish we could go home for Christmas. What I won't give for a sea-bath!"

The moment he had left I felt very old and alone. I had tried to read the anger in his face while he was still sitting there, to see if it held such ugly disregard for me; whether throughout the long cowboy movie he had refused to look at me because we were really strangers already at war. I had tried to read his breathing and his disposition each time he changed the position of his elbow, or when he stretched his legs out and drew them in again, with each firing of the cowboy's gun. But he had remained quiet. Once I even forgot that he was in the same room with me. "You know what I would like right now?" my wife was saying. "I could eat a flying fish with a dog!" I could not see exactly where the blow from the chair had landed, but I imagined it had struck him somewhere between his armpit and waist. His height and my own against his made that the likely spot. The tiresome voice of the woman beside me went on about flying fish and sea-baths . . .

The next morning he said, "I'm going swimming." The city had recently opened a swimming pool and he and the neighbourhood children went there almost every day after school. I knew he could not swim; I thought I knew he could not swim; so I wished he would drown, and then I wished he would not drown.

A week passed. My son came and went. There were no crumbs and footprints on the carpet and couch. But one afternoon I saw footprints of different sizes on the bathroom floor, along the hall and right up to the front door. My son and his friends probably had not come at all. I couldn't think he would again disobey my orders, even though I began to feel that a mark on a couch or carpet was such a small thing to lose my temper over. So these footprints on the imitation marble floor of the bathroom, and along the linoleum of the hall to the front door, could have been my own or my wife's or his, or my dream or my thoughts. They could have been my wish for his disobedience so I could punish him.

He did not drown. And on the weekend he was still with us, and my wife was lying on her stomach, beside me lying on my back. I always lie on my back. The calypso music on the radio was soft. I was remembering my life back home, and comparing that life with this house full of furniture and electric kettles and electric blenders, equipment invented to make life easier. Cobwebs were in two corners on the ceiling. The left corner and the right corner. She turned over and noticed them and explained, "With all the things this place have to offer, don't you know I have never find a cobweb broom to buy!"

"Northamerica have all the opportunities a man could ask for, girl . . ."

The calypso was one we knew and had danced to; and we listened, her leg on mine, between my legs, hands around my neck in a Boston crab of rough passionate love.

"The boy in? Go and look in his room and see if that hard-ears boy get home yet. Northamerica have everything but dis-cip-pline . . ."

I remember my wife talking as if she was dreaming, prescribing a life for her child in this city she had never grown to like or under-stand. On the one night we were home together long enough to be together, she spent all her time repeating this epiphany. That was on the Saturday night after the calypso program on CHIN-FM had ended.

Now, in all this time, remembering and relating my personal evi-dence to the woman in the law office, and remembering the inci-dent with my son, I am still just inside the door with the two locks, standing on the linoleum, leaning against the wall that separates my house from the one through which I can hear music and heavy footsteps all hours of the night and day. I am hearing the music now. And I imagine that I can smell curry. Footsteps go up and come down; and as they come down, they seem heavier . . .

I take off my winter coat and start to think of the dark suit she told me to wear in the morning at ten o'clock. And I think about asking the woman, my immediate boss, for time off; and my bank manager, Mrs. Janet White, for a loan; and Miss Elizabeth Camp-bell at the mortgage company for a little more time. I am thinking about how I would have to approach all these powerful women in my life for help and sympathy. I think too of my grandmother as I began to think of all these women controlling my life. My thoughts are as hands clinging to my grandmother's long black dress when she moved over the rocks and fallen tree branches on the path to church.

I remember when I got out of bed and went downstairs and walked along this same hallway where I'm standing now, counting all these women I must approach for mercy. Just as I reached the bottom of the stairs to look into his room, I heard the neighbours' curried music coming through the wall, as if the mallets that struck the drum had pierced its skin.

It was eight o'clock.

My wife had just got home. I was late leaving for work.

I passed over the noisy, cracked linoleum, opened the inside door to look through the peephole in the outside door with its two locks, when I saw the disfigured faces and eyes and large noses.

Through the peephole my vision of the faces was like a photograph held too close to the nose. I saw the shining buttons and the shining belt and the eyes that looked like glass; and I worked my eye down to the bottom of the hole to make the hole larger, to show me more focus on this disjointed watery picture. And it was at the bottom rim of the hole, like an eye filled with water, that I realized I was looking into the eyes of my own son.

"Pearl! Pearl!"

She came down, like the heavy bass drum next door, dressed in white oxford shoes and pink panties, and with her pink uniform ripped from the neck down to the bottom of her belly, as if she was giving rapid, violent birth. The zipper had stopped five inches from the bottom of the dress. My two screams had caught her in this Caesarean act.

I remember the police officer coming in, after showing the boy inside, and after the young Canadian woman had entered. The police officer closed the door, and I felt my living room turn into a cell. It was the first time I had been so close to a policeman. I smelled the serge and the leather and the polish of his uniform. And I saw the butt of his gun. I thought I smelled brass.

My wife sat with one hand to her mouth and the other closing the unzipped uniform. The policeman stood at attention beside my son, beside the Canadian woman.

I remember the policeman with his eyes riveted to the carpet. The Canadian woman looked around the room. Through the hallway door. Seeing things she wanted to memorize. I saw her blue eyes flick over two charcoal pictures. The Rasta man and the Rasta woman. I remember my son standing between the policeman and the woman. He looked calm, protected, and distant. He looked as though he had chosen new parents. A new allegiance grew among the three of them. I remember hearing all the words the Canadian woman spoke. She used a calm, unpointed, objective monotone. She was talking about persons I had never met. But all the time, she was talking about me and my wife and the boy. I tried to follow each word, but I couldn't understand the language she used. The meaning of her words was above my head. She was speaking in English but her words came from books. She must have read these books many times and had memorized their texts.

"As his teacher, I cannot minimize the moral responsibility I have towards the social development of this boy, and even though he may have parents of his own, in a nuclear sense, I would be remiss in my responsibility if I didn't take it upon myself to take this action and seek to protect this boy, with the help of the authorities, from the environment in which, through no fault of his own, he now finds himself, and . . ."

In all this remembering time, I am still no farther inside my house than the few feet behind the front door with the two locks. From that morning when the policeman came with the summons charging me with the criminal offence of assault to cause bodily harm towards my own son, I have been walking in a dream of frightened thoughts. I read the *Star* to see if any other father has been found guilty of this offence, to find the sentence imposed on those fathers. And when I find it, I feel lost. I find myself walking up and down at work, at home, in the kitchen as I make dinner, in front of the house, in the cold whitened garden where all the roses and flowers I've planted have now become stiff brown pieces of stick. And each time I'm inside the house, I find myself turning the pages of the Bible to the Book of Psalms, just as my grandmother had been driven to her gold-leafed Bible to search for a verse to dull the thorns of her life and problems. But I'm not seeing the words or the blurred wisdom of those words, for they are the same as the counselling the young Canadian woman had given me . . .

"Your Honour, I have been the boy's teacher in grade seven, grade eight, and grade nine. His reading difficulty was the first clue to more basic problems in the home. Lack of security and so on. When I asked the boy to read 'My father is at work,' he would read 'My father gone from home.' This invention in perception led me to investigate the assault. I noticed that his attention span was getting very short indeed. We care for all our children. So I called in the police and the authorities of the Children's Aid Society in order to protect this boy."

"Thank you, Miss Barron."

"And begging your pardon, Your Honour, if I may add one more point. The boy was an active participant before this happened. He has a healthy socialization tendency. Only after the problem I mentioned did I discover that his jaw was broken and . . ."

"Thank you."

". . . I examined the boy two days later. I found lacerations to his left side. Between the second and fifth ribs. In my estimation, the blow was caused by a sharp object. From close range."

"Could this blow or these blows have been delivered by a human hand? A fist, doctor?"

"A savage fist, Your Honour."

My wife was wearing black. I did not tell her to accompany me in this colour of the funeral, but she wore black because she wanted to look like a "good mother." She was sitting about ten seats away from me. I saw her raise her neck. And I saw her eyes fall on my hands. Your Honour had just mentioned "a human hand." My hands were in my lap, one covering the other.

The room was large and bright. There was a photograph of Queen Elizabeth II. Something like a coat of arms or a seal, complicated in its intricate design and workmanship, was on the wall. Out of the jumble of colours, white, blue, red, and green, I could distinguish only an animal. A lion. There was another animal too. It had one horn. I had never seen one of these before, and I didn't know its name. Words were at the bottom of the seal, in a foreign language. I could read only the MAL in this message. I did not know what it meant.

The room was panelled. It was quiet even when they were talking. There was a Canadian flag on the wall. A police officer stood beside me, outside the wooden dock. They had put a chair for me to sit on. I was the only person in this dock. Every now and then the men and the woman lawyer who represented me would say something in whispers. They were all smiling. I felt they all liked me because they smiled each time they looked at me. I smiled too.

A man who called himself the Crown said, "This vicious disregard for civilized practice and the principles of this country . . ." He looked at me, then he looked at the jury. Then, pointing at me without looking at me, as if he knew where I was, that I would not run from the dock, he said, "You have heard the evidence . . ."

The judge, Your Honour, sitting above us, dressed in black with some purple in his uniform, whispered something to my lawyer in Latin, then he looked at me and looked at my son, who was sitting across from me in the same row, without a wooden dock to protect him. It was as if he and I were in argument, as if he was put there to debate against me, just as I had seen people on television sit, pro and con, professional man and con man; or in the legislature down on Queen's Park, where big men in three-piece suits argue among themselves across a floor of thick carpet.

The minister of my church, the St. Clair Baptist Church, a Jamaican immigrant, had come, he and four "sisters" from the congregation, and was sitting on my left. Each time the man who called himself the Crown said "this vicious disregard," and each time the black-and-purple-uniformed judge spoke, I looked to make sure they were still there, the minister with his highly polished mahogany skin and the four sisters, and my wife dressed in black as if she was attending my grandmother's funeral. The six of them held down their heads as if they were ashamed of me each time the Crown repeated "this vicious disregard."

Another Canadian woman was now speaking. She wore spectacles with plastic frames. Her hair was thin and long and blonde. It was the same colour as her spectacles. The makeup on her lips and cheeks was red. When she spoke, the red lipstick became her words, wide, round, sharp, high, and violent. "I have seen many cases of assault in my fifteen years as a social worker at Children's Aid. And I can say that never, but *never*, have I seen a case as violent and brutal as this one. I have known many coloured immigrants. I sympathize with their problems. I understand they have to adjust to our way of life. And to our way of doing things. To our civilization and our society. But never, never, *never* in my fifteen years have I seen . . ."

I looked up in time to see her take a piece of pink tissue from her purse. She applied the pink tissue to her eyes, then her mouth. She looked now like a woman catching her breath lost by a sudden punch in the ribs.

"I've made two trips to the West Indies, to Jamaica. For a first-hand, on-the-spot study of the cultural and social derivation of West Indians living here. My conclusion is that what we in the profession refer to as the predisposition for cultural violence among West Indian parents has its origins in the harsh historical background of slavery."

When she said that, my black suit tightened around me. The dock was now a vial. I became a specimen inside that vial. I could feel the sweat under my armpits. I became embarrassed that I smelled. I could not remember if in the rushed order of dressing I had rubbed the penis-shaped bottle of Right Guard over the thick black hairs under my arms. I was sweating. The room was cold but I was hot.

The Baptist minister and the four sisters shifted on the long wooden bench. My wife stirred too. I knew she stirred because I know that noise, that special rustle of her shiny silk dress. I knew she moved the same instant I became hot.

I jumped up.

I saw my grandmother. I saw my mother. I saw the clean little house. I saw the whiteness of the sun on the road brutalizing it at the hottest time of the afternoon. The round clock on the wall said eleven. I saw myself on that warm road. And then I saw myself painted in their words, in the dock, by this brittle lady.

"Nooooooo!"

My lawyer, in a black tailored suit, with her gold chain catching the light, got up from her chair and tried to cut me off; and then in a quick movement she apologized to the Crown and to Your Honour in case I said too much, to make it bad for her and for myself.

"No!"

"Take the accused away."

It was the man in the black and purple, Your Honour, as they called him, who said it. He used a voice that was the same as if he had said "take the cream away." He must have used those four words many times. There was no emotion, no passion, and no feeling in his manner. I thought he would have at least turned red, become angry, and used the same anger in his words to match the faint protest in mine, or even to match my passion. I wanted to remind him that I was this boy's father, and as his father, I could discipline him. My grandmother had disciplined me.

The court was silent now. My word of objection had cut the tongues of the court's sanctity and whispering dignity.

"Take the accused away."

I was a dried fallen leaf that had to be raked away to keep the lawn pleasant and clean. Or a piece of banana skin kicked out of the way with a well-timed movement of the foot, to remove its slight danger from the path of law-abiding pedestrians who take cleanliness and safety for granted.

The police officer came into the wooden dock. With a sharp, short, practised click, he snapped the handcuffs on. With an equally practised push, I was on my feet and moving down to the basement cells, as if I had been released through a trapdoor.

As I was going down, they were still saying things about me.

"This is his first offence, yes, sir."

"He is at present employed."

"Checking with his neighbours, we learn that he stands in his garden talking to the flowers."

"I would recommend a light sentence, under the circumstances, Your Honour."

"They must be taught a lesson, that they're not back in the West Indies."

"I recommend a psychiatric examination."

I don't know where I am. I don't know who I am. All I know is that I'm alive. I'm on a white bed, a bed with white sheets and a white pillow. And I'm wearing white pyjamas. I'm happy, and sometimes I feel like a child, like the little boy I was in Barbados when my mother would say, "Boy, you hungry? You hungry, ain't you?" And she would feed me, and I would smile and eat whatever she gave me. It is like this, in this large room, with many small beds, all the same size; the same cleanliness, the same white walls with no pictures or photographs on them; and the bright clean light from the fluorescent bulbs. A woman with hair that is strong and looks like bright steel comes every morning since I've been here. She's dressed in a rich brown suit and brown shoes that shine. She asks me questions, and I give her answers by nodding my head and smiling.

"You feel lonely in this place, don't you?"

I nod.

"You hate this place, don't you?"

I nod.

"You don't think very much of our system, do you?"

I nod.

"The system has done you harm, hasn't it?"

I nod.

"And you would do anything, anything at all, to get back at the system, wouldn't you?"

I nod.

"Even destroy it?"

I nod.

"You're paranoid. Don't you feel paranoid?"

I nod.

"You're a violent man. You resort to violence to settle things which you can't settle with words, don't you?"

I like to nod my head. I nod nicely and properly, so she won't be annoyed with me. I like to make her happy. Each time I answer, she smiles and looks very happy and writes something in her book. And she smiles with me after she's written these things in her small, black-bound book. I smile and she smiles some more.

"Now, let me ask you a serious question, may I?"

I nod.

"If your son left potato chips on the couch or on the carpet again, would you knock him down? You would knock him down again with your fist, wouldn't you?"

I nod.

"If he came home later than ten o'clock on weekends, after you told him to get home by eight, you'd hit him with a chair again?"

I nod.

"And even break four or five or six ribs, more than the first time?"

I nod.

I like this small lady with the steel-grey hair and brown suit and shiny brown shoes. She reminds me of my grandmother.

One morning she brought me a chocolate bar. It was a Kit-Kat. My grandmother bought me a Kit-Kat chocolate bar every other Saturday when she went into town. I used to suck off all the chocolate until the bar became the colour of bone, and then squeeze the rest of the bar between my tongue and the roof of my mouth until it disappeared. It lasted longer that way.

"If you had your way, if you had it in your power, you'd do something to the teacher, wouldn't you? You don't like her or the lady from the Children's Aid Society or the entire legal system, do you?"

I nod.

And it went on like this, these happy mornings with the lady in the brown suit who'd come and ask me these questions. And I'd nod my head all the time because I wanted her to like me and feel I was a God-fearing, obedient man. I wanted her to feel that I myself was obedient as a little boy, just as I wanted her and all the others to feel that my own boy should be obedient.

And then one morning she didn't come.

When I was tired of waiting for her and was about to drop off into a doze, they awoke me and told me to dress in my black suit, that I was going back.

They made me think I was going back home.

When I got back, I would clean up my garden and paint the front door black and take off one of the locks because it was getting warmer now and I wouldn't freeze my fingers to the bone trying to find two slits in the door. And I was going to see the minister and thank him for losing two days' work by coming to court. And I would see my wife again, and we'd lie on the bed on Sunday nights and listen to calypso music and look at the ceiling to see if the two cobwebs were still there. And I would write to my mother and tell her that if God spare life, we'd be coming home for Christmas with the boy. She has never seen the boy.

And I would call my employer and tell her I'm sorry but this nice lady in the brown suit was asking me a lot of questions and I wanted to be nice to her; and since there were so many questions, I had to skip work longer than I expected . . .

But they put me in the back of a yellow panel truck, locked from the outside. It had chicken wire and bars at the top of the back door. Through this I saw people disappearing from me, getting smaller, Chinese and Japanese in size; and even those walking with their faces towards me were going backwards. They were all cut into small pieces by the mesh and iron on the door. Travelling backwards like this, I was soon between tall buildings and then underground. I could smell the fumes and the dust of parked cars and moving cars, all of which came through the chicken fence. I started to hear music.

It was loud music. Music from my part of the world. Did the neighbours who cooked curry and others know I was in this yellow panel truck? Underneath the heavy, stubborn, and fatal beat, a beat like the determination of tribal drums—heavy wooden gavels on thick animal skin, and iron on iron—I heard these words: *Yuh running and yuh running and yuh running away . . . Yuh can't run away from yourself . . . Must-have-done, must-have-done something wrong . . .* I was in a dream. I was in an elevator. The light around me became better. I was now standing between two police officers. I wished the lady in the brown suit was with us.

The two police officers did not speak with me; and in the elevator they looked up and down, reading the numbers of the floors to themselves; and there was only the humming, the soft murmuring of strained muscles in the contraption that made the elevator rise with our weight.

I was back in court. When I entered, all conversation was cut short and heads turned in my direction.

The words of the underground song, *Yuh running and yuh running and yuh running*, and the gavel beating on heavy skin and the striking of iron on iron were running through my mind, and I began to feel the peace in the soft questioning voice of the lady in the brown suit.

The man dressed in black and purple began to speak. It was a soft voice, a voice I felt contained no feeling and no sympathy; a voice that I had now become used to hearing, even when people said the worst things about you, when people made decisions that sent you unemployed through a winter, when they said things that did not help you understand that your telephone had been cut off, that your heat had been stopped . . .

". . . in view of the psychiatrist's report, it is the opinion of the court that the defendant shows a tendency . . ."

He must have been talking for some time, for I could see my lawyer lean back, sit up, shift in her seat, adjust to the ceremony of words.

And then it was over. It was over without a stir. It was over without confusion. In this room with no wind blowing, with the temperature even at the breathing point, with no coughing or clearing of the throat, in this court with the same sacred stillness of the front pews in that church in Barbados, it was over. The last words that I heard from the man on the raised seat, Your Honour, were, "Five months . . ."

Five months. *Yuh running and yuh running and yuh running away* . . . And the lady in the brown suit who had been so understanding in her questions passed before me in a swift brown blur. And then my lawyer came over and rested her hand on my shoulder. I could not even feel the weight of her heavy acknowledgement. Her perfume was like the Kit-Kat chocolate bar. She was looking above my head, not into my eyes; and just as I looked around to see if there was someone behind me, I saw my son walking between my wife and the Canadian teacher.

The oval watch on the heavy chain was uneven around my lawyer's neck and it shone like a large teardrop. Her hand felt heavier now. The heaviness of the hand became the total weight of my body.

"Do you have anything to say to me?" She seemed to be in a hurry. Perhaps she had another man to defend.

I shook my head.

"Good!"

I nodded.

"If you'd like me to talk to the judge and tell him what you've been telling me about your grandmother . . ."

I shook my head.

"Good! Because you've already been sentenced."

"Can I talk now?"

"You can't talk now."

All the way back out, into the past of the dust and the fumes and the mysterious music with its heavy gavel on thick skin, travelling over the details of the previous journey, small people walking backwards, their faces punctuated and cut up into pieces through the perspective of the chicken wire and bars, I was now sitting between two new police officers. They were protected from me.

Both my hands were tied behind my back with handcuffs. I could not stand up to face the former journey and see the progress of the curving steel of the streetcar tracks, or the potholes in the city streets, or the hairpin bends I was now taking. The yellow panel truck slid off the parallel steel lines and forced me against one of the two police officers who twinned me in the locked embracing manacles. His hand touched mine to keep me upright and from falling on my face; and the force of that touch jerked my recollection to that path through fields of sugar canes and hedges of guinea grass and peas, winding like this road, more voluntary but disciplined, in the firm grasp of my grandmother's sticky hand as we walked that last mile to face the church.

CANADIAN EXPERIENCE

He passed in front of the oval looking glass in the hallway on his way out to go to a job interview, his first in five years. His eyes and their reflection made four. He stood looking at himself, laughing, and seeing only a part of his body in the punishing reflection the glass threw back at him. He was cut off at the neck. He laughed again. This time, at the morbidness of his own thoughts. The knot of his tie was shiny with grease. He did not like himself. He was not dressed the way he had hoped to appear, and his image was incorrect. This made him stop laughing.

So he went back upstairs to his rented room on the second floor at the rear of the rooming house. His room was beside the bathroom used by the two other tenants on that floor, and the actress on the third. He wanted to inspect his hair in the better light in the bathroom. But before he reached it, he heard the spikes of a woman's heels clambering down the rear staircase; and as he listened, they landed on the muffling linoleum in the hallway; and before he could move, the bathroom door was shut. He was not laughing now. It was the actress. She was between parts, without money, and she spent more time in the bathroom when she was waiting for auditions than on her parts after she was called.

He unlocked his door and left it slightly open, to wait his turn. He wanted the actress to know he was next in line, but he didn't want her to feel she was welcome. She liked to talk, and talk bad things about her friends, her father, and her stepmother, and laugh about her career, for hours.

He had to change his clothes. He thought of what else he had to wear. Suddenly, he heard the heavy downpour of the shower as the water began to rain. So he closed his door.

The heavy ticking of the cheap clock became very loud now. It was the only one he could afford, and he had bought it in Honest Ed's bargain basement nearby. He had got it mainly for its alarm, not for its accuracy of time, which he had to check against the chimes of a rock-and-roll radio station. And he listened to this station against his better musical taste whenever he wanted to be punctual, which was not often. For he had been between jobs a long time.

This morning he had to be punctual. He was going to a job interview. It was on Bay Street in the business district of banks, brokerages, and corporations. For all the time he had lived in Toronto, this district had frightened him. He tried to pacify his fear of it now by laughing at himself.

The job he was hoping to get was with a bank. He knew nothing about banks. He was always uncomfortable and impatient whenever he had to go into one. The most he had ever withdrawn was twenty dollars. The most money he had ever deposited at one time was fifteen dollars.

For three months now he had been walking the seven blocks from his rooming house on Major Street to the reference library on Asquith Avenue to sit in the reading room, to watch the women, and to peruse the classified advertisements in the pages of the three daily newspapers, searching for a job. The *Star* contained about ten pages of advertisements which the paper called "Employment Opportunities." He was looking for a job, but he was still able to laugh at his plight. The *Sun* had three pages. Sometimes he would see the same "employment opportunities" in this newspaper as in the *Star*'s pages, and he would laugh at their stupidity of duplication. He needed a job. And the *Globe and Mail*, which he heard was the best newspaper in the country, carried three pages. He did not like the *Globe and Mail*. There was no laughing matter about its print, which was too small. And it dealt with subjects beyond his understanding and interest, and even if he could smother a laugh about that, he found its small print bad for his deteriorating eyesight; and this made him depressed and bitter. Besides, the "positions" which the *Globe and Mail* advertised were for executives, executive directors, industrial engineers, administrators, and managers of quality assurance. He did not know what they meant. But he knew he wanted a job. Any job. His clothes had been in the cleaner's for three months. And his diet, which had never been balanced, was becoming even more topsy-turvy with each succeeding month of joblessness.

It was, however, with an irony he himself could not fathom, but about which he smiled, that in the very pages of the *Globe and Mail*, he had seen the advertisement of the position for which he was promised an interview this Monday morning at ten.

His noisy clock, with a silver-painted bell on it—and white face and black luminous numerals of the Roman kind—said it was nine o'clock. His room was still dark.

The *Globe and Mail*'s ad read

> We require an energetic junior executive to take a responsible position in our bank. The successful candidate must have a university degree in business or in finance, or the equivalent in business experience. Salary and benefits to be discussed at interview. Reply to the 14th floor, 198 Bay Street.

He was a man past thirty. But he could not, even at his age, argue about taking this "junior executive" position, because his desperate circumstances were forcing this stern necessity upon him. Junior or senior, he had to take it. And when he got it, he knew it would not be a laughing matter. Necessity would make him bitter, but thankful.

He had only to remember his old refrigerator, which took up one-eighth of the floor space in his room, and which hissed and stuttered whenever he turned on his electric hot plate. The refrigerator contained a box of baking soda, which the talkative actress had told him would kill the smells of food; and on the top shelf,

cold water in a half-gallon bottle that had once been full of grapefruit juice; a half-pint carton of homogenized milk, now going bad;
his last wieners from Canada Packers, like three children's joyless
penises; six hard slices of white bread in soft, sweating plastic
wrapping from "Wonder Bread," which was printed below the
blonde-haired child who persisted in smiling on the package. And
three bottles of Molson's beer. In these circumstances of diving
subsistence, he knew he had nothing to lose—and nothing to laugh
about—concerning the "junior executive" position.

He did not come to this country to attend university. Experience of the world, and his former life at home in Barbados, were
his only secondary education. He had come here against his father's
bitter wishes. But he was not unschooled. He had attended the St.
Matthias Elementary School for Boys, Barbados. *For Boys*, he wanted
to remember to impress upon his prospective employers, since he
was not a believer in the North American practice of having boys
going to school with girls. He was a staunch supporter of the
British system of public-school education. And even though the
St. Matthias Elementary School for Boys was not, in fact, a public
school, it was, nevertheless, a school that was public.

He laughed at his own cleverness of nuance and logic. Besides,
no one in Toronto would know the difference. Toronto has Upper
Canada College for boys, Trinity College School for boys, Bishop
Strachan School for girls, and Havergal College for girls. Boys with
boys. And girls with girls. His logic was so acerbic and sharp, he was
already laughing as he heard himself telling them that St. Matthias
Elementary School for Boys was a . . .

But he stopped himself in the tracks of his hilarity: "I had-better
leave out the elementary part and just tell them St. Matthias School
for Boys." It was a satisfactory and imaginative rendering of the facts.
Bay Street, if not the whole of Canada, he had discovered in his time
here, was filled with people of imagination. The actress had been
telling him that imagination is something called a euphemism for lies.

But he couldn't take the risk of failure. Failure would breed cyn-
icism. Instead, he had said on his application that he was educated at

Harrison College, "a very prestigious college for men in Barbados, and founded in 1783, which produced the leading brains of the leading leaders in books and banking, of the entire West Indies." Had he twisted the facts a little too much? Laughter and reassurance about the imaginative men on Bay Street, liars, as the actress called them, and who became quick millionaires, told him he had not stepped off into fraud. Not yet.

In spite of his lack of formal education, he still considered himself well-read. Newspapers, magazines, the *Star* newspaper, and *Time* magazine did not escape his daily and weekly scrutiny, in the reading room of the public library, even long after he had fallen upon the debris of the country's unemployed, in *decreptitude*. "Decreptitude" was the word he always used to the actress when they talked about their lives, to make her laugh about the apparently irreconcilable differences between her and her own society, and also to impress her that he was not a fool. He had heard the word first on television.

And he listened to CBC radio and shortwave broadcasts of the BBC World Service, and watched four television news broadcasts each night: two Canadian and two from America. And he never missed *60 Minutes* from New York. Except for the three times, consecutive Sundays, when he had lain flat on his back, fed off the public welfare system, on a public ward in the Toronto General Hospital "under observation" for high blood pressure.

"Pressure in my arse!" he told the actress, who visited him every day, as he explained his illness.

In the eight years he had spent in this country, he had lain low for the first five, as a non-landed immigrant, in and out of low-paying jobs given specifically to non-landed immigrants, and all the time waiting for amnesty. One year he worked distributing handbills, most of which, because of boredom, he threw into garbage pails when no one was looking, and laughed, until one cold afternoon in February when his supervisor, who did not trust immigrants, carried out a telephone check behind his back, only to discover that none of the householders on the fifteen streets he had been

assigned to had ever heard of or had ever seen the brochures advertising "Pete's Pizza Palace, free delivery." After that mirthless firing,
there were three months during which he laboured as a janitor for
the Toronto Board of Education—incidentally, his closest touch
with higher learning; two months at Eaton's as a night-shift cleaner;
then two months at Simpson's as an assistant shipping clerk; until
the last job, five years ago, held along with Italians, Greeks, and
Portuguese, cleaning the offices of First Canadian Place, a building
with at least fifty floors, made of glass, near Bay Street, where he
was heading this morning.

He laughed to himself as he thought of his former circumstances.
For he was ready for bigger things. The murmuring refrigerator
could not, within reason, be any emptier.

So with the bathroom next door still occupied, he looked at
himself, at the way he was dressed. It was nine-fifteen now. His
bladder was full. Whenever he had important things on his mind,
his bladder filled itself easily, and more unusually heavy, and it
made him tense.

He wished the pink shirt was cleaner. He wished the dark brown
suit was a black one. He should not wear a yellow tie, but no other
ties he had would match the clothes on his back. And he knew
through instinct and not through Canadian experience that a job of
this importance, "junior executive" in a bank, had to be applied for
by a man dressed formally in black.

Laughter, his father had told him many times, a smile at the right
moment, melts a woman with even the meanest temperament. He
tried this philosophy now, and his attitude changed for the better.
He put more Vaseline on his hair to make the part on the left side
keener, for he had dressed in the dark. And now that the autumn
light was coming through the single glass pane, which he could not
reach even standing on a chair and from which he could never see
the sidewalk, he could see that the shirt he had thought was slightly
soiled was dirty.

The morning was getting older, the time of his appointment
was getting closer, the hands of the bargain-basement clock were

now at nine thirty-five, and he had only twenty-five minutes left to go; and he had to go badly but couldn't, because the actress was still inside the bathroom, singing a popular song. He could hear the water hitting against the bathtub and could imagine her body soaked in the hot beads of the shower, and he could see the red-faced ugly blackheads painted red, at the bottom of her spine. He had asked her once what they were, and she had told him "cold sores." He thought they had something to do with winter, that they came out in winter. He laughed each time she told him "cold sores." He could see them now, because he had seen them once before. Yesterday too, for thirty-five minutes counted by his loud, inaccurate, cheap alarm clock, he had heard the torrents of the shower as she washed herself in preparation for an audition.

He had nothing to do now but wait. The shower stopped like a tropical downpour and with a suddenness that jolted him. He opened his door. He listened. Mist floated out of the bathroom door, and he brushed through it as if he were a man seeking a passage of escape through thick, white smoke. And as he got inside and could barely see his way to the toilet bowl, there she was, with one leg on the cover of the bowl, which she had painted black, bending down, wiping the smell of the soap from between her legs and then the red, rough dots of bruises on the bottom of her spine, which she insisted were cold sores. When she named them first, he thought she had said "cold stores." He could understand that. "Cold stores," "cold storage"—it was enough to make him laugh.

"Oh, it's you."

He could not move. He did not answer. He could not retreat.

"Close the door and come in."

The mist came back, thick and sudden as fog swallowing him, debilitating him, blinding him, and he lost his vision. But he could see the lines of four ribs on each side of her body, and her spinal cord that ran clear as a wemm, with the dozen or so cold sores, fresh as the evidence from a recent lash.

"I have an audition in an hour, so I'm washing myself clean. You never know what directors're going to ask you to do."

He retreated to his room and closed the door. No mist or even warm sores could confuse him now; and he inspected the clothes he was dressed in, unable to change them, and worried about his interview, refusing all the time to think of the naked actress, and ignored her knocking on his door. Whenever he refused to answer her, she would leave a note on his door in her scratchy, left-handed scrawl.

But this time, when he reopened his door to leave, she was standing there, and he passed her, wrapped in the large Holiday Inn towel she had brought from Sherbrooke and which barely covered the red sores at the bottom of her spine. The two small nipples of her dropped breasts were left bare to his undesiring eyes.

"You're too black to wear brown," she said. He passed her as if she had the plague. "If you don't mind me saying so," she shouted at his back, moving away from her down the stairs.

This time he did not look at himself in the oval looking glass in the hall. He just walked out of the house. He wished it was for the last time.

The people at the bus stop are standing like sentries, silent and sullen. They look so sleepy he thinks it could be six o'clock. But a clock in the bank beside the bus stop says ten minutes to ten. He hurries the crowded bus on, with the urging of his anxiety.

The only sound that comes from the larger group of people going down into the subway is the hurrying pounding of heels on the clean granite steps and the rubbing of hands on the squeaking rails, polished like chrome. More people are coming up out of the subway at greater speed, as if they are fleeing the smell of something unwholesome below. He can smell only the fumes of the trains. And he wonders if it is his imagination. For he knows that the trains run on electricity. It must be the smell of dust, then. Or the people. Or the perfumes.

He watches a woman's hand as it wipes sleep and excreta from the corners of her eyes. He thinks of the actress, who cleans her face this way.

But it is still September, his month of laughter along the crowded sidewalks, amongst the fallen turning leaves. And the furious memory of growing grass, quicker than the pulse was in summer, is still in the air. There are no lambswool, no slaughtered seals, no furs, no coats yet to cover the monotony of women's movements, which he sees like the single-mindedness of sheep, one behind the leader, in single file downwards into the subway and in double file upwards.

He boards a crowded subway car and stands among the sardines of silent, serious people. Where he is, with both hands on a pole, he is surrounded by men dressed in grey and black. Some are darker and richer than others. Some of the women too are dressed in grey, some better made and better built than others. All the men in this car hold briefcases, either on their laps or between their shoes. And the women carry at least two bags, from one of which they occasionally take small balls of Kleenex.

He has just swayed farther from the steadying pole for moving balance as the train turns, and is standing over a woman cleaning her eyes and her nose with a red fingernail. And immediately, as his eyes and hers meet, she drops her eyes into the pages of a thick paperback book, as if her turned eyes would obliterate her act; and then she takes a white Kleenex from her handbag.

The second bag he sees some women carrying is larger than a handbag, large enough, he thinks, for rolls of toilet paper and paper towels. The men do not read; they watch the women's legs. And they look over their shoulders, between their shoulders, and down into their bra-less bodies, and their eyes touch the pages of the novels the women are reading; and, not certain of the enlightenment and pleasure to be got from this rapid-transit fleeting education, the men reluctantly allow their eyes to wander back to the pages of the *Globe and Mail*, which seem to hold no interest for them. Their eyes roam over the puny print of the stock market quotations, the box scores of the Blue Jays baseball team, and the results at Woodbine Racetrack.

If his own luck had been really luck—and something to laugh about—the actress told him once, he could win thousands of dollars on a two-dollar bet, as easy as one, two, three. When she told him, "One to win, two to come second, and three to come third," he laughed, thinking she was memorizing lines of a play she was auditioning for.

He had been living with so little luck in his life—three months with no money and no hope of any—that he could afford to dream and to laugh as he dreamed, and fill his empty pockets with imagined wealth.

A man beside him shakes out the pages of the *Globe and Mail* to the racing results: "and in the fifth race yesterday at Woodbine, the first three horses to come in 1, 2, and 3 paid $15,595.03 . . ."

The jerk of the train stopping pushes him against the metal pole and awakens him from his dreaming. When the doors open, he is at his station.

The air is cool. He can feel his shirt like wet silk against his body. He pulls the lapels of his jacket together to make himself feel warmer. The sun shines blindingly, but weakly, on the tall office buildings that surround him. He is walking in their shadow, as if he is walking in a valley back in Barbados. The buildings look like steel. One facing him, built almost entirely out of glass, shimmers like gold. Its reflection of his body tears him into strides and splatters his suit against four glass panels, and makes him disjointed. It is the building he is going to enter.

The elevator is crowded. The passengers are all looking up at the changing numbers of the floors. He looks up too. He can hear no breathing. A man shifts his weight from one black alligator shoe to the other. A woman changes her brown leather handbag and her other, larger bag, made of blue parachute material, from her right arm to her left. He reads BIJOUX, which is printed on it. There is only the humming of the elevator; then the sound of the doors opening; then feet on the polished floor outside; the sound of the doors closing; a deep breath like a sigh of relief or of anticipation for the next floor; then the humming of the next ascent and then silence. The elevator stops on the fourteenth floor. There is no thirteenth. He is at the front, near the door, when it opens. Five men and women are beside and behind him. Facing him is glass and chrome and fresh flowers and Persian rugs and women dressed expensively and stylishly in black, with necklaces of pearls. And chewing gum. It is quiet in the office. Deathly quiet. So he stands his ground.

BANK is written on the glass.

"Getting off?" a man beside him asks.

He stands his ground.

The door closes, and he goes up with the five of them and finds himself, gradually, floor by floor, alone, as they slip out one by one. The elevator takes him to the top. The door does not open. And when it starts its descent, he is feeling braver. He remembers the new vigour he used to feel at the end of three hours working with wax and mops and vacuum cleaners with Italians, Greeks, and Portuguese, going down the elevator. He will ride it to the bottom.

No one enters, even though it stops two times in quick succession. And then it stops once more, and the door opens, and he is facing the same office with BANK written on the glass, cheerless and frightening, and seeing the same chrome, the rugs, and the black and pearls of the women. Just as he moves to step out, the closing door, cut into half, and like two large black hands, comes at him. He gets out of the way just as the blue eyes of one of the women approaching the elevator door to see what he wanted are fixed upon him. Those blue eyes are like ice water; his are brown and laughing.

". . . this stop, sir?" is all he gets to hear of the woman's flat voice before the two black palms, like a shutter, have taken her eyes from his view and her words from his hearing.

"And you didn't even go into the office?"

"I couldn't do it."

"Sometimes when I'm auditioning, I get scared and get butterflies."

"There was so much wealth!"

"Are you a communist? I wish I had money, money, and more money. All I think about is money. But here I am in this damn rooming house with a broken shower curtain and a leaky bathtub, trying to be an artist, an actress. Do you think I'll be a dedicated actress because I live in all this shit? When last have I had a steak? And a glass of red wine? Or you?"

"I have some wieners."

"Wieners, for Chrissakes!"

Her flat voice and icy manner killed the kindness in his suggestion.

"The people on the subway looked so educated, like everybody was a university graduate. And not one person, man or woman, asked me if I needed directions."

"For Chrissakes! How would they know you don't have Canadian experience?"

"They looked on me and at me and through me, right through me. I was a piece of glass."

"Must have been your brown suit."

"Everybody else was in grey or black."

"I hope I get this part. Just to get my hands on some money and rent a decent place. But what can I do? I even get tired taking showers in a bathroom where the water leaks through the curtain. My whole life is like a shower curtain. That leaks. Oh, the landlady was here. Fifteen minutes after you left. She tells me you have to give up your room on Friday. So I tell her not to worry, that you got a job today. And you didn't even go into the office! She wants you to pay two months this month. But you didn't even face the people!"

"With all that glass and steel and chrome?"

"Do you want me to tell her you're not in? You could always slip out without paying the rent, you know. I've done it lots of times. In Sherbrooke and in Rosedale. God, I nearly broke my ass racing down the metal fire escape, carrying my box of French-Canadian plays. Everybody skips out on landlords. Try it. She'll never find you in Toronto! The one in Rosedale hasn't found me yet. And here I am, desperate to be an actress and make enough money to move back to Rosedale . . ."

"When she's coming back?"

"Seven."

"She coming in three hours? Are you saying four o'clock, too?"

"You *could* come to my room. I don't have to do the audition. I can skip it. There's a small restaurant on Church Street where a lot of television and radio types eat, and I'm thinking of applying for a waitress job there. It's an artistic restaurant. I'll even slip you a steak if I get the job."

"She said she's coming back at seven?"

"My room is open to you, as I say. Be free. Feel free. Don't you want to be free? Where could you go, anyhow?"

In his hands is a glass with a pattern on it that advertises peanut butter. It has dried specks like old saliva around the mouth. He passes his fingers around the mouth of the glass, cleaning it; and when it looks clean and is cloudy from his handprints, he pours the first of the three Molson's into it. He sits on his bed. There is no chair in the room. Only his television set, which he sits on when he is not watching *60 Minutes* or the American news. His dangling feet can barely touch the floor. On the floor is linoleum, with a floral pattern. "Rose of Sharon," the actress had told him. "I was a whiz in botany at Jarvis Collegiate."

The sun is brighter now. He can smile in this sun and think of home. He is getting warmer, too. A shaft of dust plays within the arrow of September light that comes through the window. It lands at his feet. The light and the particles of dust on the bright leather of his shoes attract his attention for a moment only. He smiles in that moment. And in that moment, his past life fills his heart and shakes his body like a spasm, like a blast of cold air. His attention then strays to the things around him, his possessions, prized so fondly before, and which now seem to be mere encumbrances: the valise he brought from Barbados and carried through so many changes of address in Toronto; heavier always in winter when he changed rooms, when he carried it late at night on his shoulder, although each time that he moved, he had accumulated no more possessions; the two Christmas cards that the actress had mailed to him, even though she was living in the same house, placed open like two tents and which he keeps on top of a wooden kitchen cupboard, used now as his dressing table. "TO GEORGE, AT XMAS" is written in ballpoint, in red, on each, in capital letters; and an unframed colour photograph taken in Barbados, and fading now, showing him with his father and mother and two younger brothers and three sisters: eight healthy, well-fed Barbadians, squinting because the sun is in their eyes, standing like proprietors in front of a well-preserved plantation house made of coral stone, covered in vines so thick that their spongy greenness strangles the windows and the doors. The name of this house in Barbados is Edgehill House. His present residence has no name. It is on a street named Major. It is a rooming house, similar in size, in build, and in dirt to the other houses on the street.

He drains the beer from the peanut-butter glass and refills it. He throws the last bottle into the plastic garbage pail, and the rattle of glass and tin is like a drunken cackle. Inside the garbage pail are the classified pages from the *Globe and Mail*, some shrivelled lettuce leaves, an empty milk carton, and the caps of beer bottles. He thinks of the woman in the bank's office, dressed in black, with the blue eyes. He thinks of the flowers and the glass in that office and of flowers more violent in colour, growing in wild profusion, untended, around Edgehill House, where he was born in a smiling field of comfortable pastureland.

His father never worked for anyone in his whole life, never had to leave the two hundred and eighty acres of green sugar cane and corn to dirty his hands for anyone's money.

"Work on this blasted plantation, boy. Put your hands in the most stinking dirt and cow-dung on this plantation, and it is a hundred times more nobler than working at the most senior position in a country where you wasn't born!"

His father said that almost every day, and more often when he learned that his son was emigrating to Canada.

"You call yourself a son o' mine? You, a son o' mine? With all this property that I leaving-back for you? You come telling me you going to Canada as a immigrant? To be a stranger? Where Canada is? What is Canada? They have a Church o' England up there? Canada is no place for you. The son of a Barbadian plantation owner? This land was in our family before Canada was even discovered by the blasted Eskimos and the red Indians. Seventeen-something. A.D.! In the year of our Lord, *anno domini*. Who do they worship up there? And you come telling me that you going up there, seeking advancement as a immigrant? In Canada? Your fortune and your future is *right here*! In this soil. In this mud. In this dirt. 'Pon these two hundred and eighty-something acres o' cane and corn!"

It is six-thirty now. Thirty minutes before the landlady is to arrive. He locks his door. He stands outside in front of it, like a man who has forgotten something inside. There is a red thumbtack on the door. The actress pins it there whenever she leaves messages that she thinks require urgent replies. Whenever there's a thumb-tack on his door, he thinks of the red cold sores on her back, and it makes him laugh. He does not know why; he just laughs.

He climbs the stairs to go to her room. He can see a red thumb-tack on her door, even before he reaches it. It is similar to the one he has left behind on his own door. She has written his name in red capital letters on a folded piece of lined white paper. He pulls the paper from the tack.

I got the waitress job at the restarant. He smiles when he sees she has spelled "restaurant" without a U. *Your steak waiteth.* She has signed it *Pat.*

He did not throw away the balled-up message, even hours after-wards, in all the walking he did that night, until he was standing on the platform of the subway at the Spadina station, where he is now.

He looks to his right and then to his left, and there is no one in sight. Across from him, across the clean cement that is divided by a black river of hard dirty steel, are two large billboards. One advo-cates "pigging-out," and the other tells women about Light Days Tampax. Suddenly, into the frame of these two boards riveted to two steel pillars comes a lone passenger, who stands on the plat-form and waits to take the train going in the other direction.

He does not know why he is in this station and why he has entered on the platform for southbound trains.

South is the office building with the glass and the flowers and the women dressed in black and BANK written on the glass. South is Bay Street, where no one walks after the Italians and the Greeks and the Portuguese have cleaned the offices and have left to take the subway north to College Street. South is nothing. South is the lake and blackness and cold water that smells of dead fish and screaming children's voices in the short summer, and machines and boats and grease.

The balled-up note from Pat, written on its soiled paper, smelling of the ointment she uses for her cold sores, was in his fist when he first reached this spot where he is standing now. He is standing in the centre of the platform, the same distance from the left end as from the right.

A rumble grows louder. Chains and machinery, iron touching iron, steel rubbing steel, the sound of the approaching train. He can never tell at the first sound of this familiar rumbling, out of a darkened tube, whether it is coming from his left or from his right. He always has to wait longer for the greater roar. Or if it is nighttime, watch for the first glare on the tracks.

He thinks the roar is coming from the southbound lines. He feels more at ease for a moment, and braver, and he even laughs, although he doesn't know why. The man on the other side stares at him from his seat on the brown vinyl between the two advertising boards, and the man remains, querulous with his staring, until his train moves northwards.

He is alone again. And more at ease. He moves to the end of the platform, nearest the tube through which the train will emerge, to a spot where he could see it clearly. He wants no surprises. He wants to see it the moment it appears out of the blackness. The blackness that is like the south and the lake. And he wants no one else to see him. He wants to be alone, just as he was alone in the descending elevator in the office building.

How comfortable and safe and brave he had felt travelling and laughing and falling so fast and so free, through the bowels of that glassed-in building!

He hears the rumble. He hears the sound of steel or iron—metal, anyhow—and the low screech of the train trying to emerge out of the darkened, curved tube.

He thinks of Pat. So he throws the balled-up note onto the tracks. And that act is her being thrown out of his life, along with her red-corpuscled sores. He sees the note fall. But does not hear it reach the surface of the black river of hard dirty steel below him. He does not hear it reach the tracks. He cannot gauge any distance now. Cannot gauge any face. The paper is very light. Almost without weight. Definitely without purpose and love.

But the train is here. Its lights reflect off the tracks, which now are shining and getting wider as the ugly red engine, like her sores, approaches. He knows that the train is as long as the platform, half of which he has already paced off. The train is here. And just as its lights begin to blind him, he makes his own eyes pierce through that weaker brightness and fixes them on the driver, dressed in a light brown uniform. He sees the driver's face, the driver's happy eyes and his relief that this is his last trip; and he himself laughs to an empty platform and station that are not listening, and he steps off the platform, just having seen that his own eyes, and the driver's, make four.

I'M RUNNING
FOR MY LIFE

She was in the bedroom when he touched the door, and did not enter. She had heard him come home earlier; had heard the front door open and close, and had panicked. She had thought of running downstairs. But she had changed her mind. He would see her; and catch her; and ask for explanations, even though he knew it was part of her job to clean the bedroom; and she knew she could not satisfy him with her explanations. She knew she would be fired. She feared being fired. She wanted to enrol in a night class at George Brown College, doing something to improve herself; and even though she had not, and could not decide which course she should take, she knew she had to take some courses, to upgrade her life in this city. And she wanted to buy Canada Savings Bonds, to invest in the future. And she wanted to take a trip to New York City with Gertrude, who liked plays and art galleries; while she, she knew, wanted to visit Harlem and Brooklyn, where she had friends. And she wanted to bring her savings up to a figure when she could more easily face the bank manager; and afterwards arrange a loan for a down payment on a small house in the East End, although she hated the East End, but the East End was the only place in this city where a woman like her, living on her own, making next to nothing in wages, could afford to have a roof over her head that she owned, before, as she always said, "God ready to take me to my grave, and the cold earth in this place become my roof everlasting!" She feared being fired before she had made a woman of herself. She wanted time. And she became sad to think that she could be fired just like that: she, who had worked for him so long; too long; too well; in dutiful, efficient, faithful service. She was like a member of the household.

It was her guilt which built these thoughts into the mountain of her fear. Her guilt sometimes turned her into salt. Just like Lot's wife. And this is how she described it to herself, in her Christian way of thinking. She knew she was certainly breaking one of the Commandments. But her nervousness did not permit her to name the exact one, in this moment of remorse. Was it the one about covetousness? Theft? Dishonouring?

When she first heard him, she was writing down a telephone message for his wife; and standing beside their night table, she had noticed the book, *The Joy of Sex*, and had wondered why it was there, and if they needed it, and used it, and why they had to use it; and she looked at the message she had written down for his wife, and at the book whose message troubled her, and could not decide if she should put the note on the cover of *The Joy of Sex*, and cover up the title of this suggestive book, or stick it to the telephone; and all this time, he is at the door, and she in his bedroom.

She had stood frozen. The second touch of his hand on the door reduced her to tears. Tears of guilt, of shame, of disobedience, of conflicting loyalties, and in the face of God. The message for his wife was left by a voice she had heard many times before. And it was only when she heard his steps retreating over the muffling thick carpet, and had already begun to picture him going down, with his hands dangling at his sides, walking like an ape, with his head bending forwards and backwards, as if he were sniffing out a bone that was buried and lost; picturing him with his feet which moved with no energy, desultorily, like a spring that had already unwound and lost its liveliness, only then did she crawl from under the bed.

Why did she hide when she knew he was going away from her? She was surprised that she did not bang her head against the iron bedstead. Did not get stuck in the space between the floor and the springs which caused the bed to sag, as if he and *she* were lying in it, reading most likely this book, *The Joy of Sex*. And she had struggled not to sneeze and disclose herself through the thick dust that rose to her nostrils, already clogged through hay fever, as it always was during December, January, and February, and made worse by the coldness in the house, whose temperature she always had to raise no matter how high the thermostat was already set. She could not bear a cold house. And first thing she did every morning when she arrived, even before she turned on all the radios and all the lights in the house, was raise the temperature five degrees. She had been praying that the elongated, weightless, and shapeless cottons of dust, silken and balled up, would not enter her nostrils.

What time is it? From the darkness under the bed, she can see the computer digits on the radio's face, telling her in red that she has spent more than one hour in their bedroom. Before her escape under the bed, she had passed her hands through the deep-layered drawer that contained *her* silk underwear: panties, camisoles, and slips. She had run her fingers over the designer dresses that filled one closet. She had touched, had opened, had re-touched, and had sampled more than three vials of perfume and scent; and had played with a gold-painted atomizer that contained cologne, as if it was a water pistol. All of these vials were expensive, she knew; for she had seen them in the magazines which *she* read; in Creed's and Holt Renfrew, where *she* shopped. She tried on the polka-dotted blue silk dress a second time, and was convinced that she looked much better in it than *her*. And with this, she possessed it in her mind; felt that it belonged to her, because *she* had so many, some of which seemed to be the same dress with the same design; and also because she felt it was wrong for one woman to have so many dresses, while others, many, many others, had none.

And even now, under the dark bed, with the dust tingling her sinuses and the silken balls of thread and hair making it difficult to breathe, one leg of her ashen-grey pantyhose was still on her left leg. It was the only covered leg. The pantyhose was marked from the heel to the bottom of the knee with a run that had walked sideways and lengthways at the same time. The delicate material of the

pantyhose wrapped her in a tangle, and tangled her up, so desperate
had she been not to be detected; and she felt as if she was handcuffed, just as they had done to poor Mr. Johnson before they shot
him and blew his head apart like a watermelon falling into the road;
and she was unable to extricate herself; and she could imagine how
foolish she looked, tied by this silk, in case somebody, in case he
came back into the bedroom, and looked down, and saw her, and
discovered her. She had seen somewhere, perhaps in one of *her*
glossy magazines, or it could have been while walking up the ravine
one morning in the summer, a worm covered in this same thin silk;
yes, it was while she was walking up the ravine to catch the streetcar; it was while she was walking, striding jauntily in the ravine,
flowers and faces, lawns and dresses swaying in the wind, and while
she herself was kissed by the redeeming freshness of warmth of life,
that she had seen the worm, as if the worm were turning itself into
silk right in front of her eyes, as if the silk were turning into a
worm. The winter had been so long. She had smiled then, and had
called it the wonders of the Lord. Now, in this mesh of the pantyhose, she did not smile. She did not think of birth, or of new life, or
of resurrection. She was thinking only of escape and of extrication.

She did not know how long she would have to remain in this
ridiculous imprisonment. How long it would take before the coast
was clear; before she could descend into the quiet house, like a
tomb with its dead head within it; dead even when he and *she* were
at home; how long before she could complete her domestic tasks
of the day, and run down to George Brown to register. Or stop
in on her friend Gertrude, who worked at a bookstore on Yonge
Street near Bloor.

The roast beef looked ugly while she was washing it with lime
juice and salt; and slapping it as she seasoned it with herbs he liked
to taste in his food; strange for a man born where he was born in this
cold and raised in Toronto, that she secretly held the belief he was
not white, entirely; and the potatoes which he wanted boiled and
then baked until their edges were brown with a golden crispiness;
this enticement for food that he had, and which made her mouth

water at its appearance; and the green peas from a can, like beads from a string that had collapsed into a mound; and the rice. Plain Uncle Ben's long-grain, which she was instructed to cook without salt, without parsley flakes; "I can't stand those damn green things!" *she* said one night, when the white-and-green mound of steaming substance was placed before her, as *she* sat like a princess in her blue polka-dotted silk dress—the same one she had tried on in the bedroom a few minutes ago—and was on her way to the opera. How long ago? Months now, maybe. But it could be years. Time was playing such tricks with her memory, since *she* had left; with overnight bag, all her credit cards, the joint chequing account empty; and the shining Mercedes-Benz, which he had just got washed at Davenport and Park Road; and *gone*.

The house was quiet. It had been quiet all the time. She listened in this silence for music, for the television noise, for movement in his room with all those books, and all she could hear, or all she thought she heard, was her own heart beating.

And then she did a strange thing. She tightened her grip on the house slipper she was wearing, and on the right leg of the pantyhose; and with the other hand on the hosed left leg, she crawled from under the bed; and she raised her head, in the same way she raised her head when she was in church, when she claimed she saw the face of God, daring, ambitious, secure, and charged with Christian righteousness and arrogance, and she traipsed down the stairs, as if nothing had happened. And as she moved, she indeed wondered if anything *had* happened, and if it was not all her fruitful imagination. She made more noise, going down, than she had ever done. She made more noise than anyone who lived here had ever done. She ignored consequences and detection. She ignored termination. She forgot ambition and educational advancement. And she went down with arrogance, in innocence, in her laughable impromptu attire.

When she reached the kitchen, the house was still empty; empty as it had been all day; empty as it is any day in August when they were away at the cottage.

She was safe now, and sinful; and she moved about the kitchen as if she owned the world. She had placed the pantyhose in her large hip pocket. She had passed the Afro comb through her hair that was like steel and was black. She had run cold water, from the restroom off the dining room, all over her face. She was a new woman.

She served his dinner. There was no noise. *Her* place had been set. He did not ask for *her*. He did not look at the knives and forks, soup spoon and dessert spoon and spoon for sweetening coffee, that were placed at the other end of the oval mahogany table. He sat at his end of the table, about four feet from the place setting. She did not hear his chewing. She did not hear his drinking, wine or water. She did not hear the chime, the tinkle, the slight pat of glass, cutlery, and napkin ring.

But she felt naked. His eyes moved with the rhythm of her body. She touched her bottom once when she returned to the kitchen, to make sure she had clothes under the housedress she wore when she served. She could feel in her tension, in her opposition to him, his hand on her waist. She could feel his fingers on her legs.

There was no noise. He made no noise when he ate. And he said nothing to her when he was in the house. Never. But she felt he was assaulting her, in this silence, with the roar and violence of his eyes.

He got up from the table, and threw one last glance in her direction, as she stood at the sink. He wished he could thank her for her efficiency, for her company, for looking after him now that he was alone. He looked at her, and straightaway, his mind was on his work. In the small mirror above the two-basined sink, she saw his eyes, and then his face, as he moved along the carpet which did not reproduce his weight, or the thoughts which she felt were running through his body. He had already dismissed her from his mind.

She turned the lamps in the dining room off. She closed the door. She did not feel safer. She took the served dinner off the mahogany table. She scraped the roast beef, the potatoes, the green marbles of canned peas, everything into the large tin garbage pail. He did not approve of leftovers. She left the plates and knives and forks

and crystal glasses of *her* place setting, on the rectangular mat that
showed the buildings of Parliament painted on them in the colors
of moss and brick and granite, where they were. And then she left,
after locking the door two times, after opening it two times, to be
sure. She dropped her pass-key into her handbag. She stood on the
slab of granite on the front doorstep, and she broke into tears. She
sighed deeply, pulled herself together, and took the steady climb
out of the ravine, on her way to the corner of Bloor and Yonge to
take the subway going west to Bathurst Street.

Time was out of joint. She could feel the presence again in the
house. She could feel it heavy and plain and hiding somewhere
inside this mansion. Perhaps, it was ghosts; or spirits. But she did
not believe in ghosts. Not she, a Christian-minded woman as she
was. But she was going to find it: find the cause, or the presence,
and its hiding place; and if the cause was in the form of a living person, or a dead body, she was going to seek it out and then try to
master it.

She went upstairs to the second floor, and looked into each room
off the flight of the banister that swung to her right in a wide, polished swath, walking slowly and with deliberate bravery, running
her palm over the banister, as if she was wiping and polishing it with
her yellow chamois cloth. On the third floor, inside the master
bedroom, she looked around, trying to determine if anyone had
entered it since she had left the evening before; trying to seek some
clue to meet the heavy and oppressing presence she could not see,
but which she knew was following her even as she perused the
house.

Everything was in order. Each item and article, clothes and
lotions in vials, and books, including *The Joy of Sex*, had remained
as she had left them, yesterday.

So, she retraced her steps, all the time finding company in the
rhythm and blues on the three radios on the first floor playing
loud. After turning on all the lights in the house, and raising the
thermostat the moment she entered, she changed the stations on

the three radios from classical music to her favourite Buffalo station, WBLK. The rhythm and blues made her happy and relaxed,
and appeased her spirit and helped her to face the long day of
work, with peace and patience. Now, however, this music was
adding to her anxiety and discomfiture. She turned each radio off.

The house was like death without the music. She endured this
silence. But she left all the lights on. She was safe and comfortable
with all the lights on. The late winter sunlight, which had no heat
to it, was still bright; and the lights hardly added to the illumination in the rooms.

She went into the library to see if the Indian blanket she had
thrown over his body last night, dead in his sleep immediately after
he had eaten the roast beef dinner, was still there. Perhaps, it is
this, this Indian blanket, taking on and inhabiting all the spirits and
the ghosts of those tribes. Those tribes, those men whom she saw
standing at the corner of Bloor and Spadina, old men, some old
before they are young; defeated warriors, with faces the same as she
had looked upon in her elementary schoolbooks back in Barbados,
identical in the fierceness with what her own history book in Standard Seven showed her; but without their spears and tomahawks.

The Indian blanket was on the floor of the library. In a bundle.
In a way that said it had been thrown off the body, during the
night. In a way a child would toss its covering off its body, no longer
cold. She took it up, and held it against her body, and folded it
while holding it against her body; perhaps bear, or fox, or caribou,
or seal. She didn't know much about these things. Her friend
Gertrude would know. Gertrude worked in a bookstore. Gertrude
read most of the books in the bookstore. The Indian blanket felt
odd, as if the animal from which it was made was still alive.

She took up the crystal Scotch glass, and the empty soda siphon.
The decanter was empty. On her way to take these into the kitchen,
she noticed the door to the basement ajar. And lights on. Terror
gripped her again. Someone was in the house. A man. An intruder.
A brute-beast. One of those varmints roaming Toronto in cars and

assaulting women in stairwells of hard, cold sex. Rapist. A thief, perhaps.

She tiptoes the rest of the way, crawling to the kitchen, her blood hot with fear and with the violence she knows she could be facing. And she drops the blanket on the clean countertop, and is about to rest the crystal glass in the sink, when it drops. The shattering glass is like sirens. The sound is like a cry of rape. A cry against rape. She cannot move. Her mind is in a hurry, confused, filled with decisions, not one of which she can make. She listens for the crash of the crystal to end, as if she is about to count the number of pieces which the Stuart crystal will dissolve itself into; but the glass is not broken. And she thinks this is an omen. It is her imagination which told her it was broken. Still, the danger lurks. Still, the presence, now transformed into a person, a rapist, a thief, remains.

She reaches for the large iron saucepan on the pegboard above the stove. But this proves too heavy and unwieldy. She chooses the large frying pan. Also of iron. And she crosses herself two times. Gertrude had told her how to make the sign of the cross, as Catholics do. She thinks of calling Gertrude to alert her, but she does not. And she never, in spite of promise, got around to taking down the Rape Crisis Centre of Toronto telephone number. But why couldn't it have been she who had left the basement door open?

And she creeps along the floor, suppressing what noise her footsteps make, through caution, no noise coming from the radio to distract her attention and her deadly intent and the deadly blow she is going to deliver, and not breathing, just in case. She should have called Gertrude. Is the Rape Crisis Centre of Toronto 911? Or 767?

When she reaches the open door to the basement, she moves her hand instinctively to the brass panel for the light switch. The switch answers her touch. And below her, through the agaped door, the entire basement is bathed in the pure whiteness of light.

She stops at the head of the stairs. She inhales. She hefts the iron frying pan. She can deliver a deadly blow with it.

And then she goes down. Step by step. For the first time realizing how noisy these steps are. Somebody had forgotten, after all these years, to line them with broadloom. Soft creak after soft creak. And still no sound from below in the bright light that blares and screams out her terror.

She reaches the bottom step. She closes her eyes quickly; opens them again, quickly, to get accustomed to the fluorescence. Still, there is no sound.

And then, she sees it. The T-shaped form made by the light, on the floor. Coming from the same closet she had stumbled upon last week. The faint yellow of the stroke from the left side of the door, going rightwards across the top of the door. She hefts the frying pan. She is holding it firmly; and *by God, whoever it is, he got to come clean! The bastard going-have to kill me, or I kill he!* The iron frying pan is weightless in her hand.

And she creeps silent, step after silent step, the frying pan raised and ready, her eyes staring, and seeing blood, her body, and the pan and her steps in a tense synchronized oneness; staring at the weak light forcing itself out of the half-open door; and clearer now, brighter now in her control of the threat and how she is going to master it, she sees that the shape of the light that comes out from the closet is not a T at all. It is an inverted L. And she moves as a yacht would move silent over swift water; and when she comes face to face with the door, she didn't know she could get there so fast and with such stealth; and she raises the iron frying pan ready, and at the same time, with her left hand, she flings the door outwards, and screams, "Thief!"

She finds herself standing over him.

He is sitting on a box marked CONFIDENTIAL. His head in his hands. Bent down in a stooped posture of complete dejection.

He was facing her. But he was not looking at her. His eyes were not looking at her. His eyes were not open. But he was awake and alert.

And then he opened his eyes, and remained sitting and staring at her, as if he had been sleeping, dead to the world. And she stood there, full with her former pity for him, and with a new tormenting and strange desire, like a feeling of love for someone who has never known love, all the time with the iron frying pan in her hand, but now at her side, her own eyes staring back in bewilderment and wonder. But most of all, with pity and with a great strange love.

She tried to control the shaking in her body with the emotions running through it: pity and love and a tinge of indecentness that she had robbed him of his privacy, even though she could not understand that he had sought to be private in a closet in the basement of his own mansion; she felt she had unsanctified the holiness of his retreat. Whatever was his problem; whatever was his misery; whatever had caused his heavy drinking and his apparent surrender even with a life of such success and wealth; whatever his misery that *she* had left him; and whatever *her* good reasons, it was his home, his mansion, his castle, and his dignity that she had ruptured because of her fears caused by fantasy and the reading of recent horrors in the newspaper beaten and slashed and driven into the flesh and psyche of women who live alone in apartments.

"My God, Mr. Moore, I could have kill you!"

"May," he said. "May." She could see that he wanted to say more.

"What're you doing in here, in a closet, Mr. Moore?"

"Oh, May."

She was holding him now, in an embrace. He had risen to reach her. And she could feel the weight of her body against his; and he could feel the weight of his head against her breasts; and the softness there, and the pulsating blood, such as he had tasted once when he was on holiday in the Bahamas where he had danced in his wildness to the beat of calypso; and could feel, as he felt then, the flesh in her back as his arms had tied the Bahamian woman too close to him, even for a dance; and in his present embrace, she was frantic and affectionate—squeezing him, holding him to her; frightened and faithful—for he was her employer and she was a woman, overcome by her grief and her pity; and pure and unsinning: she could feel her body for the first time in three years answering to the touch of a man's hands; and knowing, notwithstanding that dirty dream she had had the night before, the thought that rushed to her head like blood itself, and she knew she wanted him. She could feel his desire touch her *there*: plain, hard, and honest; and she could feel her body give in . . . for the three cardboard boxes marked CONFIDENTIAL, PICTURES & PHOTOS, and TERM PAPERS were large enough for the size and weight of their two bodies; and were soft enough and adequate enough and supple enough to accommodate them; and so, she put him to lie on his back, flat against the ridges and edges of the three boxes, and he had more than space and comfort. So, he closed his eyes, for he could not look at nor witness what was happening to him, after she had eased the tight-fitting custom-made corduroy trousers below his waist, and had pulled them down along his legs so white that she was surprised; *you should be in the sun*; passed through her mind; seeing that his legs were skinny, she left one trouser leg on, since it was too much trouble in her rush of emotion getting both over his shoes; and she raised the light blue cotton dress—her smock, as she called it, her work dress—and she pulled this up, above her waist, just below her breasts, now full and pointed at the nipples, and sat on him. It was then that he opened his eyes, that he saw the rich brown flesh, her belly with its slight bulge, and her breasts with their black circles round the nipples, stiff as two olives, and the thickness and silk of her hair betwixt her thighs. Such lusciousness he had not seen before. But deep down had always yearned for. It was when his eyes rested on her greatness that the sight was too much for him, and in shame, in surrender, in weakness, he closed his eyes. He closed his eyes also, because in his heart he was praying.

Always before, in the years of his marriage to *her*, it was fear and doubt and trepidation when they had sex on Friday nights—he was busy with his work at the office; and *her* with her social calendar— and he always ended it feeling inadequate, for she wanted to do it by the book, and she wanted him to talk, and say precisely how he liked it, and if he liked it this way or that; and she made him, and he had to spell out for her the positions into which she had taken him. This is why now, not being able, at this point, to know if there was going to be any difference, he closed his eyes. The realism was too much for him. It was like closing his eyes, momentarily, when the car approaching him has its high beams on, to avoid temporary blindness and an accident. But he preferred it with his eyes closed. And how was he to know that this would be the experience, the moment he had been waiting all his life to have; and at the same time, the time and the experience he had been running for his life to avoid.

And when it happened, when he reached his manhood and it spilled out inside her, she closed her eyes and said something like a prayer. And he screamed, "Oh Jesus Christ!"

And like a ritual, like a cleaning up after, like the practised taking up of things and putting them back into their correct places, she put back on her brassiere and her light blue smock, and without saying a word, she left the room.

He was too weak to move. He was too enervated to want to move from the three boxes marked CONFIDENTIAL, PICTURES & PHOTOS, and TERM PAPERS on which she had left him. But more than anything, it was the peace in his body which made him listless. And contented to remain lying. And wanting, in that contentment, to take his own life. To die.

She was standing in front of the double sinks in the kitchen. Her hands were moving automatically. Her face was serene. She could feel a new kind of life pump through her body. As if her blood were being taken out and changed and poured back in. She was staring into the backyard . . . and the trees were white and the jewels of snow, brightened by the bright powerless sun, took her wandering, walking, looking into the windows of shops along Bloor Street; and looking into the peaceful waves of the sea near Gravesend Beach, where she had lived in Barbados. Her hands moved over the crystal glass she was washing. And she realized she had been holding it merely, when the light took up the intricate workmanship in the glass, and the sparkles jumped and had a life of their own, like stars in the darkest night of blue. Then, the full force of her act struck her. Her mind was no longer focused on the glass. What had she done? What had been done to her? But what had she done?

When she realized what it was that she had done, she panicked. Tears poured down her cheeks, and she could feel the water and she did not feel her tears were warm, as people said. Her tears were cold. She felt cold all over. Terror gripped her, and she wondered what to do. What had she done? From her Bible it was clear what her act was. And her religion would chastise her; and she knew she would have to atone for it. She knew she could not wish away her act of adultery. And more than that, her sacred vow to herself, and to Gertrude, that no man would ever touch her body—far less violate it—not even if she had, as before, given her body in love, or in a passionate act of lust. When the weight of what she had done landed upon her conscience, she became irrepressibly depressed. The act, and her entire body, became one inexplicable lump, a large ball, some kind of encumbrance that was ugly and bad, blocking the way to her other thoughts about anything else she knew about herself, as if the act encompassed her entire being. She was now nothing more than the adultery itself.

The tears continued to bathe her face. But she also realized and faced the fact of the feeling in her body, and the newness there, and the love she had given. No one could erase that. No one could say it was not love, that it was not her gift, that it was his assault.

When she knew this, when this thought like the spirit she felt many Sunday nights in her church gripped her; when she knew this, and was this, she broke down.

She picked up her winter coat from the chair on which she had placed it, hours before, and threw it over her shoulders. And she rushed through the front door, not really knowing where she was going; ignoring her woollen hat, her scarf, and her gloves; and she ran across the circular driveway, crushing the snow and leaving pointed marks where her speed had destroyed the firmness of her footprints: running in the thick snow without her winter boots; ignoring the treachery of the ice beneath the snow. She bounded into the bookstore, rushed up to Gertrude, who was holding five books in her hand and a pencil in her mouth, talking with three customers standing beside her.

"Come! Come!" she said to Gertrude, and went behind the counter by the cash register, and grabbed her by the hand, and said, "Come!"

On the way through the door, she told Gertrude, "This is business. Woman talk."

"What about my job?" Gertrude said. They were in the middle of Yonge Street, with two lines of traffic in either direction, bearing down upon them. May ignored the cars.

"In here!" she said.

"The Pilot Tavern?" Gertrude was aghast.

One week ago, May had scolded women she saw in the Pilot Tavern, drinking liquor so early in the day, calling them sinners. "To drink?"

"Something happened."

"Wait!" Gertrude screamed. "The traffic!" It was almost too late. Brakes screeched as the two lines of traffic in two directions came to a shouting, abusive, and gesturing halt.

"They have to wait."

"Danger," Gertrude said.

They entered the bar. And walked past the line of stools on their right hand, which stretched the length of the bar counter. On their left were small round, black-topped tables, shining and placed into the spaces left by the custom-built leather seats. She guided Gertrude to the rear of the room. It was darker here. She chose a seat near a door over which was marked EXIT, in red.

"Gerts, what have I done?"

"You sure's hell cost me my job!"

"This is business, man. Woman talking to woman."

"I'm concerned about my job."

"I tried to call you."

"You just cost me my job, May."

"To tell you."

"How *could* you?"

"All morning, beginning last night, I had this feeling, like a burden on my conscience. All the lights was left on. And the radio was on my favourite station."

"How'm I going to explain this to Mister?"

"It was as if I couldn't help myself, all morning. I couldn't help myself. All morning I feeling this presence. And I went down in the basement. And there he was. There he was, Gertrude."

"God, May, how'm I going to explain this to Mister? What have you done to me, May?"

"And there he was, in a closet in the basement, sitting down on a box. Do you know what was marked on this box he was sitting on?"

"How can you do this to *me*, of all people?"

"CONFIDENTIAL! CONFIDENTIAL was marked on that damn box, Gertrude. I could have killed him *dead*, when he surprised me so. Dead, dead, dead, I tell you, this afternoon, Gerts. What you want to drink?"

"Something soft. Perhaps, a soda."

"A soda? A soda, Gertrude? Do you think I bring you in here to order a soda, in a crisis like this? Gerts, I have done something, and in this hour of my tribulation, you want to drink a soda? How the hell you could understand my transgression if I am drinking something hard, and you drinking something soft, like a blasted soda pop?"

The waiter was standing over them. He could not understand her speech. Her speech, and the accent in which it was embedded, were too strange for his Sicilian ear. He remained standing and waited.

"Bring her a brandy. And bring me one too, please."

"Coming up," the waiter said, and left.

"You can't help me to understand this burden if you're gonna stay sober, and me walking in the valley of death. Girl, drink something strong."

"I left my purse in the store."

"I have money." And she placed her purse on the table.

"And my job, May. How *could* you?"

"The CONFIDENTIAL box, Gerts. And I with a iron frying pan in my hand. And I see him there. Like a baby. Like a child. And I don't know if it was the dream about the woman-lion that I had and told you about, or the dream about the dog. As I stepped through that front door this morning, my spirit wasn't itself. It was the blanket."

"What the hell does a blanket, pardon my French, have to do with my job? You compromised me in front of my customers."

"An Indian blanket, Gerts."

"Indian from the East?"

"Indian from *here*! The Indian blanket that I wrapped him in, last night before I left. I told you about the Indian blanket, Gerts. When I could hardly control the thought of murder, remember? Well, I may not be able to explain it like you, but there was something in that blanket. I don't know anything about the cultures of people, but Gerts, something was living in that blanket. And for me, a Christian-minded person—"

"And drinking *this?*"

The waiter had placed the drinks before them.

"The cultures of people, native people, don't mean a damn thing to me, but I feel something was in that blanket. Some-damn-thing. Something living. A spirit." In one sip, she drank half of her brandy "Now, I am in the basement. He in the closet. Like a little boy. Put in a corner, for disobedience. And when I saw his eyes, and what was happening to him, concerning the wife, *her*, yuh know? Gerts, I don't know why I did what I have done. It is terrible, Gerts." She was crying now.

Gertrude, still pale and wan from the sudden intrusion, sipped her brandy, and then, feeling its power, drank it off in one gulp. She liked brandy.

"All the way up here to you, running like a damn madwoman, Gerts, and the tears pouring down my two cheeks . . ."

"You killed him, at last? You killed the bastard, eventually? That's the trick you want me to believe, eh, May? After you have gone and got me fired? 'Cause, I sure's hell can't go back to the bookstore!" She put her glass to her head. It was already empty. "Is that what you want to make me believe you did? That you killed him?"

"I *had* him."

"You *what?*"

"Had him, Gerts. I had him. Mr. Moore."

"Waiter!" Gertrude said; and motioned for another brandy. "A double, please." And she remained silent for a while, while she tried to understand what she had just heard. "Had him? Like, had sex with him?"

"Fooped him, Gerts."

"You mean . . . You mean, don't tell me, but do you mean, *sex?*"

"*Fucked* him, Gerts!"

"You? And Mr. Moore? *Sex?*"

"Fooped him. Going and coming."

"Waiter? Make that another double, please." She had, in her confusion, forgotten that she had already ordered a double.

For a time, perhaps longer than either of them realized, or could count, the bar remained still, dead, and with a silence that spoke amazement.

And when it was broken, eventually, it was by Gertrude's laughter that smashed the silence. She leaned back in the straight-backed chair, and laughed, until something like tears came to her eyes. She took a lace handkerchief from the sleeve of her brown fitted dress, and passed it over her eyes, and dabbed her cheeks with it.

"And how do you *feel* about this?"

"Is that all you can ask me?"

"Who initiated it?"

"What you mean, who initiated it?"

"He assaulted you, didn't he?"

"I, a woman, and at my age, mixed up in fornication with the man I works for, and all you can ask me, after drinking-off two brandies, is how I feel? And who initiated the fornicating?"

"Listen to me. Take it easy. I know you are distressed by this. But who initiated it? You have to tell me. He came at you, didn't he?"

"How do I feel? How do I feel, Gerts? I feel like shit. I feel dirty. I feel like a sinner. I feel like a whore, and a robber too. A woman who robbed a man. I feel also like a saviour. But in a strange, liberating way, I feel good. Damn good. But scared."

"I know. I know. In these cases, the woman takes on a terrible guilt, and sees herself the victim."

"And it is this that's worrying me, and I run to you, my only living friend in this city, in this country, to seek solace and a word of wisdom from, and *all* you can tell me, after two drinks, is *how* I feel?"

"Sexual assault! That's what it is, May. I know you're in no condition to see this clearly. I understand that. It is an assault to your body. The *unfair*, *criminal* advances of a man with power, and wealth, over a poor woman like you. You have your rights. And you have to do something about your rights. We have to do something about your rights. And if you don't, I sure's hell intend to!"

"Gerts, my life has changed, plain and simple, by this one act. And I never planned it. I never even imagined it. And with the man I work for? In a room? A closet? In a basement? And me, a woman who detests basements? And going to church twice a Sunday, and two more times during the week? I am planning to take a course at George Brown. Planning to buy a house. Planning to buy Canada Savings Bonds. And now look!"

"You have to tell me you don't love him."

"I can't answer that."

"That you feel hatred for him."

"I can't tell you that."

"That you don't know you do."

"I can't answer that, Gerts."

"Of course, you don't know! It's a matter of master and slave."

"*What?*"

"I didn't mean it that way."

"Slave? Did you say slave? Well, Jesus Christ, woman!"

"Please, May."

"You said master and slave."

"I mean power imbalance. You *know* what I mean. We watched it on television together, for nights!"

"What the hell is this power balance, when I talking woman to woman about having sex with a man. I fooped a man, Gerts. Can't you get that in your damn head?"

"I'm trying."

"Well, try harder."

"What're you going to do?"

"I thought you would know."

"You're *not* going back in that house. That's the first decision."

"And why not? I have a business lunch to prepare for, tomorrow."

"After he raped you? Are you crazy? Number two, you are going to report this, this assault, to the police. That's what you're going to do. You are in no shape to, you're in no shape to, to, to . . ."

"A sin, Gerts. A sin, yes. Fornication, yes. Perhaps, adultery. But not *that*, Gerts. I'm not a vic—What you call it? *Victim?* I'm not any damn victim, Gerts."

"We'll see about *that*."

"I'm no victim, Gerts. Don't call me a victim."

"God, May."

"It was something in that Indian blanket."

"These things do happen," Gertrude said. "Every day. On television. And in real life." She drained her glass. She took up her friend's handbag. And made ready to have her leave. "These things happen." And saying this, Gertrude made the first gesture of friendship since they had entered the bar. She reached out her hands, and placed them over May's, and tapped May's hands with her own; and then started rubbing them, sideways and upwards and downwards. May continued crying. The tears dropped on the edge of her glass; and when she saw that, she moved the glass to evade the water. But she had moved her face also, and one long drop kissed the surface of the rich brown liquid. The tears continued without effort, without her trying to stop them. And she did nothing to wipe them away. And they started to fall on Gertrude's fingers, and she too, caught up now in the soft, sad passion of the moment, allowed the tears to fall on her hands. "We're going to fix that fucking bastard!"

AN EASTER CAROL

Suddenly, I could hear my mother's voice licking-down the small room in which I slept. "Get up get up get up! Boy, you too lazy! You think the morning waiting on you? Get up and get! The sun almost halfway up in the sky, and you in there, still sleeping? This is Easter morning! Blessed Easter. The Lord rise-up outta Hell long long time, so you get up too! . . . And don't forget to clean out the pigpens and the sheep pens, 'cause yesterday morning you didn't clean the pigpens proper, and you left back all my precious milk inside them sheeps' breasts. Come, boy! Half the morning gone already! So get up!"

She had hardly taken a breath in all this time. I listened to the beautiful mountains and valleys of her surging voice; and I laughed inside my heart. I was already awake. I had been awake for about three hours. I could not sleep. For all night I could smell the fresh delicious smells seeping under my door from the kitchen: the roasted pork, the great cakes, the sponges, the bananas, the golden apples, the rum and the sweet drinks; and the new coats of varnish and polish and paint on all the ancient furniture in our house. This was Easter in our house.

Everything was cleansed. Even the pigs were given a bath, a clean, white, resurrection coat of freshness; and the front of the house was sprinkled with white marl, because there was never any snow in our village. Everything was new, was clean, was virginal. My new clothes had been bought months before; and my mother had pressed them many times over, and had hooked them on a hanger onto a nail, high in the heavens of the ceiling in her bed-room—where they could be seen, but not touched. And every chance I got, I would watch them: the seams in the short grey flannel trousers, keener than a new Gillette razor; the Sea Island cotton shirt, pressed without a wrinkle or blemish, and rich and creamy as milk from our sheep; my cork hat, white as snow (although no one in Barbados had ever seen snow, except in pictures in a book, or on the foreign Christmas cards which trickled into the village from America and England), and stiff with blanco; and my shoes, like two mounds of pitch, black and shining, Lord-Lord-Lord! like nobody's business. And the tie. My mother never trusted her fingers to tie my tie; and she never trusted mine, neither. So I always wore ties ready-tied, and with an elastic band round the neck. All my ties had a thick savage stripe in them. This was my Easter outfit: new and clean, from my underwear out.

I would be wearing it to church this morning, at five o'clock: my first day as a choirboy of the Cathedral. No achievement of mine in my eight years had had so great an effect upon my mother. Not even when, at seven, I had successfully fought off five girls, all sisters, with a thick piece of sugar cane; not even when I won the long-distance race at the church outing; not even when she and my stepfather came home tired as dogs from the fields, one afternoon, to find that I had cooked a meal for them (a meal which I wanted to stand out as a single landmark of my love), and which they inter-preted as a boast, with the result that I had cooked their meals every day since then . . . "Jesus Christ, boy! You heard me say morning here? Well, get up!" And then I heard her opening the window of her bedroom, and talking to the darkness outside. "Lav-ignia! Lavignia? You sleeping too? What time that clock o' yourn saying, darling? This blasted boychild I have in here still sleeping, thinking that the morning waiting 'pon him . . . The sun all up in the skies already! What time it saying? . . . Thanks." And she closed the window with a bang, and suddenly I could hear Lavig-nia's voice no more. And the barking of the dogs stopped; and the cackling of the hens ceased, as if someone had shot them dead.

I searched around in the semi-darkness for my home-clothes: the ragged cap, now too old for me to remember its original colour or shape; next, the shirt, patched expertly in many places and looking like the quilted robe of Joseph; and then, the trousers, my stepfather's, which were never reduced to fit me, and which warbled about my legs like an old man's underwear, wet in the sea. And then I rolled the crocus bags and the straw mattress from the floor, took them under my arms and went into the backyard to hand them over to the sun, to dry. I had wet my bed again. It was the kind of wetting I did not wish my mother to see, since it might have terrified her to think that I was growing up. But she found it out, nevertheless. "You pissing-pissing-pissing! Looka boy, you don't know you old to be pissing? You not 'shamed?" I was glad it was only three o'clock; that none of the girls in the village was awake; that nobody could hear her reproaching me for this behaviour. There must have been something about this morning, this Easter morning, which held her silent and crippled in awe. For she did not strike me with the backhand slap which she had perfected with such habit and such speed and accuracy that it landed, always, in the same fat spot of my face.

Again, the pigs and the sheep were on my mother's side: they had filled their pens with mountains of their droppings. And all the time I was cleaning the pens and washing the pigs I wondered if it was like this in Bethlehem, in that stable where Christ was born; if that stable smelled half as dirty as this; if God had purposely made that the birthplace of our Saviour, in order to remind him, always, to be humble. Or if it was to give him an inferiority complex. And I was glad I was not born in a stable.

The pigs smelled evil. After the pigs, the sheep. Rank-rank-rank sheep, whose perfume would have taken a soap factory of scrubbing to wipe off. And then I began to think of my first day in the Cathedral's choir: this morning when Christ was supposed to have come out of a grave somewhere in a country so far from my little village; and I was going to walk up the aisle of the beautiful church, up to the sacred chancel, and send my voice prancing all over the church, in a solo, in praise of Easter. And all the boys in my village and in the choir would envy me. Particularly Henry, who was only my substitute, and who—"Them pigs clean yet? You tending to the sheeps? Yesterday morning the sheeps had *my* milk left back in *their* bubbies! And you forget to sweep the yard. Boy, you think you is a man, because you is this big cathedral choirboy? But lemme tell you something. Your backside ain't so big that I can't put a proper tarring in it, this bright blessed Easter morning, eh!" I could feel the sting of the whip in the threat of her voice. And I knew she meant it. So I hurried through my work, making sure that in my eagerness to wear the rich linen ruff, the crimson cassock, and the pearly white surplice, I did not become inefficient. The sun pretended it was going to come up above the tops of the sugar canes. But when I paused and waited for it, it changed its mind, and continued to give only a golden glow over the entire village.

My work was done. And I bounded into the house.

"You don't intend to bathe? You intends to go into the white people church smelling like a pigpen? Looka boy, get outta my eyesight, and go to the standpipe, and get a clean bucket o' fresh water and cleanse yourself with, you hear?"

Who would argue with a woman like this? Who would *dare?*

Across the pitchlake stretch of the road the canes were grumbling and shaking their fists in my face. I imagined monsters coming out of them. Only last week a man had been lambasted by *the Man* in the canes. My head was swollen with monsters coming at me. I heard a rustling in the canes. And I dropped the bucket.

And when I stopped running, I was beside our paling. My dog, Rover, came panting at my side: again he had frightened me. And I wanted to kick him dead. But I only kicked him once; and was glad that he could not talk.

Holding on to his collar, I went back across the road to recapture my bucket and get the water. A few malicious windows with heads in them, and kerosene lamps beside the heads, were open. And I walked in the valley of the shadow of the canes this time (my guardian-angel dog beside me!), so they would not see me.

"I thought you wasn't coming back!" my mother shouted. "It is four o'clock. You not *riding* that bicycle outta this house today, bright Easter morning. You *walking* to church, 'cause I slave-and-slave on them clothes o' yourn, and no damn bicycle seat and bicycle spokes ain't going mash-up my labour, you hear me?" It meant walking two miles, two miles of canes, two miles of *Men* in the canes. In all that distance I would pass only ten houses, until I approached the square in which the Cathedral was built. I would pass only ten street lamps, which seemed to have been burning since the day the island was discovered, and which were never repaired, and which seemed ready to go out any minute. I would be alone in all that time, all that terrible distance, with only the brightly lit church in my heart and the rich beautiful music in my ears.

You not riding that bicycle outta this house today. No passenger buses ran in my part of the island on Easter morning. At least, not at five o'clock. And the villagers were so poor that only one family was rich enough to own a broken-down car. But that family was not a church-going Christian-minded family, and I could not hope for a lift. I was the only one in my village who belonged to the Church of England. My mother, who was brought up in that church, had recently started to attend the Church of the Nazarene because she felt its services were more like a part of her life, were more emotional, more exciting, more tragic and more happy: something like that holy day when "them twelve mens gathered up in that room upstairs, and talked in twelve different complete language and dialect, Christ, like nobody's business!" There, she could stand up in her small congregation, and open her heart to God, and to them, and tell the whole world that yesterday, *God stepped in and Satan stepped out, Amen! and I was brought through, pretty and clean.* There, she could testify how God helped her *when I didn't know where the hell I could get six cents from to buy flour and lard oil to make bakes for my child.* There, she could clap her hands and stomp her feet till the floorboards creaked with emotion, and jump up in the air and praise God. And for all that, feel as if God was indeed listening. But in the Church of England she was regimented to a sit-and-stand exercise of dull religious drilling. And she always complained to Lavignia that she did not understand one word of what the parson was talking about. He used words that simple, common, poor people could not understand. And never, never "have I see anybody stand up in the Church o' England, and say Amen, Halleluliah to God!" It was such a strange church to her.

My mother then began the careful ceremony of dressing me. My hair was ripped by the horse-comb, which, this morning, seemed too fine-toothed to plough the tough roots of my rebellious hair. And each time the plough stuck, my mother cursed and said she didn't understand why the hell I couldn't have good black people's hair like everybody else. After the combing came the greasing. My hair would shine like the stars in the heavens. Then the talcum powder under my arms, and the bay rum to make me smell "nice and proper." And the new silk vest, with the price tag still on it. And then the underwear. And all these things she dressed me in, suspicious always that I would destroy them. At eight years of age, she did not think that I was fit to dress myself on an Easter morning, to venture unto the powerful Church of England's God.

On went the three-quarter grey stockings, with a rim of blue and black. When I reached under the bed for my shoes, I heard her warning voice breaking my eardrums: "No-no-no! You is not mashing-up them shoes! You are putting on them shoes, *last* thing! I want them shoes to return back inside this house without *one* bruise, you hear me, boy? If I see a *mark* on them, *one* mark—well, God help you!"

And she meant it. I had suffered because of this, many times before. And all I was guilty of was that I had walked *in* them. But she had examined the shoes, and had decided that I had not walked in them "properly." This time she would take no chances.

My shirt was the next piece of vestment in this robing. I was made to stand like a piece of wallaba tree trunk, still, not breathing, while she threaded the shirt through my arms and buttoned every button herself. I could smell the richness of the cotton, and feel its warmth on my washed body. The ready-tied tie went on next. And

then the trousers. Carefully I put one leg through, and then the
other, making sure not to touch the trousers themselves. She pushed
the shirt gently into my trousers, and snapped the buckle.

Only my shoes remained! But I knew what to expect. For weeks
she had made me drill about the house, walking on old newspapers
so that the soles would not be soiled, stretching the shoes, which
she always bought *too small*. I could never understand why. And
even though she insisted that my feet were too big for my size, that
"big shoes don't look nice 'pon a small boy's foot," I couldn't really
imagine she would purposely force me into these undersized shoes
just for the sake of her belief.

But I inhaled deeply. I rested my hand on her shoulder as she
commanded me, balanced myself on one leg, and got ready for the
punishment and torture. The shoe was too small. But that was not
the point. It looked nice! My toes went in. I could feel a savage sting
against my instep. The heel refused to go in. And as I touched the
back of the shoe, to see what would happen, my mother shrieked,
"Good Christ, boy! Don't step on the back o' the shoe! You want
to throw my money down the drain? You are mashing it up. And
suppose I have to take them back . . ."

But I knew she would never take them back. Intransigence
would never permit her pride the blow of taking them even to
Woody, the shoemaker across the road, for a stretching. I would
have to make my feet get smaller. "Come-come, eat this little
food." I pulled a chair from the table, and was preparing to sit
down, when I heard her voice again, "Good Jesus Christ, boy,
I didn't tell you to *sit* down and eat! Not in them trousers that I
slave-and-slave so hard over to press and make look nice for you,
like if you is somebody decent. *Stand up!* Stand up and eat. It can't
kill yuh; it can't kill yuh!" And so I had to stand up and eat the *little
food*: about two pints of green tea, warm and thick and rich with
sheep's milk; a loaf of bread as big as a house, and a wedge of
roasted pork, enough for two persons; and a banana. My mother
believed in bananas. "They make your skin nice and smooth," she
would say.

I soon felt the heavy load in my belly; and I felt good. I would wear *any* shoe now. Even a size seven instead of a ten. "Come-come!" she said, "Belch! Belch! You belch good and proper, whilst you home, 'cause I don't want to hear that you belch-out, or break wind, in the white people church, or in the public road, like if you don't have no manners, hear?" And I granted her her belch. A smothered, respectable belch, which, although it did not satisfy her, yet made her say nothing, since it assured her that I had already belched at home.

Now, the shoes! My hand was resting on her fat shoulders. I was balancing all my weight on my left foot. My right foot was said to be slightly larger than my left foot—although she never told me why. I knew the shoe would never fit. But I was not such a fool as to tell her. "Put yuh weight on your instep, boy, do! Don't put all yuh weight on the whole shoe, 'cause the shoe won't go on then."

Exasperated, she grabbed my foot and forced it into the pincers of the shoe, while I remained silent, and in agony. "Hold there! Don't move!" she commanded. And she left me. Coming back with the large pot-spoon which we used as a shoehorn, she said, "Push! Push hard! But don't mash-down the instep. Push hard, boy, like you have life!" The more I pushed, the smaller the shoe became. My face changed from black to blue to purple. Still my judgement warned me not to comment on my pain, and certainly not on the smallness of the shoe. She would never believe. "Push! You pushing, or you standing up there with your face like some ram-goat own?"

At last, through some miracle, the foot went in. Never to come out again! Lord have mercy, I prayed in my heart, as the pain whizzed through my body. And when the other shoe was rammed on, I was sweating. The perspiration was changing my Sea Island cotton shirt into plastic. And she noticed it, and wanted to know *why* I was sweating. "You intend to sweat-up this clean shirt that I just put-on on your back, boy?" And I tried hard to stop sweating; tried very hard, as if to stop it I had only to turn off a faucet. "Walk off and lemme see how the shoes look on your foot, boy!" I held my breath, pushed my chest out, and asked God for strength. The shoes crucified me. I would never be able to walk on the smooth marble in the Cathedral. But I wanted to be at church this Easter morning. This was *my* Easter morning.

"Okay! You ready now." And she dusted my handkerchief with some Evening in Paris perfume, tucked it into my shirt breast pocket, and secured it with a gold-coloured small safety pin, which I was permitted to wear only to funerals and weddings. "Now, turn round and let me see you. Christ, boy, you look real good! You look just like the manager of the plantation's son. Just like a little doctor. Now, I want you to grow up fast, and be a doctor, hear?" And I knew that if I did not answer yes, she would want to know why. "Yes," I said, wishing that I was already grown up, and thousands of miles from there.

She looked at me again and again, and then she took me into her bedroom, and showed me my reflection in the life-sized looking glass. Back in the living room, the white, sparkling white, blanco-cleaned cork hat with the green undersides was clamped on my head. I was now ready for the Easter world!

"Since you not riding that bicycle outta here, this blessed Easter morning, I am going to give you twelve cent to put in your pocket. Now, *walk* down. I want you to look fresh when you enter that cathedral church. Now, seeing that it is Easter, and you have friends, you must buy a penny in sweets . . . No, you better buy lozengers to make your breath smell nice; and a pack o' sweeties . . . For every child like sweeties, and you ain't no different. And keep the rest of the change for bus fare *back* home. You could afford to climb in a crowded bus, *after* church. It don't matter then if your trousers crease-up a trifle. Now, come back inside this house looking tidy. Not as if you went through a pig mouth, you hear me?"

She put the twelve-cent piece into my hand, as if it was the last part of her fortune, and which I was to cherish for the rest of my life. I looked up at her, so large, so beautiful, so lovely, and so black —a mysterious queen or something, from Africa, with her hair braided neatly and long; with her old white dress, which she washed three times a week, clutching to the feminine twists and turns of her full body. She looked at me, and she looked at my thoughts; and she smiled. She drew me close, close to her breasts and her rolling soft stomach, where I could feel the love and the blood pumping through her body. And she kissed me on each cheek and said, in a voice that came from the bottom of her heart and her belly, "I praise the Lord that I didn't throw you in no blasted dry well when your father left me pregnunt with you, seven-eight years ago in this terrible world with not even a half-cent to buy milk with. God bless yuh, son. I proud o' you!"

I was ready to go now. Outside the morning was glorious. The sun had eventually decided to come up. And I could see its rays setting the tops of the canes on fire with a golden flame. And the dogs and the chickens and the small children were quarrelling for their breakfast. My own breakfast felt good and heavy and safe in my belly.

"When you go 'cross the road, and you see Jonesie, say good-morning. Say goodmorning to Stella. And to Lavignia. I am going to call Lavignia now, and let she see how nice you look." And she moved from me, and went into her bedroom, and called out for Lavignia.

"Why you don't let me say my prayers to God in peace this blasted morning, eh, Mistress Carlton? I here on my two knees, before God, asking Him, who the hell He intend to send to lend me a shilling to buy milk with this Easter morning?"

"He coming out now," my mother said, with pride.

"Who? God?"

"The bridegroom coming! Come outside, and see how he look."

And Lavignia, apparently convinced that her prayers would be in vain, left her spiritual complaining and came out in front of her house to see me *dressed like a little doctor*.

"Oh Christ, Mistress Carlton! This boychild o' yourn look first class! Boy, you should be eternally grateful you have such a nice mother. I hopes to Christ you don't intend to forget this mother o' yourn when you come to be a man, eh? 'Cause if you do, the birds o' vengeance going *pick-out* your blasted eye!"

And I had to answer Lavignia with as much respect as I would have answered my mother, and say, "No, please, Miss Lavignia. I won't never forget my mother."

"Good," she concluded, and adjusted my tie, although it was already adjusted properly. "Now, you go on down in the name o' the Lord, and sing that solo like if you is a angel. Mistress Carlton, wait, you give this boy some fresh crispy biscuits to help out with the voice? Biscuits good for the voice. If you don't have fresh ones, I have some. Come, boy, take these biscuits. They does do wonders for yuh voice. Eat them whilst you's singing, and the people in that cathedral church going think that you is Michael, the Archangel!"

I took the biscuits and mumbled on them, all the way down the road with the canes bordering it, mumbling, mumbling, trying to take my mind off the torment of the shoes and the threat of the canes. But the canes moaned and the shoes burned.

I walked in the middle of the creaking road, forcing my mind from my present predicament and focusing it on the musty-smelling Changing Room in the loft of the Cathedral. I could see the ruffs sparkling white. I could smell the starch in them; and they were ironed so many times by Henry's mother that they shone, and when you ran your fingers over them they were as smooth as glass. And the crimson robe. And the white linen surplice, all made to fit me, all mine, so long as I remained with an unbroken voice in the choir of this heavenly Cathedral. And I could see myself coming down the steps from the Changing Room with the other choristers, and standing at the entrance of the church, while the Lord Bishop and his assistants waited for a few late worshippers to settle in their seats. And in my mind, I could see the faces of that vast congregation: almost half the population of the island, who came to the Cathedral in droves whenever the Bishop was preaching. Some came to church as they would every Sunday, because they liked church; others, because they liked the resplendent robes, with the hoods of the universities of the ministers—all colours under the sun; so pretty and so impressive; and so learned. And more than once I myself wanted to become a minister in God's Church of England, to swish my long, flowing robes, and adjust my hood and hat and large ruby Cyclops ring every second of the service; and pour communion wine at the rails; and mumble those few important indistinguishable words, while the sinners knelt before *me*, and prayed to *me*, and asked *me* forgiveness, because they could not see God, nor talk to Him, unless they had first asked *me* forgiveness, and recognized me as His right-hand man.

Now, I was walking up the aisle in my mind . . . so long and so smooth, with its marble shining from the long underpaid hours of scrubbing by the cathedral sexton, my voice warbling; and the men and women at the ends of the pews nearest the choir nodding their heads, and complimenting. How they would raise their heads from their unmelodic hymn books, and nod, and turn slightly with their eyes to locate the voice; and I, seeing them, would raise my voice a little bit higher, a little bit sweeter, until the organ seemed silent and voiceless as the dumb man who opened his mouth and sang aloud his soundless praise to God, every Sunday, at matins. And then my solo. The old heads would be nodding, and smiling, because they could not applaud in God's presence, in God's church. And the organist, like a spy, glowering at me through his motor-car mirror above the organ keys, anticipating a wrong key, or a blunder . . . and Henry, envious with praise.

And then, when it is all finished, the choir, and the Lord Bishop, and the ministers walking down the whipped, chastised church, with the congregation dumb and washed out by the sermon and the presence in the church of Christ's body come from the dead . . . rejoicing, because this is Easter.

And then the benediction said by the Bishop, and the sign of the cross, which he always made as if he was chasing flies from his face; and the limp people kneeling, to say a last something, a word or two, in thanks to God.

I passed the first street lamp and continued into the desolate black morning, cramped by the thick, unsympathetic fields of canes which refused to let the sun through to keep me company. On and

on, in perpetual misery from my shoes. At last I had to give in. I
took them off. I tied the laces together. I strung the shoes around
my neck. I pushed the stockings into my pockets. My feet were so
numb they felt they had disappeared in seawater. And then I ran,
hurrying to the Cathedral before the street became too crowded,
before I could be seen, and detected, and laughed at. But nothing
happened all the way.

I reached the vicinity of the Cathedral: the tall tombstones like
diminutive skyscrapers, and the trees in the graveyard of the church,
and the black birds playing hide-and-seek from tree to tree, and the
houses coming alive . . . and finally, the Cathedral itself, facing me
like my mother, unapproving.

I would have to put my shoes and stockings on before I could
cross the threshold of the West Portico. But I had to find some
place to sit down, first.

The bells were ringing now. I looked up to see them, and they
filled my heart with joy. And I yearned to be in the choir, in the
chancel, singing my solo.

The congregation was arriving. From where I stood, outside
the church wall, I could see women dressed in the white of angels:
white hats, white shoes, as if they were proud to be part of this
great resurrection morning, as if they had remained new brides,
new virgins, all their lives. They were standing in the West Portico, waiting for the service to begin, waiting for their friends
and enemies to see their new clothes, waiting for the men to pass
and whisper, little controversial words for their ears. And most of
the men, in the black of the funeral, wearing their suits of long-
ago black, which fitted them like coats of armour, and walking stiff
and proud in the morning sunlight spinning through the lazy
leaves—they hovered around the North Portico, talking about the
test match which ended in a draw.

I could see Henry, my arch-enemy, standing near them, and
with him were some of the boys in the choir. I lingered near the tall
wall that kept the Cathedral hearing-distance away from the fish-
cries and the whore-cries of the nearby market and the street of

floating women. How was I to get into the churchyard and sit on a tombstone and put my shoes on my feet again?

The organ began to rant and swell, breathing its powerful cruel chords into the ears of the disinterested congregation. Everything was fresh. Everything was new. The organ was breathing now like a monster. Somebody important was arriving. From where I stood, looking over the tip of the wall, over the tops of the short croton trees, and over the head of the white angel, silent and stationary in polished marble, I could barely make out the roosters sitting on the helmets of the governor of the island and his party. The Lord Bishop, with his robes fluttering like the Union Jack in the breeze, came out to meet His Excellency at the North Portico. I could see the prime minister of the island and some of his ministers standing uncomfortable in their official clothes; and the lords and ladies of the island, all untitled, but all rich and white, coming to this cathedral church old as Christopher Columbus, so early in the morning. And they all seemed half asleep to me.

As they disappeared into the church, I threw my shoes over the church wall and jumped behind them, onto the soft dew in the grass, near a dead sailor who slept in a tomb. It said he was an ensign.

They were coming towards me now, coming up the aisle, as I peered through the west window. The important people, and the choir. I saw Henry grinning into the pages of his hymn book. I saw the choir pass the multitude of people of all colours: the black, the brown, the light-skinned, the light brown, and approach the front pews of the church, where the Governor and the white people and the rich black people always sat.

I was fighting with my shoes.

And as they filed into their seats and into their stalls, all that was left was the wide white aisle, like a swath in a cane field, running straight out into the road, through the east gate.

There was a beggar-man standing in the silhouette of the gate, in the road, drinking from a small paper bag, with which he was conducting as the music romped and played.

I was fighting with my shoes.

   And all the time my tears were falling on the clean, freshly ironed cotton shirt, and into the shoes, as I tried in vain to get them back on my feet. And when I looked up and the film of sadness dropped with the tears, and I could see, I saw Henry step into the middle of the aisle, in the chancel, and my heart broke. And straightaway I saw my mother, standing at the entrance of the gate, waiting: waiting to examine my shoes.

A SHORT DRIVE

This Saturday afternoon at three, with the first real light, and the first cleansed skies washed so blue after the rains, there was a constant breeze and upon the breeze came the coolness and the strong smell of patchouli and summer flowers. It was tantalizing as the smell of saltiness and of fresh fish brought out of the sea on a beach in Barbados. Gwen was a woman with a touch of this saltiness on her breath. And the woman back in Toronto, on Lascelles Boulevard, she too carried a trace of the smell; but her real smell was of lavender.

Calvin sat nobly and like an emperor, stiff, with the pride of new ownership, behind the steering wheel, reduced to the size of a toy wheel against his imposing size, of the Volkswagen which he had just bought, "hot," he said, for seventy-five dollars. He called it his "Nazzi bug." And he too looked clean, as the skies. His skin, on his arms up to his elbow; his neck, right into the V of the black dashiki; his legs from below the knee and down to his toes, all this flesh was "oiled, Jack," he said. He had "shampooled" his round-shaped Afro, and it was glistening although he had used Duke Greaseless Hairdressing for Men. He had given me some, but my hair did not accept the same shine as his. He looked clean. And he looked like a choice piece of pork seasoned and ready for the greased pan and the oven. He would not like this comparison. But I have to say he looked clean.

His legs were thin and had no calf. This was the first time I had seen Calvin dressed in anything but grey-green plaid trousers and blue blazer. Today, he was in cut-down jeans, which gave me the first glimpse of his legs. I could not believe his long stories over beer in frosted mugs and Polish sausages, about playing running back for the college football team. The black dashiki with its V-neck and sleeves trimmed in black, red, and green, tempered somewhat the informality of his casual dress.

"Pass the paper bag. Glove compartment. Take a sip, brother," he said, holding the steering wheel with his left hand, and a Salem in the other. "And keep your motherfucking head *down*. In case the *man*."

The puttering VW rollicked over the gravel road at a slow pace. Its dashboard was cluttered with additional things which Calvin had installed. Cassette tape deck *and* eight-track tape deck, AM-FM radio and a shortwave radio, a contraption which looked like a walkie-talkie, and two clocks. One he said gave the time in the Northeast, and the other the time of the South, of the city of Birmingham, Alabama, where we were, and had been together since the beginning of the summer semester. Looking at this dashboard, I was reminded of the glimpse of the cockpit of the plane in which I had travelled two months earlier from Toronto to teach the summer course, in which Calvin was an auditor. I had never heard that term before. But Calvin was my student. And as the heavy Southern nights spun themselves out into greater monotony, he became my guide to where the action was, and almost my friend. The noisy VW moved slowly over the rutted road, and I could see in the distance the sights and substance and large properties, the grace and the Southern architecture in the residential exclusive district we were passing on our right hand. We were driving so slow that I thought it was a mistake, that Calvin lived in this district, and that we would turn into one of the magnificent gates, any minute now. One of these mansions I had passed, in the dark last night, searching in vain for Gwen's apartment. I now could see the structure I had mistaken for the house. It is a white-painted gazebo with Grecian pillars. And in the gazebo is a child's swing and a white-painted iron chair and iron table. There is no child in the swing, now.

"Ripple?" Calvin said, after a large gulp, wiping away the evidence with the hand that held the Salem, just in case. "This is the real shit." Last night, at the bar with the frosted beer mugs and huge Polish sausages, Calvin ordered two gigantic T-bone steaks and two bottles of Mommessin red wine, both of which I paid for. This Ripple wine, which cut into my throat like a razor blade dipped in molasses, must have been a ritualistic thing to go with his cut-down jeans and the dashiki. Or it might have been cultural. I took a second swig from the bottle hardly concealed in the brown paper bag, and squeezed my eyes shut, and shook my head. "This be the real shit," he said, disagreeing with my reaction.

On our left hand, we were passing men, slow as in a shutter speed to capture even the whiz of movement, men bent almost in the shape of hairpins, doubled-up, close to the grass which was so green it looked blue; they resembled gigantic mushrooms painted onto the sprawling lawns, in their broad-brimmed hats necessary to protect them against the brutality of the sun, and the exhaustion that the humidity seemed to sap from their bodies. I could see them move their hands as if they were playing with the grass, but at the completion of each piston-like action, the effort in their movements appearing slowed down by the encompassing grandeur of the afternoon. When this act of slashing the blades of grass was completed, a shower of grass lifted itself on impact, a blade of steel flashed like lightning, and the grass was scattered harmlessly over the lawn.

"Mexicans," Calvin said, as if he didn't like Mexicans, and with some bitterness; and as if he was pronouncing a sentence not only on them, but also upon their labour.

They were soaked to their backs and their shapeless clothes made them look Indian to me. But the formlessness of their shirts and pants was the designer's label of hard labour. They could have been Chinese standing up to their ankles in water and growing rice.

"Amerrikah! Home of the motherfucking *free*, Jack!" Calvin said. "This South's shaped my personality, and this university's fucked it up, with the result that I don't know *who* I am. I was happier in Atlanta on 'Fayette Street in the black area." I did not know what he was talking about. I was admiring the Mexicans. They looked now like figures in a tableau, painted against the bluegrass lawns; and the manner in which they had thrown out the proficiency and precision of the power mower by the bare strength of their hands made me deaf to Calvin's protestations. And it seemed that they were showing the superiority of their knowledge of nature and things and their own past, in this temporary but scorching menialness of labour, and expressing their own protest, as Calvin was with words, with the violence of their muscular arms.

Calvin was now slouched behind the steering wheel, as if the Ripple had suddenly changed the composition of the blood in his veins. His right arm was extended so that his fingers just touched the steering wheel, as if he wanted no closer association with it. As if he was despising the wheel, the VW, along with the statement he had just made about rejection. "What the fuck am I getting a college education for? And writing academic papers on reductionism for?" I still did not understand what he was talking about. But he brought the VW to an uncertain stop. We were under a tree. Calvin had told me the name of this tree. They were all over the South; and they cluttered the path through the woods to a building on campus where convocations were held. The first time Calvin told me the name of this tree, he told me about a woman named Billie Holiday. I did not know whom he was talking about; but he started to sing the words of a song, "Strange Fruit," and we were inhaling the sweet smell of the magnolia trees and the wind was unforgiving in bringing the strong Southern smell to our nostrils. I would have trouble remembering the name of the woman who sang this song, and more often the title of the song slipped my memory. But I remembered one line, only one line of the song about Southern trees. *Blood on the leaves, and blood at the root.* Calvin had sung the entire song from memory. He sang it off-key. And now, this afternoon, the VW stopped uncertainly because he had never accumulated the thirty dollars to fix the brakes, we were stopped under a tree. I looked up into the thick branches of the trees under which we had walked to the place which served beer in frosted glasses and huge Polish sausages, and only the raindrops accumulated on the leaves dropped into my face.

"What kind of tree is that? I don't think we have these trees in Toronto."

"The size, or the name?" Calvin asked.

The mouth of the Ripple bottle was in his mouth. A little of the wine escaped his lips, and it ran slowly down into his beard, but I could still see the rich colour of red, like blood.

"The name."

"Poplar. This be a poplar tree."

We were shaded by the tree. And I was beginning to feel great relief from the humidity which embraced me like a tight-fitting shirt.

Southern trees bear strange fruit.

Calvin's singing had not improved in the month since I had first heard it. I smiled at his rendition.

Black bodies hanging in the Southern breeze.

We remained in the shade, and I could feel the breeze, making my body cool, as if I was being dipped slowly into seawater. I was comfortable. But Calvin was not: sadness appeared in his eyes. His lips formed themselves into a sneer. He moved his body, and the bottle of Ripple became heavy and caused the seat and the leather to cry out. The leather on the seats of the VW was the most valuable feature of the old rumbling automobile. He moved his body in the small space we shared, and I could smell his perspiration, and his breath laden with the menthol from the Salems, and the sickening sweetness of the Ripple.

"Dualism, my brother," he said. He leaned over, took the bottle from me, and drained it dry. "What the fuck? I've seen the ass-whuppings in Selma, Bamma, Little Rock."

The breeze stopped. In the languor of the afternoon we were once more lumbering over the road, which turned to hard, dried, uncared-for dirt. It was sad. The sadness was like the sudden fall of dust under the low-hanging trees, when the scent of magnolia rises like shimmering zzz's you see, if you kneel down, rising from a hot tarred road.

"What do you want to be, then? What do you want to make of your life, if not be a scholar?"

"Miles!"

"Away from Birmingham?"

"Miles Davis!"

I did not know what to say to this: Calvin's feelings and fantasies seemed to inflate his thin body, making him large and grand and strong as the running back he always boasted he was when he played for his college football team.

"As Barry White says, bro', *let the music play*. Let the music play on. Let the motherfucking music *play*, Jack! I be Miles. I am Miles. Or, I am Coltrane. Trane. I am Otis. I'm Nina Simone. And I am 'Retha! And I am on a stage at the biggest theatre in the South, but not the Opry, and *thousands* are out there in the dark screaming my name. My toon. My voice. My riffs. My trumpet. My tenor horn. It's the same fucking thing, Jack. Let the music *play*."

The smell of Calvin's Salems, the old odour that had settled inside the VW, filled my nostrils; and with these smells was the smell of clothes that are wet, and drying in the back seat. I could also smell the oiliness of Southern-fried chicken from Chicken Box Number Two. We had eaten chicken many times in the VW, deliberately not eating in restaurants, as if we were still suffering from the segregation of accommodation. Eating in the VW allowed us greater ease of checking out the beautiful women coming out of the women's residence in their pink shorts, and white shorts, and blue shorts. Perhaps we had left some uneaten boxes in the back seat.

We were by ourselves on this road of dried mud now, running by a field in which grew something I could not recognize. Corn came to mind, as this place shared the geography of that island where I came from. Corn came naturally to mind, but there was not the lusciousness in the endless spread of green that made me feel we were adrift on the sea; we were alone, although far to the right I could see the smudged whiteness of the pillars and other parts of the architecture from colonial times; and closer on our right, some small houses, and from them sentinels of rising white smoke that turned blue as it reached high above our heads. And still the sun was shining.

And then in the distance, like the call of my mother's voice, miles away, but only a few yards from the makeshift cricket pitch we had gouged out of our own mud to play the game, my mother's voice calling me home for dinner: rice cooked with few split peas because there was a war on, and served with salt fish from the Grand Banks of Newfoundland, thin and flat and full of bones, but transformed by the improvised wisdom in these things of my mother, and soaked in lard oil, tangy from the cheap butter it was said we imported from Australia, to us in a commonwealth of nations, friends; and tomatoes picked from our backyard; that welcoming call, that wrenched me from my friends and playmates, disappointed that I had not hit the ball for six, or four, or even a single in the hot, hot-competing afternoon. So did this sound come to me, unanchored in this vastness of living, thriving green, in the rickety VW with a stranger, drinking Ripple concealed in a brown paper bag from the eyes of the sheriff.

In the blue-white distance I heard the heavy rumbling of a train. A freight train. I followed the train as it wriggled its way like a worm through the greenness on the land, as it moved like a large worm, and in my mind, through the history its approach was unravelling and through the myths of trains, men on the run travelled on them; men fleeing women and wives and child payments hid on them; and men in chains and those who escaped from chain gangs were placed on them. The best blues were written about them. The rumbling of this train, like the rumbling of that train in the cowboy movies of the Old West, seemed interminable as a toothache that comes at sunset and that lasts throughout the groaning night, like a string pulled by a magician from the palm of one hand, like the worm you pull from the soft late grass-covered ground that does not end, and that makes you late to go fishing. I heard a siren. Or a whistle? There were so many sirens I was hearing this summer in Birmingham because of civil rights and fights with sheriffs, that I sometimes mistook the sound. I heard a siren. The siren killed the sound of the train.

"Police cruiser?" I asked Calvin. "Or ambulance?"

"In this neighbourhood, could be either. Both. Chitlins and hog maws. One goes with the other."

"Cops coming through the grass?" I still did not know what was planted in the growing vastness surrounding me.

. Calvin lit another Salem. The VW was immediately filled with smoke. This lasted for one moment. Then, it was filled with a tingling, sweet, and bitter smell. It was not the Salem that Calvin had lighted. It was not a Salem. But he filled his lungs with the smoke, and then shot two unbroken thin and fierce jets of white from his nostrils, making him look, in that moment, like a walrus; speaking through smoke and coughing at the same time as if his thinness meant tuberculosis, and with his breath held, he said, "What can we in the South do, with this dualism thing? Before it fucks us up?"

"Education could never be so destructive."

"Spoken like a true West Indian who knows nothing about the South, and Amerrikah."

"Education is freedom."

"Spoken like a man who's never lived in Birmingham, or in any city in the South!"

"You need education."

"We need a black thang. We don't need no education, brother. A black thang. And a black conclusion."

"And what about your seminar on reductionism?"

"Shit! Can you see me discussing that at my mother's Sunday dinner table? She be calling the cops thinking this nigger's crazy!"

The VW became quiet, still filled with the strange smoke. The words Calvin was using were larger than the capacity of the small "Bug," too bulging with the possibility of explosion and violence. I went back to the Mexicans on the lawns. I began to have the sensation of being rocked from side to side. But it could have been the vibration of the freight train, which had not yet come to its end from within the tunnel created by the endless fields of growing things. Looking outside through the steam of smoke from Calvin's fag, I saw pieces of cement and concrete and paper blowing along the narrow sidewalks and into the street. The light here was harsh. There were no flowers. There were no poplar trees. The trees here were stubby, but they did not shade the blinding, shimmering waves that came off the surface of the sidewalk. I wished, at that moment, that I was back in Toronto among the red brick, the dirty red brick and cobblestones, passing shops that sold the *New York Times* and the *Times Literary Supplement*, and that sold Condor and Erinmore pipe tobacco and French cigarettes and French leathers or letters—I never knew which was the proper term—things I was accustomed to, and knew how to handle, among the buildings that were not so imposing and the short streets. Space there was more manageable. I wished for the softness of streets shaded by small trees, and lined with cars, many of which belonged to students and were broken into; with garbage pails of green and other wrecks; and I wanted the softness of the northern seductive and betraying nights, and to be among the unthreateningness of broken-down homes with cloth at their windows and with unpainted boards nailed across the windows and the doors, derelicts from the nights of rioting in the cities in the North—Detroit, New York, Washington, D.C.; and missed by Toronto.

Calvin must have been buried in similar thoughts of wanting to be elsewhere, must have come to a conclusion of similar importance, or to some agreeable compromise with his thoughts about education, for he straightened his back, and the vigour and youth of his years came back into his body. His eyes were bright again; and the whiteness in them shone. The dashiki he was wearing made him look noble like an emperor, stiff and proud with knowing where he was.

"This is the very last time I be laying this paranoid shit on you, brother. You are my guest here in this city. I am a Southerner, and we Southerners 're hospitable people. I'm gonna show y'all some real Southern shit now, y'all!"

He had lit a Salem before he spoke. He was the kind of man who could not make a serious statement before he had first lit a cigarette. Smoke streamed through his nostrils, and he looked like a walrus again.

"I'm an Amerrikan. This is my motherfucking country."

"You were born here, man."

"I'm a Southerner. So, let's have some Ripple. Let's drink this shit."

It was a long road. There were no street lights. Dust swirled round the tires of the VW, as it pierced its single weak headlamp through the oncoming darkness. "If the man don't get me for this Ripple, he sure's shit gonna get me for this light!" The moon was a dark sliver of lead, far off to the right. Calvin was still in his cut-down jeans and dashiki. But I had changed. I was in white. White Levi's and a white dashiki, bought from the Soul Brother Store. When I went into the store, dark and musty and smelling of old cigars, the owner greeted me, "Brother, come in, brother!" He charged me twenty dollars more than the price I had seen on the same clothes in two other, white stores on the same integrated street. But I did not divulge this to Calvin.

"Lay it on me, brother!" Calvin had said in admiration and in approval, when he picked me up.

"Be cool, man," I had told him, trying hard to be cool.

"Gwen's opened your nose!" he said, meaning that Gwen was educating me in the ways of the South.

"Shee-it!" I said, hoping it came out right, and heavy, and properly Southern.

"Shit!" Calvin said. His speech was like a crisp bullet in my chest.

Now, driving along this road, in the middle, there was no dividing line, and if there was, we could not see it; in the swirling flour of this thin road, cramped in the VW, with the smell of smoke, a trace of leather, and the acrid and sweet languor from the fumes of Ripple, making less speed than the rattle of the muffler suggested, and hitting stones in the middle of the road, the two of us, rebellious and drunk in our joy, were like escaped prisoners; but I, like a man redeemed, Gwen had said, when I was at the door like a gentleman, "Shee-it, you ain't leaving here to walk those

dark streets, at this hour, man. This is the South," saying it with
a pronounced West Indian accent; we were now, Calvin and I,
screaming and hollering as if we were both born in the ecstasy of
mad Southern Saturday nights in Birmingham.

Calvin slapped an eight-track tape into the player. "My Favorite
Things" came out. The hymn-like introduction, like a chant, coiled
around the jazz solo, reminded me of matins at St. Matthias Anglican Church in Barbados, and especially evensong and service. I could
picture myself walking in that peaceful sacred light, one hour after
the sun had gone down behind the tall casuarinas, trees that
reached the sky, in my imagination, when there was slice of a moon,
like this one here in Birmingham, and walking between thick green
sugar canes in my black John Whites that kicked up almost as much
dust as the tires of this old VW. And each time Coltrane repeated
the main statement of the tune, I could hear and recall the monotony of the tolling bells. There, my mother walked beside me, in
contented sloth of age, of sickness, and of Christianity. Here, I
bent my neck to the charmed pull of the music.

Calvin is silent beside me. This music is his. I have heard this
music before, probably, all the places and things and colours that the
music is showing me I have faced in Toronto. The tape is scratched
badly.

In the distance, pointed out to us by the weak left headlamp, is
a barn, or a factory, perhaps something that was once used as a
portable camp for soldiers. Soldiers are always on my mind in
Birmingham, this summer. The Civil War, a magazine swears in its
cover story, is about to be fought again: white people versus black
people. Soldiers with muskets, vertical straps of leather aslant their
shoulders, fighting for the *other* cause. And the flag of their con-
federation with its own two vertical blue slashes across its broad
bloodied shoulder, signifying something different. This building in
the shortening distance sits in a square stubbornness in the middle
of the single headlamp, with no grace of architecture like the
white-painted gazebo. From this distance it is black. It soon looks
brown. Light from inside the building is being forced through small

windows that are covered by blinds made of sacks for sugar, not for Bohemian style, but from economy. And as we get nearer still, the truth of its dimension, size, and colour, is exposed to us.

Coltrane's tenor saxophone reminds me of the singing of old women, repeating the verse of the hymn as if their age has crippled their recollection of succeeding verses. So, I begin to think again of my mother, leading the song at the Mothers' Union service, going over it again. "Rock of Ages." This saxophone is not speaking of such desperation, though.

We are approaching Gwen's wooden house.

Calvin stops the VW, for no reason; and I realize he's always doing this, but this time he parks it, and it rocks forward and backward, just before the engine dies. We are now bathed in the light from the naked fluorescent bulb on Gwen's porch. I did not see this light the night of the party. The rain was too heavy that night.

"You're really into Trane playing 'Love Supreme'!" he said.

"Not 'My Favorite Things'?"

"'Love Supreme,' brother."

How many other things in this city of Birmingham, this South, in this culture, in this short time here had I got wrong? I had heard a train, but was there a train rolling through the green fields like a lawnmower? I had seen a moon, but now that we were stopped, there was no moon.

"*A love supreme, a love supreme, a love supreme,*" Calvin said. "Nineteen times Trane chants it." I can see movement in Gwen's house, at the side, for the bedrooms are at the side.

Calvin got out, leaving me in the car, slammed the door shut, and stood beside the car. A splattering of water hit the gravel. I imagined steam rising. I could smell the sting of the water. And then I too got out, and shook my legs, each one, to straighten the seams of my tight-fitting jeans. Calvin was still peeing and shaking. Some men can pee as long as horses. But it looked more as if he was being shaken by the peeing, in short spasms of delight and relief. Each time I thought that Calvin was finished, he shook again. I was wrong about the name of the tune on the eight-track. I was wrong about my mother. It was not "Rock of Ages." It was not even the walk through the country lane going to St. Matthias Anglican Church for evensong and service that had pulled those memories from me. It was I myself. As a chorister in the St. Michael's Cathedral, singing a song of praise. Was it Easter I was thinking about? Easter? Or Christmas? Rogations Day? Quinquagesima Sunday? Could it have been Lent? *O, all ye beasts of the sea, praise ye the Lord. O, all you fish of the sea, praise ye the Lord*? Could it have been that? Yes. That was the comparison of the repetition which the beauty of the saxophone ought to have brought back.

"Every time I hear Trane playing 'Love Supreme,' I gotta have me at least *one* smoke, and . . ." He seemed short of breath, all of a sudden. His words were cut short. Nevertheless, there was a lingering, a drawing out of the enunciation of his words. His words would be cut off. In mid-sentence. As if he were struggling. For breath. And trying to talk at the same time. The middle door on the porch opened and light flowed weakly out, and I could see Calvin's eyes, now red and fierce and, at the same time, peaceful, and filled with water. But he was not in tears. He was happy. "Want a joint? Can you handle this shit, brother?"

"I'm cool, man."

"Shit'll kill you. It's a motherfucker. It kills the black artist, and the black musician."

"I'm cool, man."

"Know something? Let's not waste time with these chicks. Forget Gwen." I was wondering what kind of a man Calvin was. "Let's talk, brother. You're going back up to Toronto, next week, and when you're gone, ain't nobody I can talk to, nobody on this campus, in this city, in this fucking country. Let's talk. And I gonna cut out all these 'motherfuckers' and 'shits' in my speech, and just talk." I was sure he was reading my mind. But I was getting accustomed to his speech, peppered with this Southern or American violence. "I've been checking you out back there, while you were talking to yourself, as Trane was grooving. Bet you didn't realize you were talking to yourself? 'Love Supreme' is a motherfuc—is a fantastic piece, freaks me out too, every time I listen to it. At least five times a day. And if I have a joint, shee—well, it's fantastic." He took the last, deep, noisy pull on the cigarette, now no longer than his fingernail. "'Love Supreme' brings back memories of something my grandmother used to hum, just after she lit the kerosene lamps every evening. Some white folks calls this shit a canticle. Took me years to stop confusing canticle with cuticle. Heh-heh! But, anyhow. This canticle thing has a Latin name. Man! I kicked more ass, I was superior to everybody in my class in Latin in high school. Hate the thing now, though. But I know it all, by heart. Had to learn it by heart. Been learning it by heart from hearing my grandmother, singing it for years. Listen. *O, all ye works of the Lord, bless ye the Lord; praise him, and magnify him forever.* Want to hear more?"

"Didn't know you were Anglican."

"Baptist! To the bone. But I read that shit in a book that had words like *works*, *nights*, *days*, *whales*, *water*, etcetera, etcetera, and all were spelled with a capital letter. Isn't that something? The English be strange motherfuckers. Strange people. In the South, right here in this city of Birmingham, we worship the English, culturally I mean. The English use colons like Coltrane uses the E-flat! Baptist to the bone! Baptist to the bone. And anti-English, except culturally." He threw the marijuana cigarette, now smaller than his fingernail, through the window. The VW's engine started as if the whole car was about to explode. It stuttered, and finally, it turned over. "Life is better without chicks around. Sometimes. We're going to the Stallion Club, where there's the best rib sandwiches and fried chicken in the whole city of Birmingham! If not in the whole South!"

Pandemonium, sweet as pecan pie and ice cream, struck me full in the face, the moment the door of the Stallion Club was opened, when Calvin pushed me inside, first. The room was dark. Bodies were moving. The laughter was loud and sweet and black and jocular and exaggerated. Smoke was rising and swirling. And above the lighter darkness of the bodies in the room, the smoke remained there like halos. The music was climbing the walls. Music such as this I had never heard. It was like a baptism, a final submergence in the hidden, secret beauty of the South. Loud and full, enunciating each vowel, each nuance possible of behaviour, each instrument, each riff. I heard a voice pleading, "*Didn't I do it, baby? Didn't I? Didn't I do it, baby?*" and I looked towards the stage, in the deeper darkness there, through the large, slow-moving dancers, expecting to see Aretha Franklin in the flesh. What a victory it would be, to know her, in this thick-fleshed Southern, warm night! I was overcome by the music. I could feel my entire body relax. I could smell the odours around me. I could feel my blood. I could feel the difference, and the meaning of my presence in the South. The fried chicken. The barbecued ribs. The tingling, sweet nausea of burnt hair. The cosmetics and lotions in the glassy, bushy "pompadoos," as Calvin called them, on the fat, healthy jowls of the men and women dancing. I could feel my own body give off a stifled exhaust of smell. I could feel the sweat and the excitement under my armpits. A housefly was in the room. It came and rested on my top lip, and I did not brush it away. I was, for the first time, at home in the noise, the smells, the fragrance, the sounds and the voice of this city of Birmingham. And they all made me nervous, as they made me good. "*Didn't I do it, baby? Didn't I . . .*" I was like a man drowning in this foam of a wave that one moment ago had been wafting me in its freshness; I was moving towards the front of the swaying crowd that was coupled in its own sweetness. I looked into their faces. And those faces that were not buried into the necks and shoulders of men and women wore flat expressions. Masks. No one was smiling. No one was grinning. No one was laughing as he danced. No teeth showed in this relaxed, coagulating, heavy, and soft coupling of the music with the voice. It was as if the voice was giving them a message they all knew and desired. I could feel and taste the powerfulness in the large room. It was like a country. A country of men and women, all of the same colour, the same breathing. And this became my baptism: I had never imagined it was possible to be in a room so large with only black people. Never in Toronto. Never even in Barbados. I looked around to see, just in case. And there was none, not one white person. It was a beautiful sensation, and it frightened me. This is why I thought of powerfulness. And now I knew what it meant. I could feel it in my blood. Two large women, heavy in their thighs, heavy in their bosoms, heavy in their arms, heavy in their waists, each one about fifty-five years old, were tied together in the slow almost unmoving dance; their breasts pressed against each other, thighs glued together beneath their miniskirts, looking like logs of mahogany polished to a high magnificent sheen, arms lassoed to arms like tentacles, or in a Boston crab, and with the weight of their waists pressed together, begrudging space and denying any man's hand from forcing itself between their impenetrable love, close as if they were Siamese; love for the music and for the voice that pumped this love from one into the other, blood through veins, these two women moved in their heaviness like oil on shining glass, oblivious to the fact that there were hundreds dancing along with them. They moved as if they were on ice. They moved, only because I had seen them leave one spot small as a dime, and occupy another dime's area, not that they themselves could ever know that they had moved. They were close to me now, and I stood for a moment and watched them. I watched them grinding out their satisfaction and their ageless joy in this heavy, segregated world, in this black section of this city, safe amongst numbers, and amongst blackness created through the dance. *Didn't I do it, baby?*; a black world and a black poem which the dance itself had formed and had drawn a circle around. "This is a black world," Calvin said, having to shout to be heard.

I was now only three paces from the stage. I stood. I had to stand, for the bodies were not moving now. They were grinding. I was the only one who moved. I was the only one out of the rhythm. Inching to the stage, I was the only one out of place.

"Didn't I do it, baby?"

The face of the singer was bathed in black perspiration. It was like the water of baptism and of revival. And it was growing out of the body, like strength. Not dripping like an exertion. The thin, tight body looked as if it was being tormented. I could see this through the slits of space in the crowd as the dancers moved. I could see it as a slice of a fish, a slice of a human being, slithering in the shimmering sequins on the long dress that was like an extra skin. She was bathed in the white material of the dress, like a dolphin. *"Didn't I do it, baby?"*

"This sister can whup Aretha's ass any . . ." And Calvin's voice was blocked out, for a moment, by the passing of the two women between us. ". . . any mother—any day!" Here in this room, I needed space even to hear. The song came to a perspiring end. It was a soft end. And it was followed by an explosion of applause. Handkerchiefs, fingers, and Kleenexes came out to repair the cheeks, and wipe away the beads that had damaged the neckline and the collar and the forehead for the duration of that lovemaking rendition. And before the women and men had completed the renovation of their cosmetics, the mermaid of a woman on the stage began another song. *"A midnight train to Georgia . . ."* Without warning, without even a desire to join in this dance and in this circle, for I was out of place, inarticulate, foreign, without speech and gesticulation, one of the fat ladies took me into her arms. It was like a mother knowing before the expression of pain is moaned, how to take her child into the safety of her breast and bosom. I sank deep and comfortable in the billows of her love, as her arms wrapped my smaller body in embrace so much like my mother's that I felt I could fall off into a sweet slumber and surrender myself to her; except that the song was raging through the magnolia and pine and poplar woods of a land that held such frightening memories. And Calvin was there to witness my surrender, and perhaps, in a seminar on black behaviour, live to tell the story. But she held me close. She held me tight. She held her left arm round my waist, and her right hand on the softness of my bottom. I began to travel all those miles between the never-ending rails of steel, going from one place I did not know, to a place which was even farther removed from my present; but to a place which was identifiable, as I was able to *know* where I am now. And so, I buried myself in her flesh, her perfume acting as a mild chloroform, and I found that Gwen and the woman in Toronto climbed into the sweet delirium along with the woman holding me, and I paid no regard to those two encumbrances, and allowed myself to be moved so very slowly by her, by her body that was guiding me, and by her blood which I thought I could taste. But that would have been, in addition to the unseemly, unnatural acts, incest. I was dancing with my mother. The smell of her body, and the strength in her legs, which were tightened round my left leg, was like the tightness of a thick towel after a bath deep in winter. I could hardly breathe. But I could just as easily have died in her arms.

The housefly I had seen earlier returned and lighted on the woman's mouth. She pursed her lips, unwilling to release one hand and let go of my body; and the fly fled. It probably had learned, through its ugly leaden antennae, what thunderous violence her anger would give rise to, in the slap the woman would have used.

Her lips were rouged in a deep red. Like the blood inside her body which I felt I could feel and taste. But I was not entirely passive in my enjoyment. My eight fingers were pressed deeply into her soft flesh. With difficulty I tried to move to the music, in my own slow, sweet time. It was like poetry; and I thought of poetry. *And green and golden I was huntsman and herdsman . . .*

"Are you screwing me, nigger?" she asked. And then laughed. A breath of Jack Daniels came to my nostrils when she spoke. I could feel her weight. I had made a wrong step, and her weight fell upon me. And I wondered what it would be like, if by accident, I were to make another wrong step, and she were to fall on top of me. "You want me?" She whispered this into my ear. I smelled her lipstick. I smelled her Jack Daniels again. "You're screwing me, ain't you?" Her mouth was at my ear. I smelled her perfume, and the cosmetics and the treatment in her processed hair. She tightened her grip on me. She tightened her grip more. My breathing became more difficult. And then she groaned, in a short spasm. *My wishes raced through the house-high hay, and nothing I cared . . . that time allows.* "You like me, don't you, small-island man?"

Whatever Georgia was, whatever was the ruggedness of its landscape, whether of rocks or of stones, green fields of sugar cane or of cotton and corn, the concluding journey was before me. The singer was washed in perspiration, pouring out of her body with a sensual righteousness; the sequins in her dress moved as she breathed, from her ankles to her covered arms, like pistons on the very train that was pulling into Georgia, long after midnight. *Oh as I was young and easy in the mercy of her means, time held me green and dying though I sang in my chains like the sea.*

"I want you, nigger. I have to have you."

I could feel it. I could feel the soft inside of her thighs. I was hard. The singer was coming home. Two sequined arms dropped at her side, in victory like that which concludes exhaustion of the flesh. And sudden so, the strong feeling thundered down. The rain had arrived.

"You want me, don't ya? I want *you*."

"No, I don't want you," I said.

"Well, fuck it! Nigger, you's *mine!*"

"*Clovis!*" It was Calvin, like a referee forcing himself between two locked boxers. "Clovis! Take your motherfucking hands off the brother! The brother's with me, motherfucker!" And Calvin ripped at Clovis's head, as if he was delivering a jab to the face. And when Calvin's hand returned from the face, in it was the wig which had contained such allure and fragrance of Duke Greaseless Hair-dressing for Women. His head was shaven bald, and was shining, and he was shaking with anger; and he said in a huskier voice, "Shit, Cal! I thought the nigger was mine!"

"Motherfucker!" Calvin pushed him off.

A few men and women danced close to us, looked at me and danced away. I stood looking at Clovis's shining head.

"Motherfucker, this is a Yale professor!"

"I could've *swear*, Cal, honey, the nigger was mine. I am very sorry, sir, I am very sorry," Clovis said, offering me his hands. I remembered his hands were very soft. But by this time, I was feeling the eruption in my bowels; and Calvin, sensing this, and intent upon freeing me from this assault, this offence, and knowing that I had lusted after the wrong person, was easing me with some force through the thick of the crowd, to the entrance. On the way out, I barely recognized Clovis's voice, as he stood where he was, saying, "I knew the nigger looked strange, as if he didn't belong here, weren't one of us, weren't from the South, so what the fuck was I supposed to think?"

I could not wait until I was on the gravel patch in front of the entrance of the Stallion Club, before the vomit spewed down on my white dashiki, onto my white cotton Levi's, into my shoes, with the noise and the slime and the bad taste, and Calvin talking and talking.

"Shit, brother, couldn't you *tell*?"

"How?"

"Didn't you see the motherfucker didn't have no breasts? Couldn't you see?"

"How? I was mesmerized by the woman singing 'Midnight Train to Georgia.'"

"That motherfucker was a man too, brother!" The vomit punctuated whatever else he was about to say. It was coming out with pain and with violence, as if I was trying to rip something awful, something vile, some sin, some hurt clean from my insides.

"I was in love with the woman singing 'Midnight Train.'"

"The woman singing is also a man," Calvin said. Pity and disappointment in me registered in his explanation. "The woman is a motherfucking man, brother! This be the South. Birmingham. In the South, it be so fucked up, you can't tell one motherfucker from the next."

"I thought the man was a woman."

"It's a motherfucking *man*, Jack! A *man*!"

He lit a Salem. "Sure's hell ain't Toronto, Jack!"

GRIFF!

Griff was a black man from Barbados who sometimes denied he was black. Among black Americans who visited Toronto, he was black: "Right on!" "Peace and love, brother!" and "Power to the people!" would suddenly become his vocabulary. He had emigrated to Toronto from Britain and, as a result, thought of himself as a black Englishman. But he was blacker than most immigrants. In colour, that is. It must have been this double indemnity of being British and black that caused him to despise his blackness. To his friends, and his so-called friends, he flaunted his British experience, and the "civilized" bearing that came with it; and he liked being referred to as a West Indian who had lived in London, for he was convinced that he had an edge, in breeding, over those West Indians who had come straight to Canada from the cane fields in the islands. He had attended Ascot many times and he had seen the Queen in her box. He hated to be regarded as just black.

"Griff, but you're blasted black, man," Clynn said once, at a party in his own home, "and the sooner you realize that fact, the more rasshole wiser you would be!" Clynn usually wasn't so honest, but that night he was drunk.

What bothered Griff along with his blackness was that most of his friends were "getting through": cars and houses and "swinging parties" every Friday night, and a yearly trip back home for Christmas and for Carnival. Griff didn't have a cent in the bank. "And you don't even have *one* blasted child, neither!" Clynn told him that same night.

But Griff was the best-dressed man present. They all envied him for that. And nobody but his wife really knew how poor he was in pocket. Griff smiled at them from behind his dark green dark glasses. His wife smiled too, covering her embarrassment for her husband. She never criticized him in public, by gesture or by attitude, and she said very little to him about his ways in their incensed apartment. Nevertheless, she carried many burdens of fear and failure for her husband's apparent ambitionless attitudes. England had wiped some British manners on her too. Deep down inside, Griff was saying to Clynn and the others, *Godblindyougodblindyou!*

"Griffy dear, pour your wife a Scotch, darling. I've decided to enjoy myself." She was breathing as her yoga teacher had taught her to do.

And Griffy said, *Godblindyougodblindyou!* again to Clynn; poured his wife her drink, poured himself a large Scotch on the rocks, and vowed, *I am going to drink all your Scotch tonight, boy!* This was his only consolation. Clynn's words had become wounds. Griff grew so centred around his own problems that he did not, for one moment, consider any emotion coming from his wife. "She's just a nice kid," he told Clynn once, behind her back. He had draped his wife in an aura of sanctity; and he would become angry to the point of violence, and scare anybody, when he thought his friends' conversation had touched the cloud and virginity of the sanctity in which he had clothed her: like taking her out on Friday and Saturday nights to the Cancer Calypso Club, in the entrails of the city, where pimps and doctors and lonely immigrants hustled women and brushed reputations in a brotherhood of illegal liquor. And if the club got too crowded, Griff would feign a headache, and somehow make his wife feel the throbbing pain of his migraine, and would take her home in a taxi, and would recover miraculously on his way back along Sherbourne Street, and with the tact of a good barrister, would make tracks back to the Cancer and dance the rest of the limp-shirt night with a woman picked from among the lonely West

Indian stags, his jacket let loose to the sweat and the freedom, his body sweet with the music, rejoicing in the happy absence of his wife in the sweet presence of this woman.

But after these hiatuses of dance, free as the perspiration pouring down his face, his wife would be put to bed around midnight, high up in the elevator, high off the invisible hog of credit, high up on the Chargex card, and Griff would be tense, for days. It was a tenseness which almost gripped his body in a paralysis, as it strangled the blood in his body when the payments of loans for furniture and for debts approached, and they always coincided with the approaching of his paycheque, already earmarked against its exact face value. In times of this kind of stress, like his anxiety at the racetrack, when the performance of a horse contradicted his knowledge of the *Racing Form* and left him broke, he would grumble, "Money is *naught* all."

Losing his money would cause him to ride on streetcars, and he hated any kind of public transportation. He seemed to realize his blackness more intensely; white people looking at him hard— questioning his presence, it seemed. It might be nothing more than the way his colour changed colour, going through a kaleidoscope of tints and shades under the varying ceiling lights of the streetcar. Griff never saw it this way. To him, it was staring. And his British breeding told him that to look at a person you didn't know (except she was a woman) was *infra dig. Infra dig* was the term he chose when he told Clynn about these incidents of people staring at him on the streetcars. The term formed itself on his broad thin lips, and he could never get the courage to spit it at the white people staring at him.

When he lost his money, his wife, after not having had dinner nor the money to buy food (the landlord locked the apartment door with a padlock one night while they were at a party), would smile that half-censuring smile, a smile that told you she had been forced, against the truth of her circumstances, to believe with him that money was "not all, at-all." But left to herself, left to the ramblings of her mind and her aspirations and her fingers over the new broadloom in her girlfriend's home, where her hand clutched the tight sweating glass of Scotch on the rocks, her Scotch seeming to absorb her arriving unhappiness with the testimony of her friend's broadloom, or in Clynn's recreation room, which she called a den, in her new sponge of happiness, fabricated like the house in her dreams, she would put her smile around her husband's losses, and in the embrace they would both feel higher than anybody present, because, "Griffy dear, you were the only one there with a Master of Arts."

"I have more brains than *anyone* there. They only coming-on strong. But I don't have to come on strong, uh mean, I don't *have* to come on strong, but . . ."

One day, at Greenwood Racetrack, Griff put his hand into his pocket and pulled out five twenty-dollar bills, and put them on one race: he put three twenty-dollar bills on Number Six, *on the fucking nose—to win, eh!* (he had been drinking earlier at the Pilot Tavern); and he also put two twenty-dollar bills on Number Six, *to show*. He had studied the *Racing Form* like a man studying torts: he would put it into his pocket, take it out again, read it in the bathroom as he trimmed his moustache; he studied it on the sweet-smelling toilet bowl; he studied it as he might have studied laws in Britain; and when he spoke of his knowledge of the *Racing Form*, it was as if he had received his degrees in the laws of averages, and not in English literature and language.

And he "gave" a horse to a stranger that same day at Greenwood. "Buy Number Three, man. I read the *Form* for three days, taking notes. It *got* to be Number Three!" The man thanked him because he himself was no expert; and he spent five dollars (more than he had ever bet before) on Number Three, *to win*. "I read the *Form* like a blasted book, man!" Griff told him. He slipped off to the wicket farthest away; and like a thief, he bought his own tickets: "Number Six! Sixty on the nose! Forty to show!" And to himself he said, smiling, "Law o' averages, man, law of averages."

Tearing up the tickets on Number Six after the race, he said to the man who had looked for him to thank him, and who thanked him and shook his hand and smiled with him, "I don't have to come on strong, man, I *mastered* that *Form*." He looked across the field to the board at the price paid on Number Three, and then he said to the man, "Lend me two dollars for the next race, man. I need a bet."

The man gave him three two-dollar bills and told him, "*Any time, pardner, any time!* Keep the six dollars. Thank *you!*"

Griff was broke. Money is *naught* all, he was telling the same man, who, seeing him waiting by the streetcar stop, had picked him up. Griff settled himself back into the soft leather of the new Riviera, going west, and said again to the man, "Money is naught all! But I don't like to come on strong. Uh mean, you see how I mastered the *Form*, didn't you?"

"You damn right, boy!" the man said, adjusting the tone of the tape deck. "How you like my new car?"

The elevator was silent that evening, on the way up to the twenty-fifth floor; and he could not even lose his temper with it: "This country is uncivilized—even the elevators—they make too much noise; a man can't even think in them; this place only has money but it doesn't have any culture or breeding or style, so everybody is grabbing for money, money, money." The elevator that evening didn't make a comment. And neither did his wife: she had been waiting for him to come from work, straight, with the money untouched from his monthly paycheque. But Griff had studied the *Racing Form* thoroughly all week, and had worked out the laws and averages and notations in red felt-pen ink; had circled all the "long shots" in green, and had moved through the "donkeys" (the slow horses) with waves of blue lines; had had three "sure ones" for that day; and had averaged his wins against heavy bets against his monthly salary: it was such a "goddamn cinch"! He had developed a migraine headache immediately after lunch, slipped through the emergency exit at the side, holding his head in his hand, his head full of tips and cinches, and had caught the taxi which miraculously had been waiting there, with the meter ticking; had run through the entrance of the racetrack, up the stairs, straight for the wicket to bet on the daily double; had invested fifty dollars on a long shot (worked out scientifically from his red-marked, green-circled, blue-wavy-lined *Form*), and had placed "two god-damn dollars" on the favourite—just to be sure!—and went into the clubhouse. The favourite won. Griff lost fifty dollars on the first race. But he had won two dollars on his two-dollar bet.

"I didn't want to come on strong," he told the man, who was then a stranger to him. The man could not understand what he was talking about, and he asked for no explanation. "I didn't want to come on strong, but I worked out all the winners today, since ten o'clock last night. I *picked* them, man. I can pick them. But I was going for the long shot. Hell, what is a little bread? Fifty dollars! Man, that isn't no bread, at all. If I put my hand in my pocket now, look . . . *this* is bread! . . . five *hundred* dollars. I can lose, man; I can afford to lose bread. Money don't mean anything to me, man; money is no *big* thing! . . . Money is *naught* all."

His wife remained sitting on the Scandinavian couch which had the habit of whispering to them, once a month, "Fifty-nine thirty-five owing on me!" She looked up at Griff as he gruffed through the door. She smiled. Her face did not change its form, or its feeling, but she smiled. Griff grew stiff at the smile. She got up from the couch. She brushed the anxiety of time from her waiting miniskirt ("My wife must dress well, and look *sharp*, even in the house!"), she tidied the already-tidy hairdo she had just got from Azan's, and she went into the kitchen, which was now a wall separating Griff from her. Griff looked at the furniture, and wished he could sell it all in time for the races tomorrow afternoon: the new unpaid-for living room couch, desk, matching executive chair, the table and matching chairs where they ate; desk pens thrown into the bargain the sales-man swore he was giving them, ten Friday nights ago down Yonge Street; scatter rugs, Scandinavian-type settee with its matching chairs, like Denmark in the fall season, in style and design; he looked at the motto, "Christ Is the Head of this Home," which his wife had insisted upon taking as another "bargain"; and he thought of how relaxed he had felt driving in the man's new Riviera.

He took the new *Racing Form*, folded in half and already notated, from his breast pocket, and sat on the edge of the bed, in the wisteria-smelling bedroom. The wife had been working, he said to himself, as he noticed he was sitting on his clean folded pyjamas. But he left them there and perused the handicaps and histories of the horses. The bundle buggy for shopping was rolling over the polished wood of the living room floor. The hinges on the doors of the clothes cupboard in the hallway were talking. A clothes hanger dropped on the skating rink of the floor. The cupboard door was closed. The bundle buggy rolled down from its prop against the cupboard and jangled onto the hardboard ice. Griff looked up and saw a smooth brown, black-maned horse standing before him. It was his wife.

"Griffy dear? I am ready." She had cleaned out her pocketbook of old papers, useless personal and business cards accumulated over drinks and at parties; and she had made a budget of her month's allowance, allowing a place in the tidied wallet section for her husband's arrival. The horse in Griff's mind changed into a donkey. "Clynn called. He's having a party tonight. Tennish. After the supermarket, I want to go round to the corner, to the cleaner's, and stop off at the liquor store for a bottle of wine. My sisters're coming over for dinner, and they're bringing their boyfriends. I want to have a roast. Should I also buy you a bottle of Black & White, Griffy dear?" . . . *They're at post! They're off!* . . . *As they come into the backstretch, moving for the wire . . . it's Phil Kingston by two lengths; Crimson Admiral; third, True Willie . . . Phil Kingston, Crimson Admiral, True Willie . . .* but Griff had already moved downstairs, in the direction of the cashier's wicket: "Long shot in your arse! Uh got it, this time, old man!" *True Willie is making a move. True Willie! . . . Phil Kingston now by one length, True Willie is coming on the outside! True Willie! It's True Willie!*

"It's almost time for the supermarket to close, Griff dear, and I won't like to be running about like a racehorse, sweating and per-spiring. I planned my housework and I tried to finish all my house-work on time so I'll be fresh for when you came home. I took my time too, doing my housework, and I took a shower so I won't get excited by the time my sisters come, and I didn't bother to go to my yoga class . . ." *It's True Willie by a neck! True Willie! What a run, ladies and gentlemen! What a run! True Willie's the winner, and it's now official!* " . . . and I even made a promise to budget this month so we'll save some money for all these bills we have to pay. We have to pay these bills and we never seem to be paying them off and the rent's due in two days—no, today! Oh, I forgot to tell you that the bank manager called about your loan, to say that . . ." *It's True Willie, by a neck!*

Griff smashed all the furniture in the apartment in his mind, and then walked through the door. "Oh, Griffy dear! Stooly called to say he's getting a lift to the races tomorrow and if you're going he wants you to . . ."

Griff was standing in the midst of a group of middle-aged West Indians, all of whom pretended, through the amount of liquor they drank, and the "gashes they lashed," that they were still young black studs.

"Man, when I entered that door, she knew better than to open her fucking mouth to me! To *me*? *Me*?" The listening red eyes understood the unspoken chastisement in his threatening voice. "Godblindyou! She knew better than *that*. Me? If she'd only opened her fucking mouth, I would have . . ." They raised their glasses, all of them, to their mouths, not exactly at the same time, but sufficiently together to make it a ritualistic harmony among men. "As man!" Griff said, and then wet his lips. They would, each of them, have chastised their women in precisely the same way that Griff was boasting about disciplining his. But he never did. He could never even put his hand to his wife's mouth to stop her from talking. And she was not the kind of woman you would want to beat: she was much too delicate. The history of their marriage had coincided with her history of a woman's illness which had been kept silent among them; and its physical manifestation, in the form of a large scar that crawled halfway around her neck, darker in colour than the natural shade of her skin, had always, from the day of recovery after the operation, been covered by the neckline of each of her dresses. And this became her natural style and fashion in clothes.

Sometimes, in more daring moods, she would wear a silk scarf to hide the scar. "If my wife wasn't so blasted sickly, I would've put my hand in her arse, *many times!* Many times I've thought o' putting my hand in her arse, after a bad day at the races!" He had even thought of doing something drastic about her smile and about his losses at the track and at poker. It was not clearly shaped in his mind; and at times, with this violent intent, he could not think of whom he would perform this drastic act on. After a bad day at the track, the thought of the drastic act, like a cloud over his thoughts, would beat him down and take its toll out of his slim body, which itself seemed to refuse to bend under the great psychological pressure of losing, all the time.

He had just lost one hundred dollars at Woodbine Racetrack, when one evening as he entered Clynn's living room, for the usual Friday night party of Scotch and West Indian peas and rice and chicken, which Clynn's Polish wife cooked and spoiled and learned how to cook as she spoiled the food, he had just had time to adjust his shoulders in the oversized sports jacket, when he said, braggingly, "I just dropped a hundred. At Woodbine." He wet his lips and smiled.

"Dollars?" It was Clynn's voice, coming from the dark corner where he poured drinks. Clynn was a man who wouldn't lend his sister, nor his mother—if she was still alive—more than five dollars at one time.

"Money don't mean anything, man."

"A *hundred* dollars?" Clynn suddenly thought of the amount of Scotch Griff had been drinking in his house.

"Money is *naught* all."

"You're a blasted . . . Boy, do you lose *just* for fun, or wha'?" Clynn sputtered. "Why the arse you don't become a *groom*, if you like racehorses so much? Or you's a . . . a *paffological* loser?"

"Uh mean, I don't like to come on strong, or anything, but, money is *naught* all . . ."

"Rasshole put down my Scotch, then! You drinking my fucking Scotch!"

And it rested there. It rested there because Griff suddenly remembered he was among men who knew him: who knew his losses both in Britain and Canada. It rested there also, because Clynn and the others knew that his manner and attitude towards money, and his wife's expressionless smile, were perhaps lying expressions of a turbulent inner feeling of failure. "He prob'ly got rasshole ulcers, too!" Clynn said, and then spluttered into a laugh. Griff thought about it, and wondered whether he had indeed caused his wife to be changed into a different woman altogether. But he couldn't know that. Her smile covered a granite of silent and apparent contentment.

He wondered whether he hated her, to the bone, and whether she hated him. He felt a spasm through his body as he thought of her hating him, and not knowing about it. For so many years living together, both here and in Britain; and she was always smiling. Her constancy and her cool exterior, her smiles, all made him wonder now, with the Scotch in his hand, about her undying devotion to him, her faithfulness, pure as the sheets in their sweet-smelling bedroom; he wondered whether "I should throw my hand in her arse, *just* to see what she would do." But Clynn had made up his own mind that she was, completely, destroyed inside: her guts, her spirit, her aspirations, her procreative mechanism—"Hysterectomy all shot to pieces!" Clynn said cruelly—destroyed beyond repair, beneath the silent consolation and support which he saw her giving to her husband, at home among friends and relations, and in public among his sometimes silently criticizing friends. "I don't mean to come on strong, but . . ."

"You really want to know what's wrong with Griff?" Clynn's sister, Princess, asked one day. "He want a *stiff* lash in his backside! He don't know that he's gambling-'way his wife's life? He doesn't know that? Look, he don't have chick nor child. Wife working in a good job, for *decent* money, and they don't even live in a decent apartment that you could say, 'Well, rent eating out his sal'ry.' Don't own no record player. *Nothing.* And all he doing is walking 'bout Toronto with his blasted head high in the air! He ain' know this is Northamerica? Christ, he don't even speak to poor people. He ain' have no motto-car, like some. Well, you tell me then, what the hell is Griff doing with the thirteen thousand Canadian dollars a year in salary? Supporting racehorses? No, man, you can't tell me that, 'cause not even the *most* wutless of Wessindians living in Toronto could gamble-'way thirteen thousand dollars! Jesuschrist! That is twenty-six thousand back in Barbados! Think o' the land he could buy back home wid thirteen thousand Canadian dollars. And spending it 'pon a racehorse? What the hell is a racehorse? *Thirteen thousand?* But lissen to me! One o' these mornings, that wife o' his going get up and tell him that she with-child, that she *pregnunt* . . ." ("She can't get pregnunt, though, Princess, 'cause she already had one o' them operations!") ". . . Anyhow, if his wife was a diff'rent person, she would 'ave walked-out on his arse *long ago*! Or else, break his two blasted hands! And she won't spend a *day* in jail!"

When Griff heard what Princess had said about him, he shrugged his shoulders and said, "I don't have to come on strong, but if I was a different man, I would really show these West Indian women something . . ." He ran his thin, long, black fingers over the length of his old-fashioned slim tie, he shrugged the grey sports jacket that was a size too large, at the shoulders, into shape and place, wet his lips twice, and said, "Gimme another Scotch, man." While Clynn fixed the Scotch, he ran the thumb and index finger of his left hand down the razor edge of the crease in his dark brown trousers. He inhaled and tucked his shirt and tie neatly beneath the middle button of his sports jacket. He took the Scotch, which he liked to drink on the rocks, and he said, "I don't have to come on strong, but I am going to tell you something . . ."

The next Friday night was the first day of fete in the long week-end. There hadn't been a long weekend in Canada for a long time. Everybody was tired of just going to work, coming home, watching CBC television, bad movies on the TV, and then going to bed. "There ain' no action in this fucking town," Clynn was saying for days, before the weekend appeared like raindrops on a farmer's dry-season head. And everybody agreed with him. It was so. Friday night was here, and the boys, their wives, their girlfriends, and their "outside women" were noisy and drunk and happy. Some of the men were showing off their new bell-bottom trousers and broad leather belts worn under their bulging bellies, to make them look younger. The women, their heads shining like wet West Indian tar roads, the smell from the cosmetics and grease that went into their kinky hair and on their faces, to make them look sleek and smooth: all these smells and these women mixed with the cheap and domestic perfumes they used, whenever Avon called; and some women, wives whose husbands were "getting through," were wearing good-looking dresses, in style and fashion; others were still back-home in their style, poured in against their wishes and the better judgement of their bulging bodies; backsides big, sometimes too big, breasts bigger, waists fading into the turbulence of their middle age and their behinds, all poured against the shape of their noisy bodies into evil-fitting, shiny material, made on sleepy nights after work, on a borrowed sewing machine. But everybody was happy. They had all forgotten now, through the flavour of the calypso and the peas and the rice, the fried chicken, the curry-chicken, that they were still living in a white man's country; and it didn't seem to bother them now, nor touch them now. Tonight, none of them would tell you that they hated Canada; that they wanted to go back home, but that they were "going to make a little money, first"; that they were only waiting till then; that they were going to go back before "the blasted Canadian tourisses buy-up the blasted Caribbean"; they wouldn't tell you tonight that they all suffered some form of racial discrimination in Canada, and that that was to be expected, since "there are certain things with this place that are not just right"—not tonight. Tonight, Friday night, was forgetting night. West Indian night. And they were at the Cancer Club to forget and to drink and to get drunk. To make plans for some strange woman's (or man's) body and bed, to "spend some time" with a real West Indian "thing," to eat her boiled mackerel and green bananas, which their wives and women had, in their ambitions to be "decent" and Canadian, forgotten how to cook, and had left out of their diets, especially when Canadian friends were coming to dinner, because that kind of food was "plain West Indian stupidness." Tonight, they would forget and drink, forget and dance, and dance to forget.

"Oh-Jesus-Christ, Griff!" Stooly shouted, as if he was singing a calypso. He greeted Griff this way each time he came to the club, and each time it was as if Stooly hadn't seen Griff in months, although they might have been together at the track the same afternoon. It was just the way Stooly was. "Oh-Jesus-Christ, Griff!" he would shout, and then he would rush past Griff, ignoring him, and make straight for Griff's wife. He would wrap his arms around her slender body (once his left hand squeezed a nipple, and Griff saw, and said to himself, "Uh mean, I won't like to come on strong about it, but . . ." and did nothing about it), pulling up her new minidress above the length of decency—worn for the first time tonight—exposing the expensive lace which bordered the hem of her slip. The veins of her hidden age, visible only at the back of her legs, would be exposed to Griff, who would stand and stare and feel "funny," and feel, as another man inquired with his hands all over his wife's body, the blood and the passion and the love mix with the rum in his mouth. Sometimes, when in a passion of brandy, he would make love to his wife as if she were a different woman, as if she were no different from one of the lost women found after midnight on the crowded familiar floor of the Cancer.

"Haiii! How?" the wife would say, all the time her body was being crushed. She would say, "Haiii! How?" every time it happened; and it happened every time; and every time it happened, Griff would stand and stare, and do nothing about it, because his memory of British breeding told him so; but he would feel mad and helpless afterwards, all night; and he would always want to kill Stooly, or kill his wife for doing it; but he always felt she was so fragile. He would want to kill Stooly more than he would want to kill his wife. But Stooly came from the same island as his wife. Griff would tell Clynn the next day, on the telephone, that he should have done something about it; but he "didn't want to come on strong." Apparently he was not strong enough to rescue his wife from the rape of Stooly's arms, as he rubbed his body against hers, like a dog scratching its fleas against a tree.

Once, a complete stranger saw it happen. Griff had just ordered three drinks: one for his wife, one for himself, and one for Stooly, his friend. Griff looked at the man, and in an expansive mood (he had made a bundle off the long shot in the last race at Woodbine that afternoon), he asked the stranger, "What're you drinking?"

"Rum, sah!"

"I am going to buy you a goddamn drink, just because I like you, man."

The stranger did not change the mask on his face, but stood there, looking at Griff's dark green lenses. Then he said, "You isn' no blasted man at all, man!" He then looked behind: Stooly was still embracing Griff's wife. It looked as if he was feeling her up. The man took the drink from Griff, and said, "You is no man, sah!"

Griff laughed; but no noise came out of his mouth. "Man, that's all right. They went to school together in Trinidad."

"In *my* books, you still ain' no fucking man, boy!" The stranger turned away from Griff; and when he got to the door of the dance floor, he said, "Thanks for the drink, *boy*."

The wife was standing beside Griff now, smiling as if she was a queen parading through admiring lines of subjects. She looked, as she smiled, as if she was under the floodlights of some premiere performance she had prepared herself for a long time. She smiled, although no one in particular expected a smile from her. Her smiling went hand in hand with her new outfit. It had to be worn with a smile. It looked good, as usual, on her; and it probably understood that it could only continue to look good and express her personality if she continued smiling. At intervals during the night, when you looked at her, it seemed as if she had taken the smile from her handbag, and had then powdered it onto her face. She could have taken it off any time, but she chose to wear it the whole night. "Griffy dear?"

she said, although she wasn't asking him anything, or telling him anything, or even looking in his direction. "Haiii! How?" she said to a man who brushed against her hips as he passed. The man looked suddenly frightened, because he wanted his advance to remain stealthy and masculine. When he passed back from the bar, with five glasses of cheap rum and Cokes in his hands, he walked far from her.

Griff was now leaning on the bar, facing the part-time barman, and talking about the results of the last race that day; his wife, her back to the bar, was looking at the men and the women, and smiling; when someone passed, who noticed her, and lingered in the recognition, she would say, "Haiii! How?"

A large, black, badly dressed Jamaican (he was talking his way through the crowd) passed. He stared at her. She smiled. He put out his calloused construction hand, and with a little effort, he said, "May I have this dance, gal?" Griff was still talking. But in his mind he wondered whether his wife would dance with the Jamaican. He became ashamed with himself for thinking about it. He went back to talking, and got into an argument with the part-time barman, Masher, over a certain horse that was running in the feature race the next day at Greenwood. Masher, ever watchful over the women, especially other men's, couldn't help notice that the calloused-hand Jamaican was holding on to Griff's wife's hand. With his shark-eyes he tried to get Griff's attention off horses and onto his wife. But Griff was too preoccupied. His wife placed her drink on the counter beside him, her left hand still in the paws of the Jamaican construction worker's, whom nobody had seen before, and she said, "Griffy dear?" The man's hand on her manicured fingers had just come into his consciousness, when he wheeled around to give her her drink. He was upset. But he tried to be cool. It was the blackness of the Jamaican. And his size. Masher knew he was upset. The Jamaican reminded Griff of the "Congo-man" in one of the Mighty Sparrow's calypsoes. Masher started to laugh in his spitting *kee-kee* laugh. And when Griff saw that everybody was laughing, and had seen the Congojamaican walk off with his wife, he too decided to laugh.

"It's all right, man," he said, more than twice, to no one in particular, although he could have been consoling the Jamaicancongo man, or Masher, or the people nearby, or himself.

"I sorry, suh," the Jamaican said. He smiled to show Griff that he was not a rough fellow. "I am sorry, suh. I didn' know you was with the missis. I thought the missis was by-sheself tonight, again, suh."

"It's no *big* thing, man," Griff said, turning back to talk to Masher, who by now had lost all interest in horses. Masher had had his eyes on Griff's wife too. But Griff was worried by something new now: the man had said "by-sheself tonight, again, suh"; and that could mean only one thing: that his wife went places, like this very club, when he wasn't with her; and he had never thought of this, and never even imagined her doing a thing like this; and he wasn't sure that it was not merely the bad grammar of the Jamaican, and not the accusation in that bad grammar . . . *But language is a funny thing, a man could kill a person with language, and the accusation can't be comprehended outside of the structure of the language . . . Wonder how you would parse this sentence, Clynn . . . A Jamaican fella told me last night, "by-sheself tonight, again, suh." Now, do you put any emphasis on the position of the adverb, more than the conditional phrase?* Griff was already dozing off into the next day's dreams of action, thinking already of what he would tell Clynn about the accident: *Which is the most important word in that fellow's sentence structure? "By-sheself," "again," or "tonight"?*

"Never mind the fellow looks like a cane-cutter, he's still a brother," Griff said to Masher, but he could have been talking into the future, the next day, to Clynn; or even to himself. "I don't want to come on strong; he's a brother." The CBC television news that night dealt with Black Power nationalism in the States. The Jamaican man and Griff's wife were now on the dance floor. Griff stole a glimpse at them, to make sure the man was not holding his wife in the same friendly way that Stooly, who was a friend, would hold her. He thought he would be able to find the meaning of *by-sheself*, *again*, and *tonight* in the way the man held his wife. Had the Jamaican done so, Griff would have had to think even more seriously about the three words. But the Jamaican was about two hundred and fifty pounds of muscle and mackerel and green bananas. "Some other fellow would have come on strong, just because a rough-looking chap like him held on—"

"Man, Griff, you's a rasshole idiot, man!" Masher said. He crept under the bar counter, came out, faced Griff, broke into his sneering laugh, and said, "You's a rasshole!" Griff laughed too, in his voiceless laugh. "You ain' hear that man say 'by-sheself tonight, again'? If I had a woman like that, I would kill her arse, be-Christ, just for *looking* at a man like that Jamaikian-man!" Masher laughed some more, and walked away, singing the calypso the amateur band was trying to play: *Oh, Mister Walker, uh come to see your daughter* . . .

Griff wet his lips. His bottom lip disappeared inside his mouth, under his top lip; then he did the same thing with his top lip. He adjusted his dark glasses, and ran his right hand, with a cigarette in it, over his slim tie. His right hand was trembling. He shrugged his sports jacket into place and shape on his shoulders . . . *Oh, Mister Walker, uh come to see ya daughterrrrrr* . . .

He stood by himself in the crowd of West Indians at the door, and he seemed to be alone on a sun-setting beach back home. Only the waves of the calypsonian, and the rumbling of the conga drum, and the whispering, the loud whispering in the breakers of the people standing nearby, were with him. He was like the sea. He was like a man in the sea. He was a man at sea . . . *Tell she I is the man from Sangre Grande* . . .

The dance floor was suddenly crowded, jam-packed. Hands were going up in the air, and some under dresses, in exuberance after the music; the words in the calypso were tickling some appetites; he thought of his wife's appetite and of the Jamaican's, who could no longer be seen in the gloom of the thick number of black people; and tomorrow was races, and he had again mastered the *Form*. And Griff suddenly became terrified about his wife's safety and purity, and the three words came back to him: *by-sheself, tonight, again*. Out of the crowd, he could see Masher's big red eyes and his teeth, skinned in a mocking laugh. Masher was singing the words of the

calypso: *Tell she I come for she* . . . The music and the waves on the
beach, when the sun went behind the happy afternoon, came up
like a gigantic sea, swelling and roaring as it came to where he was
standing in the wet white sand; and the people beside him, whispering like birds going home to branches and rooftops, some singing,
some humming like the sea, fishing for fish and supper and for
happiness, no longer in sight against the blackening dusk . . . *She
know me well, I had she already!* . . . Stooly walked in front of him,
like the lightning that jigsawed over the rushing waves; and behind
Stooly was a woman, noisy and Trinidadian, saying "This par-tee
can't done till morning come!" like an empty tin can tied to a
motor-car bumper. All of a sudden, the fishermen and the fishing
boats were coming back to shore, climbing out of their boats, laden
with catches, their legs wet up to their knees; and they walked with
their boats up to the brink of the sand. In their hands were fish.
Stooly still held the hand of a woman who was laughing and talking
loud: "Fete for so!" She was like a barracuda. Masher, raucous and
happy, and harmless, and a woman he didn't know, were walking
like Siamese twins. One of his hands could not be seen. Out of the
sea, now resting from the turbulent conga drumming of the waves
in the calypso, came the Jamaicancongo man, and Griff's wife.

"Thank you very much, suh," he said, handing Griff his wife's
hand. With the other hand, she was pulling her miniskirt into place.
"She is a first-class dancer, suh."

"Don't have to come on *strong*, man."

"If I may, some other time, I would like to . . ." the man said,
smiling and wiping perspiration from his face with a red handkerchief. His voice was pleasant and it had an English accent hidden
somewhere in it. But all the words Griff was hearing were *I know
she well, I had she already . . . by-sheself again, tonight* . . . and there
were races tomorrow. His wife was smiling, smiling like the everlasting sea at calm.

"Haiii!" she said, and smiled some more. The Jamaican man
moved back into the sea of people, for some more dancing and fish.
The beach was still crowded; and in Griff's mind it was crowded,

but there was no one but he standing among the broken forgotten pieces of fish: heads and tails, and empty glasses and cigarette butts, and some scales broken off in a bargain, or by chance, and the ripped-up tickets of losing bets.

Masher appeared and said into his ear, "If she was *my* wife, be-Christ, I tell you . . ." and he left the rest to the imagination.

Griff's wife's voice continued, "Griffy dear?"

Masher came back from the bar with a Coke for the woman he was with. When he got close to Griff, he said into his ear, "Even if she was only just a screw like that one I have there . . ."

"Griffy dear, let's go home, I am feeling . . ."

". . . and if you was *something*," Masher was now screaming down the stairs after them. Griff was thinking of the three little words which had brought such a great lump of weakness within the pit of his stomach.

"Masher seems very happy tonight, eh, Griffy dear? I never saw Masher quite so happy."

". . . you, *boy*! . . . you, *boy*! . . ."

"Masher, Haiii! How?"

"If it was mine," Masher shouted, trying to hide the meaning in his message, "if it was mine, and I had put only a two-dollar bet 'pon that horse, that horse that we was talking about, and, and that horse *behave' so*, well, I would have to *lash* that horse, till . . . *unnerstan?*"

"Griffy dear? Masher really loves horses, doesn't he, eh?"

They were around the first corner, going down the last flight of stairs, holding the rails on the right-hand side. Griff realized that the stairs were smelling of stale urine, although he could not tell why. His wife put her arm around his waist. It was the first time for the day. "I had a *great* time, a real ball, a *lovely* time!" Griff said nothing. He was tired, but he was also tense inside; still he didn't have the strength or the courage, whichever it was he needed, to tell her how he felt, how she had humiliated him, in that peculiar West Indian way of looking at small matters, in front of all those people; he could not tell her how he felt each time he watched Stooly put his arms around her slender body; and how he felt when the strange Jamaican man, with his cluttered use of grammar broken beyond meaning and comprehending, had destroyed something, like a dream, which he had had about her for all these fifteen years of marriage. He just couldn't talk to her. He wet his lips and ran his fingers over the slim tie. All she did (for he wanted to know that he was married to a woman who could, through all the years of living together, read his mind, so he wouldn't have to talk) was smile. That goddamn smile, he cursed. The sports jacket shoulders were shrugged into place and shape.

"Griffy dear? Didn't you enjoy yourself?" Her voice was like a flower, tender and caressing. The calypso band, upstairs, had just started up again. And the quiet waltz-like tune seemed to have been chosen to make him look foolish, behind his back. He could hear the scrambling of men and crabs trying to find dancing partners. He could imagine himself in the rush of fishermen after catches. He was thinking of getting his wife home quickly and coming back, to face Stooly and the Jamaican man; and he wished that if he did come back, they would both be gone, so he wouldn't have to come on strong; but he was thinking more of getting rid of his wife and coming back to dance with a woman and to discuss the *Racing Form*; and tomorrow was races, again. He imagined the large rough Jamaican man searching again for fresh women. He saw Stooly grabbing some woman's hand, some woman whom he had never seen before. But it was *his* club. He saw Masher, his eyes bulging and his mouth wide open, red and white, in joy. And Griff found himself not knowing what to do with his hands. He took his hands out of his jacket pockets; and his wife, examining her minidress in the reflection from the glass in the street door they were approaching, and where they always waited for the taxicab to stop for them, removed her arm from his waist. Griff placed his hand on her shoulder, near the scar, and she shuddered a little; she placed her hand on his hand; and then he placed both hands on her shoulders; and she straightened up, with her smile on her face, waiting for the kiss (he always did that before he kissed her), which would be fun, which was the only logical thing to do with his hands in that position around her neck, which would be fun and a little naughty for their ages, like the old times in Britain; and his wife—expecting this reminder of happier nights in unhappy London, relaxed, unexcited, remembering both her doctor and her yoga teacher—and in the excitement of her usually unexcitable nature, relaxed a little more, and was about to adjust her body to his, and lean her scarred neck just a little bit backwards to make it easy for him, to get the blessing of his silent lips (she remembered then that the Jamaican had held her as if he were her husband), when she realized that Griff's hands had walked up from her shoulders, and were now caressing the hidden bracelet of the scar on her neck, hidden tonight by a paisley scarf. She shuddered in anticipation. He thought of Stooly, as she thought of the Jamaican, as he thought of Masher, as he squeezed, and of the races—tomorrow the first race goes off at 1:45 P.M. And the more he squeezed the less he thought of other things, and the less those other things bothered him, and the less he thought of the bracelet of flesh under his fingers, the bracelet which had become visible, as his hands rumpled the neckline. He was not quite sure what he was doing, what he wanted to do; for he was a man who always insisted that he didn't like to come on strong, and to be standing up here in a grubby hallway, killing his wife, would be coming on strong: he was not sure whether he was wrapping his hands around her neck in a passionate embrace imitating the Jamaican, or whether he was merely kissing her.

But she was still smiling, the usual smile. He even expected her to say, "Haiii! How?" But she didn't. She couldn't. He didn't know where his kiss began and ended; and he didn't know when his hands stopped squeezing her neck. He looked back up the stairs, and he wanted so desperately to go back up into the club and show them, or talk to them, although he did not, at the moment, know exactly why, or what he would have done had he gone back into the club. His wife's smile was still on her body. Her paisley scarf was falling down her bosom like a rich spatter of baby food: pumpkin and tomato sauce; and she was like a child, propped against a corner in anticipation of its first step, toddling into movement. But there was no movement. The smile was there, and that was all. He was on the beach again, and he was looking down at a fish, into the eye of reflected lead, a fish left by a fisherman on the beach. He thought he saw the scales moving up and down, like small billows, but there was no movement. He had killed her.

But he did not kill her smile. He wanted to kill her smile more than he wanted to kill his wife.

Griff wet his lips, and walked back up the stairs. His wife was standing against the wall by the door, and she looked as if she was dead, and at the same time she looked as if she was living. It must have been the smile. Griff thought he heard her whisper, "Griffy dear?" as he reached the door. Stooly, with his arm round a strange woman's body, took away his arm, and rushed to Griff, and as if he was bellowing out a calypso line, screamed, "Oh-Jesus-Christ-Griff!"

Masher heard the name called, and came laughing and shouting: "Jesus Christ, boy! You get rid o' the wife real quick, man! As man, as *man*." Griff was wetting his lips again; he shrugged his sports jacket into place, and his mind wandered . . . "Show me the kiss-me-arse *Racing Form*, man. We going to the races tomorrow . . ."

THE MAN

The man passes the five open doors on two floors that shut as he passes, moving slowly in the dark, humid rooming house. Slowly, pausing every few feet, almost on every other step, he climbs like a man at the end of a double shift in a noisy factory, burdened down also by the weight of time spent on his feet, and by the more obvious weight of his clothes on his fat body, clothes that are seldom cleaned and changed. Heavy with the smell of his body and the weight of paper which he carries with him, in all nine pockets of trousers and jacket and one in his shirt, he climbs, leaving behind an acrid smell of his presence in the already odorous house.

When he first moved into this house, to live in the third-floor room, the landlady was a young wife. She is widowed now, and past sixty. The man smells like the oldness of the house. It is a smell like that which comes off fishermen when they come home from the rum shop after returning from the deep sea. And sometimes, especially in the evening, when the man comes home, the smell stings you and makes you turn your head, as your nostril receives a tingling sensation.

The man ascends the stairs. Old cooking rises and you think you can touch it on walls that have four coats of paint on them, put there by four different previous owners of the house. Or in four moods of decoration. The man pauses again. He inhales. He puts his hands on his hips. Makes a noise of regained strength and determination. And climbs again.

The man is dressed in a suit. The jacket is from a time when shoulders were worn wide and tailored broad. His shoulders are padded high, as his pockets are padded wide by the letters and the pieces of paper with notes on them, and clippings from the *Globe and Mail*, and envelopes with scribblings on them: addresses and telephone numbers. And the printed words he carries in his ten pockets make him look stuffed and overweight and important, and also like a man older than he really is. His hips are like those of a woman who has not always followed her diet to reduce. He meticulously puts on the same suit every day, as he has done for years. He is a man of some order and orderliness. His shirt was once white. He wears only shirts that were white when they were bought. He buys them second-hand from the bins of the Goodwill store on Jarvis Street and wears them until they turn grey. He changes them only when they are too soiled to be worn another day; and then he buys another one from the same large picked-over bins of the Goodwill store.

He washes his trousers in a yellow plastic pail only if a stain is too conspicuous, and presses them under his mattress; and he puts them on before they are completely dry. He walks most of the day, and at eight each night he sits at his stiff, wooden, sturdy-legged table writing letters to men and women all over the world who have distinguished themselves in politics, in government, and in universities.

He lives as a bat. Secret and self-assured and self-contained as an island, high above the others in the rooming house; cut off from people, sitting and writing his important personal letters, or reading, or listening to classical music on the radio and the news on shortwave until three or four in the morning. And when morning comes, at eight o'clock he hits the streets, walking in the same two square miles around his home, rummaging through libraries for British and American newspapers, for new words and ideas for letters; then along Bloor Street, Jarvis Street, College Street, and he completes the perimeter at Bathurst Street. His room is the centre of gravity from which he is spilled out at eight each morning in all temperatures and weather, and from which he wanders no farther than these two square miles.

The man used to work as a mover with Maislin Transport in Montreal. Most of the workers came from Quebec and spoke French better than they spoke English. And one day he and a young man dressed in jeans and a red-and-black checked shirt, resembling a man ready for the woods of lumberjacks and tall trees, were moving a refrigerator that had two doors; and the man said, "Lift." He misunderstood the man's English and began to turn left through the small apartment door. He turned old suddenly. His back went out, as the saying goes. And he developed "goadies," a swelling of the testicles so large that they can never be hidden beneath the most restraining jockstrap. That was the end of his moving career.

This former animal of a man, who could lift the heaviest stove if only he was given the correct word, was now a shadow of his former muscle and sinews, with sore back and calloused hands, moving slowly through a literary life, with the assistance of a private pension from Maislin Transport. He had become a different kind of animal now, prowling during the daytime through shelves of books in stores and in libraries; and visiting slight acquaintances as if they were lifelong friends, whenever he smelled a drink or a meal; and attending public functions.

His pension cheque came every month at the same time, written in too much French for the rude bank teller, who said each time he presented it, even after two years, "Do you have some *identification?*"

He used to be sociable. He would nod his head to strangers, flick his eyes on the legs of women and at the faces of foreign-language men on College Street, all the way west of Spadina Avenue. He would even stop to ask for a light, and once or twice for a cigarette, and become confused in phrase-book phrases of easy, conversational Greek, Portuguese, and Italian.

Until one evening. He was walking on a shaded street in Forest Hill Village when a policeman looked through the window of his yellow cruiser, stopped him in his wandering tracks, and said, "What the hell 're you doing up here, *boy?*" He had been walking and stopping, unsure along this street, looking at every mansion, each of which seemed larger than the one before, when he heard the brutal voice: "Git in! Git your black ass in here!"

The policeman threw open the rear door of the cruiser. The man looked behind him, expecting to see a delinquent teenager who had earned the policeman's raw hostility. The man was stunned. There was no other person on the street. But somehow he made the effort to walk to the cruiser. The door was slammed behind him. The policeman talked on a stuttering radio and used figures and numbers instead of words, and the man became alarmed at the policeman's mathematical illiteracy. And then the cruiser sped off, scorching the peace of Forest Hill, burning rubber on its shaded quiet streets.

The cruiser stopped somewhere in the suburbs. He thought he saw DON MILLS written on a signpost. It stopped here, with the same temperamental disposition as when it had stopped the first time in Forest Hill Village. The policeman made no further conversation of numerals and figures with the radio. He merely said, "*Git!*" The man was put out three miles from any street or intersection that he knew.

It was soon after this that he became violent. He made three pillows into the form of a man. He found a second-hand tunic and a pair of trousers that had a red stripe on them, and a hat that had a yellow band instead of a red one, and he dressed up the pillows and transformed them into a dummy of a policeman. And each morning at seven when he woke up, and late at night before he went to bed, after he washed out his mouth with salt water, he kicked the "policeman" twice—once in the flat feathery section where a man's testicles would be, and again at the back of the pillow in the dummy's ass. His hatred did not disappear with the blows. But soon he forgot about the effigy and the policeman.

Today he had been roaming the streets, as every day, tearing pieces of information from the *Globe and Mail* he took from a secretary's basket at the CBC, from *Saturday Night* and *Canadian Forum* magazines. And the moment he reached his attic room, he would begin to compose letters to great men and women around the world, inspired by the bits of information he had gathered.

And now, as he climbs, the doors of the roomers on each floor close as he passes like an evil wind. But they close too late, for his scent and the wind of his presence have already touched them.

With each separation and denial, he is left alone in the dim light to which he is accustomed, and in the dust on the stairs; and he guides his hand along the shining banister, the same sheen as the wallpaper, stained with the smells and specks of cooking. He walks slowly because the linoleum on the stairs is shiny too, and dangerous and tricky under the feet.

Now, on his last flight to his room for the night, his strength seems to leave his body, and he pauses and rests his hands, one on the banister and the other on his right hip.

The cheque from Montreal will arrive tomorrow.

He feels the bulkiness of the paper in his pockets, and the weight of his poverty in this country he never grew to love. There was more love in Barbados. On many a hot afternoon, he used to watch his grandfather rest his calloused hand on his hip as he stood in a field of endless potatoes, a field so large and quiet and cruel that he thought he was alone in the measureless sea of green waves, and not on a plantation. Alone perhaps now too, in the village, in the country, because of his unending work of bending his back to pull up the roots, and returning home when everyone else is long in bed.

And now he, the grandson, not really concerned with that stained ancestry, not really comparing himself with his grandfather, stands for a breath-catching moment on this landing in this house in which he is a stranger. He regards his room as the country. It is strange and familiar. It is foreign, yet it is home. It is dirty. And at the first signs of summer and warmth, he would go down on his hands and knees in what would have been, back home, an unmanly act, and scrub the small space outside his door, and the four or five steps he had to climb to reach it. He would drop soap into the water, and still the space around the door would remain dirty. The house had passed that stage when it could be cleaned. It had grown old like a human body. And not even ambition and cleanliness could purify it of this scent. It could be cleaned only by burning. But he had become accustomed to the dirt, as he was accustomed to the thought of burning. In the same way, he had become accustomed to the small room which bulged, like his ten pockets, with the possessions of his strange literary life.

He is strong again. Enough to climb the last three or four steps and take out his keys on the shining ring of silver, after putting down the plastic bag of four items he bought through the express checkout of Dominion around the corner, and then the collection of newspapers—two morning and two afternoon and two evening editions. He flips each key over, and it makes a dim somersault, until he reaches the last key on the ring, which he knows has to be the key he's looking for.

Under the naked light bulb he had opened and shut, locked and unlocked this same blue-painted door, when it was painted green and red and black, so many times that he thought he was becoming colour-blind. But he could have picked out the key even if he was blind; for it was the only key in the bunch which had the shape of the fleur-de-lys at its head. He went through all the keys on the ring in a kind of elimination process. It was his own private joke. A ritual for taking up time.

He spent time as if he thought it would not end: walking along College Street and Spadina Avenue when he was not thinking of letters to be written; looking at the clusters of men and women from different countries at the corner of Bathurst and Bloor; at the men passing their eyes slowly over the breasts and backsides of the women; at the women shopping at Dominion and the open-air stalls, or among the fibres of cheap materials and dresses, not quite pure silk, not one hundred per cent cotton, which they tore as they searched for and ripped from each other's hands to get at cheaper prices than those advertised at Honest Ed's bargain store. And he would watch how these women expressed satisfaction with their purchases in their halting new English.

And now, in the last few months, along those streets he had walked and known, all of a sudden the names on stores and the signs on posts had appeared in the hieroglyphics of Chinese. Or Japanese? He no longer felt safe, tumbling in the warmth and shouts of a washing machine in a public laundromat in this Technicolor new world of strangers.

He had loved those warm months and those warm people before their names and homes were written in signs. They were real until someone turned them into Chinese characters which he could not read. And he spent the warm months of summer writing letters to the leaders of the world, in the hope of getting back a reply, no matter how short or impersonal, with their signatures, which he intended to sell to the highest bidder.

He came from a colony, a country, and a culture where the written word spelled freedom. An island where the firm touch of the pen on paper meant freedom. Where the pen gripped firmly in the hand was sturdier than a soldier holding a gun, and which meant liberation. And the appearance of words on paper, the meaning and transformation they gave to the paper, and the way they rendered the paper priceless, meant that he could now escape permanently from the profuse sweat and the sharp smell of perspiration on the old khaki trousers and the thick-smelling flannel worn next to the skin. This sweat was the uniform, and had been the profession of poor black grandfathers. Now pen and paper meant the sudden and unaccountable and miraculous disappearance from a colonial tradition where young bodies graduated from the play and games and beaches of children into the dark, steamy, and bee-droning caverns and caves of warehouses in which sat white men in white drill suits and white cork hats, their white skin turning red from too much rum and too much sun, and from their too-deep appetites for food and local women. For years before this graduation, he could find himself placed like a lamp post, permanent and blissful in one job, in one spot, in one position, until perhaps a storm came, or a fierce hurricane, and felled him like the chattels of houses and spewed him into the gutter.

So he learned the power of the *word*. And kept close to it. When others filled the streets and danced in a Caribana festival and wore colours hot as summer in a new spring of life, this man remained in his isolation; and he cut himself off from those frivolous, ordinary pleasures of life that had surrounded his streets for years, just as the immigrants surrounded the open-air Kensington Market. He thought and lived and expressed himself in this hermitage of solitary joy, writing letters to President de Gaulle, President Carter, Willy Brandt (whose name he never learned to spell), to Mao Tse-tung, Dr. Martin Luther King, and Prime Minister Indira Gandhi.

The few acquaintances he called friends and met for drinks at the eighteenth-floor bar of the Park Plaza Hotel, and those he visited and talked with and drank with in their homes, all thought he was mad. And perhaps he was mad. Perhaps his obsession with the word had sent him off.

The persons to whom he wrote were all unknown to him. He did not care about their politics or their talent. But he made a fortune out of time spent in addressing them. It was an international intrusion on their serious lives: *Dear Prime Minister, I saw your name and picture in the Toronto Globe and Mail this morning. I must say I was most impressed by some of the things you have said. You are one of the most indispensable personages in this western world. This western world would come to its end of influence were it not for you. You and you alone can save it and save us. Long may you have this power. Yours very sincerely, William Jefferson.*

"Look what I pulled off!" he told Alonzo. He held the glass of cold beer bought for him on the account of friendship, and a smile came to his face. The smile was the smile of literary success. He had just promised Alonzo that he would defray all his loans with the sale of his private correspondence. A smile came to Alonzo's face. It was the smile of accepted social indebtedness. "The university would just *love* to get its hands on this!" *This* was the reply from the Prime Minister: a plain white postcard on which was written, *Thank you very much, Mr. Jefferson, for your thoughtfulness.*

He would charge the university one hundred dollars for the reply from Prime Minister Gandhi. Perhaps he could sell them his entire correspondence! Why not? Even publish them in *The Private Correspondence of William Jefferson with the Great Men and Great Women of the Twentieth Century*.

Alonzo did not know whether to continue smiling or laugh right out. He could not decide if his friend was slightly off the head. He needed more proof. The letter from Mrs. Gandhi, which he did not show, could supply the proof. But it was a man's private business, a man's private correspondence; and not even the postman who delivered it had the right to see it. If this correspondence went on, Alonzo thought, who knows, perhaps one day he may be drinking beer and associating with a man of great fame, a famous man of letters, hounded by universities to get a glimpse of this correspondence . . .

While the man is trying to unlock his door, the urge overtakes him. The keyhole had not answered the key. And the urge to pee swells over his body like a high wave. This urge would overcome him almost always when a porcelain oval hole was not immediately available. It would take him into its grip and turn his entire body into a cramping, stuttering, muscle-bound fist. Always on the wrong side of the street too.

He was on Bloor Street once, in that stretch of shops and stores and restaurants where women wear furs and carry merchandise in shopping bags with CREED'S and HOLT RENFREW and BIRKS proclaimed on them, where the restaurants look like country clubs and the shops like chapels and banks, where he could not get the nerve to enter the stained-glass door with heraldry on it, jerk a tense glance in *that* direction, and receive the direction to *there* or get a sign to show him the complicated carpeted route to WASH-ROOMS printed on a brass plate. Not dressed the way he was. Not without giving some explanation. Not without alarming the waitresses dressed more like nurses and the waiters who looked like fashion models.

Once he dashed into Holt Renfrew. It was the last desperate haven. The water was heavy on his nerves, on his bladder. His eyes were red and watery. He barely had strength to speak his wish. Experience with this urge had cautioned him, as he stood before the glass case of ladies' silk underwear, that to open his mouth at that moment, when the association of this urge with ladies' panties was in full view, meant a relaxation of his grip on the water inside him. Then it would pour out onto the carpeted floor of Persian silence, perhaps even dribble onto the feet of the young clerk whose legs he could see beneath the thinness of her almost transparent dress.

The young woman saw his stiffness and posture, and with a smile and a wave, showed him the nearest haven. It had EMPLOYEES ONLY inscribed on the shining brass. When he was finished, he could not move immediately. The loss of weight and water was like the loss of energy. "Have a good day, sir!" Her smile was brighter then.

He was still outside his room. The key was still in the hole. He did not have the strength to go down two flights of stairs to the second-floor bathroom beside the room of the woman who lived on welfare.

To have to go back down now, with this weight making his head heavier, did something with his hand, and the key turned.

He was safe inside his room. Relieved and safe. He did it in the pail. He keeps this pail in a corner, under the table, on which is a two-ringed hotplate. In times of urgency he uses it, and in times of laziness and late at night. He adds soapflakes to the steaming liquid to hide its smell and composition, and when he carries the plastic pail down, the woman on welfare cannot smell or detect his business. He relishes his privacy.

Sometimes he has no flakes of soap, so he drops a pair of soiled underwear into the urine and walks with it, pretending there is no smell; and if the coast is clear, he bolts the lock on the bathroom door and does his business and laundry like a man hiding from his superstition.

He had heard that a famous Indian politician used to drink his own pee. And it overcame him.

He is safe inside his room. He breathes more easily now. He is home. His room relaxes him. It is like the library of a man obsessed with books and who is eccentric about the majesty of books.

Red building bricks which he stole two at a time are placed in fours at each end of the white-painted three-ply shelves. And the shelves end, as a scaffold should, at the end of available space, the ceiling. The same construction occupies all four walls. There are books of all sizes, all topics, all tastes.

The space between the bottom shelf and the floor is crammed with newspapers which are now yellow. There are magazines with their backs missing through frequent use. Each new magazine goes into the space which can get no larger. Statements of great political and international significance, the photograph of a man or a woman to be written to, are torn out from their sources and pinned to the three-ply shelves with common pins; and there are framed photographs of writers whom this man regards as the great writers of the world. No one else has heard of them.

He has collected relics of his daily passage through the city, in the same two square miles, not going beyond this perimeter. He has never again ventured into that part of the city where the policeman picked him up. Among his relics are jars and bottles, and one beautiful piece of pottery that looks as if it had been unearthed in an archeological digging somewhere in the distant world. It is brown and has a mark like antiquity around its swelling girth; and where it stands, on an old trunk that could have belonged to a sea captain, or to an immigrant from Europe or the West Indies, large enough to transport memories and possessions from a poorer life to this new country, this little brown jug gives age and seriousness to the other useless but priceless pieces in his room.

In all the jars and bottles, and in this brown "antique" jug, are dried branches of trees, flowers, sprigs, and brambles. Dead beyond recognition.

The man collects dead things. Leaves and brambles and flowers and twigs. And he must like this death in things, because there is nothing that lives in his room. Nothing but the man himself. He does not see them as dead things, or as meaning death.

He has five clocks. They are all miraculously set at the same, precise time, with not a second's difference. Every morning, using the time on the CBC radio as his standard and barometer, he checks and rechecks each of his five clocks; and when this is done, he sits on his old-fashioned, large and comfortable couch, upholstered in green velvet that now has patches like sores in the coat of a dog, with knobs of dull mahogany at the ends where the fingers touch, or rest, or agitate (if he is writing or thinking about a letter to an important personage in the world). He would sit here, now that he has set his time, and listen to the ticking, secure ordering of the meaning of time; pretending he is back home in the island that consumes time, where all the clocks ticked in various dispositions and carried different times. Canada has taught him one important discipline. And he has learned about time. He has learned always to be *in* time.

Paper bags are stuffed between books, folded in their original creases and placed there, anxious for when they can be used a second time. A cupboard in the room is used as a clothes closet, a pantry, and a storeroom. It contains more paper bags, of all sizes, of all origins, from all supermarkets; but most are from Dominion. They are tied and made snug and tidy by elastic bands whose first use he has obviously forgotten. On the bottom shelf of the cupboard are plastic bags imprinted with barely visible names of stores and shops, folded in a new improvised crease and placed into a large brown paper bag.

All this time, he is walking the four short lengths of floor bordered by his books, stopping in front of one shelf, running his fingers absentmindedly over the titles of books. The linoleum floor is punctuated by the nails in his shoes that walk up and down, late into the night of thoughtfulness, of worrying about a correct address or a correct salutation. Now he stands beside a large wooden table made by immigrants or early settlers on a farm, in the style of large sturdy legs, the size and shape of their own husky peasant form.

This table does not move. It cannot move. On it he has store-roomed his food and his drinks, his "eatables and drinkables," and it functions as his pantry of dishes and pots and pans. At one end of the table is the gas hotplate, the only implement for cooking that is allowed in this illegally small living space.

On the hotplate is a shining aluminum saucepan battered around its girth by temper, hunger, and burned rice.

He uncovers the saucepan. The food is old. Its age, two or three days, has thickened its smell, and makes it look like wet cement. The swollen black-eyed peas sit permanently among hunks of pigtails. He is hungry all of a sudden. These two urges, peeing and eating, come upon him without notice and with no regard to the last time he has eaten or peed. So he digs a pot-spoon into the heart of the thick drying cement of food and uproots the swollen hunks of pig-tails, whose oily taste brings water and nostalgia to his eyes, and he half shuts his eyes to eat the first mouthful.

He replaces the lid. He puts the pot-spoon between the sauce-pan rim and the lid, and pats the battered side of the saucepan the way a trainer would pat a horse that has just won on a long-shot bet.

He takes off his jacket. It is two sizes too large. Then he takes off his red woollen sweater; and another one of cotton, and long-sleeved; and then a third, grey, long-sleeved, round-necked and marked PROPERTY OF THE ATHLETIC DEPARTMENT, UNIVERSITY OF TORONTO.

He is a man of words, and the printed claim of ownership on his third pullover never ceases to amaze and impress him.

Stripped now of his clothes, he is left in a pair of grey long johns. And it is in these that he walks about the wordy room, ruminating as he struggles late into the night to compose the correct arrangement of words that will bring him replies from the pens of the great. Sometimes his own words do not flow as easily as he would wish. And this literary constipation aborts the urge to pee. At such times he runs to his Javex box, where he keeps all the replies he has ever received. He reads them now, praying for an easier movement of words from the bowels of his brain.

Dear Mr. Jefferson, Thank you for your letter.

That was all from one great personage. But it was good enough. It was a reply. And an official one at that. A rubber stamp of the signature tells you of the disinterest or the thick appointment book of the sender, that perhaps the sender does not understand the archival significance of the letter he has received from Mr. William Jefferson.

This is to acknowledge receipt of your letter.

Another reply from a great personage. Even the stamp, print, and address are reproductions of the original. But the man believes that some value lies even in this impersonal reply.

Dear Mr. Jefferson, We are very glad to know that, as a Barbadian, you have introduced us to the archives of the University of Toronto, which is considering maintaining a Barbados Collection. We wish you every success in your significant venture.

This is his most valuable letter. It is signed by someone who lives! A human hand has signed it. But he cannot untangle the name from its spidery script. He does not know who has replied to him. For typed beneath the script is only the person's official position: *Secretary.*

He understands more than any other living person the archival importance of these letters. And he treasures them within a vast imagination of large expectations, in this large brown box which contained Javex for bleaching clothes before it fell into his possession, to be put to its new use as a filing cabinet.

He has been nervous all week. And this nervousness erupted in strong urges to pee, strong and strange even for his weak bladder. The nervousness was linked to the price of his collection. This afternoon he had spoken to someone at the university. Over the telephone the voice told him, "Of course! Of course, Mr. Jefferson. We'll be interested in seeing your collection." It was a polite reply, like the written ones in his Javex box. But as a man obsessed by relics, who attaches great significance to their esoteric value, he inflates that significance. He is also a man who would read an offer to purchase in such a polite reply from the university, dismissing him. He is a man who hears more words than those that are spoken.

He starts to count his fortune. This letter to him from a living prime minister would be the basis of his fortune. His friend Alonzo would get a free round of beer at the Park Plaza roof bar. He would pay his rent six months in advance. He would have more time to spend on his private correspondence with the great men and women of the world.

He holds the Prime Minister's letter in his hand and examines the almost invisible watermarks on which it is typed. He studies the quality of the official stationery, made in Britain and used by the West Indies, and compares it to that of Canada and the United States. He decides that the British and the West Indies know more about prestigious stationery. He continues to feel the paper between big thumb and two adjoining fingers, rubbing and rubbing and feeling a kind of orgasm coming on; and in this trance, he reads another letter.

Dear Mr. Jefferson, Thank you for your kind and thoughtful letter. Yours, Prime Minister's Office.

Above this last line, *Margaret Thatcher* is stamped in fading ink. Still, it is a mark on history; "a first" from a woman, once poor, whom history had singled out to be great.

When he is in his creative mood, he moves like a man afraid to cause commotion in a room in which he is a guest, like a man moving amongst bric-a-brac, priceless mementos of glass and china and silver locked in a glass cabinet. He moves about his room soundlessly, preparing his writing materials and deepening his mood for writing.

His stationery is personalized. *William Jefferson, Esquire* is printed in bold letters at the top of the blue page. And below that, his address. He writes with a fountain pen. And when he fills it from the bottle of black ink, he always smiles when the pen makes its sucking noise. This sucking noise takes him back years to another room in another country, when he formed his first letters. And he likes the bottle that contains the ink. It has a white label, with a squeezed circle like an alert eye; and through this eye, through the middle of this eye, is an arrow which pierces it. PARKER SUPER

QUINK INK. PERMANENT BLACK. It suggests strength and longevity. It is like his life: determined and traditional, poised outside the mainstream but fixed in habit and custom. Whenever he uses this fountain pen, his index finger and the finger next to that, and his thumb, bear the verdict and the evidence of this permanent blackness. This *noir*. He sometimes wishes that he could use the language of Frenchmen, who slip words and the sounds of those words over their tongues like raw oysters going down the throat!

"What a remarkable use of the tongue the French have! That back of the throat sensation!" he told Alonzo one afternoon, but in such a way as if he were speaking to the entire room in the Park Plaza Hotel bar.

Noir.

Many years ago, in 1955, the minute his feet touched French soil at Dorval in Quebec, the first greeting he heard was "*Noir!*" The sound held him in its grip, and changed his view of ordinary things, and made him fastidious and proper and suspicious. The only word he retained was *noir*. It was not a new word to him. For years even before that greeting, and in Barbados on a Sunday afternoon after the heavy midday meal, he used to sit at the back door looking out on to the cackling of hens, one of which he had eaten earlier, inhaling with the freshness of stomach and glorious weather the strong smell of Nugget shoe polish as he lathered it onto his shoes and onto his father's shoes and his mother's shoes and his grandfather's shoes. So he had already dipped his hands into *noir* long before Canada.

He had known *noir* for years. But no one had addressed him as *noir*.

He likes the *noir* of the ink he uses, as he liked the *noir* in the Nugget which gave his shoes longer life and made them immortal and left its proud, industrious, and indelible stain on his fingers.

Tomorrow the University of Toronto is coming to buy his papers. He runs his hands over his letters in the Javex box, hundreds of them, and thinks of money and certified cheques. He empties all his pockets and puts the papers contained there on the table. He picks up each piece like a man picking flesh from a carcass of bones. Who should he write to tonight?

The silent books around him, their words encased in covers, do not offer advice. But he knows what they would answer. He finds it difficult to concentrate. Tomorrow is too near. The money from his papers, cash or certified cheque, is too close at hand. He spends time spending it in his mind. And the things contained in tomorrow, like the things contained in his Javex box, have at last delivered him, just as his articulate use of the pen confirmed the value of the word and delivered him from the raving crowds of new immigrants. He has gained peace and a respectable distance from those aggressive men and women because of his use of the word.

"Should I write to the president of Yale University?"

The books, thick in their shelves around him, and few of which he has read from cover to cover, all these books remain uncommunicative and have no words of advice.

"Should I write to President Reagan?"

His five electric clocks continue to keep constant time, and in their regulated determination, refuse to disclose a tick of assistance.

"The prime minister of Barbados?"

Barbados is no longer home. Home, he had told Alonzo ten years ago, "is where I pee and eat and write."

He gets up and turns on the flame of the hotplate under the saucepan. "While the grass is growing, the horse is starving," he tells the saucepan. He smiles at his own wisdom. The heat makes the saucepan crackle. "While the grass is growing . . ." The thin saucepan makes a smothered crackling sound. The hotplate seems to be melting the coagulated black-eyed peas and rice and pigtails. The hotplate is crackling as if it is intent upon melting the cheap alloy of the saucepan and turning the meal into soft hot lead, and then spreading its flame over the letters on the table, and then the table itself, and then the room. He lowers the flame.

"Fire cleans everything," he tells the hotplate. The saucepan stops laughing with the heat. His meal has settled down to being recooked.

But he is soon smelling things. The nostalgia of food and the perspiration from his mother's forehead as she cooked the food, and the strong, rich smell of pork. He smells also the lasting wetness of flannel shirts worn in the fields back on the small island.

He gets accustomed to these smells. And he thinks again of new correspondence, since all these on the table before him would be gone by tomorrow, sold, archived among other literary riches. A hand-rubbing enthusiasm and contentment brings a smile to his face.

"I'll write the prime minister of Barbados!"

The smell comes up again. With the help of the smell, he is back on the small island, witnessing spires of blue smoke pouring out from each small castle of patched tin and rotting wood where his village stood. He can hear the waves and the turbulent sea, so much like the turbulence of water he boiled in the same thin-skinned saucepan to make tea. As he thinks back, his eyes pass over used teabags spread in disarray, an action caught in the midst of an important letter, when he would sometimes drop a used teabag into the yellow plastic pail.

Dear Prime Minister . . .

He reaches over to the hotplate and raises the flame. He sees it change from yellow to blue, and smiles. "The horse is starving . . ."

Certain important universities have asked me to act as a liaison to encourage you to submit your . . .

The fragile aluminum saucepan is losing its battle in the heat of warming the food. But it is the smell. The smell takes his mind off the letter, and off the great sums of money, cash and certified cheques. He is a boy again, running home from school, colliding with palings and dogs and the rising smells of boiled pork reddened in tomatoes and bubbling over rice like the thick tar which the road workers poured over a raw road under construction.

He can taste his country now. Clearly. And see the face of the Prime Minister, greedy to make a name for himself in a foreign institution of higher learning, and obtain foreign currency for his foreign account.

. . . I have lived a solitary life, apart from the demonstrations and protests of the mainstream of immigrants. I have become a different man. A man of letters. I am more concerned with cultural things, radio, books and libraries, than with reports . . .

Something is wrong with his pen. The flow is clogged and constricted, just like when he's caught with his pants up in a sudden urge to pee, and having forced it inwards, cannot get it outwards. And he gets up and heads downstairs. Just as he's moving away from his door, still on the first three or four steps going down, he turns back. "My pen is my penis," he tells the door.

He picks up the yellow plastic pail. He throws a shirt and underwear into the brown stagnant water. It looks like stale beer. Before he goes through the door again, he picks up the unfinished letter to the Prime Minister of Barbados, and in his long johns, armed with pail and paper, he creeps out.

The stairs are still dim. And he smiles. He moves down slowly, hoping that when he reaches the second floor, the woman on welfare who occupies the toilet longer than any other tenant would not be there.

The saucepan has now begun to boil, although there are more solids than liquids within its thin frame. Popcorn comes into his mind. He doesn't even eat popcorn! He doesn't even go to the movies! The saucepan is turning red at the bottom. If he were in his room, he could not tell where the saucepan's bottom began and where the ring of the hotplate ended.

He thinks of roast corn as he reaches the closed door of the only bathroom in the house. He stands. He listens. He smells. He inhales. And he exhales. He puts his hand on the door and pushes gently, and the door opens with a small creak. He stands motionless, alarmed to see that the bathroom is indeed empty. Where is the woman on welfare?

. . . at night, back home, in the crop season when the sugar canes are cut and harvested, they burn the corn over coals . . .

Right then, above his head, the saucepan explodes. He doesn't hear it. The black-eyed peas and rice burst out, pelting the lid before them, and the tabletop is splattered with careless punctuation marks. It falls on his fine blue stationery.

The explosion comes just as he holds the yellow pail at a tilt, over the growling toilet bowl. In the same hand as the pail is the unfinished letter. The urine is flowing into the bowl and he stands thinking, when he sees the first clouds of smoke crawling down the stairs, past the open bathroom door.

The smoke becomes heavier and makes tears come into his eyes. He is crying and passing his hands in front of his face, trying to clear a passage from the second floor, through the thickening smoke rising like high waves. Up and up he goes, no faster than when he entered the house earlier that afternoon, struggling through the smoke until he reaches the steps in front of his door. And as he gets there, it seems as if all the books, all the letters, all the bags of plastic and paper shout at once in an even greater explosion.

Before he can get downstairs a second time, to call for help from the woman on welfare, he thinks he hears all five of his clocks alarming. And then, in the way that a man who has been struck by a deadening blow waits for the second one to land, he stands, expecting the five clocks to do something else. It is then that he hears one clock striking the hour. He counts aloud until he reaches eight, and then he refuses to count any longer.

A SLOW DEATH

It began very slowly, almost imperceptibly, his hating the house in which he had lived for fifteen years, and without warning, like the melting of the stub of snow at the end of his walk that signalled in the spring. This hatred became a rage, an explosion, and it consumed his mind. It happened soon after his wife died. Her scent and her spirit remained in the house, quiet at first, and like an aggressive tenant afterwards, taking up most of his time and his space, although he was now occupying the three-storeyed house by himself.

He told the young, vivacious saleswoman that he had to sell the house because it had become too large for him. He did not tell her about his wife.

He showed her through the house, the three floors of rooms which he had recently cleaned and painted. Linoleum was nailed down the very morning it was bought from Bloor Hardware. The heads of the nails were still shining and visible. When he took her into the bathroom, the fresh, high, pungent smell of the small white balls he had taken from the storeroom at work returned his wife's smell, the smell of camphor.

He had mourned for three weeks, with the help of Canadian Club rye whisky. And he would have mourned longer if the rye had sat less heavily upon him, and hadn't made him drop off in dozes in the middle of the day, and hadn't built up a pallor of ennui around his entire personality. He felt tired all the time. Cigarettes and more rye did not help.

He became suddenly tired, almost exhausted, by climbing the three flights of stairs. He began to hate her and her gnawing memory each time he got drunk. And he was drunk these days more often than the evenings of the weekend, which had been his time for relaxation and the occasional drink.

The saleswoman smiled all the time. He could not guess at her seriousness or interest in his home. But at the end of the showing, she said, "I'll take it off your hands." He did not like the way she said it. He did not like the way she was dressed. During the interview she had pulled the tape measure from the neck of her cashmere sweater, like a snake unfolding, dropped it in one corner of the bedroom, after having kicked aside a shoebox, and then she bent down without bending her knees, so that the ridge of her behind faced him as she certified the size of the room. It was in the bedroom in which his wife had died that she bent down this way for the first time. He was still aware of his wife's presence in the room.

Whenever he saw her legs and the colour of her panties, he turned his eyes away. But he had taken a full appraisal of her young body and sensual legs; and his age told him he could be her father, and therefore he had probably called the wrong real estate company. She said her name was Jennie Cambull. But she was pretty. He tried to see a comparison between her and his wife, but he could not remember when his wife looked as young as this self-assured woman in the transparent dress. The shoebox she had kicked aside contained his wife's jewels.

Nevertheless, he signed the agreement to sell. "I'll take it off your hands," she said again, and then left.

On the subway going back to work in the east end, he was sad. He had agreed to sign his life away, and would probably be lonely and desolate and would have to enter a home for the aged. He wished he had had children. He would happily live in one room and give the children the run of the rest of the house. He wished the city would transfer him to the park across the street from his house. From his house to the city park where he worked as a gardener, down in the Beaches, was a daily journey of almost one hour by streetcar. At five o'clock it took almost twice as long. But the time spent travelling whetted his thirst for rye, and it also kept him away from the house.

Many nights soon after she died, he would walk up and down the house, talking to her, which he never did when she was alive, rearranging her clothes and playing with her jewels in the shoebox.

The weekend was upon him. It was Friday afternoon. As he got off the streetcar near the racecourse at Greenwood, a clock on a large brick building said two. He would have the weekend to himself, all of Friday night, all Saturday and Sunday, but he could not face another weekend alone in the house that seemed filled with echoes of a past, unhappy life. He had already done all those small jobs that old men occupy their hands with, leaving their minds to wander and be oppressed by loneliness and advancing helplessness. He had always feared, even when he was fifty, that he would have a hard time going to the toilet and that there would be no one to clean him afterwards. This was one reason he hated her for dying before he did. And now all he had to look forward to were the rough hands of an indifferent, unrelated public nurse in a home for the aged. But that was better than living in this large house alone, to be lathered in his own excrement and be found dead. He wondered if the smell of his excrement would be the same he would give off when he was found dead. This Friday evening he stifled these thoughts with a half-bottle of Canadian Club.

He had chosen this house because of the park. The park and the price of the house. He had lived for ten years in a flat in a rooming house opposite; and when the FOR SALE sign was nailed into the snow in mid-February, he saw it early. That afternoon he was walking through the park. Sibelius Park was as lovely and boisterous with snow and children's laughter as was the music of the composer after whom the park was named. He had saved three thousand dollars in ten years. Once a month, on each payday, with a constancy that matched his wife's attendance at the Shaw Street Baptist Church, he went to his bank to make his deposit. This regularity impressed the bank manager. When the time came for purchase and a loan, the bank manager gave him the extra three thousand dollars to make the down payment. "You're a steady man," he told him. The price was twenty-five thousand dollars.

When he came home that night, he announced his good fortune to his wife. He was the first in both their families to own the roof over their heads. He poured himself a rye and ginger, and poured one for his wife. And together they stood at the window of their flat on the third floor of the rooming house and looked across at their new home. He dreamed of improvements and flower beds and green-painted fences and red roses and new linoleum.

He faced the new life before him—new, but only as large as the width of the quiet dog-deserted street—with the same bravery as he had faced the steps of the Air Canada plane that brought him here from Barbados twenty-five years ago.

Fifteen years ago this house was on a street whose houses had an ordinary beauty and working-class charm. The street was inhabited by Jews and Anglo-Saxons who were still trampling through snow to catch a five-o'clock streetcar in the morning; by people of modest means and fair-sized families, with children who played safely in the park. But all of a sudden the street became popular, enviable and expensive; and just as suddenly the neighbourhood became known as the Annex. He never found out what it was annexed to. But the droves of refugees from the suburbs and from Europe's poorest countries transformed it into a village.

"Townhousing" sprang up like the bulbs he nurtured in the city parks. He watched the street change from a stable, working-class district to one made up of lawyers, university professors, and architects. They filled the sidewalks in front of his house and his shared laneway with the guts of their renovations. Dust and brick and broken plaster lay for days all over the demolished front lawns. And in the racket of the improvements, he remained silent and disapproving, suffering from long bouts of sinus caused by the dust of regenerated homes.

The owners, wallowing in new money, delighted in destroying the old gracious charm of these houses bought by the sweat and blood of ambition; and they resold them after one year for small fortunes, and the street became infested with transients who bought and sold and had no time for families and for sitting amongst the flowers and the playing children and the barking dogs in the park.

The first thing he did when he moved into his home was turn the volume of his Seabreeze record player up as loudly as it would go. He stood with a broad smile on his face, laughing with his wife, who covered her ears with her hands, and he cried out, "I am now a man!" She shrugged and moved away, but there was a smile on her face.

He experienced new privacy. He used the bathroom with the door wide open, and the sound of his passing gas went from the second floor to the first, where she was washing the dinner plates. "Ahhh! I wanted to do that for ten years! Excuse me."

As the years passed, he loved the park more and it became a vacationland of his imagination. In winter the crystals of leaves and icicles shone white and splendid, and he sat by his bay window and watched this magic, helped on by the strength of his rye and ginger ale.

In the spring, which it is now, he counted the erupting new life of plants and flowers, Dutch bulbs and green grass around him; and at his job in the east end, he wallowed in these new shoots of life and felt himself getting younger. Every year at this time, and for years now, he pestered his supervisor for a transfer. "Everything takes time," his wife would say, but it only made him more impatient and angry with her. "A man like me, used to watching and waiting on bulbs and plants and things to grow, and that is *all* you could say?" She did not understand him, did not understand his anger, his ambition for their success, his ambition to be his own man.

On this Friday night, as on every Friday night since she had died, he did the shopping for the groceries and topped off the plastic bag that had a large red D with two forty-ounce bottles of Canadian Club. He already had a case of ginger ale in the cupboard beneath the sink. He took a shower and put on a green long-sleeved shirt and green trousers, the same as the uniform he had to wear to work. "City" was stitched in large letters on his left-hand breast pocket. He threw the uniform which he had worn during the week, and which fitted him no better than the fresh one, into the dirty-clothes hamper. He did not close the lid.

After the news and the first television movie, after five drinks, he still faced a long night. So he got up from his favourite leather chair that grew higher and longer when he sat upon it at a certain angle, and embarked on his nightly roaming through the house. He touched the backs of chairs and ran his calloused hands over the crocheted antimacassars on the heavy upholstered furniture. Grease was left on them. He went to the third floor in the voiceless house, to the room where he'd been sleeping since she died, and took out the ten suits he owned. He had bought the material cheap in the garment district on Spadina Avenue and had given it to a West Indian tailor. The suits were all of wool, made in the same style, and with waistcoats. He never wore nine of them; and the one that touched his back was worn only once. But every Sunday morning, in the spring and in the summer, he put them on the pink plastic clotheslines in his backyard to get the sun and the air. Mothballs were in all the pockets of each suit. And in the lapel of the black serge suit was the white carnation, dried and dead now, which he had worn to his wife's funeral.

He sat on the bed, with five suits on each side, and ran his thick birthmarked palms delicately over the rich material. He smiled as he discovered the tailor's bill in the breast pocket of one of them, the subway transfer in the waistcoat of another; and these two mementos did not bring back any clues to a life that seemed to have ended long ago. He replaced the bill and the transfer.

Even when she was alive he had delighted in these expeditions. His delight was no less this Friday evening. He used to put his father's suits on the line to sun when he was a boy. His father had two suits, a black one for funerals and church, a dark brown one for weddings and "services of songs" and dances, which were called balls in those days.

"Any cockfight," he said, as if he were talking to his wife, and as he had joked with her each Sunday morning before she left for church as he prepared his suits for airing, "any cockfight, and I can't be caught with my pants down! I prepared for any cockfight. Funeral or wedding."

He didn't know that the funeral would be his wife's.

Even now he wondered whether he hadn't, by his harmless words, brought on her death. She had taken ill on a Wednesday, called the doctor on a Friday, and the following Thursday she was dead. It was cancer. She had borne it silently for one year before she confessed her pains to the doctor. Cancer.

But he must not think of her long, silent suffering and swift departure now. The house was still in mourning.

At the bottom of the clothes closet from which he had taken the ten suits was a line of shoes, black and brown, stiff from lack of wearing, and shining bright from the weekly polishing he gave them. They were perforated at the instep, and they all had rubber heels. He hated noise. These he took out, all twelve pairs, and as he had seen his father do every Sunday morning, he polished them with Nugget, black and brown, and spat on them twenty-four times to improve their shine.

He's in the bedroom where she died. He brushes the dust from her large black Bible. He rests his hand on its cover, like a man swearing to tell the truth, and for the first time he has a strong urge to open the Bible. The pages, trimmed in gold, fall apart, dividing the book almost in half, and he sees the lines: *The sleep of the labouring man is sweet, whether he eat little or much: but the abundance of the rich will not suffer him to sleep*. Was she trying to tell him something? It could not have been an accident that his eyes would fall upon this passage. The pages had fallen open on their own when he held the bible. It was as if the bible had reorganized its weight to be balanced in two almost equal halves.

He began to remember how her voice wheezed when she read. A soft, almost bronchial whispering. And then he noticed the smell of her bathwater, Bournes Bay Rum. It was the smell of death too, that same smell he had noticed in the funeral parlour. And although his friends from the city parks department had sent fresh flowers and wreaths that took up one entire pew, her smell, body and bath-water, was stronger.

What is the time now? The bottle is less than half empty. He looks out onto his former landlady's house. He knows her profession because he knows her, and they say good morning to each other every morning. But the men and women and children in all the other houses have remained strangers. He does not see them except on weekends. His hours are not theirs. And no one except his former landlady has ever come to ask how he is now that he's alone. Perhaps they do not even know he's alone. Perhaps they do not even know she's died. At home in Barbados the coffin and the funeral service would be in the front room, and the whole village would know and would mourn. But here in Toronto, her body was placed in the balmed safekeeping of a funeral home. Out of sight, out of memory. Could he die in this house and nobody would know until the gas company came to read the meter?

The street is quiet and ordinary. There's only the normal activity of people passing. No one pauses, no one's aware of him, no one looks up and sees anything different. Their lives have not changed. A woman passes with a plastic bag of groceries. A foreign car stops, turns off its lights, and the driver locks the door and disappears in the larger darkness. That's the man who wears a beard and walks with books in both hands. The woman with the plastic bag enters the house beside his through a heavy black door that has brass rectangles on it. Perhaps she's a lawyer.

Three Indians pass. One of them drops the bag from which he's eating. He casts his eyes right and left, above and behind, then digs his left hand deep into the seat of his trousers, shivers, and walks on. He laughs. Perhaps his companions have seen him in the shadows at the second-floor curtain. They're all wearing cloth wrapped around their heads, and the street light turns the cloth into shimmering silver.

He had never seen them on this street before. He wondered where they were born. He was glad they did not live on the street.

How much more could he bear?

He does not watch much television, even though he turns it on every night, for there's too much crime and murder coming into his living room. Last week a nine-year-old girl was missing from the park; and after searching for her for two days, they found her cold in an unused refrigerator, strangled and raped and buckled in two, like a flying fish, to suit the size of her attacker's whim. The refrigerator was still plugged into the wall. Every week in the *Toronto Star* you read that a man killed a man or a woman, and sometimes two or three; and on television you see thousands killed or starving to death. In Africa, which he doesn't know and doesn't care to see but which he hears a lot about, the television shows him images of ribs and dried flesh, and flies on black faces. And before the story ends—the suffering on the faces or the images on the screen—he shuts it out and turns it off.

But there was one night when he could have borne more. That was the night, many years ago, which he relives even now. The smell of meat in old oil had disappeared. The house was still. Rose and pine, the smells his former landlady favoured and kept in a green bottle, drifted from the first floor up to him on the third. The two bottles of smells for the house had a wick that looked like a grey tongue. He liked this mixture of smells more that night than in the ten years he had lived in her house. That was the night he bought this very house in which he now stands looking out at his unknown neighbours.

Quietly as the creaking linoleum allowed, he had walked down from his flat to use the bathroom. It was beside the communal kitchen. For ten years he had used caution and was always conscious of the smells and the noise when he was inside that cold room. He always ran the water at full blast to stifle the explosion and the smell. Down the steps of green indoor-outdoor carpeting, then over the thick broadloom leading him to the first floor, where he stood noiselessly inside the screen door of glass and chicken wire. He stared at it through the peephole. His house. It appeared circular, almost round within the restriction of the peephole. The house was like a womb. His eyes were watery from the strain of looking. He could hardly breathe. The landlady's television started to play "O Canada." He waited until the national anthem was over, until the martial music became a hum and then silence. And in that cold white silence he took a last look at his house. The broadloom changed back into the indoor-outdoor carpeting, he was back again in the area of his flat, linoleum creaking on the uneven stairs. He could hear each step. He did not know until he had reached his flat that he had walked so heavily. He was still wearing his construction boots. And before he closed the door, he laughed aloud. Three doors somewhere in the rooming house opened and he could hear the inquisitive steps into the hallway, then the slamming of the doors in disgust. He stared at his wife's worried eyes, and he heard his own laughter and then hers, rejoicing at his success.

He believed she was a religious woman. He believed she was a weak woman. He watched her practise her religion day and night with a Christian silence, as if she was doing it to give him a whipping. He remained at home, shining shoes and airing his suits, when she took her Sunday-morning journeys to the Shaw Street Baptist Church. She wore brown against her brown skin, with the only relief being the glossy silver of her hair. And a string of pearls. And he followed her out of the corner of his eye, out of the right side of the second-floor window, as she set out for the ten blocks to Bloor and Shaw streets.

In his imagination he would follow her down the incline, at which point she always had to slacken her pace because, as she complained after each Sunday, she had "symptoms and pains." It was unbearable to hear her speak this way, as it was when he watched her try to turn the pages of her bible. Every afternoon, when other women would read the *Star*, she read her bible. And sometimes she read aloud, as if she was telling him a bedtime story. "*The sleep of the labouring man is sweet . . .*"

And he would be on the couch dozing in front of the television, the half-empty glass of Canadian Club at an angle ready to crash on the coffee table, and he would be saved each time by the scoring of a goal and the explosion of noise in the Gardens, and would wake to hear " . . . *will not suffer him to sleep."*

"You really miss her, don't ya?" His former landlady was sitting on his verandah. It was a summer afternoon. He was watering his roses. The aluminum chair in which she sat was his wife's favourite.

He was pouring too much water over the chrysanthemums. The water was breaking off their stalks.

"You really miss her."

He washed the mould from his hands and joined her.

"How's your nephew?"

"This place's too big. You should move to a smaller place. Even a room. Or back in with me! What you say to that? My nephew's moved out. Sammy. My first sister's first boy. Had to ask him to leave. But he's not far from me. Just over there at Golden Acres on Bathurst. He likes it there." She paused at the end of each piece of information she gave him, as if she wanted him to fill in the rest for himself. He did not know whether she would go on. "That's the best place for someone with his condition. Cancer, ya know. I can't be bothered looking after him. Too much time and too much work. I have my church, as you know. Keeps me busy. I just had to get him in a nice home. Now he's his own man. But I make him visit me every Saturday. My church keeps me busy all Sunday. This cancer is such a bad thing. A person needs attention all the time . . ."

He was thinking of the broken stems. When this woman left, he would prop them up with sticks. She got up, pulled out the part of her dress that was stuck in the crease of her behind, raised her dress high enough for him to see her legs, and prepared to leave. He saw the thick blue veins, like wandering worms in the fat parts inside her knees. "I'll get my nephew to come over and keep you company. He's coming Sunday this time. On Sunday I have to run down to the hospital to visit a church member."

As night closed in and he was into the last fifth of the bottle of rye, feeling the full weight of loneliness which he experienced every night in the summer, at sunset, the same heaviness that he knew so many years ago in Barbados, as if the word "dusk" meant that dark scales or ashes from a nearby fire were falling all around him, he began to do what he always did at this time of night, whether in Toronto or in Barbados. He began to touch things: objects that made him remember brighter times.

He brought his old copies of *Popular Mechanics* from the basement and put them into boxes. Next, he packed his winter boots and the two pairs of old workboots. He threw them back onto the concrete floor of the basement, and with a cigarette dangling at the corner of his mouth, and rye and ginger in hand, he went upstairs. The natural light of day and the light in the house was now mixed. At this time of day, when he was a small boy, his mother had always asked him to shut the windows in her bedroom, to keep out the mosquitoes. And always, wherever he was, he would enter his bedroom at this time of day, not knowing why, until this Saturday evening when he stood in the bedroom where she died.

The white crocheted bedspread, now turning grey, was as she had left it. Some necklaces of beads, large as red grapes, were on the frame of the mirror on her bureau. Her copies of *The Light of Life*, *Living a Christian Life*, and *The Watchtower* were piled neatly, month by month, on the floor beside the bed. Her embroidery— palm trees growing out of red earth, and two pieces of needle- point with "God Bless This House" in shaky script—were on the bureau top. Hanging in the clothes cupboard were all her dresses, untouched for eleven months from the day she had ironed them. They now looked like carcasses of slaughtered, undernourished animals. In circular wooden frames, there were other pieces of embroidery, mere outlines, drawn in pencil on cloth. Her winter boots with the fur trimming and woollen balls at the ends of the laces stood upright like the two ushers at the funeral parlour. And the monthly *Baptist Messenger*, which she stacked in a neat pile after reading twice.

He was too close to her while he sat on her bed. But he was drawn to her, in a headiness of exciting adventure, as a climber ignores the perils of height for the sake of exploration.

In his hands is the shoebox. In it is her jewellery. When will he
hear from the saleswoman? Bright gold-coloured brooches, clusters of luscious fruits and bouquets of flowers. They do not remind
him of his gardens in the city parks. Some are silver-painted stars
of glittering waterfalls, and buttons and pins given to her for her
attendance at church with relentless frequency and for her Christian devotion. He puts his hand deeper into the box and fingers
her jewellery. When he was a child, at the beach, he used to dig
into the soft, wet sand until he reached the water below. Into his
grasp came a strand of pearls. He had bought them for her. Was it
a birthday or an anniversary? She wore them every Sunday over her
brown skin. The skin of the pearls was peeling now. He should have
buried her in this necklace.

The long slithering necklace ran through his fingers, like soft
sand, bead after peeled bead, and he measured the months of loneliness with each bead.

Her bureau drawers were filled with her underclothes. Some he
had never seen before. Her pink corset, its metal stays covered in
silk corrugated cloth, was like a rack of ribs in his hands. He threw
it back into the drawer, slammed the door, and left.

When he sat in his chair with the white embroidered headrest, a
rye in his hand, the television took over his senses and he was soon
in a deep sleep.

It was a beautiful morning when he drew the window curtains
apart. He was in the first-floor living room. He had slept in his
work uniform again. The sun came in like a bullet. His spirits were
high. He felt vigorous and he added up the things he wanted to do.
It was as if he was among his flower beds in the east end park. If
only they would approve his transfer soon . . .

Sibelius Park was ablaze with colour and already filled with
children. A green Frisbee sailed from one end of his window
and disappeared out the other, leaving a rainbow of excitement and
children's laughter. His former landlady faced him, coming up the
walk. An old man was scraping behind her, his shoes sounding like
iron on the cement. He remembered the old man's cancer. He

must be walking in pain. He looked terminal inside his oversized suit. But he was smiling.

"Here's Sammy!"

Her nephew's face was red. Did they leave him out in the sun on the verandah over at Golden Acres and forget to take him in?

"Sammy, tell Mr. Trotman about Golden Acres. I won't be gone a minute . . ." She was already at the end of the walk. "He caught me unawares. I thought he was coming tomorrow . . ."

But he was glad for the company.

Sammy was a silent man. Whenever he had seen him passing and had waved at him, he was smiling and dressed in a three-piece suit which was always too big for him. Did the cancer cause the padding in the shoulders to droop?

Sometimes the pain in his body came over his smiles, like bacteria on a leaf. It seemed to stab him now when he moved his body to take the three steps to reach the door.

They sat without talking, looking out at the park. A pink Frisbee joined the green one. And a dog ran and jumped after it.

"Ya want one of these?" Sammy asked. He turned his head to see Sammy take a short flat brown bottle from inside his breast pocket, unscrew it, and put it to his lips. His swallow-pipe jumped like a piston, up and down. "Jeez!" He passed the back of his hand lightly across his lips. He pressed his lips tightly, and shook his head and squeezed his eyes shut. When he opened them, they had taken on a look of pain, rebuke, and fear. "Jeez!" he said. His face was washed in a smile.

He left Sammy smiling and went into the kitchen. He returned with glasses, ice, a bottle of ginger ale, and a bottle of Canadian Club. A larger smile broke out, like the sun, on Sammy's face. The children in the park were screaming for joy at the elusive Frisbees.

"Jeez!" he said again.

They drank the first one in silence.

"The bitch," Sammy said. He took another drink. And with each sip, he did the same thing with his lip, his eyes, and his head. The silence returned between them, strong as an old bond. He could see long afternoons of loneliness and few words and deep memories in Sammy's watery eyes.

"Here's to Golden Acres!" Sammy said. "Jeez!" His laughter was a blend of coughing and a splutter. He clapped his chest. "Golden Acres!" His words were like two plates dropped on cement. He held the bottle, and his hand grew tense around its neck, and the blue veins swelled in that hand and became prominent, as if they were about to burst, as if he was about to break the neck of the bottle. "Jeez!"

He unscrewed the bottle. After he poured himself a drink, he placed the bottle on the table, and his hands relaxed, and his body relaxed and went almost dead; all feeling went from his face, and the skin looked like sagging layers of leather, his eyes like the circles left by the two glasses of water on the table. He sat like that, his hands dropped to his sides, and breathing heavily. "The bottle," he said, lifting the glass, "and my cigars"—taking a package of White Owls from his pocket—"is the only two things they left me with. Best two things in the world. Keeps me from going mad. Or killing that bitch. Or setting the place on fire."

He did not know if Sammy meant Golden Acres or his aunt's house.

"So you're selling this place!" He filled up his bottle with Canadian Club and then put his bottle into his breast pocket. He forced life out of his body and sat limp, summoning another thought about Golden Acres before taking on the exertion of talking. "You coming to Golden Acres? You coming to be a goddamn inmate like me?" He was dead again.

Sombre and flushed with the rye, he watched Sammy slide almost onto his back, slouched under the weight of his memories and the drink. Sammy sat up, poured a large drink from the Canadian Club bottle, and said, "You sixty yet?"

"Sixty-one," he lied.

"Jeez!" Sammy said, and immediately he appeared younger. "Better be going." He seemed very sad now, and resigned. He took something from his other breast pocket and sprayed it into his mouth. "Jeez! You're from Jamaica, ain't it?" He sprayed his mouth a second time.

"Barbados."

The smell of peppermint lingered on the verandah long after he left.

The new week began like a Dutch bulb in bloom. His foreman had approved his transfer. And he spent the rest of that Monday morning amongst children and flowers in Sibelius Park. He did not care that they had given him only one helper. He was within sight of his home.

The saleswoman came twice that day with prospective buyers, all of them wealthy even by appearance. But he had now changed his mind about selling the house and was about to tell the saleswoman when she smiled and said, "I'd like a spare key. You shouldn't have to leave your job to let me in."

All that night he drank and went from room to room, pulling the blinds shut as a watchman closes doors. He retraced his steps, room by room, and turned off all the lights except those in her bedroom. He walked around the bed many times, each time crossing his reflection in the oval mahogany mirror on the bureau laden with her beads. He could not conquer the space in the rest of the house, and so he confined himself to the small room, the third-floor bedroom. But he could not sleep.

He went down to the first floor and sat in his favourite chair in the dark. He held the shoebox with her jewellery in his lap. He sat and drank and spent a long time sifting through the box, letting the strand of pearls fall through his fingers, until it slithered to the end where she had attached a silver cross. He had not noticed this before.

When the telephone rang, it was already morning and he was still in the chair, dressed in his green work clothes. The contents of the box were scattered on the floor, but in his hand was the cross.

"Congratulations!"

He did not know what time it was. He did not recognize the voice. Then, he thought it was his wife talking to him. But it was only the telephone. He thought he had just dozed off.

"Good morning!"

The voice was more pleasant now.

"I have a buyer for you."

It was the saleswoman. "We're coming over right away. You have an offer to sign. What a lovely day!"

She arrived just as he was leaving for the park. The buyer came through the door without greeting him, and immediately praised the possibilities of the house. "Great! This wall will come out! The whole wall. I'll townhouse it. These stairs have to go. A winding staircase right here. Right up to the third floor. After I tear out a couple more walls, you know, open it up to let it breathe . . ."

He could feel the dust in his nostrils, and his sinus returning, and he relived the first years of his ownership of the house when this was a working-class street, before it was transformed by renovation trucks, heating trucks, gas installation trucks, contractors' trucks, and garbage trucks.

"How soon can you move out?"

He had given the buyer immediate occupancy.

"The sooner the better," she said.

He could see the line of her brassiere. He could see the line of flesh above her bikini panties. And he could see the complete outline of her panties. They were not the same colour as her lightweight dress. Although he had signed, he still did not like her.

He went back to his park. As he cleaned the garden beds, children threw Frisbees into the air, and some of them landed beside him.

He had cut the last thread of his connection.

He looked up and saw them leaving.

Children walked gingerly in and out of his garden beds at the far corner of the park, and each time a ball or a Frisbee landed, he threw it back to them. The black-and-white soccer ball came to him, and at the last moment it swerved away. "Pardon!" As he bent down to kill a grub, he watched a young man stomp on a cluster of Dutch bulbs, trying to pick up a Frisbee. A dog stepped lightly through the bed of chrysanthemums and bent down. But before the thin brown sausage was out of its shivering body, he threw a rake at him.

He looked across the street and saw two vans parked in front of his house. One was marked TEPERMAN RENOVATIONS and the other MARVEL LANDSCAPING. Disregarding the rake and the children and the dog, he rushed across the street. He couldn't believe they would come so soon!

The buyer and the saleswoman and the men from the renovations and landscaping companies were walking through rooms, pushing furniture aside, measuring, running lines of cord along walls and making small dots with a pencil. He was standing just inside the front door. Their voices came down to him from her bedroom. They did not know he was home. He heard their gleeful voices, sounding surer, it seemed, than his own fifteen years ago when he acquired the house.

"You got it for a song!"

Their footsteps were over his head.

"I'll take care of your kickback." He recognized the buyer's voice.

"I didn't tell him you were a developer." He recognized her voice.

They were coming down now. She was the first to appear. She saw him standing there and she flashed a smile.

He went back outside. He discovered that they had walked through his garden beds. Chalk marks that roads department men make on sidewalks when they're measuring for sewers were all along his walk.

He had left her memory inside. And he had left her shoebox, and all her clothes, her private accumulation of fifteen years. And now these strangers were drawing lines on the walls of her bedroom and along the floors she had walked so silently and painfully on. Their hands had touched her bed. And their footprints were in his flower beds.

He heard the front door bang. The saleswoman was running out behind him. He walked away without answering.

Back in the park, he sat on a bench. Children were all around him.

She came out ahead of the three men. The buyer stood with his arms akimbo. The two workmen shook hands and drove off. She left in her silver-grey BMW. Only the buyer remained. He moved from one side of the house to the other, bending down at basement windows, all the time jotting things in a book. At last he left. But he saw him come back in a black Cadillac, drive slowly up to the house, stop, and then move on. The buyer passed beside him sitting on the bench in the park.

A dog was at his feet, licking his construction boots. It was the same dog he had chased earlier. The dog came closer and sat between his boots.

As the warmth went out of the day and the children ran home, as if a bell of hunger and obedience had summoned them, he was left alone in the park with the dog still sitting between his muddy boots. The flowers seemed to make one last shiver before the night air bent them slightly for their long sleep. All around him lights came on in houses, but he remained sitting there, motionless in the large sea of grass as the park seemed to turn into a lake and he was anchored to the bench which moved only with his imagination.

Sammy would already be in his room for the night, with a bottle of rye under his pillow for company and warmth.

He could no longer see his house, for it had become submerged in the same darkness in which he and the dog sat. But he imagined it was still there.

The shoebox was all he would take to his new place, whether that place was the rooming house or Golden Acres.

The dog jumped up beside him on the green bench and put its head between his legs.

Shapes moved in the windows on the border of the park. The dog nudged closer to him to say goodnight with a warm licking tongue, or goodbye, and was soon lost in the darkness. His eyes followed its first trotting steps in the shadows and then could not find it among the trees and the tool shed.

He got up and collected his tools and took them into the shed. He walked to the far corner of the park where his helper had left the lawnmower; he rolled it backwards and locked it up. He walked the few dark yards to his house, but when he stood in front of it and saw its own darkness and absence of life, he turned away and walked instead to Bathurst Street. He bought a bottle of ginger ale, a bottle of Canadian Club, and some cigarettes. He went along Bathurst, just walking and thinking, until he found himself beside Golden Acres. The entire building was ablaze with fluorescent lights. He wished he knew which was Sammy's room. He walked to the front door, past the nurse sitting at a desk reading the *Star*. "You're getting in rather late," she said.

He was climbing the stairs, looking into empty rooms where the lights were fierce as in the lobby. In one, there was an old man motionless on a small white bed. In another, an old woman was sitting upright on a white sheet and her lips were moving. There was no other sign of life on that floor. He walked along another corridor, hearing only his construction boots on the grey linoleum, until he reached the top floor. It was noiseless there too. He retraced his steps. On the way out, the nurse looked up and nodded and said, "Oh, you're just visiting . . ."

He was back on the bench in the park. The dog had not returned. He opened the door of the tool shed. The bulb in the small cement room was weak and he tripped among the hoses. He moved some tools aside and some snakes of hoses and forks before he found the can which contained gas for the lawnmower. He filled an empty bottle and left. He walked slowly with the three bottles, ginger ale, rye, and gas.

He entered his house and left the front door wide open. He turned on the lights in each room, right up to the third floor. He went back to the kitchen and poured himself a rye and ginger, and sat with the shoebox on the kitchen table. The house was quiet. The house was bright. He had missed Sammy's room. Perhaps it was the one in darkness.

He took the bottle with the gas back to the third floor and, just as he would do with plant fertilizer in his own garden or in the park, he sprinkled the gas around the edges of the rooms, one room at a time, some on the bed, some on the white crocheted doilies she had made, all down the stairs to the first floor. He doused the kitchen and the bathroom more lavishly, more carefully, as if he was coaxing young plants. He washed his hands under the cold-water tap with Sunlight soap. It felt as if small snakes or worms were pulling at his skin, as if his skin was tightening.

Now he could not find his cigarettes. He could not find his matches. He didn't know which floor to light first. He hadn't thought about that. Should he light the third floor, and then run down to the second, and then the first, and then run outside and go back to the shed, which he had forgotten to lock? In twenty years he had never been so careless.

He took another drink. He always had to take a second drink to help him unknot a problem. The cigarettes and matches were on the table. The shoebox was hiding them. Was she in the room with him? She was always there to tell him where he had misplaced his cigarettes. She was always so careful!

He lit the cigarette. He threw the match into the sink. He got up with the shoebox and his drink. And immediately, as the glass touched his lips, so too did the flame kiss the gas and fly up and engulf him; and before he could think of where the front door was, the explosion came.

He could not move. He could not see. He could not cry out. There was no smoke. Only the orange of fire, bright as the colours of spring in the park. And the last thing he heard, or thought he heard, was the terrified yelping of a dog, arrived too late, scampering from the rage of the fire.

THEY'RE NOT COMING BACK

On the second night, the day after it happened, the house was dark. She was surprised to hear the six o'clock news on television as she closed the front door. She could not remember whether she had left the television on for security or whether she'd wanted to hear voices in the empty house when she came home. The bottle in the big brown paper bag nearly slipped from her hand. The liquor store closed at six. The bottle was her sustenance for the night. She was a Catholic. She went to church irregularly, but devoutly, if that is possible. And always, she read books of devotion at night or *The Lives of the Saints*, especially when she needed something steadfast in her life. She was doing well: confident in her new job; saving when she could; dressing smartly; and she kept in touch with her friends and family. What grieved her was her husband.

She'd always said it was a bad marriage, but she could offer no certain act, no one thing for blame. She knew she was unhappy. And that was the only important thing. When she'd left him in the house—her house, the house her parents had "given" them for one hundred dollars—she said it was a decision she'd made three years earlier. But she'd taken with her, though she'd tried differently, countless problems from the small renovated bungalow, built in the same style as the one she now rented: she'd taken with her pains and anger from the past two years; unpaid bills and balances on his credit cards, personal debts now changed into consolidating loans;

her fifty percent obligation to all these debts; and the two girls, one sixteen, the other nine.

The new house was now full of their absence. The girls were as beautiful as their mother, though larger in their limbs, and more mature and grown-up than their ages suggested. It showed on their faces and in their actions, just as their mother's pains and anger showed in her face. And the fact that they were not here tonight, welcoming her, as they did every other night, with complaints about the school day and each other, filled her with anxiety. She was a woman waiting for something bad to happen. She did not know what it would be, but she was certain it would happen. And there was the emptiness.

Five days ago he'd said he would come and take them from her, and drive them to their former home, now his, with his new young daughter, only two months old, and his new woman, their step-mother, who occupied the space she had said was sacred, the space that was the result of the sweat that had poured off her father's face while he worked for twenty years digging trenches, lifting heavy objects until the strain pulled something in his body and made his testicles grow large, the size of a grapefruit. Her father and mother had given her the small bungalow as a wedding present, marrying that "bastard Kit, 'cause I can't tell you I like the bastard and the way he treats my daughter"; and it was where her mother and father had lived, in the basement, for the first years of his retirement, until they moved to a little place in Florida for six months. They lived in a home for the aged the other half-year.

Yes, five days ago he said he would come and take them. It was an experiment. It was for the sake of the two girls. The elder child had told her mother she wanted to live with Daddy. The previous Sunday, when he'd brought them back earlier than usual because he had "things to do," just as she was preparing a dinner of roast beef and mashed potatoes with thick brown gravy, the older daughter declared, "I want to go live with Dad." She heard the words go into her heart, into her abdomen, into her womb. She went over and over all the things she had done in the sixteen years of her daughter's life, doubting her method of bringing her up, doubting whether she had put the child to lie on the right side, the correct side, whether she should have persisted and fed her from her breasts in spite of the gland problem that had developed. No one ate more than the first spoonful of supper, and then the roast beef and mashed potatoes with thick brown gravy were shoved aside.

"Can we go to the store and get chips and bubble gum?" the sixteen-year-old said.

She knew what it meant for them to come home from school at three or half-past three five days a week and find the bungalow empty, with the lights turned on for company, and the radio blaring out their favourite rock music. She knew what it meant for two young girls to be in this neighbourhood in this house that stood in a long line in the long street, identical to the others in red brick; and she knew too what it meant for them to be alone in the house, large and eerie on this side of the street of men who did not go to work during the day, men who worked during the night and were home during the long, boring, and tempting day.

A man of forty-nine had entered a bungalow when the single parent was at work, taking possession of both the house and the child. It was on the front pages and on television. The little girl was fifteen years old. Blood stained the street for months while mothers wrung their hands and the police, diligent as worm-pickers, trudged in the snow and found nothing but a brown plastic haircomb. She knew how it felt. She knew how it could happen. She had left her children alone one night to meet a man. During the passionate hour with the man she had bristled with resentment because she did not have the leisure to enjoy making love, which she loved to make, and was filled with guilt and doubt: could the sixteen-year-old look after the nine-year-old, and remember to keep the television loud, and remember not to answer the door, and if she answered the telephone, remember *not* to say, "Mom is not here," but say, "She's busy at the moment"? Those fears had left her shaking in all her limbs, so long untouched, so long tense, so long pure.

At the age of seventeen, because the boy with whom she was in love for life had left the small town to make his fortune in the city, and had not said he would return and take her with him while he made his fortune, she gave up boys, and gave up all pleasure and buried herself in books, and homework, and knelt in the crimson-draped confessional and whispered to the priest that she was entering a nunnery.

"I want to enter a nunnery," she said, hardly audible, so great was her devotion.

The priest whispered, "You want to be a nun?"

"I want to enter a nunnery."

She smelled incense, she heard liturgical music in her heart. She felt the boy's hands on her breasts, her body shaking as she shook the night when she'd left her children alone.

"I want to enter a nunnery."

The priest, knowing young girls, told her to think about it for a week and come back. When she did go back, to the same priest, in the same small box, with the same crimson velvet curtain, she said to him, in the same whispering voice, "Father, I think I am pregnant. But he has promised to get married before the baby shows."

"Are you still thinking of becoming a nun?"

The house was dark. She could hear her own footsteps on the linoleum, and her heels sticking to it because she had not mopped up the orange juice and milk spilled on the previous morning at breakfast with her daughters. She dropped her briefcase, rested the brown paper bag on the table, and walked towards her bedroom. Normally, she stopped in the kitchen, put her manicured hands into the thick oily water full of plates and saucers and coffee mugs and knives and spoons and her one crystal martini glass. She washed the three sets of dirty dishes, unable to understand why the three of them used so many, and she would stand looking at them, plates half-submerged in the murky water. When done, almost every evening, it would be close to ten o'clock. No one would have an appetite: neither she nor the two children.

Free of that chore, she headed for her bedroom, and felt the emptiness there. Sometimes the younger child, tormented by the older, would seek refuge on her mother's bed. It was a welcome show of affection, even when she had to sort out the quarrels and secret beatings. Tonight, there was no child on the bed. And in a flash of hope and forgetfulness, she wondered why.

She went down the wooden steps, almost too narrow even for her small body, into the basement, and along the cement floor, past the furnace-room door to the largest bedroom, the room her elder daughter had commandeered when they had moved into this house. The bed was made. In the middle of the single mattress was a book. The girl was always reading. At seven o'clock on that night, she had just put the book down when the car horn sounded. The book was open and turned down. She had always scolded her daughter about damaging the spines of books that way. She went to the small closet and opened the door, saw the empty shelves, and the wire hangers, some of them bent into shapes to suit her small-size blouses, brassieres, and denim jeans. On the bookcase, there was only a white envelope. Nothing was written on it. A ballpoint pen sat beside the envelope.

All around the room, cool in the summer and warm in the winter, large and bright for a basement room, her eyes wandered, picking up her daughter's presence, her movement and posture, the sound of her small feet when she walked in her bare feet after her bath, when the floor was spotted by water. She sat on the bed, and before she rose, she turned her face away from the bed, left her right hand on it as if she were patting it goodbye, as if the closeness of the body that slept in it was still on the blue sheet patterned with daisies.

She hurried back upstairs. At the top of the stairs, she paused, as if catching her breath, but she was young and in good health. She paused and put her hand to her head, to think of the heavy presence in the empty house, and of loss.

"Are you sure you want to do this?"

"Sure!"

"You realize of course that it could be seen, perceived that you are giving your children up, and—"

"I'm not *giving* my children up."

"I know that. But—"

"Suppose, just suppose the arrangement is for a few months, till I catch myself, till I am more in control of myself. And we can have an agreement saying that it is for a few months and at the end of this time, they'll come back to me, and—"

"I understand what you mean, and I understand what you want, but I have to advise you that the perception—"

"The perception is one thing. I know about perception. But the reality is that he's taking them for a trial period. It is the decision of my daughter to go and live with her father."

"What're you going to do with the little one? Send her too?"

"How can I separate the two of them? What is he making me do? What is he up to? Does he want me to send the older one to him, and me keep the younger? I won't have it. I won't do it. I don't trust his motives. What does he want me to do?"

"Suppose . . . suppose before the time ends, they want to come back to you? Suppose only one wants to come back before the trial period ends? Or, now that you're moving to a more economical place, suppose, before the five-month arrangement ends, one of them wants to live with you?"

"You mean . . . ?"

"Yes."

"You mean *that*?"

"Or when the time ends, they don't want to stop living with their father?"

"You mean, they're *not*?"

She took a Kleenex from her purse and spread it on her knee, and then put it to her face. She had been biting her lip. She could feel her muscles tighten.

"How's your concentration at work?"

"Fine."

"And your nights?"

"Just fine."

"You know, a little snort . . . a spot of brandy. Are you sleeping well?"

"My doctor gave me something."

"Sleeping pills?"

"Something to relax."

"To relax you? I'd be careful."

"I'm fine."

There was a slip of yellow paper, a paper a little bigger than a postage stamp, in her shoe. She recognized the handwriting of her sixteen-year-old. She closed her eyes, refused to read it, feared its message, and tore it from the insole of the shoe, balled it up, put it into the pocket of her skirt. She had arranged all her shoes at the bottom of the cupboard according to the fondness she had for them; and she ran her hand along the metal bar that held the wire hangers with her dresses. She wrenched the hangers to the left, not liking how they looked, and then wrenched them in the opposite direction. She looked at her bed, saw how large it was for the room, and promised to call her sister and take back the smaller bed and mattress she had left there. She looked around the bedroom, hating that she was forced to move out of her home, more comfortable than this even when the family was four, plus a dog that had fleas, and two cats.

Her eyes were sore; she must take out her lenses. She blinked, held on to the top of the dresser, placed the third finger of her right hand to her eyeball, flicked her lid, and extracted the miniature piece of plastic; and she placed her left hand, not seeing clearly, on the white bottle that contained lens solution, and her fingers touched a small slip of paper, the same yellow colour as the first, and before she used the liquid, straining her eye to see, she saw the hand-writing again, and this time, she had no excuse for not reading it.

Mummy, I still like you. Your daughter.

She used no Kleenex this time. She allowed the suppressed feel-ings of hurt and disappointment that had welled up for three days to spill out: and she sat on the edge of her unmade bed, allowed the tears to fall, and did not seek to control them.

Why didn't she write "love"? Did her daughter not love her? *Why didn't she say she loved me?* She felt the parting note was too formal, too distant, after only three days. On the door of the fridge was another note. It repeated the same longing and liking. And when she took the plastic holder with the ice cubes for making her martini from the fridge, there was another note. It was frozen into the ice.

The martini she made was pure gin. Luckily, she'd found Bombay Sapphire. And she had an old bottle of olives in the cupboard. If she was in any doubt about the potency of the pills her doctor had prescribed, she would wash them down with the first martini.

"In a way," she said to herself, "in a way it's good the kids are gone. I don't have to worry about supper." She corrected herself. "If they were here, I would not be able to have this martini." She liked the revision.

On the night she'd left the girls unattended, going to see the man, she'd known she was going to have sex, not make love, because, as she said to herself, "I can't make love to a man I don't know." It had been such a long time since she had had sex with a man. It had happened only with her husband, it had happened whenever he came to see how the kids were taking it; and each time she broke down. He promised to change his ways and told her that it was "just for a time," and that he intended to give her some space and distance. In that confused understanding, he took her upstairs into her new bedroom, where her clothes were still in boxes and some of them strewn over the uncovered mattress, and he took her and did not pay attention to the spots and smudges on the grey-striped single mattress, so thin that he thought he could feel the boards of the bedstead in his steady, hard, unloving pushing against her eager body. Yes, it was to have sex, to remind herself that she had not entered the nunnery and that her body, as the body of a woman, needed that nourishment. He knew it. And she knew it.

She believed that with the other man, whom she has not spoken to or seen since that hectic night, the sinfulness of the act was mollified by the urgency of her body's need. She was not going into a nunnery. And after all, she said, breaking the speed limit to get back to her unattended children, "I'm a free woman."

When she got back to the house, the sixteen-year-old was sitting on the couch in the living room. The television was a steady scene of falling snow. When she saw the screen, it reminded her of the plunging water at Niagara Falls. In the lap of the sixteen-year-old was the nine-year-old. Both were wrapped in sleep. Each had a smile on her face, oblivious to the risk her mother had taken. Both were in the rapture of sleep, as she had lain in rapture for five minutes in the man's arms, after he had screwed her, and had sunk into a doze.

She went back over these things. The clothes she had worn to work for the past five days were dropped over chairs, and some of her underclothes were draped over the back of the toilet. The shoes she'd worn were scattered, kicked off as soon as she had come through the door. "Feet killing me!"

She had seen the state of the kitchen: the uneaten meals, the fragments of toast, the dishes left unwashed in the stagnant water. Ashtrays were filled with cigarettes stubbed out, twisted, and some were hardly smoked at all. In some cigarette packages, she had left matches and cigarettes and telephone messages which she never returned.

The liquor she'd bought, the brandy, the Bombay Sapphire, and the sparkling wine, stood arranged in a triangle of bottles in the cleared kitchen counter space. The water glass was filled with cubes. The crystal glass, the only one she had washed from the cluttered sink, sat sparkling among them.

The first taste of the martini struck her stomach, exploding all the hurt and pain and self-crucifixion at the sight of the notes from the sixteen-year-old, notes pinned against her heart. She walked through the house, ignoring the evening news on the television, and the announcer screaming about the success of the Blue Jays, who were playing in Oakland. She sipped her martini. She could not feel the touch of her feet on the carpet. *I have to vacuum.* Dust had risen; she could see it in the beam of light from the floor lamp. She swore to herself that she would shift a framed photograph, remove a dried bunch of flowers. Everywhere she looked she saw a note left by her child. She had three more martinis and cried herself to sleep.

She fell asleep on the couch. Very early the next morning, the dishes were still unwashed. She found more notes from the sixteen-year-old. One was in her panties in the drawer. She discovered one stuck to the blank cheque in her book that was to be sent to the landlord. She sat down now and drank two more martinis, and as they did not stimulate her, she poured herself a brandy, looking at the morning news, and a game show and a talk show. She was about to take a sleeping pill, but realized it was nine in the morning. For the second time that week, she called in sick, saying she had to take the kids to the doctor. But they had been with their father for three days now. She took *The Lives of the Saints* from under the jumbo box of Kleenex and opened it, but before she had read the first paragraph, her vision became blurred by her tears. She was thinking of sin and of the time she'd sat in the small confessional and whispered to the priest, "I want to enter a nunnery." She cried and she wondered if she was losing her mind. And how was she to stop it?

She filled the house with noise from the radio, the television, and the stereo. But her best balm was the martinis. She loved martinis, and drank them in generous quantities. They were a part of her sophistication. Other women, her sister and friends in the office, drank white wine. She held that for a woman to drink martinis showed a sign of class.

Now, she was sitting in the living room on the large couch. The gin was gone. She passed her hand over the couch's silk material and noticed stains left by her children. She made a mental note to wash them with detergent and a cloth; better still, send the whole damn thing to the cleaners. No, not the cleaners; to the upholsterers. And she decided that the other couch, which was too large for the living room, should be sent to the upholsterers too. Then, she made up her mind to throw them out and replace them with furniture that she, as a new woman, demanded. A new, fresh, virginal beginning. She looked at the coffee table, and then at the end table, and the large dining table, and the television, her reliable friend, sworn to keep her company. All were discarded. She was sipping Courvoisier now. She became tense, with a pain that entered her stomach and went up into her chest. She thought of stress. She thought of ulcers. She thought of her heart. She inhaled deeply six times, taking deep, deep breaths, trying to hold them. She knew people held their breath in these circumstances. She couldn't. She put the snifter down on the coffee table and said to herself, "These things could be my death." She stood up and felt better. She poured herself a more generous Courvoisier, in which floated four snippets of lemon peel. She had eaten a bottle of green olives.

It was late now. Still, only half of her body was tired. Fatigue did not touch her mind. She thought of things to do the next day at work; she thought of plans for the transformation of her bungalow; she thought of plans, not really plans but plottings, to get her children back with her; and she thought of the new richer life she would lead, as a result of this rebirth.

The movie on television was in black and white. There were women in long dresses that reached to the floor. And men were wearing formal clothes, with stiff collars cutting into their necks, just below their chins. Their necks were red, though she could not see that colour; she had seen such men during her holidays in Florida, when they spoke to her. And there were servants coming and going. She had spoken to women like them at the bus stop. She could picture herself in that grand living room. The amount of drink being served made her comfortable. It was her place. She was born to be like this.

When she was five months pregnant with her first daughter, he'd been kind and attentive. He'd sat with her on the hospital-room floor where she and six other mothers-to-be were on mats, and one day a week they'd pretended that they were giving birth. He would breathe with her, rub her belly, and have an erection, impatient to take her back home to jump on her belly, sometimes forgetting that his seed was buried already inside it.

And he was in the room when the pains really started. And he held her hand when they increased. And when his first daughter was born, he saw it all, and did not leave the room until he had to. That night he called her mother and her father, her sister and brothers, and distributed expensive cigars. And then he went home.

He was home for fifteen minutes before the woman arrived. She parked her car in their garage. She went through the front door, straight to the bedroom. The pink baby booties, bonnets, sweaters, nightgowns, and suits lay undisturbed at the foot of the bed, which his wife had made up minutes before he had driven her to the hospital. And the infant's garments remained undisturbed, by some miracle, while he "fucked the living daylights outta her," which is how he put it to his friend at the desk next to his the following morning, holding open the almost empty box of Tueros cigars, celebrating his firstborn child.

She heard about this years later from her husband's friend when they were no longer friends, when the friend wanted to assure her that that friendship had ended, after he made a pass at her, as he told her what a bastard her husband was, had been, and would always be. It was the same man she had gone to on that night when she had left the nine-year-old in the babysitting hands of her older sister.

She gets up, tired and sure, and she takes up the telephone.

"How are you?" It is her mother she is calling. "I haven't spoken to you in a long time," she says. And she has to repeat her words, because her mother cannot hear them distinctly.

"You been drinking, darling? I know what you're going through. And a glass *does* help. I won't like to know you're overdoing it, though. Are you all right?"

"I'm fine. I'm fine."

"You know, darling, when you were a little girl, and you came home from school and I would ask you how school was, you always said, 'Fine,' just like you're saying now. Everything I asked you about, you always said, 'I'm fine.' I knew things weren't fine. Because things're never fine, all the time."

"I'm fine."

She could not remember if she had asked her mother to come over. She could not remember when it was that she had made the suggestion, if in fact she had.

She went into the bedroom and took the plastic vial from the medicine cupboard. She did not have to look at the writing on the bottle. And she did not have to spend any time selecting this bottle from all the others there: Aspirin, vitamins, and pills pre-scribed months ago for other medical ailments, which she never completed taking according to the doctor's orders.

She took a few, put them into her mouth, and took a sip of her brandy. She passed a brush through her hair. And she examined her face in the small looking-glass in the bathroom. She cleansed her face with Noxzema cream, applied makeup, and even brushed one of the four colours from the Cover Girl case across her eyelids.

It was past midnight. She'd made her face pretty. She'd made her appearance appealing. And she did this even though it was only her mother coming over to see how she is. And she knew that her mother would be gone in fifteen minutes, for it is so late; and there is really no need to fix herself to meet her mother. She *is* her mother. And mothers understand that love and appreciation are not measured in this kind of facial preparation.

She raised her skirt, hooked her fingers into the elastic at her waist and lowered her pantyhose. She chose a fresh pair of panties. The pills started to make her feel relaxed. She will sleep tonight. The pills and her martinis. And she will usher her mother out, nicely, after a few minutes. Before she put her panties on, she took her silk dressing gown from the nail behind the door of her bedroom. It was rich in colour, a pattern of dragons and beasts that could be from the sea or the vast land of China. It was warm on her soft beautiful body, no longer old and tired as it had been a few minutes ago when she rose from the couch. She drew the skin-coloured silk underwear over her legs, and she felt a slight irritation. A piece of paper. And she pulled them down, and a page from her personalized stationery, folded into the size of a large postage stamp, fell out.

She unfolded it, was passing her eyes over the uneven letters, in capitals, the uneven pencil strokes telling her, *We are not coming back coz you send us away,* when the doorbell rang. She jumped. She wondered who would call at this hour. She wondered if it was her husband. She wondered if it was the man, her husband's friend. She wondered if it was her children. She had forgotten she had spoken with her mother ten minutes ago.

She crept to the door, looking through the hole, and saw the disproportioned face of the woman standing on the other side. She looked old, and ugly from the magnification, and frightening. But it was the eyes, her mother's eyes, that told her she was safe. She was safe again, safe always when she was with her mother. She was safe in all those years of her bad marriage whenever her mother called, or came over and sat with her, holding her face in her lap, and sometimes, her mother would have her lean her head against her shoulder and pass her hand over her forehead, as if she knew she had a headache.

The note was still in her hand when she opened the door, taking the chain in her hand, pulling back the bolt, unlocking the deadbolt.

"What have you got there, dear?"

She showed it to her. "My dear! Leah wrote this?"

She did not answer. Her body was weak, too weak for the exertion of words and explanation. And water had already come to her eyes.

"The *little* . . ."

Her mother did not complete her sentiment. There was no need to.

"Where're you going this hour?"

She had noticed how properly her daughter was dressed, hair in place, every strand of her dark brown hair; and the makeup and eye shadow; and she mistook the silk housecoat for a cocktail dress.

"You young people wear such crazy styles, child, I thought you were on your way out! What would make Leah write a thing like this?"

"You want a drink, Mom? I only got cognac."

"Your father would think I was out to meet a man, at my age!" And she laughed her full-throated laugh. And her daughter laughed too. And was happy for the duration of that laughter.

"Oh, Mom!" she said. "Oh, Mom!"

And then tears engulfed her, and washed over her, and gave her the feeling of holiness that she had known in her childhood years of accepting the ritual of being a young Christian-minded child. She knew that powerful feeling that swept over her when she attended Mass, like the warm water of the sea when she and her mother went on their holidays. And she could feel the spirit she knew was inside her body when she knelt and said her personal prayers, after the priest had given the Benediction.

"Oh, Mom!"

"What're you doing to yourself, eh, child?"

"Oh, Mom!" She reached for the snifter.

"Why don't you put an end to this, dear?"

"Oh, Mom!" she said in the whisper she'd used when she said she intended to enter the nunnery. "Have I disappointed you, Mom?"

"You are my daughter," she said. And drew her body closer, and rested her daughter's head on her shoulder. "You smell good. What is it?"

"I'm using Chanel No. 5 now, Mom."

"That's a good scent."

"Oh, Mom!"

"Now, first thing in the morning," her mother began, passing her hand with the three gold rings on the wedding finger over her daughter's forehead, and then along her neck, "first thing in the morning, you and me, we're going to see somebody for you to talk to." And she could smell the scent, and the shampoo her daughter had used. And she could feel the muscle on the left side of her neck. And she could feel the softness of the silk of her housecoat.

The time passed slowly. Her mother sat silently and paid no attention to the movie on television. Soon there was snow on the screen. All she could hear was the taking in and letting out of breath from her daughter's warm body and the sudden, short, startled moving of the body. Once, instead of a shudder, there was a sigh. She went back over the years of struggle with the six children she'd borne the man she loved, and still loved; how she'd cut and contrived and got them all through high school, and all but one in college and university; attending graduations and birthday parties, and weddings and christenings, and hockey and basketball practice.

And you were always my favourite, out of all my children; you were always my star, and I can still remember the nights I stayed up with you, seeing you through measles, mumps, cutting your teeth, toothache, earache, everything, until you met that man you married and threw away your life, you the star, my favourite out of all the children I carried in my womb.

And time passed without her notice, for she did not know the body was no longer so warm, and she thought of raising the thermometer . . . these bungalows where the workmen worked so fast and didn't know one thing about insulation.

Time, passing without sound. And there is no longer the spasm that tells of life, and there is no longer the soft whisper of sleep.

It is quiet. And this quiet is felt not in the motionless sleeping body she is holding, not from anything inside this house, but through the sound of the leaves and a branch rubbing against the house. And it becomes cold. Her own body is cold and she draws her daughter closer still to her body.

In all the time, and with all these children, all of them out of my womb, you, you, Claudette, were always my star, and my joy. Out of all of them, I loved you the most. All these years, all these years.

But this time, it is different. The weight is lighter, but the burden is heavier. Her right shoulder is numb, bearing this sleep that is like a solution. First thing in the morning, I will take you to somebody to talk to you.

It is still. It has been like this for a while now, and still she continues to pass her hand with her wedding rings on it over and over her daughter's forehead that smells so seductively of Chanel. And her hand, like her shoulder, loses its life and feel, the circulation gone out of it, until she opens her eyes. And looks. And sees the beautiful tranquil face. "Sleep. Sleep, my darling."

Her face is soft and relaxed. There is a smile across her lips. Her lips, the smear of the lipstick. The mascara. Her face is soft and relaxed; and the beauty that defines it is young and innocent. "Sleep."

ON ONE LEG

Alexander came into the beverage room like a soldier. Like a general in full dress. With his chest full and broad with the ribbons and medals of his fifty years of experience and battles. Alexander's battles were fought on the battle-scarred field of everyday life. He walked with a heavy step. And as he walked, you knew he was a man of some substance. He looked so. Perhaps it was the experience that decorated his face with lines and age. This same experience had ruffled his hair with the fingers of its tragedies. And it had marked his face in circles and crow's feet, like the boulders crawling at the bottom of a mighty long and slow river would have marked the river.

When he sat down, his body from his waist up to his neck was as stiff as a wooden leg. His head would lean forward, always his head, as if he regarded any aspect of the conversation of his drinking friends to be so important. In the men's beverage room of the Selby Hotel, where he drank every afternoon straight from work with a ritualistic regularity, his head would follow the meandering slurring vocabulary of his friends, like a child's pencil following the outlines of a picture-book drawing.

All the men in the Selby liked Alexander. He was like a general to all of them. They thought he was a bit aloof, but they knew that he liked them too. He carried in his heart a feeling for them that was equalled only by the love and affection which soldiers who have survived wars and close calls have known. The men in the beverage room were like soldiers to Alexander.

He was always anxious to get there. And when he sat down, it seemed as if he had prepared his system and his appetite the whole day, from nine until five in the afternoon, just for these few hours of being together among men.

"I've been with men," he told his tired, complaining, callous-handed wife one night as he entered the mothballed house after an evening of drinking beer that stretched out too long, long as the tales of his battles at work, and in the mine in northern Ontario where he had worked for some time. But this did not appease her. She did not know anything about men, she said.

"They was *men*," he insisted.

He would talk to them as men talked to other men. He would talk about his job, and he would dress his job in important phrases and give tragedy, if not drama, to the sorting of letters, which bored him eight hours a day in the main post office downtown, but which he would never admit to his drinking companions. As far as they were concerned, it was a job, like tactical manoeuvres. As far as he was concerned, he was like a general putting little flags of many different colours on a very complicated map, and directing from this apparently simple movement of flags and hands a theatre of combat whose proportions were great enough to involve the lives of many thousands, of many millions of people: the entire population of Toronto.

"You have to observe," he was telling his friends one afternoon. "You should see me in that occupation. There's one thing about handling the nation's mails . . ." And he would sip a bit of his beer and allow them to grasp the full meaning of his last words. "You have to be a man of a certain level of intelligence and education to work in this job I have." And he would again pause and permit them time to raise their glasses to their heads, and he would not continue until each man had swallowed, along with his drink, all that he had said up till then. "Now, I'm a man who didn't go to university. But I have seen college kids come to work there in the summer, in the post office, and this job that I do, it gives them a hell of a lotta trouble just to learn the fundamentals."

All the men would breathe easier and they would look important, as if *their* jobs were shining in their faces, because none of them
had gone to university either; because many of them had not even
finished high school. But each one of them could tell a similar story
of a university student to whom they had taught a summer job.

"It could be a serious thing. Imagine. The slightest mistake, the
slightest miscalculation, and a letter could go to the wrong person.
And people stealing so much nowadays! They could even open a
letter and take out the money, if it had any, 'cause people nowadays,
particularly the young ones, the ones you see in Yorkville with long
hair, hippies—you understand what I'm talking about . . ."

The men would all nod their heads. They understood. They
understood because they had all felt this way about the young men
with long hair walking about Toronto "like living deads," as Alexander called them.

"I would take on the youngest o' them right now," he said on
another afternoon, "and I lay a sawbuck on it that he couldn't
throw me!"

The men nodded and cheered with their eyes. Alexander was
talking like a real, honest, hard-working man. "Not one o' them!
If I had a son still living, who'd be twenty this year—ten years he
died—but if he himself was living today, *he* couldn't throw me!
And I am his father. I am a man now, going into my—" But he
thought better of the idea and did not tell them how old he was. "A
man my age is no pup," he said with a grin.

The men grinned too. They nodded their heads faster and more
vigorously to show him, like a kind of illustration of sympathy, that
they too were old men, but strength and vigour and marrow hadn't
gone out of their bodies, their spirits, or their bones.

"Yeah!" one of them, Joe, said a bit too loud, for they were sitting at a round table, close together as poker players. "Yeah, Lex!
Men!"

He was the only one who dared to call Alexander "Lex." And
he too fell silent and allowed Alexander to fill up the beverage
room with the real meaning of sweat and sinews and muscles and

hard-nailed boots and potato chips, chomped like pieces of dried bramble.

Alexander liked these beer-drinking gatherings. Whatever problem he might have had at work would be set aside, just as he always pushed the loaded ashtray of spit-stained cigars and plain-tipped cigarettes from in front of his seat, and in his easy and unstudied movement made it seem as if the ashtray were the last fistful of letters placed correctly into the pigeonhole at the post office.

He had therefore successfully pigeonholed one branch of his slowly moving life, and had skipped enthusiastically into the turbulence of this artery which bubbled in the beverage room of the Selby Hotel. He would rub his hands together like two slabs of board covered with sandpaper, slap them firmly but not loudly, and not in any real rhythm of jubilation, but as if to say, "Good! Time for a good, cold beer."

He came into the beverage room this Friday afternoon and brushed aside Joe's ashtray that was in front of his usual seat, although nobody had ever decided upon any order of seating. He slapped his callouses and said, "One here, Bill!" *One* was his favourite drink. Beer. And Bill was the waiter. It was not his real name, but they had all christened him Bill. It saved them the complication and the mincing of tongue and beer and words and enunciation to pronounce Sudzynowski, which Bill told them in his halting English was the name his Polish godmother had given him, back in the days across the Atlantic Ocean when he was a baby.

"*Fairy* godmother!" Alexander jeered with his mouth full of broth and beer and smoke. "Eh? Eh? Eh? *Fairy* godmother!" He screamed with laughter, the beer dripping down his mouth. Sudzynowski began to teach them how to pronounce his name correctly, for he preferred to be called by it. But they laughed and he decided to forget it.

"Ahh, what the hell. We'll call you Bill," Alexander said. The others nodded in agreement. "'Smore friendly. What you say, Bill? What you say, fellas? You see, we're a friendly people, eh? Eh?"

Sudzynowski nodded his head and shrugged his shoulders and went away saying something in Polish. It was not very friendly.

"Another one here, Bill," Alexander said five minutes later, when the waiter was within hearing distance. "Bag o' chips while you're at it. Worked like a slave today, fellas. All day. I want to tell you fellas something, something I never told you before in all the months we been joking and drinking together in this place. Pack o' Exports! A's! Worked like a slave today, and all the time I watching some young fellas sneaking off to the can to get a rest and a smoke. There I was with not a man, not none o' them young fellas man enough to match me, to stand up to me. Those bastards with long hair, they won't take a bath; got the whole goddamn post office smelling like a urinal in the train station, I swear to God! If my boy was still living, and he ever showed me his kisser with that kind o' hairdo, I smack him one!" Bill, the rechristened waiter, was approaching with the beer and cigarettes. "Eh? Eh? Eh? What you say, Bill? You like hippies? You're a Polack hippie, ain't ya? Eh?"

Bill smiled, and inside his smile he wished them dead. He placed the beer courteously on the shining black tabletop, set Alexander's chips and cigarettes before him, smiled again, waited for the ten-cent tip he always got from Alexander—nothing more, nothing less, regardless of the amount of beer he drank—and then left, cursing Alexander and all the men at the table, in his mind, in his own language.

"Any o' you fellas ever worked in a mine? I mean a *mine*. Underground. You go down on that lift five o'clock every morning to work your shift, your lunch pail in your hand, your heart in your goddamn mouth, though you can't show it to the other fellas, and you know, as your buddies know, that one o' these days none o' you might see the light o' day again when that shift ends. Never again. That's what I call *work*. Well, I was a miner once. Twenty years of it. After the war. Worked in the McIntyre. Timmins. Best goddamn gold mine in the world one time. That's my opinion. Best goddamn high-grade miner you see sitting right in front of you. Worked like a bitch in those days. Made money too. Good money. Spent every goddamn penny on women, whisky, and poker. But I had me a ball! I mean a mine! McIntyre. In Timmins. Wasn' a woman in town who escaped my wrath!"

The men roared. The waiter, standing by the counter, looked up from watching television.

"Used to shack up with a Indian woman in them days. Best goddamn woman in the North too! In the world. Kind as anything to me. Worked like a bastard and ate like a horse, I did. Shot me a moose twice every winter. My Indian woman acted as my guide all through the bush. Like say, for two months. November, December, January, February, and March we lived like a goddamn bear inside that shack we called our home. Me and my goddamn woman. *Lived*! I was a man then. Screwed like a bitch too. Them days I had my wife living in a town fifteen miles south. Porcupine. Lived like a man, I did!"

He whetted his tale with a large draught of beer and dried it with a smack of his lips. The others, waiting on his cue, raised their glasses to their lips; and as they settled down to listen again, they wiped their melting moustaches of beads and beer.

Alexander made them cry and he made them bawl with laughter and sympathy at his stories of the North. They laughed at his jokes about the women he had conquered like a real general, and they saw him as a general. He was a great man, a great goddamn buddy, they said in words and in looks. And they would always wait for him, should they arrive at the Selby before him; and they'd order just one beer each and nurse it until Alexander came through the door and into the darkened beverage room, already noisy before he entered, with the footsteps of sand on the floor and television soap operas which none of them watched except Joe, though they insisted it always be on.

He would come in like a soldier. And when he sat down, it seemed as if they had gathered their breaths and attention in one long intake. And they would wait until he was settled in his scraping chair. He told them, careening over the years of his life in the Canadian army, of his conquests, especially his personal conquests of women in Italy, in North Africa, in the Suez, and in Britain. But the woman he talked most about was his Indian woman from Timmins.

"One night my missus sneaked up on me! And, goddamn, fellas . . . well, I don't have to tell you the rest!" They laughed like men would laugh at this kind of joke; and they blamed his wife, whom none of them knew, for being so goddamn thoughtless as to sneak up on him. A man like Alexander deserved a better wife, a more thoughtful wife, a wife who could understand such things, who could understand that she was living in the company and sleeping in the bed of a great man, a general.

"Women and wives can be clumsy sometimes," Joe said.

Alexander looked at him with an expression which Joe did not understand. But inside, Alexander was saying to himself, *Joe, you ain't even a goddamn man, so how could you know?* And then he relieved the tension in his cruel expression, and the tension around the table was relieved. He punched Joe playfully on his arm, and the men, like poker players after having diagnosed a bluff, relaxed and sipped their beer and smiled.

"Yeah, men, yeah," Joe said. This time he was complimenting himself. He had had two wives. Both of them had divorced him for mental cruelty. He shrugged this memory out of his mind, remembered that Alexander still held the floor, and said, "That's right, Lex. You're right."

Alexander felt good again. He had regained his prestige and their loyalty, and he had regained their attention without having to demand it. He thought he would play with them a while and tell them the story about the winter weekend he was lost in the bush in Timmins. But instead of telling them the truth—that he had cried like a child while his Indian woman left to go back to the camp for help—he decided to tell them it was he who had *insisted* she go back, while he lay in the snow for forty-five hours with his right leg frozen like an igloo. And of course they believed him. When he told them the story, they nodded and patted him on his back with their smiles and with a free round of beer. Every man bought him a beer. Alexander never bought anybody a round.

"My Indian woman fell sick on the way back to the camp, so they had to leave her behind. At the camp. Then they went and lost their way; those bastards lost their goddamn way. Took the bastards five hours more than I figured it would take them to find me. OPP even sent in a helicopter. And there I was in the goddamn snow, my right foot feeling like a ton o' bricks, lifeless. And you know what? I'd just killed me a rabbit and was eating it raw when they arrived. And they said—"

"*A rabbit?*" Joe shouted, enjoying the story. "Hey, you hear that, fellas? A rabbit!"

The men were not the outdoor type. None of them had ever lived in the North. It was doubtful whether they knew the kind of animals to be found in the northern bush. But they laughed anyhow. It was a damn good story, they said. A damn fine story. And Alexander told it like a master, like a man, like a real man, which they all thought he was.

Now it was time to go home to his wife.

Alexander pushed his glass with some beer still in it, warm like plain tea, from in front of him. He made the first gesture to stand. And the others immediately scratched their chairs on the noisy sand on the floor and got up. They all began to talk about their wives being annoyed because supper had to be put into the oven to keep warm. But Joe, who wasn't married now, merely commented upon what an enjoyable Friday afternoon it had been listening to Lex. If it wasn't so late, and if they didn't have wives, and if they hadn't kept their wives waiting for supper and Friday-night shopping, he would invite Lex to return later in the evening and ask him to tell some more stories. But it was late now, they all agreed. Eight o'clock, and they hadn't gone home to their wives with their wages.

"If you fellas were *men*, you won't have to . . ." Alexander began, and he finished the rest of his opinion in a hoarse laugh filled with the pebbles of his deep voice and the bubbling suds of too much beer on an empty stomach.

"Yeah, yeah!" Joe chimed in. "Tell 'em, Lex; you tell 'em! If they was men . . . Christ, when I was a married man and my wife ever so much as opened her—"

Alexander scraped his heavy feet on the sand and straightened himself. "Well, men," he said, putting an Export into his mouth, "thanks for your company." Joe had raised his lighter to Lex's cigarette. "S'long, fellas!!" He slapped each of them except Joe on his back, as he had done every evening when he was leaving, as he had seen army sergeants do on television. And then he left.

Joe caught up with him as he turned the corner to walk along Sherbourne, in the direction of the rooming houses with their dark foreboding hallways, where women sat on front steps with their blue-veined legs tucked into the crux of their cheap cotton dresses, white like their legs. Alexander hadn't looked back for Joe. And Joe, mumbling in his words and in his walk, the beer making rubber of his legs, was chipping along a step behind Lex, as if his feet were spades scraping the sidewalk.

"You really told 'em back there, Lex. You really socked it to 'em. I like that one 'bout the time you got lost. And they couldn't find you! And you stayed there, like a giant! Like a hero! Waiting for help. And all the time you was waiting, all the time you're waiting in that damn cold, you was there, cool as a goddamn cucumber. Eating a raw rabbit!" He laughed. He was coughing. He started again to laugh and cough. And then he was coughing and trying to laugh, and all the time he was saying, "A rabbit! Imagine that! A goddamn raw rabbit!" And he would splutter into a coughing and laughing fit and touch Lex with his elbow, trying to do all these things and still keep up with Alexander's pace. "A goddamn rabbit!" He spluttered some more. Saliva and stale beer touched his lips. He brushed it away with the back of his hand, and then he spat into the gutter. He nudged Lex with his elbow and said, "You know something, Lex? You wanna know something, old buddy?" Alexander continued walking, thinking of his wife waiting for him at home. "You know what, Lex? I wish I was like you. Really. No, really. I wish I was like you."

Something was bothering Alexander. But the way he walked, a little in front of Joe, made Joe think that he was worrying him, that Lex didn't want to talk any more, that he was probably thinking about very important things. And Joe thought he was not deferential enough to Lex.

"Now, don't get vex, Lex, old buddy. But I mean to say that, sitting down in that beer parlour, lis'ning to you talk the way you talked about the old days, it made me wish that my life was like your life, that I still had a woman at home, even a woman with a ring on her goddamn finger, even a wife, man! And I know that if I was just like you, I could be like you in that kind o' thing, having a wife, just like you have a wife. I know that I would be the boss in the house, that I won't make that mistake I make two times in the past and let her wear the goddamn pants. Not in my house. You understand me, Lex, buddy?"

Something wooden and staunch in Alexander's movement was now taking Joe's attention off what he wanted to say. Alexander seemed tense. He seemed to be angry that Joe was talking so much. To Joe it looked as if his steps were getting stiff . . .

It could have been the frostbitten leg tightening up, could have been the amount of beer he had drunk. But Lex can take his liquor, man. Lex can drink any man under the table! Nobody could take his liquor like Lex!

Alexander was moving away from him. And as Joe was thinking about Lex's rugged character, his man's rugged character, in that split second when his words and thoughts wrapped him inside Lex's skin and he was Lex, that moment of acclaim and idolization . . . that same moment of approval was when Alexander shifted his weight off his right leg, off the sidewalk, and was heading for his home, a desolate brown brick building with a woman past middle age sitting on the front steps looking at the cars and people going home along Sherbourne. The woman was sitting with her greying shanks propped up to show the blueness of veins around her knees.

Joe had never walked him home before, and didn't know he lived so close to the Selby Hotel. He had only sat with him and the other men in the dying-light-bulbed room where you couldn't really see a man's face, where you didn't really know a man by complexion or features, both of which were dimmed in the light which the proprietor called "cozy." And Joe had never walked so close, so long, beside Lex before. But today he had been carried away by some of the things, some of the drama of the strong man's views contained in the story about the raw rabbit. Now he had dared to walk with Lex and confess that if no other man around the shining black table was impressed, he was.

Joe had come out of his dream of worship in time to see Alexander turn off the sidewalk and head for the woman sitting on the steps with her hands concealed in her lap.

The woman shifted her body ever so slightly. She was like a boxer moving her large hips over the cement of the steps to let Alexander pass.

Seeing his friend about to enter the house, Joe said, "Lex, I don't mean to bug you, but I hope you didn't mind me walking home with you like this, without you inviting me or anything, but I just want you to know that what you was telling me and the fellas back there in the beer parlour made a strange impression on me. I don't know how to say this, Lex, buddy, things like this I can't say too well, but I want to tell you that you made me feel like a man today. You did. You make me feel, well . . . that's why I had to walk all the way over here with you, so that when you come to drink with the fellas tomorrow, even before you come, I want you to know you have a friend in me, and that I see a man in you, and that's why——"

The fat woman on the steps turned her bulky body around and said, as if she was talking to the wind, "Ya better go in now before it's too late, son. She been——"

"Look, I gotta go in, Joe," Alexander said with an earnestness in his voice, a tinge of fear too, that Joe had never noticed before. "I wish we could talk now. You and me. As men. But maybe tomorrow, eh?" He looked scared. He would have said more but he knew he didn't have the time. He looked like a man giving a final important farewell. "Maybe tomorrow, eh? Tomorrow?"

At that moment they could hear the marching of feet from down the dark hallway coming towards them. And the voice, as if it was just then being released from the throat, soft at first with the distance and the darkness of the house, and finally screaming, and the woman, a thin piece of a stick of a woman, was saying, "I thought I told you last night! Last night I said, make it the last time . . ."

But she did not finish her threat. Instead, she came down the two steps at Alexander. Joe was standing stupidly beside him, not knowing what to do, not knowing if there was anything to do. The woman came at Alexander and shouted, "*Stanstill!* Come, boy, stannup! *Stand up!*" in two distinct bullets.

And Alexander, Lex, the man who had waited so long in the snow, put his right hand dutifully on her shoulder while she bent down to his height.

She gripped his right leg. She pulled his trousers on that side of his body down, down, down, until it exposed a large canvas-type belt like those that sawmills use. And without another word she unbuckled some smaller belts and buckles. Alexander's heel struck the floor. Joe smelled sausages cooking inside.

With his hand still on the hardness of his wife's back, Alexander buried his face in the floor of linoleum, while the wife pulled the lifeless, eternally frostbitten and snow-devoured right leg out of the khaki trouser leg. Joe smelled the sausages inside and his eyes began to water. He was crying.

The woman sitting on the front steps did not even look back. She sat, and her relaxed fat back, flabby in the cotton dress, said that it had happened many times before.

Alexander's wife pulled the other trouser leg off. She kicked the wooden leg inside the dark hallway. And she said to Alexander, standing in his one-legged underpants, "*Move*, bugger! Move! Now!" It was like four more bullets. Joe saw Lex stumble. Then he put out his right hand to touch the doorpost. And when he could feel the strength of the post, he lowered himself down to the floor, onto his hands. On one leg. In this posture he moved down into the further darkness of the dark house.

Joe did not want to see any more, and still he wanted to watch. He had turned his face away when Lex first bent down to reach the floor. And he was going to look back to see whether Lex resembled something, some animal he knew, something that Lex himself had talked about in many of his stories. But, instead, he walked back down the steps, past the woman watching the traffic along Sherbourne Street. She sensed when he was beside her, and without moving a muscle in her billowy body, she said, "Goodnight now."

THE
MOTOR CAR

That Canadian thing you see laying down there in that hospital bed is Calvin woman, I mean *was* Calvin woman. Calvin wash motor cars back in Barbados till his back hurt and his belly burn, and when the pain stop in the body it start up fresh in his mind. Good thing Calvin was a God-faring man, 'cause if not he would have let go some real bad curse words that would have blow way the garage itself. But instead o' talking to the customers 'bout the hard work, instead o' talking to the boss 'bout the slave work he was making Calvin do in 1968 in these modern days, Calvin talk to God. Calvin didn' know if God did really hear him, 'cause the more he talk to God every morning before he went to work on his old Raleigh green three-speed bicycle, and after work when his head hit that pillow, the more the work did get harder. One day Calvin take in with a 'bout o' bad-feels, and the moment he come outta the fit or the trance, or the hellucinations, as his boss call it, right that very second Calvin swear blind to God that he leffing Barbados. One time. For good. First chance. Is only the governorship or the governor-generalship that could get Calvin to stay in Barbados. That is the kind o' swearing he put 'pon God. And it ain' really clear, even at this time, if God really understand the kind o' message that Calvin put to him. But Calvin didn' care. Calvin decide already. Calvin start to work hard, more harder than he ever work in his life, from the very day after he decide that he pulling outta Barbados. And is to Canada he coming. Now the problems start falling 'pon top o' Calvin head like rainwater.

First problem: he can't get a Canadian visa. He seeing Canadian tourisses morning noon and night all 'bout his island, walking 'bout like if they own the blasted place, and if you don't watch-out, they getting on as if they want to own Calvin too. Calvin hit a low point 'o studyation. The work done now and he pack already, two big-big imitation leather valises; and he manage to buy the ticket too, although there is a regulation down there in the island that say a black man can't buy a one-way ticket 'pon Air Canada saving he have a job and a roof to come to in Canada, or he have family here, or some kind o' support, cause Trudeau get vex-vex as hell 'bout supporting the boys when they come up here and can't find proper 'ployment. Calvin walking 'bout Bridgetown the capital all day telling people he leffing next week for Canada. Next week come, and he still walking 'bout Bridgetown. He ain' pull out in trute, yuh; he like he ain' pulling out at all, man; that is what the boys was beginning to whizzy-whizzy. They start laughing at Calvin behind his back, and Calvin grinning and telling them, "Gorblummuh, you laugh! *Laugh!* He who laugh last, laugh . . ." And for purpose, he won't finish the proverb at all; he only ordering a next round o' steam for his friends, but his mind focus-on 'pon a new shining motor car that he going buy up in Canada before he even living there a year. He done make up his mind that he going work at two car-wash places, and if the Lord hear his prayers, and treat he nice, he going hustle a next job on top o' them two too.

Well, the more the boys laugh, the more Calvin decide with a bad-mind that he going buy a brand-new Chevy, perhaps even a custom-build Galaxie.

And then, all of a sudden, one night when the fellas drink three free-round o' rum offa Calvin, Calvin really start to laugh. He push he hand inside his pocket, and he pull out a thing that look real important and official, and all he say is, "I taking off at nine in the morning." Calvin then throw a new-brand twenty-dollar bill 'pon Marcus rum-shop counter, and the fellas gone wild, be-Christ, 'cause is now real rum-drinking going begin. Calvin stand up like a man. Every one that his best friend Willy fire, Calvin fire one too.

Willy, who didn' lick he mouth too much 'gainst Calvin going-
'way, when he reach the fifth straight Mount Gay, Calvin was right
there with him. Is rum for rum. Drink for drink. They start eating
raw salt fish, and Calvin iamming the codfish as if he catch it himself
off the Grand Banks o' Newfoundland in the same Canada that he
heading out to. The fellas eat off all o' Marcus bad half-rotten salt
fish, and then start-on 'pon a tin o' corn beef and raw onions, and
you would have think that Calvin had been on a real religious fast
during the time he was worrying 'bout the Canadian visa. "I going
tell you fellas something," Willy say, for no conceivable reason at
all, 'cause they was just then telling Calvin that he ain' going see no
good cricket when he get up in that cold ungodly place call Canada.
"I going tell you fellas something now," Willy say, after he clear
his throat for effect, and to make the fellas stop drinking and eating
and listen to him. "Godblummuh! Calvin is the most luckiest one
o' we, yuh! Calvin lucky-lucky-lucky as shite!" He say the last three
lucky like if they was one word. Anyhow, he went on, "Calvin is a
king to we!" Now, nobody ain' know what the arse Willy trying to
say, cause Willy is a man who does try to talk big and does talk a lot
o' shite in the bargain. But this time, solemn occasion as it be, the
fellas decide to give Willy a listen. "We lis'ning, man, so talk yuh
talk. We lis'ning." Willy take a long pull 'pon the rum bottle, and
he stuff 'bout a half-pound o' corn beef inside his mouth, with the
biscuits flying 'bout the place like big drops o' spit. "You see that
salt fish that we just put 'way? Well, it make up in Canada. Tha's
where Calvin here going. Now understand this when I say it. I only
say that to say this. Comprehend? The salt fish that we does get
down here, send-down by Canada, is the same quality o' salt fish
that they uses to send down here to feed we when we was slaves. It
smell stink. You could tell when a woman cooking salt fish. We
even invent a term to go 'long with this kind o' salt fish and this
kind o' stinkingness. We does say to a person who uses profine
words, 'Yuh mouth smell like a fucking salt-fish barrel.' Unner-
stand? I going to lay a bet 'pon any one o' you bastards in here now,
drinking this rum. I going wager five dollars 'gainst a quarter that

the brand o' salt fish Calvin going get to buy and eat up in that place call Canada is a more better quality o' salt fish. It bound to be, 'cause that is where it produce. And if you ever study Marx, you would understand the kind o' socialism I talking 'bout." Nobody ain' answer Willy for a time, all they do is laugh. "Laugh! Laugh!" Willy say with scorn, "'Cause godblindme . . . !" And then Calvin say, like if he didn' really want to say the words at-all, "Be-Jesus Christ, when you see me leff this blasted backwards place call Barbados, that is the last time I eating salt fish. I eating steaks!"

Well, they poured Calvin on 'pon the Air Canada, next morning, nine sharp, drunk as a flying fish. Good thing Calvin mother did pack the fry dolphin steak, a bottle o' cod liver oil, in case the bowels do a thing and give trouble in that cold ungodly climate, as she call Canada; and she pack some Phensic for headache, just in case; she pack some miraculous bush, for medicine, "'cause they ain' have doctor no place under the sun who know the goodness in this mirac'lous-bush tea as we does, so you tek it along with you, son; you going up in that strange savage place, and you far from me, and I ain' near enough no more to run to you and rub your face with a lime and some Limacol, and tie it up with oil leaves and candle grease . . ."; and she put in half-dozen limes and two bottle o' Limacol; man, is a good-good thing that Calvin mother had the presence o' mind to pack these things for Calvin whilst Calvin was walking 'bout Broad Street in Bridgetown like if he was one o' them Canadian tourisses. Calvin mother do a real good job, and when she done pack the things, and she inspect the clothes that Calvin carrying 'way, she tie-up the two valises with a strong piece o' string, although they had brand-new locks 'pon them. "Good!" is the last thing she say to Calvin, as she was holding them over the kitchen door, whilst Willy was revving up the hired car and blowing the horn—which of course Calvin pay for, the hired car, I mean—plus dropping a ten-dollar bill inside Willy hand for old times sake. "Go 'long in the name o' the Lord, and make yuh fortune, son." A tear or two drop outta she eye too; but she was glad-glad in she heart that she boychild was leffing Barbados. "Too much foreigners and

tourisses and crooks living here with we now, son. Canada more
brighter than here." Calvin get vex-vex when he see the water in
his mother eye, and he was embarrass as hell, 'cause he always use
to brag how nothing he do, or don't do, could make his mother
belly burn she. Good thing Willy had the car motor revving, 'cause
Calvin get in such a state over the tears and heartbreak on the part of
his mother that he almost forget that deep-down he is a Christian-
minded man and say a bad word, whiching, as he did know full-
well, God would be vex as hell with him for. The motor car was
making good time, moving like hell going up the airport road, and
everybody Calvin know, and everybody that he barely know in the
twenty-nine years he born and living in Barbados, he hold half of
his body out through the car window, and yell out, "Boy, I going
this morning! Canada, in your arse!" All the people who see and
hear, wave back and grin their teet', if they could hear from the
distance and through the speed; and some o' them say, "Bless." If
everybody in Barbados, down Broad Street, at the airport, didn'
know that Calvin pulling out for Canada at quarter to nine that
morning, by nine o'clock the whole world did know. Friend or no
friend, every time he see a face, or a hand, he saying, "Well, I won't
be seeing you for a while, man. I going up." And they did all know
what he meant, 'cause it was a time when all the young boys and
young girls was pulling outta the island and going to Amurca and
Britain, although Britain begin to tighten up things for the fellas
because o' Enoch Powell; and some o' them start running up in
Canada. And they was more Air Canada planes all 'bout Seawell
Airport in Barbados in them days . . . you would have think that
Barbados did own Air Canada. But is the other way 'round. Anyhow, drunk as Calvin was when he step 'pon that plane, and the
white lady smile at him and say, "Good morning, sir"—first time in
Calvin life a white woman ever call him that, that way—well, Calvin
know long time that he make the right move. "Canada nice," he say
in his heart; and he end it up with, "Praise God." Canada now gone
straight to Calvin head, long time and with a kind o' power, that
when the airplane start up Calvin imagine that he own the whole

blasted plane along with the white ladies who tell him, "Good morning, sir"; he feel that the plane is the big motor car he intend to own one year after he land 'pon Canadian soil. The plane making time fast-fast, and Calvin drink rum after rum till he went fast asleep and didn' even know the plane landing in Toronto. The white lady come close to him, and tap him soft-soft 'pon his new tropical suit and say, "Sir?" like if she asking some important question, when all she want is to wake up Calvin outta the white people plane. Well, Calvin wake up. He stretch like how he uses to stretch when he wake up in his bed in his mother house. He yawn so hard that the white lady move back a step or two, after she see the pink inside his mouth and the black and blue gums running all 'round them white pearly teets. Calvin eyes red-red as a cherry from lack o' sleep and too much rum drinking, and the body tired like how it uses to get tired and wrap-up like a old motor-car fender. But is Canada, old man! And in a jiffy, before the white lady get to the front o' the plane to put down the last glass, Calvin looking out through the window.

"Toronto in your arse!" he went to say to himself, but it come out too loud, as if he was saying it to Willy and the boys who didn' think he was really going to come through. "Toronto in your arse, man!"

The plane touch down, and the first man outta the plane is— well, no need to tell you who it was. Calfuckingvin! And he pass through the Customs like if he was born in Toronto. The white man didn' even ask him a question. Something like it was wrong, 'cause Calvin did know as far away as in Barbados that the Immigration and Customs men in Toronto is the roughest in the world, when they see a black face in front o' them. But this white gentleman must have been down in the islands recently, 'cause all he tell Calvin was, "Don't tell me! Don't tell me! You're a Bajan!" For years after, Calvin wondering how the hell this white man know so much 'bout black people.

Before the first week come and gone, Calvin take up pen and paper and send off a little thing to Willy and the boys: . . . *and I am going to tell you something, this place is the greatest place for a working man to live. I hear some things bout this place, but I isn't a man to complain, because while I know I am a man, and I won't take no shit from no Canadian, white, black, or red, I still have another piece of knowledge, namely that says that I didn't born here. So I controls myself to suit, and make the white man money. The car only a couple of months off. I see one already that I got my two eyes on. And if God willing, by the next two months, DV, I sitting down in the drivers seat. The car I got my eyes on is a red one, with white tires. The steering wheel as you know is on the left hand side, and we drives on the right hand side of the road up here, not like back in Barbados where you drive on the left hand. Next week, I taking out my licents. I not found a church I like yet, mainly because I see some strange things happening up here in churches. You don't know, man, Willy, but black people can't or don't go in the same church as white people. God must be have two different colours then. One for black people and one for white people. And a next thing. There is some fellas up here from the islands who talking a lot of shite bout Black Power, and I hear that one of them is a Barbadian. But I am one man who don't want to hear no shit bout Black Power. I am here working for a living and a motor car, and if my mother herself come in my way and be an obstacle against me getting them two things, a living and a motor car, I would kill her first by-Christ . . .* Calvin was going to write more: about the room he was renting for twenty dollars a week, which a white fella tell him was pure robbery, because the white fella was paying ten dollars for a more larger room on the ground floor in the same house; and he didn' write Willy 'bout the car-wash job he got the next day down Spadina Avenue, working for a dollar a hour, and when the first three hours pass he felt he been working for three days, the work was so hard; he didn' tell Willy that a certain kind of white people in Canada didn' sit too close to him on the streetcar, that they didn' speak to him on the street . . . lots o' things he didn' worry to tell Willy, cause he did-want Willy to think that to the boys back home he was really a king, a champion, for emigrading to Canada.

Willy send back a post card with a mauby woman on the colour side selling mauby, and on the writing side, in his scribbly hand-writing, *As man!* But be-Christ, Calvin didn' care what they do, he was here for two purposes: one, living; and number two, motor car. "If they touch my motor car, now, well, that would be something else" . . . and Calvin work hard, man; Calvin work more harder than when he was washing-off cars back in Barbados. The money was good too. Sal'ry and tips. From the two car-wash jobs he uses to clear a hundred dollars a week, and that is two hundred back home, and not even Dipper does make that kind o' money, and he is the fucking prime minister! The third job, Calvin land like a dream: night watchman with a big-big important company which put him in a big-big important uniform and thing; big leather belt like what he uses to envy the officers in the Volunteer Force back home wearing 'pon the Queen's Birthday parade on the Garrison Savannah; shoes the company people even provide; and the only thing that was missing, according to what Calvin figure out some months afterwards, was that the holster at his side, join-on to the leather belt, didn' have-in no blasted gun. He tell it to a next Barbadian on the job that he make friends with, and the Bajan just laugh and say, "They think you going shoot your blasted self, boy!" But Calvin did already become Canadianified enough to know that the only people he see wearing them uniforms with guns in the leather holster was white people; and he know he wasn' Canadianified so much that he did turn white overnight. "Once it don't stop me from getting that Galaxie!"

Work, work, work; a occasional postcard to Willy, 'cause envelopes was costing too much all of a sudden, and postage stamps was going up too; no pleasure for Calvin: he went down by the Tropics Club where they does-play calypsos and dance, one time; and he never went back 'cause the ugly Grenadian fellow at the door ask him for three dollars to come in, and he curse the fellow stink and leff. But the bank account was mounting and climbing like a woman belly when she is in the family way. Quick-quick so, Calvin have a thousand dollars 'pon the bank. Fellas who get to know Calvin and who Calvin won't 'sociate with because "'sociating does cost money, boy!"—them fellas so, who here donkey years, still borrowing money to help pay their rent; fellas gambling like hell, throwing dice every Friday night right into Monday morning early, missing work and getting fired from work; fellas playing poker and betting—"Forty dollars more for these two fours, in your rass, sah! I *raise!*"—them brand o' Trinidadian, Bajan, Jamaician, Grenadian, and thing, them so can't understand at-all how Calvin just land and he get rich so fast. "I bet all-yuh Calvin selling pussy!" one fella say. A next bad-minded fella say, "He peddling his arse to white boys down Church Street." And a third fella who did just bet fifty dollars 'pon a pair o' deuces, and had get broke at the poker game, say quick-quick before the words fall-out o' the other fella mouth, "I going peddle my ass too, then! Bread is bread." Calvin start slacking up on the first car-wash work, and he humming as he shine the white people car, he skinning his teet' in the shine and he smiling, and the white people thinking he smiling 'cause he like the work and he like them, 'cause his hands never tarried whilst he was car-dreaming, and they would drop a little dollar bill 'pon Calvin as a tip, and a regular twenty-five-cent piece, and Calvin meantime continue pinching 'pon the groceries, eating a lotta pig's feet and chicken necks and salt fish—"I gotta write Willy and tell him 'bout the brand o' salt fish in this place. Willy was right!"—Calvin won't spend thirty cents 'pon a beer on a sinner; only time he even reading is when he clean out a car in the car wash and the car happen to have a used newspaper inside it, or a throw-away paperback book. But Calvin decide long time that he didn' come here for eddication. He come for a living and a motor car. A new one too! And he intend to get both. And by the look o' things, be-Christ, both almost within his grasp. Only now waiting to see the right model o' motor car, with the right interior colour inside it, and the right mileage and thing. The motor car must have the right colour o' tires, right colour o' gear shift, and in the handle too; and it have to have-in radio; and he see a fella in the car wash with a thing inside his Cadillac, and Calvin gone crazy over Cadillacs until he walk down by Bay Street and College and price the price of a old one. He bawl for murder. "Better stick to the Galaxie, boy!" he tell himself; and he do that. But he really like the thing inside the white man Cadillac and he ask the man one morning what it was, and the man tell

Calvin. Now Calvin *must* have red Galaxie, with not more than 20,000 miles on the register, black upholstery, red gearshift, radio —AM *and* FM, *and a tellyfone* . . . Them last three things is what the man had inside his Cadillac.

Calvin working even on a Sunday, bank holidays ain' touching Calvin, and the Old Queen back home, who send a occasional letter asking Calvin to remember the house rent and the poor box in the Nazarene Church where he was a testifying brother, preaching and thing, and also to remember "who birthed you"—well, Calvin tell the Old Queen, his own-own mother, in a letter: *Things hard up here, Ma. Don't let nobody fool you that because a man emigrade to Canada, that it mean that he elevate. That isn't true. But I am sending this Canadian money order for five dollars, which is ten dollars back home, and I hope that next week I would find myself in a nice job, and then I am going to send you a little something more, more regular. Your loving son, Calvin. P.S. Pray for me.* Calvin start thinking that maybe the Old Queen had a bad mind for him; he start one long stewpsing, and the fellas at work even had to ask him if he sick or something; he even stop laughing and chumming around with the Canadians at work; he refuse to play Frisbee and throw the ball in the other fellas' mittens; he even stop begging the German fella for a lift home after work. Calvin start getting ingrown like a toenail: pressure in Calvin arse. The studya-tion take a hold o' him and one weekend it capsize him in bed, Friday night, Saturday morning and Saturday night, Sunday, and right into Monday morning, half-hour before he is to leff for work. Landlady couldn' even come in and change the filthy linens and bedsheets. But Calvin make sure he went to work that Monday. "Can't lose that money now, boy!"

Willy was the next joker at this time o' hardship and studyation. Willy send a letter registered and thing, in a real pretty envelope with the colours o' the Union Jack, to Calvin, saying in part, *. . . and if it isn't asking too much, Calvin, I wonder if you can see your way in sending me down a piece of change. I am thinking bout emigrading too, because Barbados is at a standstill for people like me, people who don't have no high school education, no big kind of skills and no kiss-me-arse godfather* *in a big job in the civil service. My kind of man in Barbados is loss. I hope I am not imposing when I ask you if you could see your way in lending me the passage money, one way only, and I am going to open a new bank account with it and take a picture of it and show it to the Canadian Immigration people down here, because another fellow promise to do the same thing for me with the return part of the passage money. The Canadian High Commission place in Trinidad giving the fellows a hard time. But we smarter than any number of Canadian Immigration people they send down here. So I asking this favour for old times sake, because, not that I hard on you, but I don't want to remind you of the time when you had the accident with the motor car that didn't belongts to you, and you was in hospital, and you know who help you out, so* . . . Calvin get in a bad-bad mood straightaway, thinking that everybody back home think he is a millionaire, everybody back there getting on like crabs, willing to pull him down the moment he come up for air: "Be-Christ, but not me!" And in that frame o' mind Calvin take up a piece o' stationery he borrow from a Jamaican fella who had a job in the Toronto General Hospital, and a envelope to match, with the hospital name on both, and he ask a next fella who had a typewriter to write this letter back to Willy: *Dear Willy, I have been laid up in this hospital for two months now. I am getting a friend who is in the hospital too, but who is not confine to bed, but who can barely walk around, to post this letter to you for me. Things really bad, man* . . . "because all my friends back home think I is a arse or something; they see me emigrade to this place and they think that I get rich overnight, or that I don't work hard as shite for my money. But that ain' true!"

Willy didn' answer back immediately; but a month and a half later, two days before Calvin decide he see the right automobile, a card drop through the door of the rooming house where Calvin living, address to Calvin: *What are you doing up there, then? Canadians buying out all the island. You standing for that? Send down a couple of dollars and let me invest it in a piece of beach land for you, Brother. Power to the people! Salaam and love. Willy X.*

Calvin get blasted vex, damn vex, and start cussing 'cause he sure now that Willy gone mad too, like everybody else he been reading 'bout in the States and in England; black people gone mad, Calvin say, over Black Power; and he get more vex when he think that it was the landlady, Mistress Silvermann, who take up the postcard from the linoleum and hand it to him, and he swear blind that she hand it to him *after* she read the card; and now she must be frighten like hell for Calvin, cause Calvin getting letters from these political extremists, and Black Power birds of a feather does flock together; and she thinking now that Calvin perhaps is some kind o' political maniac, crying "Black Power!"—all this damn foolishness 'bout power to the people, and signing his name *Willy X*, when everybody in Barbados know that that damn fool's name is really William Fortesque. Calvin get shame-shame-shame that the landlady thinking different 'bout him, because sometimes she does be in the house all night alone with only Calvin; and she must be even thinking 'bout giving him notice, which would be a damn bad thing to happen right now, 'cause the motor car just two days off, the room he renting now is a nice one, the rent come down like the temperature in May when he talk plain to Mistress Silvermann 'bout how he paying twice as much as the other tenants. But what really get Calvin really vex-vex-vex as hell is that a little Canadian thing in the room over his head come downstairs one night in a minidress and thing, bubbies jumping 'bout inside her bosom, free and thing and looking nice-nice, and giggling all the time and calling herself a women's-liberation; all her skin at the door, and the legs nice and fat just as Calvin like his meats; and Calvin already gone thinking that this thing is the right woman to drive-'bout in his new automobile with, this Canadian thing coming downstairs every night for the past month, and out of the blue asking him, "You'll like a coffee?" When she say so the first time, coffee was as far from Calvin mind as lending Willy twenty-five cents for the down payment for the house spot 'pon the beach back home. Now, be-Christ, Willy X, or whatever the hell that bastard calling himself nowadays, is going to stay right there down in Barbados and mash-up Calvin life so! Just so? Simple so? Oh God no, man! But the landlady couldn' read English; she did only use to pretend she is a bilingual person; the Canadian girl is who tell Calvin not to worry; and one night when they was drinking the regular coffee in the communal kitchen, the Canadian girl say, "Missis Silvermann is only a DP. She can't read English." Calvin take courage. The bank book walking 'bout with him, inside his trousers all the time, he counting the digits going to work, coming from work, in the back seat alone 'pon the streetcar, while waiting for the subway early on a morning at the Ossington station, and then he make a plan. He plan it down to a T. Every penny organize for the proper thing, every nickel with its own work to do: the bottle of wine that the Canadian girl gave him the name to; the new suit from Eaton's that he see in the display window one night when he get hold of the girl and he get bold-bold as hell and decide to take she for a lover's walk down Yonge Street; the new shoes, brown-brown till they look red to match the car; and the shirt and tie—every blasted thing matching up like if he is a new bride stepping down the aisle to the Wedding March. And he even have a surprise up his sleeve for the thing too. He isn' no longer a stingy man, 'cause he see his goal; and his goal is like gold.

The car delivery arrange for three o'clock Saturday; no work; the icebox in his room have in a beer or two, plus the wine; and he have a extra piece o' change in his pocket—"I going have to remember to change the money from this pocket," he tell himself, as if he was talking to somebody else in the room with him, "to the next pocket in the new suit"—and he have Chinese food now on his mind because the Canadian thing mention a nice Chinese restaurant down in Chinatown near Elizabeth Street. Calvin nervous as arse all Friday night; all Friday night the thing in Calvin room (here of late she behaving as if she live in Calvin room!), and Calvin is a man with ambitions: one night she tantalize Calvin head so much that he start talking 'bout high-rise apartment to put she in; perhaps, if she behave sheself good, he might even put a little gold thing 'pon her pretty little pink finger . . . the girl start asking Calvin if he want *some*; not in them exact words, but that is what she did mean; and Calvin get shame-shame and nearly blush—only

thing, as you know, black people can't show really if they blushing
or if they mad as shite with a white person—and Calvin turn like
a virgin on the night before she get hung in church, and in the
marriage bed, and he saying all the time, because his mind 'pon
the mileage in the motor car, "Want some o' what?" And the girl
laugh, and she throw back she head and show she gold fillings and
she pink tongue and the little speck o' dirt on she neck; and she
laugh and say to sheself, "This one is a real gentleman, not like what
my girlfriend say to expect from West Indian men, at all." And you
know something? She start one big confessing to Calvin about her
previous life: ". . . and do you know what, Calvin? Would you like to
hear something that I been thinking?" Calvin thinking 'bout motor
car, and this blasted white woman humbugging him 'bout sex!
Calvin get vex; he play he get vex 'bout something different from
the woman and she sex, and he send she flying back upstairs to
her own room. He get in bed immediately as she leff. But he ain'
sleeping. He wide awake in the dark like a thief. And his two eyes
open wide-wide-wide like a owl eyes, and in the darkness in that
little-little room that only have one small window way up by
the ceiling and facing the clotheslines and the dingy sheets that the
landlady does spend all week washing, Calvin see the whole o'
Toronto standing up and clapping and watching him drive by in his
new motor car—with the Canadian thing squeeze-up 'side o' him
in the front seat!—dream turn into different dream that Friday
night, because he was free to dream as much as he like, since Saturday wasn' no work. Saturday is the Day of the Car. Motor-car day.
He have everything plan. Go for the motor car, pick she up, drive
she home, pick up the Canadian thing, go for a spin down Bloor as
far as Yonge, swing back up by Harbord, turn left at Spadina, take
in College Street, and every West Indian in Toronto bound to see
him in his new motor car before he get back home. Park she in
front o' the house—*let everybody see me getting outta she, come in, have
a little bite, bathe, change into the new suit, give the Canadian thing the
surprise I have for she, and whilst she dressing, I sit down in the car*—"And
I hope she take a long time dressing, so I would have to press the car

horn, press the horn just a little, a soft little thing, and call she outside, to see me in the . . ."

Morning break nice. It was a nice morning round the middle o' September, fall time in the air, everybody stretching and holding up their head cause the weather nice. Even the cops have a smile on their fissiogomy. Calvin get up at five, take a quick look at the alarm clock, curse the clock for being so damn slow, went back to sleep, had a dream in which he see Willy as the garage mechanic at the car place taking too long over the Galaxie; he curse Willy in the dream and nearly didn' get up in time, then turn 'round and curse Willy for coming into his dream. He left without drinking tea.

Travelling with the Canadian thing half-'sleep beside him, and gone fast 'pon the subway at Ossington along Bloor, along Danforth, for the machine. The salesman-man smile and shake Calvin hand strong, and give Calvin the history of the bird, although Calvin had already-hear the bird history before. The salesman-man come outta the office still smiling, holding the motor-car keys between his index finger and the big thumb, and he drop them in Calvin hand. Calvin make a shiver. A shiver o' pride and ownership.

Galaxie in your arse! He say that in his mind, and he thinking o' Willy and the boys back in Marcus Rum Shop. He get in the car. He shuffle 'bout a bit in the leather seat. He straighten his two trouser creases. He touch the leather. He start up the motor. Listen to the motor. It ticking over like a fucking charm. He put the thing in gear. And he make a little thing through the car lot, and he would have gone straight back along Danforth to Bloor, to Ossington, if the Canadian thing didn' wave she handbag in the air, to remind Calvin that she come with he, 'cause Calvin had forget she standing up there looking at a white convertible Cadillac, which she say is the car for Calvin, that there is lots o' "Negro men driving Cadillac cars, even in Nova Scotia, where I come from," and that Calvin should have buy one o' them.

You start spending my blasted money already, woman! This is mine! He didn' tell she out loud in words what he was really thinking 'bout she, but he was thinking so, though. The Canadian gash get in the motor car, 'cause driving in a Galaxie more better than walking behind a Cadillac, and she sit down so comfortable that it look like if she own the car, and that it was she who was giving Calvin a chance to try she out, and that it wasn' Calvin own-own money that pay-down 'pon the car. Calvin didn't like that at all; he want she to sit down in the front seat like if *he* own the motor car.

But Calvin gone up Danforth with new motor car and white woman beside o' him, like if he going to a funeral—"Got to break she in gently, man"—and the Canadian thing not too please that Calvin didn' listen to her advice as a woman should advise a man, and buy the Cadillac; but she still please and proud that Calvin get the Galaxie. She sitting in it like if she belong there by birth. And Calvin don't really mind, 'cause he have the car, and it driving like oil 'pon a tar road back home. He make a thing along Danforth as far as Bloor, turn 'pon Yonge and tack-back as far as Harbord—the itinerry ain' exactly as he first think it out, but it would do—make a thing along Harbord and meet up with Spadina, and continue according to plan. And in all this time so, not *one* blasted West Indian or black person in sight to look at Calvin new car and make a thing with his head, or laugh, or wave. When he make a right 'pon College at the corner o' Spadina, a woman with a bag mark HONEST ED'S start walking through the green light, drop a tomato, stannup in the middle of the road and bend down to pick it up, and Calvin now, whether he looking for the woman tomato or he looking the wrong way, nearly run over she. Jesus Christ! *Blam!* Brakes on. The Canadian thing nearly break she blasted neck 'gainst the windshield. Calvin rattle bad like a snake. Police come. Police look inside the car. Police see Calvin. Police turn he eyes 'pon the Canadian thing, who now frighten as hell, and the Police say, "Okay, move along now, buster!"

Calvin shaking till he get the Galaxie in front of the landlady rooming house, and he ain' remember nothing 'bout what he plan to do when he bring home the prize of a motor car; the Police upset him summuch that he trembling more than the Canadian woman. "Give me a drink o' water," he say to the Canadian thing. She rubbing she neck all the time like if it really break in truth, and she get out, and she didn' even look back at the new car, whiching, as you would understand, is what Calvin expect any man who just have a new motor car to do: yuh have to walk out of the door, close the door soft-soft because it ain' the same thing as getting out of a taxi, make sure the door close, and when you know it close, open it again to show yuhself that it close good, and then really close it a next time; then walk off, look at the car, turn yuh head right and left like if you escaping from a light jab to the head, rub yuh hand over the chrome, walk round to the door where the passenger does sit down, open that door too, close it, and open it, and then lock it. Then yuh does have to forget something inside the car, so yuh could have a chance to open the doors a next time and play with the car, hoping in the meantime that somebody who never see you before with a car, see you now with this new one, and would say something like "My! How much horsepower?" because, according to Calvin, "A car in some ways is like a woman; yuh does have to care she!" Calvin do all these things, and he didn't forget to walk to the back o' the Galaxie, stoop down and play he looking at the tires, give them a little kick with his shoes to see if they got-in enough air, look under the car to see what the muffler look like, and things like that, although he know full-well that he don't know one blasted thing 'bout motor cars except how to wash them off, or that yuh does drive them.

He do the same thing when he walk 'round to the front o' the car. The Canadian thing gone inside the house long time; and Calvin remember the glass o' water and he walking up the front steps. Not one blasted person on the whole street look out at Calvin new motor car. Then the landlady, Mistress Silvermann, walk out the front door, look at Calvin, but not at the car, and say, "Don't forget, Mr. Kingston, today your rent is due." Calvin tell her in his mind something bad, and as she eventually look at the car as she reach the sidewalk, without looking back, she say, "Do you know the owner of this car, Mr. Kingston? Tell him to move it, please . . . I don't want cars blocking my driveway . . ."

Well, Calvin gone mad now. He walk in the house, and he catch the Canadian thing sitting down in his room, with the glass o' water in her hand, as if she dreaming, just sitting and looking at the water in the glass as if it was a little aquarium. He drink the water. But it was like drinking miraculous-bush tea the Old Queen uses to make him drink when the bowels was giving trouble back in Barbados. Calvin, all of a sudden, think 'bout the Old Queen, put the Old Queen outta his head, and start dressing. He noticed that something was wrong with his dresser: perhaps the landlady was looking for her rent; perhaps the Canadian thing was—"That's why she didn' come back outside with the water! Anyhow . . ." He put on his clothes, the new suit, shoes and tie and shirt new and matching the Galaxie outside shining in the sun, and meantime the Canadian thing gone upstairs to her own-own room.

Calvin finish dress, take up a old kerchief—"Gotta have a shammy-cloth; gotta buy one Monday!"—and he gone outside polishing the motor car. Back inside, he gone up to the Canadian thing room, knock soft, the door open, and out from behind his back he take a thing, and say in a sweet loving voice, "I buy this for you."

Ohhhhhhh! Myyyyyyyyyyyyyyyy!

"You shouldn't, realllllllyyyyyyy!" But all the time she did know it was a dress Calvin buy for she for the occasion, 'cause when she went inside for the water, she start searching all the man things, and she had a nice peep at the dress. She even know it cost twenty-nine dollars without tax; and she wonder if Calvin really love she so much. Well, they dress-off and they coming out like bride and groom going to the church. The Galaxie smiling too, like if the Galaxie itself in love with the two o' them too. The dress nearly red like the car, woman and motor car in red, and looking nice. Calvin steal a peep at the Canadian thing and she look good-good-good, like something to eat! He inspect the tires a next time, though he just done looking at them, but what the hell, it is his motor car; and then he check the gas tank and the tank say, "Let's go for a long one, man!" And Calvin get in, fix the two creases in the new trousers, adjust the tie, look at the knot in the mirror, fix the mirror two times, and then ask the Canadian thing if she comfortable.

"I'm fine, thank you!"

Calvin rev-up the thing, she turn over nice, and he ready to go. "You not nervous?"

She smile. A dimple and a gold filling show when she smile. Nice. She ain' nervous.

"Don't mind what happen just now by Spadina, eh?" She smile nice again. She ain' mind what happen by Spadina. "Darling" come to she lips with the smile. Calvin happy as hell now. He think he might treat this Canadian thing nice, and do the right thing with a gold ring even.

"I take those things in my stride usually, but now it seems like an omen," she say, just as they turn on to Bloor.

Calvin ain' thinking 'bout omen, 'cause the only omen he know 'bout is that he pray for a Galaxie and he get a Galaxie! And the horses under the bonnet roaring like hell. Well, they drive and drive like if they was two explorers exploring Toronto: through Rosedale, where the Canadian thing say she would *just love* to own a house; and in his mind, Calvin promise she going get one in Rosedale; through the Bridle Path, where she say the cheapest house cost a million dollars; through Don Mills, where they see the big tall Foresters' Building, all up there by IBM.

"You should get a job at IBM, dear." ("Doing wha'? Cleaning out the closets?" *This Canadian thing like she is the wrong kind o' woman for me*, Calvin thinking. *I hads better get a black woman!*) All this she talk as they driving back on the Don Valley Parkway.

The highway nice. The motor car open a new whole world to Calvin, and he love Canada even more better. Damn good thing he leff Barbados! The Galaxie like a horse, prancing 'pon the white people road. Night fall long time as they travelling, and Calvin experimenting with the dip-lights and the high beam. It nice to play with. The FM radio thing ain' working good, cause Calvin never play one o' them radios before, and he forget to practise 'pon it when he was visiting the car in the lot after he pay-down something 'pon she, so that the salesman would keep it for him. So he working the AM thing overtime. A nice tune come on. Before the tune come on, he thinking again that the Canadian thing maybe the right woman for him: she nice, she tidy, and she quiet. And he was raise-up to like quiet women; his mother tell him so: "Never married a woman who ain' quiet, son, and that don't like church."

The tune is a calypso, man. "It's a nice calypso," Calvin say. "Sparrow, in your arse!" he shout, and he beg the Canadian pardon, he real excited because it is the first time he hear a calypso on the radio in Canada. He start liking Canada bad-bad again. "Look at me, though! New car! A Galaxie, and you beside me . . ."

The Canadian thing start wukking-up her behind beside o' Calvin; she start saying how she been going down in the islands for years now, that how she have more calypso records than any white woman in Toronto, and that she wish she had the money to take her boxes o' calypso records outta storage and play one or two for Calvin. She start singing the tune, and wukking-up some more. Calvin vex as hell. He don't like no woman who does sing calypso. His Old Queen didn' even let him sing calypsos when he was a boy in Barbados. And he is a *man*! Besides, the calypso that the Canadian thing singing the words to and wukking-up bad-bad to is a thing 'bout . . . *three white women travelling through Africa*!, and something 'bout *Uh never had a white meat yet*! and look at this nice woman, this simple-looking Canadian girl who know all the words, and she wukking-up and enjoying sheself *so*, and Calvin thinking that Sparrow watching him from through the AM radio speaker, and laughing at him, and he vex as shite, 'cause the calypso mean that certain white women like black men to lash them, and— "Don't sing that!" he order the thing, as if he talking to his wife; and the Canadian thing tell him, in a sharp voice, that she isn' his damn wife, so "Don't you be uppity with me, buster!"

Well, who tell she she could talk-back to a Bajan man like Calvin? Calvin slam on the brakes. The motor car cry-out *screeennnnchhhhhh!* The Canadian thing head hit the windshield, *bram!* and she neck like it break this time, in truth. The motor car halfway in the middle o' the highway. Traffics whizzing by, and the wind from them like it want to smash-up Calvin new Galaxie. Calvin vex as shite, but he can't do nothing 'cause he trembling like hell: the woman in the front seat turning white-white-white like a piece o' paper, and the blood gone outta she face; Calvin ain' see no dimples in she face; and she ain' moving, she ain' talking, not a muscle ain' shiver. Traffics whizzing by and one come so damn close that Calvin shut his two eyes, and ask God for mercy. "Look my blasted crosses! And my Galaxie ain' one kiss-me-arse day old yet!"

He try to start-up the motor and the motor only coughing like it have consumption. The woman meanwhile like she sleeping or dead or something. The calypso still blaring through the AM radio, and Calvin so jittery he can't find the right button to turn the blasted thing off. And sudden so, one of the traffics flying by turn into a Police. Calvin hear *weeeeeeeeeeeeeeeeeeennnnnnnnnnnnnnnnnnnnnnnn!* Sireens! A Police car in the rear-view mirror. Calvin stop shaking sudden-sudden. He start thinking. White woman deading in his new motor car, the car new, and he is a stranger in Canada. He jump out, and lift-up the hood, and he back his new jacket, and he touching this and touching that, playing he is a mechanic. The Police stop. The Police face red as a beet.

"What's holding you up, boy?"

Calvin hear the "boy" and he get vex, but he can't say nothing, 'cause they is two against his one, and he remember that he black. But he ain' no damn fool. He talk fast and sweet, and soft, and he impress the Police: ". . . and officer I *just now-now-now* give this lady a lift as I pass she on the highway, she say she feeling bad, and I was taking her to the hospital, 'cause as a West Indian I learn how to be a good Samaritan, and . . ." The police ask for the licents, and when he see that the ownership papers say that Calvin only had the car this morning, he smile, and say, "Help me get her into the cruiser, to the nearest hospital. You *are* a good Samaritan, fellow. Wish our native coloured people were more like you West Indians . . ."

They lift the Canadian thing with she neck half-popped outta the Galaxie and into the cruiser, and Calvin even had a tear in his eye too. But the police take she 'way, and the sireen start-up again, *weeeeeeennnnnnn* . . .

Calvin manage to get the Galaxie outta the middle o' the road, the traffics still flying by, but now the new motor car safe at the side o' the road. He put back on his jacket, and he shrug the jacket in shape and to fit his shoulders; he turn off the AM radio thing with the calypso—it was playing now another calypso—and fix the two creases in his trousers, look back on the highway in the rear-view mirror, and try to start-up the Galaxie. The Galaxie only coughing, and stuttering; not turning over at-all, at-all; and more traffics blowing their horn to tell him *get the fuck outta the road, nigger*, but the Galaxie only coughing. Outta habit, he hold over to say something to the Canadian thing who he thought was still beside him, forgetting that she ain' there no more, and he say, "You think I should buy the Cadillac?" The Canadian thing handbag left-back in the car on the seat open beside o' him, and he run his hand through it, and find five single dollar bills, and he wonder how much a taxi would cost, and if one would stop . . .

DOING RIGHT

I see him and I watch him. I see him and I watch him and I start to pray for him, 'cause I see him heading for trouble.

Making money. "In five or six years, I want to have a lotta money," he does-say. "Only when I have a lotta dollars will people respect me."

I had to laugh. Every time he say so, I does-have to laugh, 'cause I couldn't do nothing more better than laugh.

"Look at the Rockefellers. Look at the Rothschilds. Look at the Kennedys."

I was going-ask him if he know how they mek their money, but before I could-ask, he would be off dreaming and looking up at the ceiling where there was only cobwebs and dust; and only God knows what was circulating through his head every time he put himself in these deep reveries concerning making lots o' money and talking 'bout the Rockefellers, the Rothschilds, and the Kennedys.

I was still laughing. 'Cause the present job he had, was a green hornet job. He was a man who went to work in a green suit from head to foot, except the shoes, which was black and which he never polish. His profession was to go-round the St. Clair–Oakwood area where a lotta Wessindians does-live, putting parking tickets 'pon people cars. Before he start all this foolishness with Wessindians' cars, he uses to be on the Queen's Park beat for green hornets.

A big man like him, over two hundred pounds, healthy and strong and black, and all he could do after eight years as a immigrant, in the year 1983, is to walk-'bout with a little book in his hand, putting little yellow pieces o' paper on people windshields. He like the job so much and thought he did-doing the right thing that in the middle o' the night, during a poker game or just dipsy-doodling and talking 'bout women, he would put-back-on the green uniform jacket, grabble-up the peak cap, jump in the little green motor car that the Police give him, and gone straight up by St. Clair–Oakwood, up and down Northcliffe Boulevard, swing right 'pon Eglinton, gone down Eglinton, and swing left 'pon Park Hill Road, left again on Whitmore, and all he doing is putting these yellow pieces o' paper on decent, hard-working people cars. When he return, he does-be-laughing. I tell him he going-soon stop laughing, when a Wessindian lick-he-down with a big rock.

"I have fix them! I have ticketed one hundred and ten motto-cars today alone! And the night I leff the poker game, I ticket fifty more bastards, mainly Wessindians."

I start to get real frighten. 'Cause I know a lotta these Wessindians living in them very streets where he does-be ticketing and laughing. And all them Wessindians know who the green hornet is. And being as how they is Wessindians, I know they don't like green hornets nor nobody who does-be touching their cars. So I feel that any morning, when one o' these Wessindians come home from a party or offa a night shift and see him doing foolishness and putting yellow tickets 'pon their motor cars, I know um is at least *one* hand brek.

Wessindians accustom to parking in the middle o' the road, or on the wrong side, back home. And nobody don't trouble them nor touch their cars. And since they come here, many o' these Wessindians haven't tek-on a change in attitude in regards to who own the public road and who own the motor cars.

So whilst the boy still ticketing and laughing, and putting his hands on people cars which they just wash in the car wash on Bathurst, I continue worrying and watching him.

One night, just as we sit down to cut the cards, and before the cards deal, he come-in grinning, and saying, "I ticket two hundred motto-cars today alone!"

"One o' these days, boy!" I tell him.

"When I pass in the green car and I see him, I know I had him!"

"Who?"

"I see the car park by the fire hydrand. The chauffeur was leaning back in the seat. One hand outside the car window. With a cigarette in tha' hand. The next hand over the back o' the seat. I look in the car, and when I look in, I nearly had a fit. I recognize the pipe. I recognize the dark blue pinstripe suit. I recognize the hair. With the streak o' grey in um. And I mek a U-turn in the middle o' the road—"

"But a U-turn illegal!"

"I is a green hornet, man!"

"I see."

"I size-up the car. And I see the licents plate. ONT-001! I start getting nervous now. 'Cause I know that this motto-car belongst to the big man. Or the second most biggest man in Ontario. I draw up. The chauffeur nod to me and tell me, 'Fine day, eh?' I tell he, 'A very fine day, sir!' And I get out. I bend-over the bonnet o' this big, shiny, black car—"

"Limousine, man. A big car is call a limo."

"Well, um could have been a limo, a hearse, be-Christ, or a automobile, I still bend-over the bonnet and stick-on one o' the prettiest parking tickets in my whole career!"

"The Premier's car?"

"He mek the law. Not me!"

"And you think you do the right thing?"

"My legal bounden duty. Afterwards, I did-feel so good, like a real police officer and not a mere green hornet. And I walk-through Queen's Park on my two feet, looking for more official motto-cars to ticket. And when I was finish, I had stick-on *five* parking tickets in their arse . . . One belongst to the Attorney General too."

"The same man who does-defend Wessindians?"

"I put one 'pon Larry Grossman car too."

Well, that whole night, all the boy talking 'bout and laughing 'bout, is how he stick-on tickets on these big shots' cars, or limousines. And to make matters worse for the rest o' we, he win all the money in the poker game too. I feel now that the boy really going-become important, maybe, even become a real police, and make pure money. Or else going-lose a hand, or a foot.

But we was feeling good, though. 'Cause the big boys in Toronto don't particular' notice we unless um is Caribana weekend or when election time coming and they looking for votes, or when the *Star* doing a feature on racism and Wessindian immigrants that illegal, and they want a quotation. So we feel this green hornet is our ambassador, even if he is only a' ambassador o' parking tickets. So we does-laugh like hell at the boy's prowess and progress.

And we does-wait till a certain time on a Friday night, nervous as hell whilst cutting and dealing the cards, to see if the boy going-turn-up still dress-off in the green uniform, meaning that he hasn't get fired for ticketing the big shots' cars. And when he *does* turn-up, dress from head to trousers in green, we know he still have the job, and we does-laugh some more. But all the time I does-be still nervous, as I seeing him and watching him.

Then he start lossing weight. He start biting his fingernails. He start wearing the green uniform not press, and half dirty. He start calling we "*You* people!"

I getting frighten now, 'cause he tell me that they tek-him-off the Queen's Park beat.

So um is now that he up in St. Clair–Oakwood, and I feel he going-put a ticket on the *wrong* motor car, meaning a Wessindian car. And at least one hand brek. Or one foot. And if the particular motor car belongst to a Jamaican, not even the ones that have locks and does-wear the wool tams mek outta black, green, and red, I know um could be *both* foots and *both* hands!

I see him and I watch him.

"I have live in Trinidad, as a police," he tell me. "But I born in Barbados. I leff Trinidad because they won't let me ticket one hundred more cars and break the all-time record. I went to Guyana after Trinidad. I was a police in Guyana before Guyana was even Guyana and was still Demerara, or B.G. They make me leff Guyana when I get close to the record. Ten more tickets is all I had to ticket. From Guyana, I end up in Dominica. Same thing. From Dominica, I went to Antigua, and um was in Antigua that a fellow came close to licking-me-down for doing my legal duty, namely ticketing cars. But in all them countries, I ticket cars that belongst to prime ministers, ministers of guvvament, priests, civil servants, and school teachers."

I see him and I watch him. I see him getting more older than the forty-five years he say he was born; and I see him drinking straight rums, first thing every morning lately, because he say, "The nerves bad. Not that I becoming a alcoholic. I only taking the bad taste o' waking up so early outta my mouth. I am not a alcoholic, though. It is the pressure and the lack o' sleep."

But he was drunk. Cleveland was drunk-drunk-drunk early-early-early every day. He had to be really drunk after he outline his plan to make money to me.

"Remember the Rockefellers, man!" he tell me. "This is my plan. I been a green hornet for eight-nine years now. They promise me that if I ticket the most cars outta the whole group o' hornets, they would send me to training school to be a police. First they tell me I too short. I is five-four. But most criminals is five-three. Then they tell me that my arches fallen. Jesus Christ! What you expect? After all the beats I have walk in Trinidad, Guyana, Antigua, Dominica, and Grenada, my arches *bound* to fall! And eight-nine years in this damn country pounding the beat ticketing cars! But they can't beat me. Not me. This is the plan I got for their arse. Tickets begin at five dollars. Right? There is five dollars, ten dollars, and fifteen dollars. Right? Twenty dollars for parking beside a fire hydrand or on the wrong side. Right? Now, I write-up a ten-dollar ticket. And I change the ten to a forty. The stub in my book still saying ten. But the ticket on the car that also says ten, I going-change from ten to forty. Then I rush down to the vehicle registration place on Wellesley Street where they have all them computers. And I tell the fellow I know from Guyana something, *anything* to get him to look up the registration for me. And then I get in touch with the owner of the said vehicle and subtract ten from forty and—"

"You mean subtract ten years from forty!"

"You don't like my plan?"

"I think your plan worth ten years."

"Okay. What about this other one? People don't lock their motto-cars when they park. Right? Wessindians is the biggest vagabonds in regards to this. Right? A fellow don't lock his car. And um is night. And I got-on my green hornet uniform. Right? Meaning I am still operating in a official capacity . . ."

I see the boy start to smile, and his face spread and light-up like a new moon. The face was shining too, 'cause the heat and the sureness that the plan going-work this time make him sweat real bad. But I watching him. I know that Wessindians don't have much money, because they does-get the worst and lowest jobs in Toronto. Only certain kinds of Wessindians does-have money in their pocket. The kind that does-work night shift, especially after midnight, when everybody else sleeping; the brand o' Wessindian who I not going-mention by name in *case* they accuse me of categorizing the race. And being a reverse racist. But *certain* Wessindians, like hair-dressers, real estate salesmen, and fellows who know racehorses backwards and forwards, good-good-good, *plus* the unmentionable brand, namely the illegal immigrants, the illegal parkers, and them who hiding from the Police, them-so would have money to burn, inside their cars that not locked.

The boy eyes smiling. I see dollar bills instead o' pupils. I even hear the money clinking like when a car pass-over the piece o' black rubber-thing in a gas station. *Cling-cling.* "Gimme just three months," he say. "Gimme three bare months, and I going-show you something."

Just as I left him and walking 'cross Northcliffe Boulevard going to Eglinton, I see a green hornet fellow standing-up in front a fellow car. The fellow already inside the car. The fellow want to drive off. But the green hornet standing up in front the man car. The fellow inside the car honk the horn. And the green hornet fellow take out his black book. Slow-slow. And he flip back a page. And hold down a little. And start to write down the car licents. The fellow honk the car again. The hornet walk more closer. He tear off the little yellow piece o' paper. And getting ready to put it on the man brand-new-brand grey Thunderbird. Just as the hornet was about to ticket the man for parking next to a yellow fire hydrand, the fellow jump out. A Japanee samurai wrestler woulda look like a twig beside o' him. Pure muscle. Pure avoirdupois. Pure *latissimus dorsi*. Shoes shining bright. White shirt. Stripe tie. A three-piece grey suit. Hair slick back. And long. Gold 'pon two fingers on each hand. Gold on left wrist. More gold on right wrist. The hornet par'lyzed now. A rigor mortis o' fear turn the whole uniform and the man inside it to pure starch, or like how a pair o' pyjamas does-look when you left um out on the line in the dead o' winter.

"Goddamn!" the man say.

"You park wrong," the hornet say.

"Who say I park wrong?"

"You park illegal."

"Who goddamn say I park illegal?"

"Look at the sign."

"Which goddamn sign?"

"The sign that say NO PARKING BETWEEN FOUR AND SIX. And NO STOPPING ANYTIME. You not only park, but you stop. You stationary too." The Indian green hornet man's voice get high and shaky. "You have therefore park."

"Ahmma gonna give you two seconds, nigger, to take that god-damn ticket off my car, motherfucker!"

"What you call me? I am no damn nigger. I am Indian. Legal immigrant. I just doing my job for the City of Toronto in Metro-politan Toronto. *You* are a blasted Amerrican negro!"

Well, multiculturalism gone-out the window now!

All the pamphlets and the television commercials that show people of all colours laughing together and saying "We is Canadi-ans," all them advertisements in *Saturday Night* and *Maclean's*, all them speeches that ministers up in Ottawar make concerning the "different cultures that make up this great unified country of ours," all that lick-up now, and gone through the eddoes. One time. *Bram!*

The Goliath of a man grabble-hold of the hornet by the scruff o' the green uniform, the peak cap fall-off all like now-so, the little black book slide under the car, the hornet himself lifted up offa the ground by at least three inches, and shaking-'bout in the gulliver's hands, pelting-'bout his two legs like if he is a Muppet or a poppet; and when I anticipate that the fellow going-pelt him in the broad-road, the fellow just hefted him up a little more higher offa the ground, and lay him 'cross the bonnet of the shining Thunderbird, holding-he-down like how you does-hold-down a cat to tickle-he under his chin; and the fellow say, "Now, motherfucker! Is you gonna take the goddamn ticket off mah Bird?"

I pass 'long quick, bo'! 'Cause I know the Police does-be up in this St. Clair–Oakwood district like flies round a crocus bag o' sugar at the drop of a cloth hat; and that they does-tek-in anybody who near the scene o' crime, no matter how small the scene or how small the crime; and if um is Wessindians involve, pure hand-cuffs and licks, and pelting-'bout inside the back o' cruisers till they get you inside the station. And then the real sport does-start! So I looking and I looking-off, knowing that a green hornet, even if he look like a Pakistani or a Indian, but is really a Trinidadian or a Guyanese, and only look a little Indian, he going-get help from the Police. Not one Police. But five carloads o' Police.

All like now-so, the road full up with Wessindians and other people, and these Wessindians looking on and laughing, 'cause none o' them don't like green hornets, not even green hornets that come from the Wessindies!

I pass-'long quick, bo'. I got to face the Immigration people in a week and I don't want nothing concerning my past or present to be a stain through witnessing violence, to prevent them from stamping LANDED IMMIGRANT or IMMIGRANT REÇU in my Barbados passport! I may be a accessory before the fact.

But I was still thinking of my friend, the *other* green hornet, so I look back to see what kind o' judgement the Thunderbird-man was going-make with the Indian gentleman from Guyana, who now have no peak cap, no black notebook, one shoe fall-off, and the green tunic tear-up. And as my two eyes rested on the scene *after the fact* I hear the Charles Atlas of a man say, "And *don't* call the motherfucking cops! I got you covered, nigger. I knows where you goddam live!"

I hope that this Goliath of a man don't also know where my Bajan green hornet friend does-live! I hope the Thunderbird don't be park all the time up here! And I start to think 'bout getting a little message to my friend to tell him to don't put no tickets on no grey Thunderbirds, or even on no Wessindian cars, like Tornados, whiching is Wessindians' favourite cars. And I start to wonder if he know that a Wessindian does-treat a Tornado more better than he does-treat a woman or a wife; and with a Wessindian, yuh can't ask his woman for a dance at a dance unless you expecting some blows. Even if he give you permission to dance with his woman, don't dance a Isaac Hayes or a Barry White slow-piece too slow and too close, yuh . . .

I waiting anxious now, 'cause I don't see the boy for days, these days. I feel the boy already start making money from the scheme. I walk all over St. Clair–Oakwood, all along Northcliffe, swing right 'pon Eglinton, mek a left on Park Hill Road, a further left up by Whitmore, and find myself back 'pon Northcliffe going now in the opposite direction, and still I can't rest my two eyes on the green hornet. Fellows start telling me that the boy does-be going to the races every day, on his lunch break from ticketing people cars, and betting *one hundred dollars on the nose* and *five hundred to show* on one horse, and leffing the races with bundles o' money. And laughing like shite.

I walking-'bout day and night, all over St. Clair–Oakwood, and still no sight o' the boy.

Then, *bram!* I start hearing horror stories.

"I come out my apartment last Wednesday night to get in my car, and my blasted car not there! It gone. Tow-'way!" one fellow say.

A next fellow say, "Be-Christ, if I ever catch a police towing-'way my car!"

"I don't like this place. It too fascist. Tummuch regulations and laws. A man can't *breathe*. I can't tek it 'pon myself and lodge a complaint with the Police 'cause I here illegal. No work permit, yuh know? No job. Now, no car! You park your car, and when you come out in the cold morning to go-work at a li'l illegal job, no fucking car?"

"I was up by a little skins one night," a next fellow say. "I tell the wife I going by Spree. I tack-up by Northcliffe at the skin's apartment. I really and truly did-intend to spend only a hour. Well, with a few white rums in my arse, one thing lead to the next. And when I do-so, and open my two eyes, morning be-Christ brek, and um is daylight. My arse in trouble now, two times. Wife *and* wuk. I bound-down the fire escape, not to be seen by the neighbours, and when I reach ground, no blasted car!"

Stories o' motor cars that get tow-'way start spreading through the St. Clair–Oakwood neighbourhood, just like how the yellow leaves does-fall 'pon the grass a certain time o' year. Stories o' fellows getting lay-off, no work permit, getting beat-up, can't go to the Police in case, and getting lock-out, all this gloom start spreading like influenza. The fellows scared. The fellows vex. The fellows angry. And they can't go and complain to the Police to find out where their cars is, 'cause, yuh know, the papers not in order. As man! And the li'l matter o' *landed* and *reçu* and so on and so forth . . .

They can't even start calling the Police pigs and racists and criminals. And all this time, nobody can't find the green hornet boy at all.

Well, a plague o' tow-'way cars rest so heavy on my mind, even though I don't own no wheels, seeing as how I is a real TTC-man, that I get real concern. 'Cause, drunk or sober, blood more thicker than water . . .

"*As man!*"

I hear the voice and I bound-round. And look. I see cars. I see Wessindians. I don't see no Police, but I frighten. I see a tow-'way truck. And I still don't see nobody I know. But I think I recognize the voice.

"*As man!*"

I bound-round again, and I see the same things.

"Over here, man!"

God bless my eyesight! Um is the green hornet man. My friend! Sitting down behind the wheel of DO RIGHT TOWING 24 HOURS. I do-so, look! I blink my two eyes. I seeing, but I not seeing right. I watching, but I having eyes that see and that watch but they not watching right.

"Um is *me*, man!"

The tow-'way truck real pretty. It have-in shortwave radio. Two-way radio. CBC-FM. Stereos. *And* CB. It paint-up in black, yellow, and white. The green hornet boy, dress-off now in overalls and construction hat cock at a angle on his head, cigar in mouth and shades on his face, like if he is a dictator from Latin Amurca.

"Remember the plan? The plan I tell you 'bout for making money? Well, I went to my bank and talk to my bank manager and squeeze a loan for this outta the son of a bitch." He tap the door of the tow-truck like if he tapping a woman. "And I had a word with a fellow who was a green hornet like me. I is still a green hornet myself, but I works the afternoon shift. This fellow I know, the ex–green hornet, couldn't take the abuse and the threats to his person of being a hornet, so he open up a little place up in Scarborough where he *enpounds* the cars I does tow-'way. And me and him splits the money. I brings in a car, and quick-so, um lock-up and enpounded. If a fellow want-back his car, fifty dollars! You want piece o' this action?"

I get real frighten.

"You want to get cut-in 'pon this action?"

"But-but-but-but . . ."

"You see that pretty silver-grey Thunderbird park beside that fire hydrand? I watching that car now, fifteen minutes. I see the fellow park it, and go in the apartment building there. I figure if he coming back out soon, he going-come-out within twenty minutes. I got five more minutes . . ."

I start getting real frighten now. 'Cause I see the car. And the car is the *same* car that belongst to Goliath, the black Amurcan fellow.

I so frighten that I can't talk and warn my green hornet friend. But even if I coulda find words, my tow-truck friend too busy talking and telling me 'bout a piece o' the action and how easy it is to tow-'way cars that belongst to illegal immigrants and get money split fifty-fifty, and to remember the Rockefellers . . .

". . . and I had to laugh one day when I bring-in a Cadillac," he tell me, still laughing, as if he was still bringing-in the Cadillac. "Appears that my pound-friend had a little altercation or difference of opinion with a 'Murcan man over a car once, so when I appear with the silver-grey Caddy, he get frighten and start telling me that nobody not going maim him or brutalize him or curse his mother, that before anything like that happen, he would go-back home to Guyana first and pick welts offa reefs or put-out oyster pots down by the sea wall . . . Look, I got to go! Time up!"

I see him, and I watch him pull off from 'side o' me like if he didn't know me, like if I was a fire hydrand. I watch him drive up to the shiny grey Thunderbird car, not mekking no noise, like if he is a real police raiding a Wessindian booze-can after midnight. I see him get-out the tow-truck, like if he walking on ashes. I see him let-down the big iron-thing at the back o' the tow-truck. First time in my eleven years living here as a semi-legal immigrant that I have see a tow-truck that didn't make no noise. I see him bend-down and look under the front o' the Thunderbird. I see him wipe his hands. I see him wipe his two hands like a labourer who do a good job does-wipe his hands. I see him go-round to the back o' the Bird and bend-down. He wipe his two hands again. I see him size-up the car. I watch him put-on the two big canvas gloves on his two hands. I watch him cock the cigar at a more cockier angle, adjust the construction hat, tek-off the shades and put them inside his pocket, and I see him take the rope that mek out of iron and look like chain and hook-um-on 'pon the gentleman nice clean-and-polish grey 1983 Thunderbird. I seeing him and I watching him. The boy real professional. I wondering all the time where the boy learn this work. He dance round to the tow-truck and press a thing, and the Bird raising-up offa the road like if it ready to tek-off and fly. I see him press a next thing in the tow-truck and the bird stationary, but up in the air, at a angle, like a Concorde tekking-off. I see him bend-down again, to make-sure that the chain o' iron hook-on good. I see him wipe his two hands in the big canvas gloves a next time, and I see him slap his two hands, telling me from the distance where I is, watching, that it is a professional job, well done. I think I see the dollar bills registering in his two eyes too! And I see him tug the chain tight, so the Bird would move-off nice and slow, and not jerk nor make no noise, when he ready to tek she to the pound to *enpound* she.

And then I see the mountain of a man, tipping-toe down the metal fire escape o' the apartment building where he was, black shoes shining in the afternoon light, hair slick back and shining more brighter from a process, dress in the same three-piece suit, with the pinstripe visible now that the sun was touching the rich material at the right angle o' sheen and shine, and I see, or I think I see, the gentleman tek-off a diamond-and-gold ring two times offa his right hand, and put them in his pocket—I think I see that—and I see how the hand become big-big-big like a boxing glove, and I watching, but I can't open my mouth nor find voice and words to tell my former green hornet friend to look over his left shoulder. I seeing, but I can't talk o' what I seeing. I find I can't talk. I can only move. A tenseness seize the moment. I do *so*, and point my index finger, indicating like a spy telling another spy to don't talk, but to look behind.

But at that very moment, the black Amurcan gentleman's hand was already grabbling my friend from outta the cab o' the tow-truck . . .

FOUR STATIONS
IN HIS CIRCLE

Immigration transformed Jefferson Theophillis Belle; and after five years, made him deceitful, selfish, and very ambitious. It saddened his friend Brewster very much; but he had to confess that Jefferson was the most successful of them all. Still, Brewster pitied him. However, Jefferson had qualities which Brewster tried to emulate, even though JTB was not a likeable man. He was too ascetic, and pensive, and his friends hated him for it. But Jefferson had his mind on other things: a house and a piece of land around the house. "I must own a piece o' Canada!" Every morning going to work, as the Sherbourne bus entered Rosedale, he became tense. The houses in Rosedale were large and beautiful; and so far as he could guess they each had a fireplace . . . *because, man, I couldn't purchase a house unless it got a fireplace . . . that fire sparkling, and playing games on my face in the winter nights, crick-crack!* . . . and sometimes, at night, Jefferson would go to Rosedale (once he went at three in the morning) to watch the house he had put his mind on. But this house was not for sale! *Gorblummuh! That don't deter me though! 'Cause one o' these mornings it must go up for sale, and I will be standing up right here, with the money in my hand.*

One Friday night in the Paramount Tavern on Spadina with Brewster, Jefferson had a great urge to see his property. He paid for the drinks; said he had to go to the men's room; slipped out through the back door; and nearly ran into a taxi driver hustling women and passengers. He raised his hand to call the taxicab. But he realized that he had already spent a foolish dollar on Brewster;

so he changed his mind, and mentally deposited that dollar bill to the $10,000 he had in the bank; and he set out on foot. The wind was chilly. *Look how I nearly throw-'way that dollar 'pon foolishness! I am still a very strong man at forty. I could walk from Spadina to Rosedale, man.* And when he heard his own voice say how wise he was, he walked even faster. Anxiously, he grabbed his left back trousers pocket; "Oh!" he said, and a laugh came out. He didn't trust anybody; certainly not Brewster. He was very glad the money was in his pocket; and yet, for a second, he imagined that the money was actually stolen, and by Brewster. So he unpinned the two safety pins, undid the button, and took out the money, wrapped in a dirty black handkerchief. His experiences with money had made him uneasy. Any day he might need it for the down payment (although he could not have known what it would be); and if he wanted a house in Rosedale, he must be prepared.

He walked slowly now (there was money in his hand) and when he came under a light, he counted it. Nine hundred dollars. This money went to work with him; went to church with him; went into the washroom at work and at home with him; and when he went to bed, it was pinned to his pyjamas. "Nine! Right!" He had so much money now, he counted only in hundreds. He put the money back into his pocket; pinned it, twice; and buttoned it down. And before he moved on, he made a promise to change the handkerchief. *Five years! Five years I come to this country, with one pair o' shoes!*

Sometimes, in weaker moments, he would argue with himself to get some education too. Coming through the university grounds once, by chance, he saw a line of men and women crossing the lawn, with the lawn strewn with roses and flashbulbs and cheers and laughter, and a few tears to give significance to the roses and the bulbs; and he felt then, seeing the procession, the power of education and of the surrounding buildings. And he had shaken his head, and run away. The three hours following, he had spent forgetting and getting drunk in the Paramount. That was five years ago. Now, he did not have to run. He walked through the grounds jauntily this time, because he had nine hundred dollars, in cash, in his pocket. And as he came out, to enter Queen's Park, he saw two shadows; and the two shadows grew into two forms; and one form was raising the skirt above the thighs of the other form; and when they saw him coming, the man covered the girl's reputation with his jacket. They remained still, pretending they were shadows, until a passing car pointed its finger at the girl's back; and Jefferson saw UNIVERSITY OF TORONTO, written in white letters on the man's jacket she was wearing. *Goddamn, he's so broke through education, he can't afford a hotel room!*

Far along Bloor Street, the boasting water-van is littering Toronto and making some pedestrians wet; and a man holds half of his body through the driver's window, and says, "'Night!" and this greeting carries JTB into Rosedale, quiet as a reservation.

Five years of hard work have brought him here, tonight, in front of this huge mansion. *I going have to paint them windows green; and throw a coat o' black paint on the doors . . . The screens in the windows will be green like in the West Indies . . . I going pull up them flowers and put in roses, red ones; and build a paling, and build up my property value . . .* And he goes up on the lawn and tries to count the rooms in the four-storey house. *Imagine me in this house with four storeys! And not one blasted tenant or boarder!* But he cannot count all the rooms from the front, so he goes through the alleyway to look at the backyard, and the rooms in the back, and . . . (a car passes; and the man driving turns his head left, and sees a shadow; and he slows down, and the shadow becomes a form; he stops, says something on the radio in the car; parks the car; walks back; and waits) . . . and Jefferson comes humming back to the front lawn, and tries again to count, and four men pounce upon him and drag him along his lawn, with hands on his mouth and some in his guts, and drop him in the back seat of the cruiser. He can hear voices, talking at the same time, coming through the radio speaker. "Good!" a living voice says. "Take him to Division Two." And they did that.

Jefferson Theophillis Belle, of no fixed address, unknown, labourer unskilled, spent a very long time before he convinced them that he was not a "burglourer"; and in all that time, his head was spinning from the questions and from the blows: because "You were walking around this respectable district, this time of night, with all that money on your person, and you're not a *burglourer*? To buy a house, eh? That doesn't even have a FOR SALE sign up? Who are you kidding, mack? And they gave him one final kick of warning; and with his pride injured (*God blind you, cop! One o' these days I'm going to kill me a cop! So help me God!*), he woke up Brewster, to see what *he* thought. *They should still be kicking-in your behind!* Brewster said in his heart, as he rubbed the sleep out of his eyes. Without compassion, he dropped the telephone on Jefferson; and when he got back into bed, his blanket was rising and falling from the breath of his laughter and unkind wishes—*should have kicked-in your arse, boy!* Brewster couldn't wait for morning and the Paramount to talk about it.

After this, Jefferson decided to visit Rosedale in the daytime only. When paydays came, every cent went into his bank; and his balance climbed like a mountain; similarly, his hate for the Police. A week later he took out a summons against Brewster, who owed him twenty dollars from three years ago. He tried to get him arrested, but his lawyer advised otherwise; so Jefferson settled for a collection agency. The collection agency got the money back, but Jefferson gave it back to Brewster. This success convinced him further that business was more important than intellect; money more important still. He had seen Jews in the Spadina garment district; he had seen Polish immigrants in the Jewish market; he had seen their expensive automobiles going *north* after a beautiful day of swelling profits; and he said, *Me, too! Soon I going north, tambien!*

He stopped drinking at the Paramount. He stopped going to the Silver Dollar for funk, broads, rhythm, blues, and jazz. He didn't want to see any more black people. He spent more time in his room, alone. On weekends he watched television and drank beer; and rechecked his bank book, *because anybody could make a mistake, but be-Christ, they not making no mistake with my money!* His actions and his movements became tense, more ordered. His disposition became rawer; and once or twice he lost his temper with his super-visor at the post office (his part-time night job) and almost lost his job; but he lost only a slice of pride apologizing.

The hate that grew in his heart because the Police presumed he was a burglar, that he could be burglarizing the house of his dreams (*God blind you, Mister Policeman. I am a man too.*), presuming that he, Jefferson Theophillis Belle, a black Barbadian, could only through crime possess nine hundred dollars in cash (*Double-blind you, Mister Ossifer! When I am working off my arse, where are . . . ?*), was systemati-cally eating away his heart and mind. In isolation he tried to find some solace. He would tell himself jokes, and laugh aloud at his own jokes. Still, something was missing. The boisterousness of the Paramount was gone. He no longer enjoyed Saturday mornings in the Negro barber shop on Dundas, where he and others, middle-aged and cronied, would sit waiting for the chair, laughing them-selves into hiccups with jokes, with the barber, about women they knew when they were younger men. He went instead *north*, from Baldwin Street to the Italian barber on College. The haircuts there were worse, and more expensive; and time did not improve them.

He had almost walked away from his past when, on that bright Saturday morning—"Goddamn, baby!"—the Voice picked him out, sneaking out of the Italian barber's, brushing the hair out of his neck. He squirmed, because he recognized the voice. It came again, loud and vulgar. "I say, goddamn, baby!" Jefferson pretended he was just one of the European immigrants walking the street. And he walked on, hiding his head in invisible shame. The Voice had disappeared. He relaxed and breathed more easily. And suddenly he felt the hand on his neck, and "Goddammit! Baby, ain't you speak-ing to no niggers this morning, you sweet black motherfucker?" All the eyes in the foreign-language heads turned to listen. Then in a voice that the eyes couldn't hear, Brewster said, "Lend me a coupla bucks, baby. Races."

Jefferson Theophillis Belle made a mental note, right then, never again to speak to black people.

He found himself walking through the campus grounds again, spending long hours pondering the stern buildings; the library crammed with knowledge in print, and the building where he had seen the lines of penguins dressed in black and white, like graduate scholars. *Education is a funny thing, heh-heh-heh! And I had better get a piece o' that, too.* He argued himself into a piece of education; but he held fast to the piece of property too. He visited some institutions, and took away their prospectuses to study . . . *These things make me out as if I don't know two and two is four, that the world round, that Columbus discover it in 1492, that that bastard sailed down in my islands and come back and called them* Indian, *hah-hah! . . . If it was me make that mistake, my boss would fire my arse, tomorrow! I am an educated man, therefore.*

And he began to see himself in the diplomatic service.

He telephoned the university to see how he could become a diplomat; and after the initial silence of shock, the woman's voice advised him to read *all* the histories of the world. He borrowed a book, *The History of the World*, from the public library on College Street, and an *Atlas of the World*, and he turned on the television set instead.

Mr. Jefferson Theophillis Belle was written on each of the four envelopes that brought more prospectuses. He felt inferior that nothing was written behind his name. So he wrote on each envelope, behind his name: *BA, PhD, MA, MLitt, DLitt, Diploma in Diplomacy, Barbadian Ambassador to Canada.* And he laughed. Then he got a basin, a new one, lit a match, and burned everything. (The last to burn was the prospectus from the Department of History in the university.) He watched all the knowledge he might have had burn and consume; and he laughed. This was on a Sunday; and he went on the couch, drinking and watching television. After a while he fell back on the couch, quite suddenly, as if the string that regulated his life was cut. The half-empty bottle of warm beer was still in his hand; the landlady passing through after bingo at her church pushed the door to say "Night-night!" and saw him on the couch. She turned off the television; she put the large "Plan of the Grounds of Ryerson" over his face; she took the bottle from his hand, and drank it off. She put two others in her coat pockets, said "Bringing them back" to the two beers, and she left.

Monday came too early. He could feel pebbles of hangover in his eyes; and the raucous shouting of his landlady: "You really tied one on last night, Mr. Jefferson Belle. You really tied one . . ." was like an enamel plate banged on stone against his temples. And then, suddenly, he came to a dead stop before his 1949 Pontiac. Some-body had scratched FACT YOU, MUCK in shaky inebriated grease on the frost of his windshield and trunk. *A thing like this couldn't happen up in Rosedale. It couldn't.* All that day, at his full-time paint factory job, and all that night at the post office, he was tense.

He soon discovered that his energy was being sapped from him. He wondered whether he should quit his night job; he had enough money now; but *no, man, the house in Rosedale, man!* He worked harder that night, and when he went home, he did twenty-three push-ups. And then it happened!

A FOR SALE sign appeared—on the house *beside* his house. This threw him into a fit, trying to decide whether to buy that house (it was empty, no furniture, and had thirteen rooms), when a letter came from home. He recognized his mother's handwriting on the red-white-and-blue airmail envelope, and refused to open it. The tension came back. He took the letter to the light bulb, to see if he could read the news inside without opening it . . . *Look, Jeff, boy! Opportunity does knock only one time in Rosedale* . . . And that was it. He called the real estate agent, and arranged the purchase.

The tenseness left him. He could see himself cutting red luxuri-ant roses he had planted; waving his hand at a beautiful woman; calling her, and pinning a rose on her bosom; but the rose he held in his hand now was the real estate agent's number; and when he real-ized this, he tore it up. The paper petals fell without a noise. But he was now Jefferson Theophillis Belle, Esquire, Landowner and Prop-erty Owner, Public School Tax-payer (he had no children!) . . . He would give his occupation in the voters list as "Engineer, retired" . . . *The letter, though, Jeff! Stop this blasted dreaming 'bout house and land and see what the Old Queen have to say, and don't let more sorrow fall 'pon your head; and remember where you beginned from, 'cause a mother is a mother, boy, 'cause—*

> *Dear Jeff, when you left this island I ask God to help you. Now, I want you and God to help me. I know He help you, because somebody tell me so, and still you have not send me one blind cent. But God understand. You did not know I was laid up with a great sickness? I have a new doctor now, a Bajan, who studied medicines up in Canada, where you is. He told me you can help me, because they is a lot of money in Canada. I need a operation. I feel bad to ask you, though. But, I am, Your Mother.*
> (signed) *Mother.*
> POSTSCRIPT: *House spots selling dirt-cheap now in Barbados. Think.*
> *Love, Mother.*
> *Don't forget to read your Bible, Jefferson; it is God words, son.*
> *Love, again, still, Mother.*

Months later, in Rosedale, he would see the page burning; and the words would haunt him, in whispers; and he would tell himself that he should have torn up the letter only; and not the bible too. But when he had put his hands to it that day, he had no idea that it was such a fragile book . . . and he should have sent the money to his mother, sick then; dead, probably, now . . . the page, the last page before the bible cried out in the fire; and the line "Remember not the sins of my youth, nor my transgressions" . . . but life in Rosedale flourished like a red rose.

An invitation card of gold embossed print was dropped through his letterbox. He did not notice the name on the envelope which he tore up and tossed away; but he read that Miss Emilie Elizabeth Heatherington was engaged to Mr. Asquith Breighington-Kelly; and they were having a party, at Number 46—next door.

This pleased Jefferson. The next day, he joined Theophillis to Belle with a hyphen. For three days, he sunned his suit to kill the evil fragrance of camphor balls. He dressed for the party, and waited behind his curtains made of newspapers to watch the first guests arriving. Everyone was in formal wear. They came in Jaguars, in Lincolns and Cadillacs. He took off his brown suit, lit his fireplace, and spent the evening sitting on an onion crate. Long after he had return-posted his invitation in the flames, in anger and disappointment, he could still hear the merriment next door. He wondered why nobody called him.

But the fire died, and he was awakened by cramp and a dream of his mother. He puttered around his house; and he drew some parallel lines on the walls of three rooms, as bookcases; and he drew books between the lines, until he could get some real books from the Book of the Month Club. Before going to bed, he decided to change his car. He must buy a new car, because *living in a district like this, and being the onliest man who does do work with his bare hands, and, and-and . . . that oil company president next door, Godblindhim!* comes along, limping on the weight of his walking stick, and smells the freshness of the grass and water and roses, and looks up and smiles and says, "Evening! Have you heard when *they're* coming back?" Jefferson always pretended he didn't understand. Another time, the old oil man said, "You're a darn fine gardener. Best these people ever had; and better than those Italians, too!" He had said this on the afternoon of the party . . . and thinking about the old man's words, Jefferson had to look at that invitation again, to see something very important on it. But he remembered he had burned both the envelope and the invitation. He vowed never again to burn anything. There were many invitations printed in the blood of ink, and many Bibles with "*Remember not the sins of my youth*" printed on every page.

He traded his Pontiac for a 1965 Jaguar, automatic. It was long, sleek, and black. After this, he dressed in a three-piece suit for work, with a black briefcase. In the briefcase were old shoes, work shirt, and overalls. He would change into these in the men's room of the East End Café, near East End Paints Ltd., where he worked as Janitor and Maintenance, General. He bought a formal morning suit *and* a tuxedo for evening formal occasions.

Some time after, the stick that walked out with the old oilman next door tapped and stopped and said, "When? Are *they* coming back?" Jefferson got mad, and told him, "Look, I own this, yuh! And the name is Jefferson Theophillis-Belle!" The man of oil stretched out his hand, grabbed JT-B's, and said, amiably, "I'm Bill!"

Jefferson has just come home on this Friday afternoon, and is changing into his night-shift clothes (there was no danger of being caught at night) when the doorbell rings. It is his first caller. He looks at the half-eaten sandwich of peanut butter, and wonders what to do with it (the doorbell is ringing); and he can feel himself losing weight; and he wishes he had filled the prescription the doctor gave him for tension . . . He stops before the mirror he had hung in his imagination on the wall in the hall, to see if peanut butter is between his teeth . . . But it is only Bill's wife, who came to invite him, for the second time, to the party on Saturday—when the scandalous Voice from his past entered and shrieked, "God-*damn*! Ain't you one big sweet black motherfu—" and Jefferson rushed out of one room and whispered, "Christ, man! Not now! Some-body here!" But the Voice, thinking past is present, said, "Man, we was looking for you for a crap game, last Sar'day night, baby! Man, those fellas drink whiskey like water!"—and Bill's wife came in, smiled, and said, "You're busy, but don't forget, Satteedee." And she left. Jefferson jumped into a rage; but the Voice merely asked, "What I do?" And after looking through the first room, and the second, the Voice exclaimed, "But wait, Jeff! Where is the blasted furnitures, man?"

In the Jaguar, speeding out of Rosedale, the Voice was silent. "You ask me what you do?" Jefferson said at last. "But it is more as if I should ask myself, what *I* do?" The Voice took a long pull on his cigarette, and said, "Baby, you made your bed. Now, goddamn, lie down in it!" And he slapped Jefferson goodbye, and said, "Let me off here. I want to get blind drunk tonight."

They were opposite the Paramount. Jefferson had forgotten the landmarks on this street; he had forgotten the smoke and vapour from the Southern-fried chicken wings fried in fat, in haste, by the

Chinaman whose face never showed a change in emotion; and in forgetting all these, he had forgotten to have time, in Rosedale, to enjoy himself . . . A party of rich, educated people of Holt Renfrew tastes; he, always, ill at ease: "Now, Mr. Theophillis-Belle, as a P.Eng., structural, I ask you, what do you consider to be the structural aesthetics of our new City Hall?"

In less champagned-and-whiskied company his answer, which showed his ignorance—"*That?*"—might not have brought cheers. And the Jewish jokes and Polish jokes, and he, Structural and Jefferson and Engineer, dreading every moment, in case the jokes change into negro jokes; or walking beneath a crystal chandelier and praying he won't touch it, and break it, and have to offer (out of courtesy) to replace it (and finding that he had to!); and standing before the mirror on Bill's wall, and suddenly seeing that he was not, after all, the fairest reflection of them all; and running out through the door . . . Jefferson turned off the car lights, and sat thinking; and Brewster appeared from nowhere with a white woman on his arm, sauntering to the LADIES AND ESCORTS entrance.

Since he has been living in Rosedale, Jefferson has not taken a woman—nor black nor white nor blue—up his front steps.

He blew his horn. Brewster looked back. The woman looked too, and said, "Piss off!" He closed the car door. He started the car.

He drove beside the Paramount, hoping to see Brewster. But only a drunk came out; and when he saw Jefferson he raised his hand, and coughed and vomited on the gravel beside the LADIES AND ESCORTS . . . Well, he might turn west for Baldwin Street, to see his ex-landlady, to see if the house is still there, or if the city or Teperman Wreckers have . . . But he turned east, for the post office. That night, he forgot to notice the letters addressed to Rosedale; he spent his time thinking of formal parties. All of a sudden he had a very disturbing vision which destroyed his joy in formal suits: instead of being at Bill's party, dressed and formal as an undertaker, he saw himself in a funeral parlour, laid out, tidy and dead, prepared for burial, with his hands clasped on the visible cummerbund; and on the cummerbund, his gold ring and his pocket watch.

Jefferson wondered who would dress him for his coffin; would the person remember to include *both* formal suits (he was thinking evil of Brewster)? Who would get his life insurance on his death? And his life savings, $300 and descending because of the new Jaguar, and the formal suits and the new curtains, and the True-Form mattress he had ordered yesterday from Eaton's, because the canvas cot was leaving marks and pains in his back . . . his hands trembling with the letters in them, for twenty-three minutes; and before he knew it, the supervisor was there. "Come with me!"

Ten minutes later, three hours before his shift should have ended, he still could not understand why he hadn't killed the supervisor; why he had stood like a fool, silent, without explaining that he was a man under doctor's prescriptions, for tension; and w*hy, goddammit! he hadn't flatten his arse with a right! or smash-in his false teeth, because I've been on this post office job more than four years, even before that bastard* . . . But he was entering tranquility and Rosedale now, and the only person he saw on the road was a black man: *a black man, in my Rosedale, at this time?* And then he saw her, close as a leech, walking beside him.

His house was empty and quiet. Tired now, he undressed, and stood for a while, thinking of what to do. He put on his pyjamas. He got into his cot. He got out of his cot; and dressed himself in his evening formal tuxedo. It was two o'clock Saturday, *A.M.*! He walked up to the full-length mirror on the wall, and smiled at the reflection the wall and his imagination threw back; and he adjusted his hat in the wall; straightened his shoulders and started walking in and out of each of the thirteen rooms, smiling at women—black women, white women, blue women—and it was *such a good evening, Miss Jordan . . . good evening, Bill, thanks . . . lovely party . . . Lady Hawgh-Hawgh, the name is Theophillis-Belle, engineer, structural and retired, haw-haw! . . . oh, Mr. Stein! I can now purchase four thousand shares at five . . . my solicitors will contact you, tomorrow, Monday . . . haw-haw! of course, it's Sunday! . . . and don't call me, I'll call thee, haw-haw! . . . well you see, Lady Hawgh-Hawgh, I was having cocktails in the*

Russian Embassy, discussing the possibility of granting nuclear weapons to Barbados and other Caribbean territories, when—Brewster entered.

Only later did JT-B notice the woman there. Brewster was saying, "Jesus God! Jesus God!" over and over. And the woman's mouth was open, in terror and pity. *Comrade, may I introduce my colleague, the African delegate from*—"What the hell you playing, boy? You don't know Brewster? I just pass you on the street!"—*and his charming wife, also from . . . Africa?* Brewster had to laugh. "Look you, you foolish bitch!" he said. "Take this." The telegram fell in front of Jefferson. "Your landlady send that. She had to open it, 'cause she couldn't find you. It's your mother. She *dead*, boy!" . . . *Thank you, thank you, comrade, for these tidings . . .* and Jefferson Theophillis-Belle continued to walk up and down the hollow house (Brewster and the woman still staring), muttering greetings in whispers to his guests, and answering himself; and holding the telegram in his left hand, that hand resting militarily on the black cummerbund, as he bowed and walked, walked and bowed, bowed and walked . . .

A FUNERAL

It was about a hundred degrees in the shade. It was about four o'clock in the afternoon. Clothes was sticking to your back. And the road was full o' people going home from work.

The long black hearse, build in the days when they was coaches, when coaches was drawn by two sweating horses, was now without horses, and had-in a six-horsepower engine. The island's biggest, the leading undertaker, or duppy agent, was driving the hearse.

It was a solemn afternoon. A final journey. And the hearse was decorated with white flowers and mauve flowers, and there was other flowers drawn-in, in white delicate paint, all over the glass panels of the hearse.

The hearse was moving slow-slow over the road, like if it was a fat, sad slug. Like a dew-wirrum.

All the roads in the capital was really crowded. Jam-packed with people. Men and women going home from work, and men who was just strolling, being as how they was unemploy, had slacken-off their pace, and stop, just to watch. Some o' them stop their bicycles, with one foot on the ground for balance. All them-so watched and waited until the procession pass them.

Rain had fall the night before. And first thing in the morning. So the road was clean. The air was clean and humid. The road wasn't clean, because o' the road-sweepers or the garbagemen, 'cause they was on strike. Um was clean mainly because of the torrents o' rain that had fall.

Yuh couldn't pass at all. Um was impossible to pass. So the people decide to wait. People who had to wait and who decide to become mourners on the spot, and the other people who had nothing more better to do, all them-so join-in in the procession.

"What a lovely funeral!" a old woman say. And straight off she make the sign of the cross. Two times on her chest. "Incidentally, who dead?"

"A gravedigger," a man say.

"I hope they have one leff-back for *his* sake," the old woman say.

And you couldn't hear anything more she say, and if she did intend to say anything else, anyhow, the crowd overpowered her words. And soon she herself was lost in the procession.

The Member of Parlment fur Sin-James East was there among the mourners who was walking. He was dress in the same formal suit that he had-on when he was first elected an MP, at his inauguration, ten years ago. Beside him was Seabert the tailor. Seabert was wearing a new formal black suit, a twin off the pattern that the MP was wearing. But being as how Seabert was a tailor, he put-on some pretty glamorous touches on the suit, to make him and the suit look more pretty. The suit that Seabert was wearing had come from the same piece o' material he had promise to sell to Sarge.

And behind the MP was Sarge, official in police black, with brass and silver crisscrossing his chest and back. Then Nathan, a friend of the dead man, in a black suit that had turn mauve through age and mothballs. And already Nathan was sweating-up the suit under the armpits.

The Guvvament had organize some real strict public relations to go along with the funeral. The man that was in the coffin was a Guvvament supporter. The Guvvament had decide to make the funeral an effective funeral and a politically beneficial funeral to boot.

Every Cabinet minister was present. The Prime Minister himself was leading the double line o' dignitaries. He had the Guvvament pass a ordnance saying that all people at the funeral, especially the officials, was to get outta their cars or hop-off their bicycles about a half-mile to a mile from the main gate o' the cemetery and *walk* on their two feet, slow-slow through the streets.

"That way," the Prime Minister had say at the executive meeting that morning, "we will be killing two birds with one rock-stone. We will be showing *pure* grief. In public. And also our concern for the *small* man."

They all laugh-out hard-hard when the Prime Minister say so.

"Be-Christ!" he went on, laughing himself, more louder than any of the Cabinet ministers. "Be-Christ, I don't even want to remind any o' wunnuh in here, none o' you. I don't want to have to remind none o' you. I don't want to say um more than one time. This party is the party of the small man. It is a small-man party. And if any o' you here present this morning, particularly one or two who I hear want to tek-over power from me and be Prime Minister, even before I resign or dead like Lionel . . . Well, lemme tell you bastards something now. If any one o' you in here now don't understand why we *walking* that last mile on foot behind Lionel coffin, that stupid bitch who couldn't do nothing more profitable than slam a domino . . . Well, ask the present MP for Westbury North, then! Ask *him*. Ask him 'bout the problems we getting down there near the cemetery. We getting more political licks in the Cemetery constituency than what John dream 'bout. So! This is a political funeral. Lionel will be buried *politically*. Hence! We walking that last mile, outta *pure* politics, on foot! And be-Christ, when they drop Lionel coffin in that hole after we walk-through Westbury North and the Cemetery constituency, I want each and every one o' you sons o' bitches here present to start crying. You hear me? *Weep!* Bawl-out with sorrow. Cry like shite! My political experience tell me that there going be more votes swinging to our man in that constituency than what John write 'bout!"

So the Prime Minister was walking at the head o' the Cabinet, followed by other party officials plus a detachment of the police force, walking slow-slow through the heat and humidity that you could almost cut with a knife, it was so damn hot.

And the moment they come into view, the people went wild and start screeling.

"Skipper! Skipper! Skipper!"

Once or twice the Prime Minister give a nudge to the MP for Westbury North, and whisper something outta the corner of his mouth, the left-hand corner, with a cynical, sly smile covering his face.

"What I tell you, man?"

The MP for Westbury North say, "Remind me, Skipper, to give you a report of a rumour I hear from a friend, who hear it from a reliable confidential source. It 'bout the two fellows in the party who planning to overthrow you, and—"

"We going break their arse!"

"*Lash-their-arse-at-the-polls!*" the people screel out.

The Prime Minister then take-off his rimless spectacles offa his face, and smile and mop his brown face, and smile some more with the people.

"*Skipper! Skipper! Skipper!*"

The Prime Minister skin was high brown. Like a piece o' polished leather. He was tall-tall. Like a athlete. And had a handsome body. The people who know and people who don't really know say that he does sleep in the beds o' more married women than what John could count or what anybody dare to 'numerate and tally. He does move like a dancer. And today, he move like one. Like a limbo dancer. Like a cat on ashes through the thickness o' the crowd, through the thickness o' the smells and body odours of the crowd.

He smelled the bodies o' the crowd. He smelled the perspiration dripping down from them, the odours, the sweat, the perfumes, and the rum smells. The crowd was too close for comfort and for the Prime Minister's aristocratic sense o' things. He didn't like smells. He didn't like them being so close.

Sometimes, working late at night in his office or driving home from the residence of one of his ministers who was overseas on Guvvament business, he would get sad, sad even to the point o' depression, when he compare his life o' graciousness, champagne and strawberries, Epsom Darby, and night life at Cambridge University to the poor-arse country with people who smell, who had no hope, who indulge in crime, a country with financial problems, when he could be cocking-up his two feet still in Hampstead or in Piccadilly Circus. The budget o' the country was never balance since he became Prime Minister. The budget could never be balance.

But now he remembered where he was, so he merely jerk his nostril in disgust. The smell of the people disappear. And immediately after, he start to smile.

"*Lick-in their arse at the polls, Skipper! Mash-them-up! Paint their arse black and blue on voting day, Skipper!*" the people went on shouting, falling in love with their leader.

He put-back-on his spectacles on his face, and he look more younger and more powerful than when he wasn't wearing glasses.

All like now-so, the procession reach 'round the last corner before entering in the main gate o' the cemetery. There was a sidewalk in this part of the walk. So the crowd grow more louder, more longer, and more larger. Space, or the lack o' space, now turn into tension and quarrelling. And the smell o' the poor people plus the smell o' the mayflower trees overhanging the cemetery, and the bougainvillea vines that was crawling over some neglected graves, these smells was mixed up and was turn into a real strong nauseating sensation.

"You walking with your gun?" the Prime Minister say to the MP for Westbury North in a whisper, outta the corner of his mouth. The left-hand corner. "I don't like this crowd, yuh. I don't like these people. And I know blasted well that these bitches don't like me. You have-on your gun in your holster? Just in case?"

"But, Skipper, you *knows* me! You knows full well that I sleeps with my wompuh in my hand! How you mean?"

"Well, I feel better, then."

The main gate was so close that it look as if it had feet and was coming to meet them. They was people like peas, like sand, in the procession all like now-so. So they had to force and push themselves through the narrow iron gates as if they was catching a passenger bus that was the last bus for the night. It take 'bout a hour to a hour and a half before all the official mourners plus the police plus the security guards plus all the people who had join the cortege could squeeze through the main gate.

The Guvvament had tell the Cemetery Board and the gravediggers that was off-duty to come to work, and that the minute after the last person who look like a real mourner step through the gate, to close the blasted gate.

And this happen like clockwork. Pretty-pretty this directive of the Guvvament was directed. This guvvament was a real efficient guvvament. Everything work. Political murders; firings from guvvament posts; the hiring o' girlfriends, kip-misses, and chossels to high guvvament positions; the slot machines whiching the people branded one-hand bandits; plus the thiefing and mispropriation o' guvvament funds; all these things-so work like if the Mafia was running the country and not ordinary, common politicians. Every-fucking-thing work. Most unlike the things that the previous guvvament did try to do; and *that* guvvament was a democratic guvvament.

The Prime Minister had personally ordered some members of his security force to pose as mourners and walk in the middle of the crowd. He didn't want to take no chances with the people. So one hundred of the roughest, one hundred of the most loyal members of the Security Force was assign to this funeral.

Reporters and cameramen from the radio station and from the three newspapers was all over the place. The Guvvament had plan to put the funeral on the radio news that night as the first item. Naturally, the Prime Minister would be on the front pages of all three morning newspapers.

So when enough of the people had reach the grave, the Dean, dress like damnation in black, from head to foot, black covering his black body, and with his tortoiseshell spectacles shining in the dying light, whiching was fighting its way to come through the large, thick leaves of the almond trees shimmering all round the graveside, then and only then did the Very Rendable Dean begin the Order of the Burial of the Dead.

At seven o'clock the morning before, the Prime Minister had telephone the Lord Bishop of the country to tell him that he want *he*, His Lordship, to officiate. In addition to the Very Rendable Dean. But the Lord Bishop, who wasn't sick, said in a weak voice, "Excellency, I sorry-sorry, sir. I have a migraine that killing me, Excellency. As you know from the last time you see me, I been under doctor's care. For two weeks now, going 'pon three. And I even had to cancel all my church app'intments, and . . . and . . ."

The Lord Bishop was a secret supporter of the opposition party.

But before he could complete his excuses and apologies and entreaties, the Prime Minister had slam-down the telephone a long time. "I waiting on His Lordship. He may know about Sodom and Gomorrah, but I have a file on his arse concerning sodomy and Gomorrah. I waiting on that son of a bitch!"

So they had to settle for the Dean only.

But the Dean did already behaving as if he did already the Lord Bishop of the country. And one night he utter a wish 'bout his ambition loud enough and in the well-chosen hearing o' some Cabinet ministers, who laughed-out and remind him whilst laughing that the Lord Bishop was not even born in the country, so anything could happen one o' these dark nights.

And the night that Lionel's murder was announce on the radio news, the Dean say to his wife, "But why it couldn't be the Bishop? Instead o' that fool, Lionel?"

Lionel had get stabbed during a argument over a game o' dominoes. The fellow who stab him say that Lionel had hide the key card, the very card he did need to beat Lionel and win the tournament. But the Bishop, as far as the Dean did know, didn't play dominoes!

Lionel, before he dead, was also the Deputy Head Gravedigger at the Westbury Cemetery. The Very Rendable Dean really like big, pretty ceremonies. Official receptions, pompous gatherings, military parades, and social events did always bring out the best in his civilize nature and properness, and proprieties concerning food. And at all these functions, he uses to behave as if he was already His Lordship.

So on this solemn occasion, he begin to use a voice that was really suited and fittable to the sombreness and the sadness of the hot afternoon. And not even the stickiness of his surplice and the stickiness in the weather did bother or take away from his standing and stature, dress-off as he was, like damnation, in heavy, long black.

He start speaking 'bout love. 'Bout family. 'Bout the family of love. 'Bout the family of the people. 'Bout the family of politicians. 'Bout politics and 'bout power.

The last thing he mention was the dead. Poor Lionel laying-down in front o' him in a mahogany coffin! But the Dean was talking real sweet when he mention something whiching he called "the politics o' love."

The Prime Minister had already know what the Dean did intend to say in the eulogy. Um was the Prime Minister himself who had tell the Dean what to say. They did discuss it in detail over some rum and sodas, and from the notes whiching the Prime Minister had write and had take to the Dean office.

Now the real poetry start to roll-off the Dean mouth:

"I am the resurrection and the life, saith the Lord: he that believeth in me, though he were dead, yet shall he live . . ."

The Dean tongue move-over the words and make them sound real pretty, like pure honey. He had a real Oxford accent too. But the play-play English accent wasn't strong enough still to muzzle the broad, flat flavour of his native speech.

"The Dean could preach *too-sweet!*" the MP for Sin-James East say to Seabert the tailor, in Seabert's ear.

Seabert had recently join the Party, and did seeking a seat in the constituency where he and Nathan was living.

"Too sweet, in truth!" the MP say.

"Like a new zipper in a pair o' new khaki pants!" Seabert say.

"Like Frère Pilgrim cane juice!" the MP say. "With a drop o' rum in it!"

Seabert start to smile, so overpowered he was by the prospect o' power.

"Sweet for days!" he say.

And at this point, the Prime Minister tek-out his handkerchief from outta his breast pocket, tek-off his rimless spectacles, and start to wipe his two eyes. He then held down his head and give everybody the impression, by the posture o' sadness, that he was serious. All the people see him doing so. A cameraman see him. And caught him. And thinking that the Prime Minister was weeping for the dead, he pop-off a flash in the Prime Minister face.

The flash from the camera light up the total immediate surroundings. It would make a real nice front-page picture, the Prime Minister say.

"I know that my Redeemer liveth, and that he shall stand . . ."

Right then, all o' Lionel family start to cry. His woman from who he had two thrildren and with who he uses to live, she start-on 'pon one loud crying. His next woman, from who he had one son and with who he didn't used to live, she too was crying. His three sisters, one of who had come in from Brooklyn, New York; his mother and his father; the members of the Darrells Road Domino Players team, all o' them dress-off in black, with handkerchiefs jutting-out outta their pocket, handkerchiefs mek outta white dots on black silk squares—Jesus Christ, *everybody* start crying now.

But the most loudest, the most body-wrenching crying that was crying did come from the woman with who Lionel did live and from who he had two thrildren. She burst in a earth-rendering weeping. She raise-up her two hands high-high-high up in the air and bawl for blue murder. She raise she voice when the Dean did emphasizing the part of the Scriptures, namely about "my Redeemer liveth." And she lower-down her lamentations when he reach the words "the Lord giveth and the Lord tekketh away." Her voice overtake all the other voices. Her voice reach right up to the tops o' the almond trees and the casuarina trees in the pit of her sadness when the Dean reach "blessed be the name of the Lord." Her voice was clearer, was higher, and was more unsettling than even the shimmering, dying light from the setting sun shining on the coconut and casuarina trees surrounding the grave, the people, and the graveyard.

Seabert, as a tailor and man o' letters, recognize the part of the Scriptures that the text was tek-from. "Joab," he say, "chapter one, verse twenty-one."

The MP from Sin-James East, for who Lionel had work in the last campaign, see a cameraman pointing his lens in his direction and he start to wipe-off his sweating face with a blue and white polka-dot handkerchief. And start to weep like shite. The flash from the bulb explode like a big-big firefly before the MP could move-'way his handkerchief from covering up his whole face.

"Man that is born of woman hath but a short time to live . . ."

Oh Lord! Who tell the Dean to say so? Who tell the Very Rendable to utter them words?

Lionel woman jump up in the air. She throw her long blue silk dress high-high over her two thighs. She raised um up in a gesture o' grief. And in the gesture, she show-off one of the sweetest, juiciest, prettiest, and most luscious pairs o' legs. And the two eyes of the MP from Sin-James East rested on them. Some other men look too, yuh. And they liked what they saw. But in the present circumstances, they put it outta their minds, for the time being. As man! 'Cause they understood.

They did understand that Lionel, alas, born as he was of woman, no longer had all o' this beautiful, nice, black flesh inside his hand to grasp and hold-on 'pon, to hold-on 'pon and slam as he like, as he uses to slam a domino in a big tournament game . . . "The Lord giveth and the Lord tekketh away, boy!" And she, a woman, pretty-pretty-pretty, and with some class, with good body and better body-line and more better thighs, was now left, poor soul, with only the sting of his death to comfort she.

And the MP from Sin-James East start thinking 'bout slamming, 'bout slamming a dom, as they uses to call the game that brought-on Lionel death. And the two eyes of the same MP was stick-on 'pon the woman legs, and he couldn't concentrate no more on the sadness of the moment. So he move over a little and rested a comforting hand 'pon the shoulder of the grieving woman. He feel the softness of her neck. And she stiffen-up, like if his hand was a stinging bee.

And she bawl-out again. And the Dean was to pause in his reading of the Order of the Burial of the Dead.

Soon after this, they start to sing a hymn. The hymn come from *Hymns Ancient & Modern*, the book they does use in the Cathedral and in all Anglican churches. Hymn 477. Hymn 477 is a hymn whiching no old woman in the whole country would ever go sleep at dusk without singing to herself.

The day thou gavest, Lord, is ended,
The darkness falls at thy behest.

"Remind me," the Prime Minister say, talking to his aide, the MP for Westbury North, all the time the people was singing, "remind me to call in the union boss of the Harbour Workers Union and the leader of the Garbage Collectors Union and get the two o' them to brek-up these blasted strikes. They strangulating the people. First thing when we get back to the office, hear?" He wiped the booby outta his two eyes. "Sarge here?" he ask his aide, who was wiping the booby outta his two eyes too. "Sarge at this funeral?" His aide nod to say that Sarge here. "I want a tail put-on 'pon Sarge. Yuh can't trust nobody these days. Not even the Police."

The singing was going-on all the time the weeping and the lamenting was punctuating the singing. And the last punctuation mark come when, in the end, the thick, black soil start hitting the top of the mahogany coffin that was polish to a high-brown sheen.

The undertaker, or duppy agent, who was a member of the Party and the largest and most expensive duppy agent in the country, this undertaker tek-off all the silver-painted handles and other decorations from offa the coffin, just as they was about to lower Lionel in that deep, dark crevice.

Four politicians and the two gravediggers on duty slipped Lionel coffin down gently-gently, with the help of three leather straps that was so big that they could have fit a giant waist.

The mould start to pound on the shiny mahogany box. The men heard the pounding and start thinking of Lionel in the flesh and how he uses to pound a key card. As the mould fall, less louder now that the crevice in the ground was fulling up, as Lionel coffin was getting cover up, the screeling and the wailing start-up more louder. And when the coffin was hidden and conceal by the crumbly mould and the Dean say "ashes to ashes," the screeling and crying come to a end.

It was strange how it come to a end. Like if the end came and nobody didn't know nor notice it. All like now-so, all you could hear was a moaning from the family. A sound like a painful, almost stifled groan cause by a toothache. One or two white handker-chiefs was tek-out by politicians and placed at their two eyes, in respect. The women in Lionel's life moved from side to side in a slow-slow rhythm o' sadness.

"We must set-up a television station soon," the Prime Minister say to his aide in a whisper. "State-own. And state-control, of course! All this nice feeling and emotion this afternoon, all this grassroot sentimentalism should be captured by a coloured televi-sion camera. It would make such lovely, nice news!"

Standing 'round them, the cameramen was clicking their shut-ters tekking pictures and mekking noise like ducks and drakes chattering in a yard full o' chickens.

"I want to have a word with Lionel woman right after the funeral. Send-round my official car for she when she get home from the cemetery. As man!"

The choirs from the Cathedral, who had march at the head of the procession, even in front o' the Prime Minister and the Cabi-net, start up now to sing the hymn, whiching if it wasn't sung, nobody would believe there was a real funeral. It was a hymn whiching if it was not sung, nobody would believe that anybody dead or that a dead was buried.

Abide with Me.

"Hymn number twenty-seven," the Dean say. "Hymn twenty-seven. Two-seven."

Man, "Abide with Me" was a immure popular song than "God Save the Queen."

The men who was singing bass and them who was playing they could touch the alto parts, these men start to make poetry with the parts. They was singing as if they was competing with themselves and with the choristers. And they was singing loud-loud to drown-out the voices of the poor choirboys. 'Cause they had already had-in some strong liquors and didn't really know the tenor part or the alto part too good. But um was pure improvisation and imagination that make them sing-so.

They was singing this burial hymn as if they was singing um at a wedding. So "Abide with Me" become, by the way they was singing it and by the way they was improvising the parts, like a national Sunday anthem.

But all the people in the country did know that the men had good reason and cause to sing it so. Things was expensive. Crime was high-high. Unemployment was more higher. So the men had good reason to sing it. Without no reservation at all. Man, they lift-up their voices, right up to the top o' the almond trees and the casuarina trees and the coconut trees and the bougainvillea, and shake-up the earth itself with their deep, sad challenge.

Shine through the gloom, and point me to the skies;
Heaven's morning breaks, and earth's vain shadows flee:
In life . . .

And when they get to "in life," the people make a pause; they paused, as if their own-own lives, the lives they been leading under this guvvamment's regime, was itself in question. As if it was a stranglehold the Guvvament had grapple 'round their neck. 'Cause everybody did know from their own circumstances that in the midst o' life, they was also in the midst o' death.

And when they reach "in death" in the hymn, they paused a next time. This pause was like if they was expressing in a gradual lowering-down the sadness that was in their very voices.

Oh Lord! When the hymn reach "O Lord," man, you woulda think that all the people in this whirl was shouting-out, compelling, telling, and calling-on 'pon God to lissen. Lissen, man, God. Jesus Christ, at least lissen to we . . .

". . . abide with me."

"The minute the news broadcast on the radio tonight," the Prime Minister say, "the minute they broadcast this funeral— bram!—we calling elections! Political savvy and funerals, boy! Politics is like a *nice* funeral. Yuh does cry like shite over the coffin, and half-hour later yuh does catch some liquors at the wake. Political savvy and funerals, boy! And this is one o' the *loveliest* funerals in the history of this country! We calling elections."

"We send-off Lionel, God bless his soul," the MP for Westbury North say, "to his final resting place this afternoon with one o' the loveliest funerals for the year, in the history o' this political party. And Lionel was only a common, half-ig'rant party supporter. A blasted yard-fowl. But as you say, Skipper. Political savvy and funerals. So we had to send-he-off with a lovely funeral. And with a pretty song, 'Abide with Me.'"

When the MP for Westbury North was saying this, um was only one hour after the funeral done. All the people at the cemetery didn't even get home yet then. But the Prime Minister had already gone in Lionel's home, or former home, with Lionel woman. He had just return to his official car after spending some time with she. It was a dark night. A dog was growling as if somebody dead, or as the old people uses to say, as if the dog seeing duppies and spirits and deads. Um was Lionel's dog too. Spot. The dog was growling. And already the elections was in full swing.

The MP from Westbury North, who had drive the car on this mission for the Prime Minister, start to sing:

A-bide with me, O Lord, a-bide with me.

The Prime Minister wipe his face and his two hands with a white handkerchief. He pass the handkerchief over his lips. And he then wipe-off each finger clean-clean-clean. And then he throw the handkerchief into the black gutter. The car was park beside the gutter. And the dog was laying down beside the gutter, beside the car. Because the dog had come to greet the Prime Minister.

"And that blasted coffin cost the Party one thousand dollars. One thousand dollar bills for a blasted coffin, for a blasted political yard-fowl! But we intend to get-um-back, though," the Prime Minister say after he spit in the gutter.

"Lionel leff-back any property?" the MP say.

"He leff-back his woman, though!" the Prime Minister say. "He dead, and leff-she-back." And then he laugh.

"As man!" the MP say.

"We send-off Lionel as if he was a prime minister himself!" the Prime Minister say. "With a lovely funeral!" He spit again, in the gutter. "How you fix for tomorrow night? You could bring me back here?"

"As man!"

And then the Prime Minister sit down on the plush leather o' the back seat of the large black car with the MP at the wheel, and he start to hum:

Shine through the gloom, and point me to the skies;
Heaven's morning breaks . . .

And for days afterwards, the people who had live near the cemetery and them who had attend the funeral as witnesses to its size and everybody connected to the Guvvament, they all say, "What a *lovely* funeral they give Lionel!"

And more than anything else, more even than the voice of the Dean, the people remember the singing of "Abide with Me." And especially one thing they remember, whiching was the way the choirs sing it and rendered it and how the people did sing the very last line, in the very last verse.

In life, in death, O Lord, abide with me.

BONANZA 1972
IN TORONTO

"Clemmie! CLEM-MEEEE! Child, you ain' know the tellyphone did want you? Child, I ringing and ringing for you,
the whole blasted morning, to tell you 'bout last night,
and Christ, you ain' answering at all, at all! You think I don't have
nothing more better to do, eh? Well, let me tell you that I am a
busy-busy person, my Missy having-in friends this evening, I have
a million-and-one things to do, and when she having-in friends,
and the friends finish eat and drink and get drunk, be-Christ, you
would think a hurricane pass through this home that I sweat over to
make look decent for her . . . But that ain' what I ringing you for,
though . . .

"Child, last night! Last night at the Holiday Inn up in Don Mills!
But let me tell you first, how I get to get up there in amongst them
high and mighty Canadian people. Well, lissen . . . seems as though
the invitement did come to my Missy. But you know *her*. She
hopping here and she hopping there, museum party tonight, art
gallery party last night, here there and everywhere, child. Well,
she says to me, 'Pinky, darling?' . . . Tha' is how she addresses me
when me and she setting horses. But don't let that fool you, 'cause
it don't fool me, and I know it don't fool you neither! I have her in
my craw up to today for what she do me since last year; and no
blasted skin-teet' can't fizz 'pon me, nor wipe-out that grief. You
know that. But I telling you 'bout last night, darling. Last night,
oh Christ, Clemmie! The free eats and the free drinks that the
Barbados touriss people back home send up to that place! And in

the midst o' my eating and drinking—'cause last night I was right there with them; I was one o' the tourisses too, like the best o' them!—in the midst o' my eating a flying-fish steak, I had was to wonder, 'How many o' we back home have a piece o' this nice fish in their mouth, this evening?'

"But the story running-'way from me. I beginned by telling you how I got there. It appears that the Missy been too busy with her own business, so she send me there in her place. Gal, I was *dedigated* to go there, yuh hear? I dressed-off in my best clothes, and the missy say, 'Pinky, since you going in my behalfs, and to such a big affair as the Holiday Inn, here is taxi fare.' Darling, I sit my behind in that back seat and watch that taxi-man drive as slow, slow-slow-sloooooowww as he blasted-well like, the dollars and cents clocking-up 'pon that damn meter in his car, and I didn' as much as pick my teet' to him. Is my Missy money I was spenning last night, soul. The blasted taxi-man make two wrong turns, on purpose, and I ain' business with him yet, 'cause it is the Missy who paying for all this. Well, eventually, *eventually, at long last*, he reach the right drive-way, and he tell me six-eighty-something, and child, I hand him a twenty-dollar bill, and on top of it, I give the bastard a fifty-cent tip! How yuh like muh? Ain't that style? Child, that is style! Last night I was *Miss* Pinky Best! I was living in style with the best o' them bitches I works for, up here in this exclusive district.

"Well, let me tell you how things was situated. First, they had this man behind a counter who takes your coat, and you pay him a quarter; then, there was these stewardess-ladies from Air Canada, smiling and thing, and asking you what your name is, and then they write-down your name on a piece o' paper, or card, which said HELLO in pink print; and child, then you stepped through that door of a big-big ballroom place, and first thing you know, a man with a butler jacket on, bring this tray in front o' you . . . just like how we serves at a party . . . and ask you, 'Please take a glass o' champagne, madam.' Child, last night was a night o' champagne! I was the onliest domestic in that company, and I held my head high as shite—pardon my vernaculer—I held up my head high-high-

high as if I was the wife o' the Governor-General back home! I was *Lady* Best last night. That was my introduct— . . . What that you say?

"You want to know what I wore? Well, child, I bathe myself in some o' the Missy best bath oil, Estuh Lauder, and for the hell of it, I throw in some Algemenge too; seeing as how I was going to a Wessindian fete, I figure that this Algemenge thing that this bitch here boast so much about, and does wear on her body as if it is water—well, what is good for her, was good enough and more proper for *Miss* Best, darling. It is a funny thing, this Algemenge. It does make the water turn blue-blue-blue, like seawater back home. Well, I was stepping-out last night to a Wessindian function, so what better bath-thing to use than one that does make the water look pretty as the blue sea we have in the Car'bean! Then I held up both my armpits and I powder them with dusting powder, and then stepped-into my pantsuit—yes! the one me and you buy together down in Simpson's, the black one, darling. It was a black-dress affair! . . . Heh-heh-heh-heeee! and not a stitch on my bubbies. Be-Christ, last night, Clemmie dear, I was bra-less like the biggest and the most prettiest womensliberationiss in Amurca. And I going tell you something else. Iffen I was not the respectable woman you know me as, Clemmie, I telling you, I woulda gone up there at that Holiday Inn without panties too. Heh-heh-heh-heeee-oh-Gaaaaaawwwwwd! Child, I was *wicked* last night! But I did, in trute, at first put on the pantsuit pants without no panties, but when I figure that there could be some men up there, who with two free Bajan rums in their arse, and feeling their oats and might try to feel-me-up—Christ! Well, I didn' want to be in a position to have to disgrace the clothes I was wearing. I ain', at my age, putting no ideas in no blasted Canadian-man head. At my age, I isn' no pup. Yes! That is what I wore.

"And when I stepped in front o' the Missy full-length looking glass, and see myself, how I look, how I was right to go without brazzieres, how at my age I ain't a bad-looking woman, not old yet—change-o'-life hasn't ask me a question yet, Clemmie—a sadness come over me, and I had was to ask myself, 'Pinky, where the bloody hell is the black mens in this town?' A woman in my position—I have a nice job, I makes a decent wage, and I have a small piece o' land back in Barbados and Canadian Savings Bonds up here—a woman in my position in life should be stepping out with a man who is proud to have me walking beside o' him! I should have a regular man. You don't think so? That was the onliest sad part o' the evening. I was looking *good*, child. Like something to eat—if I say so myself. And I stepping into the people place, by myself, be-Christ, Clemmie, and there was not even a shadow of a half o' man excorting me; there shouldda been a man next to me, any kind o' man . . . well, even a Jamakian-man, then! . . . Heh-heh-heh. Don't laugh; Jamakian-men ain' so bad! Be-Christ, you is a Jamakian yourself, so you should know what they gives. I am not able for no man to beat me up and fuck me up, and treat me like no blasted dog. This is the womensliberationiss age, so we have to get with the times, never-mind we is Wessindians. Get with the times, that is my motto for this place called Canada.

"Look, now that I on the phone, I might as well tell you the latest thing I heard 'bout *you-know-who*! Yesss! *Her*! The same one, the self-same one, gal! Didya know she manage to get pregnunt? *Preg-nunt*! After all these blasted years o' trying and failing. Been on the pill for years. Come offa the pill. Went back on 'pon the pill 'causin somebody, a nurse-friend o' hers tell her that the pill—coming off it and going back on 'pon it—would make her *you-know-how*, put some green bananas and mackerel in her arse! And as that nurse-friend said, bram! Just after Christmas, she with child. Yesss! In the fam'ly way! Start telling every-blasted-body in Toronto, she was so pleased with her little old self. 'I getting baby,' a frien' of a frien' tell me she tell them. Well, guess wha' happen, now. No, not that! No such thing as a fall 'pon the ice 'pon the sidewalk! . . . No, gal! *D-and-C*! Yes, child, in the midst o' childbirth, she was back where the arse she started from! *D-and-C*! And you could imagine how that man feel today. He wanting a child in his old age, and be-Christ, every-and-anybody who can barely wear a dress walking 'bout

Toronto with their belly big-big-big, and all his sperms throw-away in Maxwell Pond. The heartbreak!

"Well, when yuh say one thing, yuh got to say the next. This ain' no day and age for no woman to say she want thrildren. Thrildren is too much trouble nowadays! That is why I *dead* telling you I am with the womensliberationiss way o' doing things. I gets my little fun, and it end where it start. Thrildren? At my age, darling? . . . Well, anyhow, I still telling you 'bout last night . . . I hope I not keeping you on this phone too long, eh? 'Cause these employers nowadays does have everything to say when we sit down for five minutes to take a breath from their blasted slave-work, and they still paying we pennies for that hard labour.

"Child, I even forget to tell you that I put-on the Missy brown suede maxi winter coat! And, be-Christ, it fit me more better than it have ever fit her. She ain' have *half* the shape I have! . . . Anyhow, I have to hurry-up this part before she come smelling 'round my behind, asking me if luncheon isn't finished yet. The thing last night, child, it was something to see. They put slides and pictures on something which we uses to call a magic lantern back home in Barbados, and these pictures, all o' them was in Technicolor. They show the sand 'pon the beach more whiter than goat's milk, more whiter than the snow in Canada, and the seawater blue as blue, palm trees and blue skies that you born seeing and you never know before your eyes touch that magic-lantern screen, that a palm tree and a blue sky was so blasted pretty; you could look up in the sky and see a pin, and it was that pretty, child, that I could even smell the wind and the air and the sea breeze. In one o' the pictures, they show you a man, a Bajan man, bringing-out breakfast for a family o' Canadians, and you know, as a Wessindian yourself, what that breakfast consist of: fry plantain; scramble egg—with the egg tasting like real egg and not like the egg powder we buys in this place, where they are able to feed a little-little chicken from a chicken right into a big fowl, in less than three months!—real grapefruit juice, must be from Trinidad; a little fry-pork on the side . . . Thinking 'bout it now, I don't think now that the picture had-in fry-pork, but I imagine that any proper touriss worth his salt would have to ask for a little o' we fry-pork for breakfast to make the bowels feel proper and work more proper, heh-heh! . . . All these things I am seeing before my two eyes, child, and be-Christ, a bad thought strike me and I think-back to the time, just half-hour ago, when I went to check-in my coat, or rather, the Missy suede maxi, and the Canadian man behind the counter, set-up his blasted face in such a manner just becausin I ask him to hold on 'pon my woollen hat too. The bastard had the nerve to charge me a next twenty-five cents just for that. That bastard!

"You know me, Clemmie. I is not a prejudice-minded person, 'cause I understand that all kinds have got to live in this blasted world, together. But seeing the paradise that them Barbadian fellows was putting on for these Canadians, on a Technicolor screen, and I in there, as a Barbadian person, in the midst of all them Canadian people in the touriss business and from the Air Canada place, and to see how that man at the coat-checking place treat me, just like a dog, a funny thought came in my head, and I had was to ask myself, 'Why, why we ain' learn no sense yet? That we up here in this bright country, selling-out our blasted piece o' island, to a lotta prejudiced-minded Canadians, who only going down in the Wessindies for a twenty-one-day fling, their skirts over their heads.' . . . That is what it is, man, so don't you come telling me damn foolishness, Clementine! They going down there for a twenty-one-day excursion to blow off their woman-steam on we men, and be-Christ, I was born and bred there, and have live there more than twenty-one *years*, not to mention days! Could they contradict them twenty-one years that I live there? Tell me! They could come down from this place and come in my island, my country, and be-Christ, if perchance I happen to want to pass water, and perchance the nearest place and most convenient place was near a beach, and I bend down, as I uses to be able to do before the island start progressing with tourisses, and hold up my dress over my two knees and start sssssszzzzz-ing, you don't tell me that one o' these same Canadians who was up there last night at the Holiday Inn—

you telling me that one o' them bitches won't actually call a police, or a security guard to arrest me, just becausin I am easing myself on my own blasted land? Look at it that way, gal. And you would understand the kind o' purchase and sale o' my island that was going on up there at the Holiday Inn last night, right in the midst of all that free rum and with all the shaking o' hands and handshakes and smiles. Be-Christ, they was on holiday. The way they tear loose in that food, flying fish . . . When is the last day I tasted a piece o' flying fish? You know as well as hell, that I haven' been back home since I lannup in this country. That is seven years going 'pon eight.

"And I was glad to be there because somebody who I know, a maid who works in the touriss board place here, tell me in confidence, that the board was flying-up some fresh flying fish. Seven years since my mouth hasn' taste flying fish, and flying fish, in case you don't know it, is so important a stable-dish in my past and in my culture back home, that they even paint it on 'pon the Barbados coat-of-arms, and it is included too in the national anthem. So you see, Clemmie, that when I stannup there, in that push o' people last night, all o' them Canadian people, and they was rubbing and shubbing and keeping me from getting in front o' that table, and when I see this one Canadian man stannup and station himself in front o' that flying-fish table, toothpick *and* fork to boot! In case the toothpick that the touriss board provided to eat with didn' take up enough flying fish, that man stand there, and won't budge, and be-Christ, Clemmie, I could have *kill* him! Just for a flying fish! For eating-up one more mouthful of my culture and past! A man who didn' even have the manners to ask me, a stranger in that white midst, a Barbadian person who naturally couldn' be born here, but must be from the islands because o' speech and other things, that man station himself right there in front o' that table and in front o' the other ladies, laden down with the flying fish, and when he move from in front of it, the dish didn' have in nothing—not even a fish scale, then!

"Well, after I see how these Canadians could stay up here in their own country, and have a big-big-big party with all kinds o' freeness o' drinks and eats given in their behalfs, offa the Barbados Touriss Board people and on we taxpayers' money, just so! Nothing they ain' pay for, just a campaign to get more o' them to continue going down, spenning their money down in my country, and to proceed to buy-up all the whole blasted land. Seacoast gone! The best bathing places 'pon the beach gone long time! When I see how we-own Barbadian people come up here in Toronto and proceed with pictures to sell-out the island in Technicolor, to Canadian people, and the very Canadian people on the back of it, couldn' have the decency to treat me like a *person* when I went to check in my maxi coat and beg the man to hold on 'pon my woollen hat for me too, Clemmie child, I telling you that I change *there and then* from being a simple womensliberationiss-woman right into a blasted Black Panther woman!

"I stand up there, one o' the few Barbadians in a throng o' Canadian people, and see how pretty that magic-lantern thing . . . I think they call it slides in this modern age . . . I watch how that slide-thing make magic outta the pictures o' my island, and I see how a woman, a lady from Canada, or Toronto, or from somewhere in Northamerica, a *stranger*, hold-down and lift-up a handful o' white sand inside her hand, and how she look at the sand pouring through her fingers, and the feeling o' happiness and peace that come to her face as she see that sand pour through her fingers, like a child watching for the first time a hourglass, with sand coming down like how snow, here in this place, does come down offa a high roof, I see how happy she could be in my country, a strange place to her, and I stanning-up there, right in front o' her as she was in the picture, and next to others that look the same as her, and I have never felt so strange and lonely in my whole life. After watching that tragedy, the champagne in my hand went tasteless and the taste turned into bush-tea that we uses to use back home to purge our bowels with.

"Clemmie, I isn' a prejudice-minded person. And I don't hold the same racial views as some coloured Americans I have meet here in Toronto, when they come up for their holidays on Thanksgiv-

ing Day or on George Washington birthday. I have had the opportunity and the pleasure to be sitting down and exchanging one-two
ideas with them . . . 'cause some o' them, in spite o' the big car
and pretty clothes, does do the same domestic work in America as
we does do here in Toronto . . . and I would never forget what one
o' them say to me. She say, 'Sister,' . . . and the way she hold that
word in her mouth, and pronounce it as if it was a long-long-long
word, with more than two syllables in it, in its pronounciation, the
way she hold on 'pon that word *siiiiiisss-terrrr*, and bring it out,
slow, slow outta her mout', and her big Afro hair stanning-up on
top of her head like a tower . . . and she was a woman the age o' my
mother, too! . . . Well, then she say to me, 'Sister, white people is
our enemy!' Jesus Christ, Clemmie, I get so vex with that black
Yankee bitch! I was stark-staring mad! I tell her, 'Now lissen to me,
man! How the hell could you stannup in 1972 and say to me that it
ain' possible for no white person amongst the millions of Americans that they have down in the blasted States where you come
from, not *one* o' them won't do something good for you, an American yourself, in a hour o' need? If they hate we, it don't mean that
we have to hate them back.' I told her that. Clemmie, I took a turn
in her arse. And I finish it off by telling her, 'Lissen to me, lady, you
is old enough to be my mother, and I can't be rude or disrespectful
to you, 'cause we were brought up to respect people who are more
older than we. But I would have to tell you, in all respect due to your
age, that not all white American people is bastards, darling. I works
for one, who treats me like a lady. She *has* to. I demands that much
from her!' And be-Christ, Clemmie, *the very next day*, it wasn' more
than twenty-four hours after I had meet that sister from the States,
less than a day later, that my Missy didn' do something to me which
have me, from that day, watching her arse like a blasted eagle. You
should come up here, in this house, invisible as you are here, and
observe me and she: tit for tat! She gives me one, I gives her back
one. She plays the arse. I plays the arse too. And yet, I can't hold
grudges 'gainst no man, 'gainst no human being once he behave like
a human being to me. I am not a grudgeful person, Clemintine . . .

"But wait! Last time I talk with you, you wasn't no black militant, gal! What the hell is this I hearing now? For true? You been going to black militant meetings down at the UNIA hall 'pon College Street? Without me? But why the hell you couldn' call me up on the Missy tellyphone and let me accompany you down there? 'Cause I intend to talk and ask some questions concerning the Barbadian people selling out the Wessindies to the Canadians and the Americans. Child, I have to go with you, next time. And I *intends* to have a field day informing them 'bout what I think in regards o' this tourism tragedy . . .

"They had music too, yesss! But the music wasn't *we* music. It wasn' real Wessindian music. I couldn' even feel a blasted beat in the tunes they was playing the whole night. And the sad part was— the musicians was black to the last man, and from Barbados. Some red-skin fellow, one o' the big shots up there on the flatform, had the guts to tell the people, in the hearing o' me, that the group was the best calypso band in Barbados and the whole Car'bean! If they is the best, I don't want to hear the worst. A more serious thing, though, that I realize then and there, 'cause the only thing in my body that was working properly last night was my blasted brain, and it was working like I was a madwoman, thinking and having nothing to do but think. I figured out that them bastards musta been playing this way without beat and without rhythm only when they was playing for Canadian tourisses. They don't play the same music for Barbadians. The way they stannup up there on that flatform, and get on as if they was burying somebody, instead o' making a person feel a little life, a little hot blood flowing through their veins in this damn cold place! I needs rhythm and life and rhyme in my body, darling. I like to sit down, or when I am dancing, to hear that bass guitar, or the drums . . . I loves drums! I just loves drums! . . . I like to hear them drums going *boooommmm-boooommmm-boooommmm*! And the women's bodies going with the beat, or 'gainst the beat, and still everybody in time, everything match-up, you take a step outside the paling o' that music and you get back in inside that pal-ing just before the next beat play, you going and the music coming.

"But to stannup up there, last night, and to witness, to be a witness to the slides and the magic-lantern show, to see how that Canadian man eat-off all the blasted flying fish in my presence . . . I went up for that, and had to left without tasting it . . . to see how that Canadian woman from all the way behind God back could take an Air Canada, leaving me up here in the blasted cold, 'cause that is all this place have to offer me, and to go down there, just because and only because she have the two hundred or three hundred or five hundred dollars to do that, and she could stannup on my beach, my blasted beach, and hold that handful o' white pretty pure sand inside her fingers and watch the sand fall-out outta her hand, and the pleasure and joy that come to her face when she see that, and when I see and feel how they could treat me, a human being, living amongst them, to leave me here and for them to be able to go there, and live the life o' queens—child, are you telling me that that Yankee woman from the States wasn' speaking a grain o' truth?

"I went up there at that Holiday Inn place, as a pure-minded, unprejudice-minded person. And when I left, I was the biggest female radical woman they have in this Toronto. And it all happen over a little thing like a man eating a flying fish in my face, in my presence, and the attitude of his eating that flying fish and ignoring my rights to have a piece o' that flying fish, which is rightly mine, my own very culture, a fish which is native only to the sea round my island . . . By his denying me that right to get near that table o' flying fish, I reason that it really and truly was something more bigger than a mere little flying fish, which once upon a time my mother could buy three dozen of for six cents. It was a more bigger thing than a man stanning-up in front o' me, a lady, *a lady*, without the common decency o' saying, 'Lady, beg your pardon, but do you want some o' this fish?' Or even . . . seeing I am a Barbadian person, and he being a man from these parts, who naturally must have been down before in my island, judging from the way he licked his blasted fingers, and from the tan on his face, a man who taste the hospitality o' Barbados, seeing that the least o' men would have ask me, 'Try some . . .' But as I talking to you this Sarduh morning,

Clemmie, it started as a little thing, my being vex as hell with him, over a piece o' flying fish, but it turn into a mountain. Seeing that man with the flying fish and seeing that woman with the sand, *my* sand, in her hand, I feel that I did lose a baby. I start to feel just like that woman who had the D-and-C, whatever the hell that mean in hospital terms, musta feel: seeing that she born a thing, seeing something that had start to grow inside her, inside her belly and womb, and then to see it come out in a form that wasn' meant to be, and disappear in this foreign form, into something that don't have any use or life in it—Well, now I know what a D-and-C must mean for some women. My blasted belly *burned* me, 'cause I felt the same as a D-and-C woman.

"Look, child, am I talking too much for you? All I am worth this morning, after last night, is to talk to you, somebody from the Car'bean. 'Cause, if I were as insane, after seven-eight long years working for this woman, as to forget that you are there somewhere outside this house, Clemmie, I would *go mad* if I couldn' find someone like you, my own kit'-and-kin, to exchange two thoughts with. . . . But are you sure I not boring you with my talking? You will have to bear with me, because I can't take a cup o' coffee in my hand and go in the living room here, and sit down and say to my Mistress, 'Look, Mistress, I wants to talk with you.' And even if *she* could as much as say 'What about?' for me to then say, 'I wants to talk to you, 'bout myself, the way I feel here in this country, 'bout my culture,' be-Christ, Clemmie, she would hit the roof. 'Cause, as far as I am concern, she won't understand what I would want to talk about and why about *that*. So, you have to bear with me . . .

"That is another thing I had to tell you about . . . and I am glad that it is you who bring up this point, in case you start feeling that this is a one-sided conversation this Sarduh morning; or that you might find yourself thinking, after I finish talking to you, and you sit down to digest my words, I say I am glad you is the author o' that sentiment and not me, although many's the time I myself sit down in this plush palace I works in, and the poorness and poverty of my situation comes to me in leaps and bounds, and sometimes I have to open my mouth wide-wide in amazement at the narrow-mindedness that I finds myself with, at times. I am cooped up here, in a palace, working as a domestic, and within these four walls, Clemmie, darling, I have build four *more* bigger, higher, and thicker walls, to protect me from what the four walls of this palace mean to me, in terms o' myself. I won't deafen your ears concerning the material things I have accumulated through my stewardship for this lady. I won't do that to you. For me and you, both o' we is two women who find weselves in a position o' possessing things and owning things that wasn' in our lives back home. You down there, in Jamaica . . . Did yuh hear recently that Shearer, the prime minister, get his arse cut in the elections? *Good!* . . . and I, in Barbados. We are the owners and possessors o' first-class material things. But things that have to do with a person—or with a person's spirit!—we is only part owners o' that . . .

"But the point you just bring up . . . and this going have to be my last point with you this morning 'pon the tellyphone, 'cause I am still a employed person. But the point: *emigrading!* Emigrading-back to the West Indies from here! *Emigrading-back.* And we have to emigrade-back becausin we neither have the means nor the where-withal to be treated as tourisses here in Canada. Once I used to go 'round Toronto pretending I was a touriss: that I come up for a short visit, to see the snow and the new city hall, watching the subway and the tall-tall apartment buildings going up in the sky, whiching, as we have discuss over and over again, is really all that Toronto have to offer; but as you know, I couldn' pretend for *too long* that I was a touriss. For one thing, Canada don't have no touriss board down in Barbados, nor in the rest o' the West Indies —to my knowledge—to encourage Wessindian people to come up here for the winter to ski or the summer, to fish . . .

"But you looking at it that way, Clemmie? You ever see it in that fashion? Why is it that Barbados does have to send big able Barbadian men with all kinds o' degrees and certificates up here just to invite a few Canadians to go down there to my country, to buy it out, and lick it up, and give the place a bad name as a *resort* . . .

Jesus Christ! Barbados is not well-known for our literacy rate, which is the highest, the very highest in the world! Nor for the fact that Barbadians know as much Latin and Greek as any Roman from the days o' Caesar and Nero! Not for that! But as a *resort*! A resort, Clemmie, is nothing but a closet, a water closet, a WC . . . they does call it a restroom up here in Canada! The biggest enemy, and the most anti-Barbadian Bajan-man I have hear about in this world, is that bastard down there in Bridgetown, by the name o' Henry Shideaway! I can't understand why the government back home allow he to do that kind o' unfairness to young Wessindian women, by selling them at such a tender age, to all kinds and forms o' tourisses, just because the tourisses is Northamericans with money. Is that what money mean? And to get back to the point: you never-never-never see a touriss place open by the Canadians down there in the islands, asking Wessindians to come up here and walk in the snow, and take up a handful o' snow in their hand, and feel the snow, which, if I understand something I see once on the CBC television, is a way of learning a person's culture, in the same way that I watch with my own two eyes, that foreigner-woman down on that beach at Paradise Hotel in Barbados, how she could take-up a handful o' sand in her hands, and by that act, transform both herself and the sand and the place and the time where she was stanning-up, and I had a blasted difficult time remembering that I was looking at a Canadian woman and not at a native-born Barbadian-woman. At that Holiday Inn place, last night, Clemmie, darling, it was that brand o' emigrading-back in my mind that caused me, in the midst o' my presence there, dress-off in my Mistress maxi suede coat, standing in the middle of all them people, alone and by myself and seeing a bunch o' foreign people take over possession o' my island—even from this distance and through a slide in Technicolor, lock, stock, and flying fish.

"And a next thing happen. Child, I must tell you 'bout this. Outta all the fellows they bring up to sponsor and organize this big-big bonanza 1972 in Toronto, out of all o' them highly educated and successful men and women, Barbadians bred-and-born like me, Bajans who I remember, either from going to school with, or else remember through word o' mouth, walking 'bout Barbados and Bridgetown barefoot, with their backside at the door, naked, those ladies and gentlemen were too proud to pick their teet' to me, or to anybody like me, 'cause they was only businessing with the Canadians and anybody who could rent a room in their guest house . . . Outta *all* o' them the *only* Barbadian who thought enough of me to exchange two words with me, was one big tall light-skin man, by the name o' Worms, a gentleman, who, iffen he ain' really white in a Canadian sense o' shade and colour, could easily pass for one o' them up here—if he choose to—well, this gentleman stand up behind me. Before he speak to me, I don't know him from Adam. He didn't see my face yet. At least not before he speak to me. He just understand that I am a lady, somebody, who musta been some-body since I was there amongst them invited guesses. And when his voice hit my ears, I make a spin-around, pleased as hell, to at last get a greeting from one o' my own-own countrymen, and when I see the colour o' the face and the size o' the man that went 'long with the voice and the accent, I had was to hold on 'pon both his hands, and in my heart, I say to him, 'Thank you, thank you, Mr. Worms, for at least mekking me feel like a person, a lady.' He said to me, 'Miss? How are you enjoying yourself? Let me get you a rum and soda, 'cause I know you's a Bajan, like me. And I is just as lonely in the midst o' all these Canadian people as you, never mind I almost got the same colour as them . . . So look, man, come, let the two o' we Bajans get drunk as shite offa this freeness.'

"Clemmie, when Mr. Worms say that to me, water from my eye dropped into the glass with the rum and soda in it . . . just to think o' that, just to think . . . just to think . . ."

LETTER OF THE LAW OF BLACK

"Edgehill House"
Edgehill Lane
Edgehill Tenantry
BARBADOS

I am writing this letter to you now, at this rather late time, because when you left the island to go away to Toronto, there was too much emotion in the air, and talk was impossible and talking did not make sense. Most of the things that was said was what I call emotion; all that emotion was good for someone as young as you, taking up a journey in life, to another country which is strange to you, although you may forget that you were born there.

The emotion itself was not complete though, was not real emotion, and it rang a bit empty to me, because I am too old for emotion and passion, and because the one person who could have made the rafters ring for joy, that you, her only child, was going to a place where she had so many happy years, and tragic years, was not there. Then, was not the time. Then, was not the occasion to bring back memories whose only meaning and point in bringing them up, would have demanded the bringing up also of the tragedy which define those memories. Your mother.

I waited all these years also, because I wanted to be sure and certain that you got through your first year in Toronto. They tell me, and I am referring to the lawyer-fellow and the vicar who live beside me, that the first year of studying the things you are studying, is the most hardest of the four years proscribed for studying. The first year is the hardest and saddest. That is what the lawyer-fellow say. The vicar say that being in the first year, you are free from whatever spiritual responsibilities that being at home here assumes you should carry with you; and that you are alone in a new kind of freedom, and that very often you will need somebody with experience and affection, to help you confine yourself within that very freedom. It was the vicar, I think, who used the words "inner spiritualism," to make the point that I now making to you, using a summary of his words as I do so. To me, it is a more simple thing. I call it knowing and understanding what freedom really stand for.

And if I remember correctly from my own days in that country while I was on a two-year farm labourers' scheme working on farms in southern Ontario—Chatham and London and Windsor— before I forgot to report to the liaison-man in charge of checking the conditions of the farm labourers, and took a leave without leave, as you may say, and lost myself in Toronto until they tracked me down, and deported me, a man with my education at the best school in Barbados, and with all my years in the Civil Service here, things which you already know, and before they hounded me down like a dog—as it was their duty to do, the liaison-man said—and send me back here, but not before I had amass thousands of dollars for your maintenance and upkeep, I call to mind that the first year in that country, as in another country where you are a stranger, demands your complete attention to details which later turn out to be a damn complete waste of time.

You have to watch your allowance. And the allowance that the government people and the man in charge of the farm labourers used to give, was not nothing you could write home about. You have to watch your allowance, as if you are a banker or an economist. Or as if you are an investor. And the worse thing that happens, is that you bound to become, and does, a hoarder and a miser. God help you son, that you do not follow in my footsteps, as a stranger in that land, and have to be a hoarder.

For instance, being the son from my loins, you are bound to love clothes and women, not necessarily in that order. But as to clothes, you may see a shirt in a store for ten dollars, and you buy it because you think it is a saving. And the next day, you will pass another shop window and see the same shirt, on sale for half the price. And being new to Canada, you do not know, and would never think that you could take the ten-dollar shirt off your back, wrap it in a nice cellophane parcel, and return it to the store, and sneak it on the shelf and get your money back. Canadians do it every day. The Canadians taught me never throw away a receipt, even a receipt for a French letter, if you see what I mean! So, never throw away a receipt from a store, not even a liquor store.

You could tell me if Stollery's Emporium for Men still is at the intersection of Bloor and Yonge streets? I spent many dollars and more hours talking to the manager, and getting wrong advice, but the proper fit from the male clerks. Their shirts are not bad. But the best ones I wore, and still have some of, after fifteen years, were obtain at the annual Jewish Hadassah sale of clothes in the Canadian National Exhibition, or at the second-hand establishment named the Royal Ex-Toggery, near the Anglo-Saxon residential district of Rosedale on Merton Street. So, you see, I took the best. The best of the second-hand, from the best of both Toronto worlds, the two founding races, at the time. The Anglo-Saxons and the Jews. I am talking about the Fifties. Now, as I have been reading from the clippings you been sending down, and from chatting with the odd tourist on the beach, the place is a virtual potpourri of nationalities, saddle with something called a new sense of ethnic and of nation, namely multiculturalism.

The Jewish man dresses well and elegantly. It is small wonder that Hitler stole his clothes. The Jewish man who dresses, and I knew a few in my time for whom I worked illegally in their homes and in their habadasheries, dresses in good clothes. You can learn something, this and more, from the Jewish gentleman. It is not fit for me, your father, from this distance, to utter to you, what you can learn from the Jewish woman. Our own Hitler is here, wagging his tail, brushing out his fleas against my foot as I write this letter to you. Perhaps I had said the name Hitler out loud as I wrote it, and he thought I was commending him for his companionship, and for guarding the old place and protecting me from the varmints we have down here as Barbadians, now that you are away. If he could talk, and had the uses of language, Hitler would say hello to you, although if he did have that blessing of speech, years ago he would have blasted you in condemnation for your unmerciful treatment of him, and for your insistence that he lived nothing but a dog's life. "Dogs amongst doctors," I used to overhear you saying to him; and then Hitler would give out a yelp, as if trying, in his own way, to inform me that you had kicked that precept into him. A dog's life, indeed. How empty; and still how full. He is lapping up water from the blue enamel bowl in the kitchen, as I sit at the kitchen table, with the door open, writing you this letter. The pullets have multi-plied. The cocks crow and screw from sunrise to sunset. And still, I cannot find a blasted egg laid by these thirty-something hens that the two fowl-cocks master, for the thieving neighbour on my right, and the light-fingered bastard on my left. But God do not like ugly.

Nothing here has changed. I went into your room the other day and dusted the cobwebs and the dried skeletons of scorpions and bugs from off your books. The sea air and the salt in the wind are the censors of books in this island. No wonder that people in these hot, tropical countries eat up the television programs from North America, in preferences to putting their faces inside the pages of a book, and so, as a result, in consequence do not know their head from their backside. The book, my son, is moth-eaten, just as the morality of politics in this country is eaten out. Decaying. And Mannigheim, our leader, is the biggest, fattest, and most bother-some moth to fly around the eyes, and sometimes, to get into your mouth. He behaves like a moth, acts like a stinging bee.

I happened to notice the titles of your small but well-chosen library of books. I was pleased to see that although you have read the classics at Harrison College, you still had time besides all that Latin and Greek, two of the deadliest languages I can think of, to read some good literature. You should, while you are there, and during term breaks and March breaks, look at the Russians, especially Pushkin, the vicar say. You know, he was one of us! I nearly dropped dead when the lawyer-fellow told me so. He went to school in Amurca, and studied all this black thing that people about here are now talking about. If you had stuck me with a pin, not one blasted drop of red blood would have oozed from my stunned body. Pushkin is one of us. By that, I mean, a colonial man, more than I mean the obvious, namely that he was a black or coloured man. Even in your position of being in a minority, or as I read in the clippings you send down, a member of a visible minority—as if you could ever be invisible!—being in a minority through color, in a country like Canada, whose immigration policy was pearly *white* officially, up until 1950, and you can ask Don Moore if he's still living, the fact of being a coloured colonial; you young intellectuals would say "post-colonial," or "neo-colonial," but I am old, and old-fashioned, and the only university I went to was the University of Hard Knocks, and so I say *colonial*. The colonial is the fact that transcends blackness. Blackness may change when you are amongst all black students; or it may change when you are in the company of good white people. (Have you had the chance to look up Mr. Avrom Lampert yet, as I have asked you, and pay him my respects? He was extremely kind to me; and most helpful in renting me a basement. It was damp, but that was all right. Things used to crawl on the walls. I have eaten more bagels and latkees—do you spell it so?—in his home during my time in the City of Toronto, hiding from the Immigration and Farm Workers' liaison-men, than I have eaten flying fish and peas and rice. I hope he is still in the flesh. I still owe him the fifty dollars he lent me, thirty years ago, to pay a bill. Shirts, I think. And you know, I lost the receipt! However, if you see him, do not mention the fifty dollars. Time heals all debts.)

You should browse through some Russian literature. In addition to Pushkin, I would think that Dostoyevsky's *Crime and Punishment* would be worthwhile, as the vicar tell me. One winter, when I was flat on my back with fever, indisposed through health and threatened with dismissal from my job of being a janitor, and laid up in a small attic room on College Street near where the Main Public Library used to be, where I took out and read *Crime and Punishment* in two days of delirium and high temperatures, thinking it was a detective story, I got worse. They rushed me in an ambulance, with the sirens blaring, to the Toronto General Hospital. They meaning the two Canadian students who rented rooms next to me that summer, and another Canadian who used to put me on my guard Immigration-wise. Dr. Guild, the physician who saw me in the Casualty, what they call the Emergency up there, just smiled and told me to get a bottle of Gordon's Dry Gin. I had told him of *Crime and Punishment*. I hope you would not have that kind of relapse when you seek to broaden your literary horizons. If you were to read *Das Kapital* or *The Communist Manifesto*, as the lawyer-fellow say, even though you are reading it for your degree in Economics and Political Science, if you read it outside your course, *they* will say you are a communist. You should, if you read those two ideologies, be careful enough to hide their tolerance under your academic gown. Or hide their colour under brown wrappers. But if you are seen on a streetcar or in the subway reading Pushkin or *Crime and Punishment* or Tolstoy, *they* will say you are an intellectual. Even if they call you a colonial intellectual, as they have a habit of doing, such as black writer, or black artist, or black doctor, it would be different. You would, by this intelligence, be more dangerous to them, and *they* would not be able to despise, or worse still, ignore your presence, and call you a visible minority.

Who are these *they*? *They* are all the unspeakable, invisible spies, the unnameable people, people who watch you when you do not know they are watching you, do not feel they are, or should, who take it upon themselves to be your sponsors. Beware of sponsors. Beware of liberals too. Beware of patronage. Beware of fools. And beware of Gordon's Dry Gin.

The only ones you do not have to be wary of . . . I just had a silly thought, the musings of an old man. We can say "beware of," and be splendidly and syntactically correct. But we dare not say "those whom you should be beware of." English is such a blasted puzzle. Such like a young woman under thirty-three. A woman under thirty-three, who does not know how to make love when she says she is making love, is as unattractive as bad English. I do not know what that means. And I do not know why I said it. Do you? I am not, as you have guessed, talking about *all* thirty-three-year-old women, girls, up there in that City of Toronto. I am talking about those who were born in working-class districts, in London, in England, and in the East End in Toronto, of West Indian parents; those who grew up in the slums of Brixton, and do not tell you this, when luck or a football pool brings them to you, unprepared for Canada; and when they speak to you in their Braytish accent, which, if you remember listening to the BBC World Service radio news, and have been taught, as you were, by Englishmen at Harrison College here, you would readily see that their Braytish accent is nothing more refined than the cockney of a braying jackass. They are all lower class. Beware of the lower classes of all races. They spit on you because they grew up spitting on the ground. Spitting was the way of their lives. They were spitted on; and now, they spit on you.

Spitted, spat, spatted . . . spat on. *Haaawk! Kah-chew!*

Did I ever tell you of Kay? Why would I have done so? You are, after all, still my son, and while you were here, you were still a little boy, and there was no way I could, or should, have spoiled you by these disclosures, and spilled my love life and escapades, in that City of Toronto, onto your youthfulness of innocence. But now at twenty-two not quite yet, according to our customs and ethics and culture, at twenty-one, and therefore a man, not yet peeing a pee that foams the foam of manhood—nevertheless, at twenty-one and being away, abroad, overseas in that city, which gives you a certain privilege, I shall bend the moral and disciplinary precepts you learned so well at Edgehill House, and tell you about Kay.

Kay dressed well in cheap clothes. She loved clothes, but didn't have the money to accommodate her tastes. Kay talked with a Braytish accent. Kay said, "I am not a Canadian. I was born in Brayton," meaning Britain. Kay looked intelligent. Kay was affianced to a Barbadian man of unknown social background, but who had some brains, some luck, and—through the emergence of Black Power, and the unachieved importance of Eldridge Cleaver and Black Awareness—was given a scholarship to do gradual work at a university, in the Sociology of Violence. The Sociology of Violence! Did you ever hear anything like this? Beware of poor West Indians who, with changing times, find themselves in Gradual Schools, in second-rate universities, writing second-rate theses in second-rate disciplines. The Sociology of Violence! They are the worst kinds of socialists.

But to get back to Kay. Kay was courting this man, was to be married in the October, when I invited them in the September to tea one afternoon, when he brought Kay along. She was the most beautiful black woman I had ever seen. I served tea and biscuits, grapes and cheese, and then wine. *Chateauneuf du Pape*. After tea, we had pickled pig's feet and Scotch. She was very Braytish during tea. She held the teacup the wrong way. With both hands. Cupped. And she said, three times, "I like this silver teapot. These are lovely cups. Chinese? Bone cups? I like these Chinese bone cups. This is very civilized."

We had been talking about West Indian immigration to Britain and to Canada. She said, "I am Braytish." It was the second time she had declared her ancestry. When it came time to eat the pig's feet, she put up her nose. Her nose is rather flat and broad, for that kind of superciliousness. Years later, when I met her sister and her "half-sister," as she called her, and her mother, all three noses were flat and broad. But those three flat broad noses understood the ancestral dignity of design. They understood pig's feet also. Not Kay. "I've never eaten pig's feet. I am Braytish," she said, when her fiancé, embarrassed by the repetition of her exploding airs, told her about souse, probably to take the reservation out of her palate and taste. He looked at me in one of those quick nervous glances. He was mortified, as mortification mortifies a man of low class, and he told her about his "primary proposition" and about the "point he is trying to make." Beware of "primary propositions" and "points people *try* to make." I had welcomed her because I saw only her beauty. Beware of beauty. I saw her good looks. Her appearance. Beware of appearance.

"Girl, don't be a stupid bitch, do," he told her, trying to make the point that he disapproved of the passing of her airs. "Woman, what British you talking 'bout? I am doing a Ph.D. in the Sociology of Violence as It Affects the West Indian Diaspora in Britain. And I *know*. I know people like you been eating nothing but shit like fish and chips in Britain since 1950, when the first wave of immigrants washed up at Southampton. Ackee and bad salt fish. Pig ears. Pig snout. Pig tail and rice. And kiss-me-ass fish and chips! Or were you bought up on Yorkshire pudding? Look, girl, eat the blasted trotters, do!"

That was the first sign I got about Kay's problem of positive or negative self-identity. She did not tell lies at those times. She allowed people, me and my friends, to make conclusions about her, and spread them, and in turn, believe them, and she kept her silence, knowing all the time they were lies.

She graduated from McMaster in business, we told our friends. She was a trainee at a large commercial bank downtown, we told them. She was born, as I have said, in Brayton, we said. She had a nanny, we said. She went to private school, we said. She called herself a banker, we assured our friends.

She was, in fact, a teller. A junior teller. At a counter. In a small bank. It was not even the main branch. And she was born in Jamaica. She went, however, to a girls' boarding school in Clarendon.

One day, she called me. She was crying. Her fiancé had met a white Canadian woman, much older than she, much older than he, who had a child nine years old. He told his colleagues in Gradual School, in the Sociology of Violence as It Affects Department, that he was going to marry this white Canadian girl. And he did. And he regretted afterwards. But he never apologized to Kay. Never called. Never wrote a letter to save breach of promise proceedings. Never sent a message. Never sent back the three hundred dollars she borrowed on her credit card to buy his wedding shirt from Stollery's store at Bloor and Yonge. Was not mortified by the mortification of the breacher of promise, or by the Sociological Violence that her family, the three women with ancestral noses, were preparing to be wreaked on the jilter.

The church had been booked, she said. The reception, in a rec room—what a doleful term!—a rec, could it be a *wrecked* room, was booked for the reception, she said. Flowers were ordered, she said. Her girlfriends at the bank, all tellers, and of lies, presumably (not one of them a junior trainee), were invited, she said. They had bought their wedding dresses, she said. She had bought her wedding gown too, she said. White, she said. She had one child left back in England, he said. She did not have any offspring in England, she said. Everything was arranged, she said. The "wrecked" room was vacuumed twice by the superintendent of the apartment building, she said. It was situated in a dreary district in the City of Toronto where there were five factories and one slaughterhouse, for cows and pigs. Do you think that's why she did not like pig's feet?

I found myself in the ticklish predicament and role of a father figure giving fatherly advice to a young woman I wanted to take to bed. Young, because at that time, I was twice her age, plus three. Her father left her mother when she was two, in Brayton. You were not born then. I saw myself as the main character in the movie made of the novel *Lolita*, that the vicar told me about; a novel about a dirty old man, and a dirty little girl of sixteen and of monumental sexy disposition. I saw the inequality and the immorality in our relationship. She was a nymphomaniac. I was steadily on a diet of green bananas and flying-fish roe, prescribed by a woman once my age!

I found myself, after working ten hours six days a week, in a packing company as a packer's assistant, walking beside a person in blue jeans and white ankle socks, eating small plastic tubes that contained frozen ice of many colors, and artificial sugar. Holding on to a paper napkin, on a Sunday afternoon, to wipe every trace of dripping stickiness from the white hairs of my beard. (I grew a beard then, to help hide from the Immigration and Farm Workers' people.) So, walking through Queen's Park in the dead cold of winter, and leaving conflicting, contradictory, unequal pairs of footprints deep in the thick, indifferent snow. Deep, because we used to walk hand in hand, and slow, and talk. What do you talk to a woman half your age, plus three? And who likes *Chinese* bone teacups, and does not eat pig's trotters?

"I didn't know you had a granddaughter so big, man," Rufus, a fellow who had walk-away from being a farm labourer the same way I did, said to me. The son of a bitch! He had seen us necking on a bench whose colour I could not tell, the snow was so thick. He probably meant, by his salutation, that I should think of incest. Had he said "robbing the cradle," I would have been happier. Rufus is not more than five years younger than me. He had refused to grow a beard to camouflage his illegality at the time, from the Immigration people.

But she, Kay, twenty-two at the time, made me, by her sensuality, look and behave older than I was. And I, knowing my own age, seeing her look *and* behave like Lolita in the movie version, increased my consumption of green bananas and flying-fish roe from only Saturdays, to Friday, Saturday, *and* Sunday. And a Chinese man in a store down in the Kensington Market had pity on me, and gave me something Chinese to drink. My son, it was Sodom and Gomorrah, after that! Beware of twenty-two-year-old women. Lolita, as you would remember, from the book or the movie, was not the kind of person anyone could accuse of having brains. In the four years that we lived together in the townhouse, I never could accuse her of *that*. Of other things, maybe. And I accused her of many other things. But never of *that*. She was, however, infelicitous in other ways which I shall tell you about, at another time; for at the moment, I have to boil some rice with lard oil in it, and a few fish heads, for this growling dog, Hitler. Why did you ever christen this poor, unfortunate dog with the name of Hitler? Were you being intellectual? Symbolical? Or diabolical? Or ironical? Suppose Hitler had won the war? Don't you see that, all this time now, Hitler would be one dog you could not kick?

The government of brown-skinned and red-skinned men that is governing this place (there is no woman in this Cabinet!) has raised the price of propane, and since I am cooking for a dog—what a dog's life!—I have to prepare his vittles on a wood fire. The previous colonials who owned this house, before it passed into our family, through whoring and prostitution and piracy, in 18-something, were smart enough to build a solid iron grate, with a stone fireplace, so I shall be bending over a fire, blowing my guts out, to give it wind and make it burn, and cook the rice and red snapper heads, for this dog, Hitler, as if I was cooking for a person.

It is only nine o'clock in the night here, on a Friday night. A good night. But it could be after midnight, the blackness is so thick. Days in this part of the almost forgotten world are too short. When they get short, and the nights long, the lawyer-fellow and the vicar and me would deal a few hands of five-card stud. Sometimes, we play "no limit," sometimes, ten dollars a raise: highest raise, fifty dollars, and raise as much as your little heart desires. These last short days with the long nights, the vicar has been lucky. The lawyer-fellow had to tell him that the parishioners lucky too, because that demon's hands won't be in the collection plate! We three, old men, retired from life and from the tribulations of the young, with money in the bank and time to spare . . . what more— save health, praise God—do we want? But where you are, in that city at this time of year, September and autumn, the days fade more gradually, more romantically, though faster, into night than they do in June, July, and August.

So, before it gets blacker than that afternoon in 1910, with the May Dust, I still have to read the Good Book. I am reading from the front and going steadily to the back, with the help of some strong, stiff snaps of Mount Gay rum and water.

Don't ever feel you are too much of an academic to read the Good Book. And do not let "blackness" or the colonial syndrome make you feel that the only people who get something mentally nourishing from the Good Book is white people, racists, and Jews. The Good Book is beyond culture. I don't know who wrote it. And I don't care. It is like the air, the skies, the wind, and the blue sea. It is attainable. So, even if you have to wrap its cover in brown paper, and hide the title from some of the radicals and semi-atheists in Trinity College, in order not to be called unsophisticated and be called a fundamentalist—beware of fundamentalists, especially fundamentalist women under twenty-three—still do it. You can hide and read. You can't read and hide. As a matter of truth, you should enter that kind of meditation, in the privacy of your conscience.

I have finished with Genesis again—not a bad piece of writing —the vicar told me so, and I have to agree with him—and am now moving through Exodus.

"Then Jacob gave Esau bread and pottage of lentils. And he did eat and drink and rose up and went his way: thus Esau despised his birthright."

When I read these words in the evening, in this tropical part of the world, sitting under my mango tree, with Hitler beside me, and a rum and water on the bench beside me, with the stillness of the air, the smell of flowers, and the smells of all these polluting fumes from cars and buses and lorries, with the crickets chirping and the mosquitoes humbugging me, I still can't help feeling that the meaning of these words is more immediate and precise in this circumstance of climate. I read that same passage once kneeling down in St. Paul's Anglican Church on Bloor Street, just before you get to Jarvis, after you pass Church Street, one week before I was to face the Immigration people with regards to deporting me, or letting me leave on my own two oars, in case I wanted to creep back into Canada. And all I felt was that I was reading the Bible, praying for help, in order to understand, in less than twenty-four hours, the economics of my situation and the versatility of my fabricating a story to impress the Immigration officer with. I felt nothing more. It could have been like reading the *Telegram* newspaper, which was one of the best pieces of journalism ever sold in that city. But here in this island, with the vicar living beside me, with all the poverty, dead dogs, and dead crappauds in the road, untouched and unmoved for days, with all the poorness and poverty and political pillage by the government of the brown-skins and the red-skins, I feel that Moses or Mr. Genesis had just written the words for me personally to read, and had intended these words specifically for my ears. I never got this feeling of recognition, this pointing out of respect, when I read that verse, that Sunday morning in St. Paul's Anglican Church. It was damn cold too. Minus twenty-something. It was January. It is ninety-eight here.

And don't ever let me hear that you have become so modern, that you have started reading the new edition of the Good Book, which reads like the constipated prose of that American writer Ernest Hemmighway. Read it in the King James Version, *not* the Oxford edition. Me and the vicar came to words, and nearly came to blows over this same argument. Christianity is contemporary, he say, as if he was talking to a child, or was talking about manners and deportment.

Listen to how beautiful these words are: "*And tarry with him a few days, until thy brother's fury turn away*." Where but in the King James would you hear language as pretty as that?

Only a person with Kay's understanding would want such language modernized, for easier comprehension. The infelicities of the young . . .

I don't know how and why I got started on Kay. But having begun, you shall hear the end of that part of my life. I do intend, however, that the end of my life shall be slightly postponed. At seventy-one, I intend, as I have said, to begin at Genesis, and word for word, word by word, worm and work my way through, until I reach Revelations and Concordance. Another poetic word! I feel that I have reached concordance with you, my son, in the writing of this letter, at this stage, for after Hitler has been fed his rice and fish heads—hoping that no bones are caught in his swallow-pipe!— and I have read a few chapters of Exodus, I shall retire for the night, and join you again, soon, in a concordance of love and of deep nostalgia. I hope to complete both: this letter, and the Good Book, and I wonder which of the three remaining duties of my remaining days shall have been dispatched first? The Good Book? This letter? Or my life?

The feelings which I have been expressing to you, and which I have been expressing particularly with more emotion and honesty than normal, are taking hold of me, because all of a sudden, you are not here, not here in the big old house, whose emptiness echoes as if it was a rock quarry and I myself dynamiting coral stone. It is an old house. And it is larger, larger than for one man who spends almost every hour of the day and night inside it, except when I am next door with those two robbers, the vicar and the lawyer-fellow, alone. But it is a happy house, a warm house, a museum of memories and events and things which have been ourselves and our past and our aspirations. Your absence gives me the joyful opportunity, both to view these things and to rearrange them. Your absence, I hope, is merely temporary. Four years of study in that City of Toronto, which at this time of year must be forgetting the life and love of summer.

I was talking about feelings. Yes, these new feelings, which I must be expressing in my letter to you with a vengeance you had not known before, are feelings more normal for a woman, a mother who follows her child into another land, with words of love and reminiscence to express. And in the case of most women, this kind of love and reminiscence need not be pure love. It could be her transmitting the cord of birth, the maternal cord, the umbilical restriction that reminds the child, the daughter, that she owes an unpayable debt for being born. It is important that you do. I do not wish you to miscalculate my motives, even if they are devious.

I have, and I probably transmit feelings to you which state that I am not only your old, irrelevant father, but am behaving as if there is a piece of the woman, the mother, inside my advice and words. And I hope that as a wise man, with the blood of your dead mother's veins inside you, an Edgehill, that you will disregard all the advice I have been giving you, because I am speaking a different language, and breathing in a different air. Disregard it as a *modus vivendi*: but regard it as a piece of history, to be used as a comparison. Having now absolved you from all filial encumbrances of the mind, let me now incarcerate you immediately for your choice of a philosophical position which is not valid, or tenable, precisely because, as I have said earlier, you have assumed that there was not a history before your time, and you made the mistake of calling it a political situation.

You said you wrote a paper on the British Constitution, and that the professor gave you a B. You showed your paper to a Canadian friend, and he asked you to let him use it as his own submission. In the same course, you said. To the same professor, you said. The same length, you said. The identical paper, you said. The only change in the paper, you said, was that your Canadian friend put his name, a different name from yours, on the paper. You said all these things. Those are the facts of the case. And your Canadian friend got an A for the paper, you said. And you ask me now, if this is not racial discrimination, or bigotry, or unfairness. It is not so much your shock that it happened, and to you, but that there was no explanation, no regret, no forgiveness from anyone when you pointed it out to them.

I myself am shocked that you would have confronted the professor with his own bigotry. I am also shocked that you expected an apology and did not get one from him. You seem to feel that all these incidents of bad manners, all these expressions of a lower-class, peasant syndrome have only begun with your presence at Trinity College, and that Trinity is above that rawness of disposition. Had you an eye to history, to the realism and the logic that other black men before you had passed through the portals of Trinity College, you would not now be so smitten by your paltry experience.

You are, in spite of the black American Ralph Ellison, who would claim you are invisible, you are rather outstanding and conspicuous. An easy unprotectable target of whims and of deliberation. You are also a conscience. And if you know anything about consciences, then you should know that that part of our makeup, of our psyche, is hidden, is dark, is criminal, is Christian, is pure, is degenerate, and is beautiful as is Caliban.

There was a group of West Indian students at a place in Montreal, a second-rate place, called Sir George Williams College.

Montreal, as you know, and in spite of what you may be hearing these days amongst the Anglophones at Trinity, is essentially a French conscience. Why did I say this, when I am really speaking about the West Indies, and a bigoted professor of biology, and not about the culture of a place? The West Indians protested. And the Administration at Sir George, which had become during these protests a most third-rate institution, ignored their pleas of protest. The West Indians held a demonstration. They held it in a room where there was a computer. I never could understand that computer. Why did they not demonstrate in the Department of Biology? Or at the professor's home? In my estimation, it would have been better tactics, philosophically, to have done one or the other. However, the computer was damaged. Allegedly damaged by the West Indians, they said. The West Indians were arrested. All the newspapers said so. The West Indians were charged. The West Indians were later sentenced. To various prison terms. One of them is now a senator down here. Another is a senator up there. Does Trinity College have a computer? Do you wish to be a senator? Up there? Or down here?

These are not the sentiments I like to send to you, in a red, white, and blue airmail envelope, with a fifty-cent stamp on it, all the way from this island to you, up there in that City of Toronto, buried almost up to your two knees in snow, and in hostility.

I thank you for sending me the phonograph record by Lionel Richie, "Games People Play." It was also the name of a book by a man named Toffler, lent to me by the lawyer-fellow. I could not understand why so much attention was given to Toffler's book, which I have not read, and so little to the song. The Third Symphony of Beethoven's arrived without a scratch or a warp. I wonder how many postmen or post office workers have put their paws on this masterpiece before it got to me? Pearls amongst postmen!

Unfortunately, there are no pearls in the music that the Government Radio in this place plays. The music is like the voices of the politicians: vulgar. "Games People Play," which I remember dancing to with Kay, almost every Saturday night at a West Indian calypso club, The Tropics, fifteen-twenty years ago, is still fresh and contemporary; and very sensual.

If Hitler was a woman, Hitler and I would take a few steps. It is the kind of music that makes me want to dance with a dog! That never dies. Timeless. Incidentally, although I do not advocate that you become a Christian, I do insist that you find time to sit in a church, at least once a month. But preferably, in the Church of England. If you should stumble into a Catholic church, or if you are taken there, choose the best: the old cathedral at the corner of Shuter and Church. Sit inside a church. Listen to the music. Pay less attention to the sermon. The sermon is not meant for you, for our people. But the liturgy and the ritual are artistically rewarding. And so is the liturgical music. So far as Trinity College is concerned, and in case you are hungover, and desperate on Saturday nights, and cannot rise on Sunday mornings for breakfast before the dining hall closes, slip into the Chapel, take a seat near the rear, find the hymn —that shouldn't be a problem, you were a choirboy in the Cathedral church here—and sing it loudly, but not as if you are the soloist. And before the worms in your unrepentant stomach growl you out of favour from amongst the "divines," the theological students as they are called by the vicar and the lawyer-fellow, and out of favour with the sincere worshippers, the latter who are there because of the breakfast that is served after the collection plate, you may find yourself amongst the blessed, meaning the hungry poor. For the rich would not rise so early on a Sunday morning, and when they do rise, instead of oranges, bran flakes, soft honey that is grey in colour, bran bread and bran toast, warm milk, bacon done too hard, and soft-boiled eggs, the rich would rather eat eggs by Saint Benedict.

If you were here at Edgehill House, you would be partaking *our* Sunday breakfast: crab backs, stuffed with pork, and washed down with champagne. (*I found a bottle dated 1943. Dom-Pee.*) A pity it is, that I cannot put a crab back into this red, white, and blue airmail envelope, and send it to you!

"Games People Play"! It is a song that keeps coming back to my ears, whose emotion will not let me forget the sadness of love spent in Toronto. But I have to begin to move my finger as I read, along these lines of Exodus, and watch for the bones in Hitler's supper, and scratch the fleas from his back, after supper.

Hoping that the reaches of these few lines will find you in a perfect state of good health, as they leave me feeling fairly settled in concordance,

I am,
Your loving father,
Anthony Barrington St. Omer Edgehill

IF THE
BOUGH BREAKS

Where they were, on the second floor of a building that
squatted at the corner of Bay and Davenport, whose ground
floor was taken up by a store that sold milk for five cents
more than you could buy it in any supermarket in Toronto, and
beside which was a store that sold everything, these five women
were chatting while two others sat in the hairdresser's chair. The
hairdresser was a man. Christophe. A big strong man with a black
complexion, from Barbados. He had never learned French at school;
had never visited the islands in the West Indies where French is
spoken; but he understood what French meant in his business
in this city, so he changed his name from Granville Da Costa the
moment he graduated near the bottom of the class from the Marvel
School of Hairdressing; went by bus to Montreal and stayed there
for a long weekend, Labour Day weekend; and when he returned,
by train, he had the name Christophe and a new accent. He called
every customer *chérie*, which came out as "cherry." He had two
women working for him. They themselves had graduated from the
Marvel School of Hairdressing, three months ago, near the top of
their class.

On the front of the building, on the second floor where these
five women were now sitting, was emblazoned in lights, CHRIS-
TOPHE'S SALO. The lights that formed the letter N in "salon"
never worked. But Christophe was known throughout the city as
the best hairdresser, the only man, or woman, who knew how to
"fix" black women's hair.

One woman had curlers and grease in her hair; another woman's hair was lathered in shampoo, so thick and rich you could not tell her age, although she was the youngest in the salon. And the five women waiting together were all over forty and well-dressed; and two of them had foreign cars parked below; after one hour, they had given up running down the stairs to put loonies into the meters.

The girl in the chair cried out, as the shampoo ran into her eyes, stinging them, "Are you trying to blind me, Christophe? I'm too old to learn Braille, hear." She was a fourth-year student at the university. She was studying psychology. She was very good-looking. She came from a rich Barbadian family who owned a very small sugar cane plantation that grew sugar cane no longer. "I have theories to read."

"Cuddear, cherry!"

It was three o'clock, Thursday afternoon. They could hear the traffic below and the voices of people passing, for the windows facing the street were open for the breeze.

Christophe had forgotten to call the repairman to come and fix the two noisy air conditioners, taped around their perimeter with electrical tape which his friend Cox, a plumber, had left. So, the room was warm. And the five ladies were using the boxes of Kleenex, passing them from hand to hand, mopping their brows, their embroidered cotton hankies having been already saturated. And the prospect of the ironing comb, not really a comb made of iron by a blacksmith, as many of these very women used back in the West Indies, but its modern version, which performed the same function, making their hair "white," making their temples hot, threatening burns on their scalps, certainly singeing hair in the wrong places, all this made their waiting more uncomfortable than the patience they knew they must have, each time they visited this salon, always too crowded, too slow, and too understaffed. They had been Christophe's customers for years.

In, with a whiff of wind which cooled the salon, came voices of a quarrel below on the street. The room was quiet for a moment.

Then, a siren screamed through the buzz of voices, and the humidity seemed to clutch the women's bodies, and cause them to breathe more heavily. The noise increased and it seemed as if the ambulance or the police cruiser was going to climb right up the flight of stairs and join them. And in fact, it did stop in front of the entrance. The five women ran to the windows.

There was a hiss. The sirens stopped. And the hissing sound lasted a few more moments. The two assistants had dropped their instruments into some kind of liquid to make the hissing sound. They now joined the others at the windows. Christophe continued fixing the young woman's hair.

There were three large windows. The lower half of each was pulled up. So the women could lean their bodies out, and see. And they could look at one another leaning out the three windows. It was not an ambulance. There were three police cars. Stopped in the middle of the road, blocking all traffic. The owner of the store that sold high-priced milk came out to meet the policemen. They had left their car doors open. The women could hear the three radios crackling. The six policemen had their guns drawn. In the distance, coming towards them, was another cruiser, flashing in red speed and urgency.

"I bet you," one woman said, "it's some black man in there."

"And not eighteen yet," another said.

The policemen and the store owner were now inside the store.

"These *people*!" one of the assistants said. "I was walking through the Eaton Centre one night, and just as I take up my parcel with the things I bought in it, and paid for, all of a sudden I feel this hand on my shoulder, and when I turn round . . ."

"Blasted people, eh?"

Two of the policemen came back out. Between them was a young white girl. No more than sixteen. They took her to a car, and put her to sit in the back seat, while the other four officers exchanged words which the women could not hear; and then they too got into their cruisers, and drove off. The few men and women who had stopped to look walked on. One man took a red box from his pocket, extracted a cigarette, and lit it. He walked at a faster pace. A bus was coming. The wind was blowing again. The store owner came back outside with a broom, sweeping the sidewalk; and they could see, because of the stains from chopping meat and pork and roasts on his white apron that covered his body from his neck to his thighs, that he sold other things than milk.

"What you think they got her for?"

"Shoplifting."

"They begin young."

"Well, it was a good thing," the assistant continued, "that I had keep my receipt that Friday night. It was the Friday before the Caribana parade, and I was thinking of stopping at the kiosk-thing to buy a Lotto, 'cause I had had a dream the night before. But before I could walk more than two feet from the counter where I had bought the pantyhose, this blasted man's hand on my shoulder. I look round. And staring me in my face is this blasted white man. Security guard. Accusing me. Of something. Say I shoplifting. Well, I not ashamed to tell you, I let-go some bad words in his arse, that caused all the people in the Eaton Centre to stare at me. These blasted people, eh?"

"How old you think that girl is?"

"I could only see her head."

"I wonder if she have a mother?"

"From the back, which is all I could see, I would put her at sixteen."

"So young? And to have a record?"

"She's sixteen, as you say. She can breed."

"Christ, waiting here on Chris, my mind all the way up in Pickering, wondering if *my* child went home straight from school. We moved up in Pickering to get away from the crime and violence down here, but child, I tell you, up there isn't any better than down in Jane-Finch corridor, if you ask me."

"In the weekend *Star*, did you read the thing about teenage pregnancies?"

"Wonder what time Chris intends to get to my hair? Four o'clock, and school must be out a long time."

"What happened?"

"You mean the article?"

"No. The security guard and the pantyhose."

"I looked him straight in his face. The whole store watching me now. I faced him and I said, in my best manner, 'Let me tell you something, nigger-man.'"

"You called him that?"

"Was he black?"

"What was his complexion?"

"'If you want to,' I tell him, 'you could put your hand in my bag. But let me tell you something. When you put your hand in my bag, I am going to take off my shoe, and *drive* it right into your two blasted testicles.'"

"No!"

"His complexion was what?"

"Not black."

"And you called him a nigger-man?"

"He was a white man."

"*No!*"

"And what happened?"

"He didn't say another word to me."

"*No!* But the teenage pregnancies is what I want to know about."

"I didn't read the newspapers that weekend."

"Anybody have that article? Joyce, you think you still have it? You clips things from the *Star*."

"Was in the *Globe*."

"I don't take the *Globe*. The *Star* is my speed."

"Mr. Chris, how much longer before you getting-round to fixing my hair? I have a child at home waiting on me."

"And a husband."

"Had!"

"You divorced, cherry? I didn't know you and the old man had break-up, cherry."

"In name only, Mr. Chris, a husband in name only."

"That girl that we just see being arrested by the police, I am sure that they're going to take her down in that station and make that girl's life miserable, and they may even do—"

"Do what to her? Do what to her? What you mean by miserable?"

"Child, every other day in the newspapers there's stories about the police and women they have in their custodies."

"But that child, though . . ."

"She's sixteen. She can breed."

"You mean rape."

"Who said anything about rape?"

"Sexual assault. Sexual assault is the name for it nowadays. Everything nowadays is sexual assault."

"Growing up in the West Indies—"

"You're a damn liar!"

"How can you accuse me before you hear what—"

"What you're about to say? I already know it, before you even say it. You were about to say that growing up in the West Indies, we didn't have anything such as what we witnessing nowadays in this place."

"Well, how the hell could you know what I—"

"Because I know you. And I know the West Indies. And I—"

"You know too blasted much. You must be working *obeah*, that you can read my mind."

The five women were sitting again. The wind came through the windows in a slight gust, and for a moment, it was as if Christophe had fixed the air conditioners.

"Every year. Child, when you see Christmas come and the twenty-eighth is here, I longing for home. But I won't go home *before* Christmas. Christmas isn't Christmas unless you have a tree and snow."

"Child, all over the West Indies nowadays is trees, and *real* Christmas trees too! Not the artificial ones we had in our days!"

"Snow too!"

"Snow too? What the hell I hearing?"

"You didn't know? Didn't hear? For *years* now, the tourist board people in Barbados been importing snow from Canada. For years now."

"You don't mean the tourisses from Canada? You not referring to white people?"

"I am no prejudice. I talking about the snow. I understand it comes from Toronto, whiching—"

"*And* Montreal!"

"—whiching is the best snow in North America."

"Who's next, my cherries?"

Christophe removed the plastic bib from the neck of the woman who was now almost two hours in his chair. The smoke from his cigarette rose gently. He put the cigarette to his lips; pursed his lips as if he was about to kiss the woman dismounting clumsily from the high chair; put the cigarette in the glass ashtray; and said, "Who's next, my cherries?"

The five women looked at one another. They had had lunch together at the Four Seasons Hotel nearby. They had had two martinis each. And when they arrived, giggling, after discussing their children and their families and their husbands, as they did each time they had lunch, once in two weeks, they were fortified with food and drink, satisfied to wait the long wait in the old, hard, plastic-bottomed chairs. The plastic made their dresses stick to their bottoms and they could feel the lumps where the upholstery had collapsed against their soft well-cared-for skin.

"You have a child coming from school soon. You go."

"Charmaine can look after herself, man."

"You're not concern about that little girl walking the street and going home to an empty house with all this *worthlessness* you read about in Toronto?"

"Well, child, I would never allow my Suzanne to enter an empty house. Nor go to the mall with her friends. Some o' these friends, I tell you . . ."

"Charmaine's the same age as that child the police had downstairs a few minutes ago."

"Talking about bringing up children, do you believe we bring up our children better than *them*?"

"Well, you getting me mad as hell now! The evidence speaks for itself."

One amongst them, who had been quiet, now spoke up. "How you could compare *them* with we, with us? The facts speak for themselves! If it is only once, in my twenty-something years living in Toronto, I have lived to see the day when a police go in a store and don't bring out a black boy or a black girl, but a damn white girl. And all o' you spending your time taking up for that girl? I haven't heard nobody amongst you, in the two or three hours we been sitting down waiting for Mr. Chris to fix our hair, nobody, not *one* of you haven't uttered a word in support of the police! Not one of you!"

"Wait! She fooping a police?"

"She's a married woman, child."

"Her husband would break her arse if he *only* heard!"

"Are you sleeping with one o' Metro's finest, on the sly, girl?"

"The girl is a little whore!"

"She was unfaired by the police."

"Not the police. The man who own the store is who called the police. Blame *him*. *He* could be the son of a bitch."

"Who's next? Cherries? Who's next?"

"We're talking business, man."

"Just a minute, Chris, man."

"The fact that it was a white girl and not one of ours, well, that answers the question. We raise ours better than *them*."

"We had just moved to Pickering, in the house we're living in now, and it was a day like this, in late July; no, it must have been in August, 'cause we had just come back from watching the Caribana parade on University Avenue, and—"

"You see? You see? Christ, they couldn't let us go on to parade on University, 'cause University Avenue is too good for black people, so they moved us down beside the lake, where nobody can't see us, whilst they leave right-wingers like the Shriners to walk all over this city on tricycles as if they are still blasted kids! You see? You see?"

"Nevermindthat!"

"Why never mind that?"

"Nevermindthat! We had just moved into Pickering and my daughter was nine, my son was six, and my other daughter was eight, and we had just got home from sweating-up ourselves in the Caribana parade, and it was so hot and we had nothing cool in the house to drink, so me and my husband—"

"The cop you was seeing on the sly?"

"And fooping with? I did-hear that."

"Fuck you."

"Me, child? I can't do it by myself!"

"Was nothing in the house cool to drink, as I was saying, so we send the eight-year-old to the convenience store, just across the street, in the mall, to buy a large bottle o' pop, 'cause we had just got a bottle o' Mount Gay rum from a girlfriend who had gone home on holiday, and me and Percy opening this forty-ounce and waiting for the child to come back from the plaza, and when we hear the shout, these blasted sireens going like hell in front our house, and four police in three cars jump out and my child in the back seat of one o' them police cars, *handcuff*. Well, be-Jesus Christ, you shoulda seen how my husband *react*!"

"No!"

"Good dear!"

"Oh God! This happened to you?"

"And you never mentioned a word of this before?"

"Some things you have to keep to yourself, eh?"

"No! Not a' eight-year-old child, handcuff, in the back of a police cruiser! *No!*"

Christophe struck three matches before he could light his mentholated cigarette. The smoke shot through his nostrils without sound, in two long piercing white streams. The cars outside the windows were moving fast. Horns were blown in exasperation. And the women could hear a few complaining voices. When the cars passed they could hear the footsteps of people on the street, and the scratching of the broom as the store owner swept the sidewalk, and then they heard the scratching of a match on a box, and the inhaling of the first lungful of cigarette. It was one of the two assistant women hairdressers, smoking a Salem.

"Go on. Pass her a fresh Kleenex to dry her eyes."

"*My* eight-year-old. We send her to Sunday school every Sunday. From the time she was two, every Sunday as the Lord send, she was in that Sunday school class. We send her to piano lessons from the time she was five, and last year, taking the advice of a friend of ours, she's been taking ballet lessons, and—"

"*That's* the way we bring up our children!"

"And her ballet teachers at the Ballet School just down there on a side street off Church, her ballet teachers tell us that the child have a future in pirouettes. And, don't laugh, that August afternoon at five, four police have *my* child handcuff, in the back of a police cruiser, and all the neighbours looking out and pointing. When we moved up there, four months pass before the one on our left said a word to me, in regards to good morning or good evening; and the afternoon my husband brought home the new car, you should have seen them staring from behind their curtains. We shouldn't have those things. We shouldn't live the way *they* live. We shouldn't."

"What your husband did?"

"Pass her another Kleenex."

"It's too sad. It was too sad that August afternoon. It was too sad. And too shameful. I can't talk about it no more."

"Don't then. We know everything you were going to say. It happens to all of us. We know. You don't have to say any more, 'cause it is the history and the experience of each and every one of us in this room."

"Well, who's next?"

"My mind is still on that white girl."

"Are you her godmother?"

"She's a child."

"A child? She's a white girl. And she is the daughter of the four police in those three cruisers who molested this woman's eight-year-old daughter and handcuff her. She is the daughter of that landlord who didn't rent me that musty, stinking basement apartment thirty years ago, in 1961, on Walmer Road. She is the daughter of the woman at the Eaton Centre who had the security guard come up in my face accusing me of shoplifting, a decent person like me. She is the future mother of all the racists we come across in this city. She is just herself."

"Is a hard sentence, though."

"At least, she's a thief."

"I won't put that judgement on her, though, 'cause as I said, when my husband saw those four police having my daughter in the back of that cruiser, handcuff, well . . ."

"Sins of the fathers, my dear. Sins of the fathers. I didn't say it, and like bloody hell, I didn't cause it! You can find it in your Bible, if you ever read the Bible."

"And what sins have we committed in this place, since all of us were living here, coming from various parts of the West Indies? Name me one. Go right ahead and name me *one*. Name me one. The only sins we committed in this place, is obeying the blasted law. And from what I see, there is one law for us, and one for *them*."

"We raise our kids better than them."

"There isn't no argument 'gainst that, as far's I concerned."

"We're sitting down here in this hairdressing place, in at Christophe, five middle-class bitches with not one worry in the world, except if our husbands going-crawl home before three in the morning, from cattawouling."

"And with some o' these same white bitches!"

"Look at the five of us! I dress well. She dresses well. You dress well. Look at the dress that one is wearing. Five well-off bitches like us, with two-car garage, educated, decent, and have more education than most women, than the average Canadian white woman. And with *all* this, we have to walk-'bout Toronto with our head down, and—"

"Shit! Not *my* head!"

"Christ, I looks them right in their blasted eye!"

"I know, I know. Individually. But I'm speaking as a rule, as a general rule. You know what I mean. Back home, we'd be ruling the roost. We'd be women with men and husbands that make decisions and run things. But here, if it isn't some bloody parking lot attendant who hasn't been here for six months, and can't even talk English, if it is not some woman in the Eaton Centre, and don't mention Holt Renfrew or some o' them places in Yorkville Village, if it is not some damn racist cop, if it isn't some woman in a beat-up Toyota, while you or she are driving a BMW, or I behind the wheel of my husband's Benz, *anything*, any-blasted-body, we always have to explain *some* thing to them. Explain ourselves. Explain."

"My husband been driving a '68 Chev for ten years and would come home and curse *me*, and say how the cops in Toronto are the best. Last year, the son of a bitch got his hand on some insurance money from a policy we had take out fifteen years ago, and he bought this second-hand Mercedes-Benz I just referred to. It spends more time in the garage 'round the corner on Yorkville than parked in front our house. He bought a notebook from Grand & Toy. A black little notebook. Guess what he puts down in that little black book?"

"'Course, he puts down the mileage!"

"Or the miles!"

"What's the difference? Miles is mileage!"

"Not in my book, cherry," Christophe said.

"Every week. After ten o'clock. When he gets off the Don Valley Parkway. A cop. A cop in his arse! Three times a week, a cop pulls him over. As an average."

"They want him."

"Sending him a message."

"To go back to the '68 Chev."

"And here we are worrying about a little white girl that got picked up for shoplifting from a Mac's Milk. Ain't that something? We five black bitches, in a black hairdressing saloon, sitting down this lovely summer afternoon, worrying over a little white thief!"

"Harsh, though! Too harsh, cherry," Christophe said.

"How would *you* know? You ever given birth?"

"You don't have to be a woman to know that."

"A woman is a woman."

"I suppose you gonna say next that we have the same *thing* between our legs!"

"I wasn't getting personal, I was barely stating that a woman is a woman, and a mother is a mother, and—"

"A child is a child. Is that what you saying? That the one out there a few hours ago, arrested by the police, is the *same* as my eight-year-old? I bet you, I bet you *anything*, that they took her a little way down the street from the Mac's Milk, and let her go, and that poor man who owns the store will never get satisfaction for whatever it is she took."

"What she took?"

"What she could've taken to justify the way the police came, with sirens blaring?"

"That's a strange comment coming from a black woman like you! With your eight-year-old?"

"What was her crime? We sitting down here all this time, and nobody knows what is her crime?"

"*Stealing!*"

"Who's next? This is my last time, cherries!"

"And being white."

"Suppose, just suppose, they took her away for her own good. Suppose it's the owner of the store down those stairs who did that to her?"

They could hear the footsteps coming up the stairs. Another customer, probably. The breeze was cooler now. No one snatched a white tissue from the jumbo-sized Kleenex box. The thin smoke from Christophe's cigarette moved in their faces. One woman sneezed.

"Bless you!"

"Sinus?"

"Allergies."

"Is these blasted cigarettes Christophe smoking!"

The footsteps stopped. All of them turned to look. It was a young white girl. No more than sixteen. They continued looking, not speaking, not believing their eyes. In the short silence that was heavy as the earlier humidity in the room, they went back over the scene down below on the street, the police cruisers and the police-men with their hands on their guns, and the short store owner in his stained white apron sweeping the dust from the entrance of his store. And when they saw her, a gasp came from their mouths, and they were paralyzed for a moment. And then they all rushed to the little child. A newspaper was in her hand. She was sixteen perhaps, as in their recollection; but her appearance rendered her helpless, unprotected, and much smaller, a child in their eyes; and she seemed unable to move another step up the stairs. She had stopped at the round, hand-polished newel ball at the head of the banister. Christophe had tied a red ribbon round the newel last Christmas Eve, as decoration, and it had remained there ever since.

Her face was red. Red from the colour of the blows that had struck her face. Her lips were thicker than the lips of any of the five women. Her face had no expression. At first, the women could not tell whether it was fright or shame.

They were sure that what they would hear from her mouth would be tales of pain, of assault. The thought went through each of their minds at the same piercing moment and, with five slight variations, their minds sped to their homes, where they could see their own children. She looked as if she could be drugged. As if someone had given her something to drink that contained a drug. They did not believe she had taken it herself, by herself. They believed she was too innocent, too nice a little girl. She was a child. A newspaper was in her hand.

"Lisa!"

She held the afternoon *Star*.

Christophe said the name; and said it two more times. The third time he called her name, it was astonishment turning to unbelief. "*Lisa?*"

"You know this girl?"

"She's his niece. She delivers my paper."

"The corner-store man?"

"Mr. Macdonald's niece, Lisa. She lives with him."

"This girl's in trouble, Chris, you can't see that? We have to do something for this poor child, man."

"Come, come," one of the women said. "Come."

"Ask her what happened."

"Not now, man, not now. This is an emergency."

They half-carried her, surprised at her solid weight, to the chair where the last customer had sat; and they turned the tray with the shampoos and the pins and the curlers and the straightening agents to one side, and they placed two soft cushions on the black leatherette bottom of the chair, to give growth and height to her body; and someone in the meantime was filling a sink with hot water; and the steam was rising higher than Christophe's cigarette smoke; he was holding a cigarette at the corner of his mouth, with one eye closed against the sting of the mentholated smoke; and one woman stood behind Lisa and held her gently against the hard black leatherette back of the chair; and one woman stood on each side, rubbing a hand over Lisa's chest which was rising and falling as if she were running from something, while the remaining two women took turns testing the heat of the water pouring out of the hot-water tap, soaking white towels and testing the heat against their faces and gauging Lisa's ability to withstand the steam.

The hot towel made her start. And close her eyes. And it was then that they saw bruises on her beautiful skin. The towel moved over her cheeks, and she winced. She closed her eyes each time the towel touched her, but they could see the blueness of her ears. They could see the holes pierced into her ears, for earrings. They could see her teeth, pink against the strong fluorescent light pouring down from the ceiling; and when they shifted their position, running the warm towel round her neck, her teeth became sparkling white. They could see a scratch at the bottom of her neck. "Take off her dress." She still had the newspaper in her left hand.

"Not the whole dress, she's a child, after all. Just lower the blouse."

But someone raised the hem of her dress, and they saw it. For a moment, they stopped passing the lukewarm towel round her neck. They took the newspaper out of her hand, and handed it to Christophe, and he dropped it on the floor. And the women who stood at the back of the tall leatherette chair kept their hands on her wrists and on her left shoulder. Christophe stubbed his cigarette into a jar of hair pomade. The grease embedded the cigarette into itself. It was blood on her leg. On one leg.

"*Blood?*"

"Jesus Christ!"

"It's blood, all right."

The five women thought of their children, daughters and sons. The five women thought of their husbands. And one by one, but together in their fear and in their horror at the spectacle and what they knew the spectacle could mean, they went back over all those times, when their own children had been left with uncles and brothers-in-law, with close friends of their families, with their own husbands, fathers of their children, and they dared not travel back with too much memory and clarity and honesty. It was blood on her leg.

No one wanted to ask the question.

They knew the answer without having to pose the questions even to themselves. They knew it could be one thing only. One cause. One kind of violence. It was the violence they knew. That they had lived with from birth. Pain and blood. Blood and pain, in a combination of joy, of sorrow, of natural function, and, for those blessed with fertility, the pain and blood of giving birth.

"Why does it always have to be so?" said the woman whose daughter had been handcuffed. "Why does it have to be so, all the time?"

Her eyes were filled with tears. And she made no effort to hide her disconsolation. She was now holding the child's body, in her arms, and was rocking back and forth, her tears falling into the blonde hair of the child, who was now sobbing, and who had in all this time, not spoken a word. "Why is it always this way with women? And for women?"

"Call the police."

"Who have the number for the police? I never had to call the police before."

"Call any number. Call *all* the numbers. One must be the police. Call 767!"

"That is SOS on the telephone dial."

"So call it, nuh! The police *bound* to come . . ."

WHEN HE WAS FREE AND YOUNG AND HE USED TO WEAR SILKS

In the lavishness of the soft lights, indications of detouring life that took out of his mind the concentration of things left to do still, as a man, before he could be an artist, lights that put into his mind instead a certain crawling intention which the fingers of his brain stretched towards one always single table embraced by a man and a wife who looked like his woman, her loyalty bending over the number of beers he poured against the side of her glass he had forgotten to count, in those struggling days when the atmosphere was soft and silk and just as treacherous, in those days in the Pilot Tavern the spring and the summer and the fall were mixed into one chattering ambition of wanting to have meaning, a better object of meaning and of craving, better meaning than a beer bought on the credit of friendships and love by the tense young oppressed men and women who said they were oppressed and tense because they were artists and not because they were incapable, or burdened by the harsh sociology of no talent, segregated around smooth black square tables from the rest of the walking men and walking women outside the light of our Pilot of the Snows; and had not opened or shut their minds to the meaning of their other lives; legs of artless girls touching this man's in a hide-and-seek under the colour-blind tables burdened by conversation and aspirations and promises of cheques and hopes and bedding and beer and bottles; in those days when he first saw her, and the only conversation she could invent was "Haii!" because she was put on a pedestal by husbandry, and would beg his pardon without disclosing her eyes of red and shots and blots and bloodshot liquor; the success of his mind and the woman's mind in his legs burnt like the parts of the chicken he ate, he was free and young and he was wearing the silks of indecision and near-failure. But he mustn't forget the curry: for the curry was invented by people and blessings, Indians, or perhaps they were the intractable Chinese; the curry was the saviour of his mind and indigestion just as the woman guarded for no reason in the safe soft velvet of her unbelieving husband's love, guarding her in her turn as they sat opposite each other in the different callings of paint and metals and skin and negatives and thirst during all those dark days in the Pilot; the curry was the saviour of a madness which erupted in his mouth with the aftertaste of the bought beer and the swirling bowels after the beer and after the curry; she was like the lavishness in the light except that the colour surrounding her in the darkened room hid everything, every thought in his mind, just as the wholesome curry in the parts of chicken hid the unwholesome social class which it could not always distinguish from the bones any suitable dog in shaggy-haired and shaggy-sexed Rosedale would eat, and if the dog in Rosedale and the dog in him did eat them, the dog might make them, like this woman sitting with her drinking man, into an exotic meal packaged through some sense of beer and the sense of time and place, and looking at it in one imaginative sense, turn it into something called *soul food*: now, there are many commercial and irrelevant soul food kitchens these days in nighttime Toronto, and any man could, if he had no soul and silks on the body of his thoughts, if his soul were occupied and imprisoned only with thoughts of *her* sitting there badly in the wrong light of skin, he could make a fortune of thoughts and sell them like dog meat and badly licensed food to all the becauseful people who wore jeans and heavy-weave expensive sweaters walking time into eternity in dirty clothes and rags because they were the

"beautiful people," as someone called their ugliness, like *her* of soon-
time piloted to a tavern, married to a man who did not deserve
the understanding of her; these the becauseful people, people who
didn't have to do this because they didn't want to think about that,
because they were people living in the brighter light of the soft
darkness which they all liked because they were artists and people;
the becauseful people like her liked her and likened her to a white
horse, not because of the length of her legs or the grey in her mind,
but because in the lavishness of the wholesome light of the Pilot she
looked as secure and was silent as the fingers of the tumbling avoirdupois of the man who made mud pies in the piles of quarters and
dollars, mixmasterminding them in the cash register. It is so dark
sometimes in the Pilot that if you wear dark glasses, which all the
artists wore on their minds, you may stumble up the single step
beside the fat man sitting on a humptydumpling stool and where
she always sat on her pedestal of distance and protection chastised
in pickled beer, and you may not know whether it is afternoon on
Yonge Street outside, for time now has no boundaries, only the
dimensions of her breasts which her husband keeps in the palm of
his flickering eyeballs; it is so dark in the early afternoon that with
your dark glasses on, you might be in Boston walking the climb in
the street climbing like a hill to where the black and coloured people
live; or you might be here in Toronto walking where the coloured
people and the kneegrows say they "live" but where they squat,
here where E. P. Taylor says he does not live but where his influence
strangles some resident life and breeds racehorses of the people,
where Garfield Weston lives in a mad biscuit-box crumbling in
broken crackers; in the lavishness of the night thrown from your
dark glasses, you might stumble upon a pair of legs and not know
the colour of time, or what shape it is, or where you are, or who
you are: he thinks he should haul his arse out of this bar of madness
and mad dreams, drinking himself into an erection stiff to the
touch of ghosts in her legs and the legs of the tables. He had seen
her, "this young tall thing," walking to the bar through winter in
boots and rain in blue jeans and sandals, insisting without words

in the fierce determination of her poverty and dedication to nothing she could prove or do that this was her personal Calvary to the cross of being Canada's best poetic photographer, unknown in the meaning of her life beyond the tavern, unknown like the word she would use, "budgerigar," having years ago thrown out Layton, Cohen, Birney, and Purdy in the dishwater of her weather-beaten browbeaten body and heavy sweaters; he could see her mostly among women stuck to their chairs by the chewing-gum beer, free women freed by their men for an afternoon while art imprisoned the men with beer, wallpaper along the talking walls like flowers, their own flower long faded into the dust of the artificial potato chips they all ate in the nitty of their gloom because it was like grit for their reality, their "dinner" an unknown reality like her word, "budgerigar," in the despised bourgeois vocabulary and apartment-lairs of their lives; and in this garden of grass growing in their beds he had handpicked her out five years ago, this one wallflowering woman who wore large hats in the summerstreet, and cream sweaters in winter. She always sat beside the man who sat as if he was her husband; tall in her thighs with the walk of a man, this white horse-woman with the body of a bull; and the eye of her disposition through the bottom of the beer bottle warned him that "the gentlest touch of his desire might be fatal to the harmony" of the two ordered beers which they drank like Siamese twins in the double bed of their marriage. He, the watchman-man, was harnessed by island upbringing and fear in the lavishness of the dim light, ravishing her ravishing beauty with his eyes they could not see, eyes they saw only once and spoke to once when they saw him entering or leaving; for five years. For five years of not knowing whether the sun would sink in the space between her breasts, or whether butter ever dried in the warmth of that melting space, he watched her like a timekeeper. Once he saw her leaving her husband's side and he followed her spinster's canter all the way in his mind down the railing guard of parallel eyes honouring her back-side sitting on the spinning stools where the working class reigned and into the bathroom, past two washbasins and the machine that saved pregnancies and populations with a quarter, on to the toilet bowl, under the dress she had plucked with her hand and had pulled up her dress and did not soil her seat or sit on it because it was in the Pilot, and he smiled when she reappeared with fresh garlic on her lipstick mouth; and he looked at the edges of her powder, and he looked into the lascivious dimness and saw her and smiled and she smiled but the smile belonged to the mud-piling man at the cash register or to another table where they were talking about the Isaacs Gallery and the Artists' Jazz Bann where Dennis Burton's garter belts were exhibited in stiff canvas and wore houndstooth suits and the thick heavy honey of colours and materials thicker than words. He had walked around her life in circles and bottle rings of desire and of lust and she was always there, the centre of dreams frizzled on a pillow soaked with the tears of drinking; he followed her like a detective in the wishes of his dreams, and from his inspection of a future together got a headache over them and over her, and over the meanings of these dreams. *Mickey* and *Cosmospilitane* and other dream books did not ease the riders of the head in his pain, and nothing could unhinge his desperation from the wishful slumber of those unconscious nights of double broken vision. And then, like a cherry falling under the tree because the sun had failed it, after long thoughts and wishes of waiting, she fell into his path, and he almost crushed her. He remembered the long afternoons waiting for the indelible rings of the melting bottles to ripen, waiting for the departure of shoppers who lived above the Rosedale subway station to stop shopping in the Pickering Farms market so he could shop and not have to listen to the loud-talking friendly butcher in the fluorescent meat department, and whisper loud under the suntanned arms of the meaty housewives and commonlaw wives, "One pound of pig's feet, chicken necks, and bones—for soup," and hear the unfeeling son of a bitch, "Er-er! Who's next?" behind the counter dressed like a surgeon with blood on his chest, saying, "You're really taking care of that dog, ain't you, sir?" Godblindyou, dog! Godblindyou, butcher! This meat is for the dog in front of you; and he remembered her now, single, on this summerstreet

under the large hat, as she was five years ago under the drinking
mural under the picture of hotdogs and fried eggs that some heart-
less hungry painter drew on the wall where she sat beneath when
she was in the Pilot. He fell into the arms of her greeting like an
apple to the core and he looked down into her dress and saw nothing, not even one small justification for the long unbitten imprisonment of his mouth and his ambition, thinking of the nut-seller
selling his nuts next door. She was away now from the Pilot. And he
did not even know her name: not for five years; he never was introduced to her name. "Hurley or Weeks . . . Weeks or Hurley . . ."
Either one would do? "They are both mine, and I use either one any
time," but Weeks is her maiden time; although she was no longer a
maiden, though single and with no husband for weeks and months
now. There was no large gold ring on the finger of her personal
self-regard, which she said ended mutually on a visit of her once-
accompanying husband warming radically, like forgotten beer, into
her haphazard lover; there was no bitterness in the eyes of her
separation because she missed only the cooking which he would
do every evening, when she said she was too tired, or couldn't be
bothered to cook, which was every evening, when he would do the
cooking in her kitchen and leave her afterwards like the dishes,
panting from thirst and a thorough cleaning, so her eyes said on this
summer afternoon, hungry in the frying pan of their double-bed
bedroom, where he kept the materials of his stockings, feet and
trade, his love of meddling with medals and metals and sculpture,
and where she kept a large overgrown blow-up of her brother's
success in the cowboys and movies in the West, shooting the horses
over the head of the never-setting bedpost, her brother with a gun
in his hand, a gun loaded at the ready to be fired at the nearest
rivalry of bad men and bad women, a gun which he gave her, a gun
which remained nevertheless loaded, hung-up, cocked, and frus-
trated and constipated from no practice or trigger-happiness; and
this she talked about; she did not stay in one place, she said she was
rambling, not along the streets, because she did not like to walk,
but that she was rambling and that she had to be alone in the consti-

tutional of her thoughts, from one bar to the next bar; she admitted she might have a problem, but it was not this problem which changed her husband's heart into a dying lover drifting apart at the semen in the widening sea of her jammed ambition: "I do not know what I want to do; I know what I don't want to do, and that is stay married, but I don't really know what I really want to do." She bore her wandering in her hair, loose and landing on her broad shoulders like the rumps of two cowboy horses; and her dress was short, short enough for the eyes to roam about in and follow her over all her landscape at a canter—that's how she was put away; she was put away as if she could be put to pasture for work and for love and for bearing responsibility: "I know I don't want to have a child. What am I going to *do* with a child? I know I can have children and I know I can have a child. I want a child, but not now, because a child *needs* love . . . and and and I I I haven't any left right now for . . ." He looked at her and wandered and wondered why she couldn't give a child a chance, a chance of love, with all the pasture in her body, all her body, with all her breasts, with all her milk bottled in brassieres that had no bones stitched in them, with all her thighs that spilled over her dress hem, "A-hem!"—but perhaps she was really talking about another kind of love and another need for love, which was not the same as the need for love her lover-husband needed from her when she was a child in his arms late at night, and was crying with him in the double-minded cradle of his sculptures. *Haii! Austin!* He looked into her eyes and made a wish that her body under his eye would not be completely bloodless as her hands sometimes seemed five years ago when she was fresh from the basement washroom, and the snow on the women walking out of the cold corner of Yonge and Bloor in the arctic months; that her body would not reveal the theft he had in mind to put it through, the theft her husband had put it through; that she would not be like Desdemona and wax, but that she would be a queen from the entrails of Africa and Nefertiti, plucked out in olive blackness luscious to the core of her imagined seed, like the Marian from the alligator troughs of Georgia. He dreamed a long dream standing

there on the street with summer before her, and he killed the colour
of her body because it needed too much Eno's before it could go
down; and he wrapped her in a coffin stained in wood in blood, and
made her again to look like Marian from way across the bad lands of
enroped and ruptured Georgia. *Haii, Austin!* He was back in those
good old days, good because they had no responsibility for paying
the good deeds artists incurred in debts and made them bad, bad
debts and artists on the segregation of walls and memories; he was
here and he was there in Georgia in the double ghost of a second,
for artists were bad for debts and for business in those young days
when he was free and the only silk was his ambition; he remembered her in those days, and on this summer afternoon already
obliterated in the history of the past, nights in the crowded Pilot
Tavern, searching the faces of the girls and women for one face that
would have a meaning like Marian's, and he could not find one head
with truth written in its clenched curled black peppers of hair, one
mask with the intelligent face of Nefertiti, the history of Africa
from Africa, not from the store on Yonge Street, "Africa Modern,"
selling blackness cheap to whites, written brazenly upon its ivory;
a mask, a mask from that land not unlike Georgia; he had watched
for one face like a timekeeper keeping a watch that had no end of
time in it, and he had to paint the faces black, blacken them as he
had blackened the red clay sculpture a woman did of him once, like
an Indian in his blood, and had made it something approaching the
man he wanted to be, something like the man Amiri Baraka talked
about becoming in the later years of his new Muslim wisdom; he
remembered the sweet-smelling Georgia woman in those soft
nights when the bulbs were silk as moths among the books overhead
like a heavy chastisement to be intelligent, like a too self-conscious
intention; with the sherry which she drank in proper Southern
quantities, like bourbon warm to the blood; and her fingers were
long and pointed and expressive, impressing upon his back, once,
her once-beautiful intent, as they writhed in pain with glory and
some victory, after she lay like a submarine in a watery pyre of soft
soapy suds, white flowers of Calgon upon her black vegetation,

going and coming, he remembered her in the shiny cheap stockings
proclaiming her true colour of mind and pocket and spirit and
background and intention: *a black student*; a black woman, black
and shining in that velvet of time and black skin, a black woman,
black and powerful down to her black marrow; there was something
in the ring of her laughter, perhaps in the gurgle of her bourbon, in
the *ding*ing of her voice when she laughed in two accents, northern
and Southern, something that said she was true-and-through beautiful, and because she was black, and because she was beautiful, she
was beautiful; she could withstand any ravages of history, of storms,
of stories that wailed in the rope-knotted night of Georgia; she
could stand on a pedestal under any tree which no village smithy in
white Georgia would dare to stand up to: a man who had no burning
conviction could not put his arms as high as her waist, for she had
seen certain sheets of a whiteness which were wrapped around a
black man's testicles in a bestial passion play, and she had seen, in her
mother's memories, this play as it showed the germ of someone's
bed linen made into sheets that were worn as masks of superiority,
testing a presumption that some men would always walk on all
fours like a Southern lizard. *Haii, Austin!* This woman standing
on the summerstreet in the silk of time stopped without desire;
and that woman lying in the rich water with her smell, whom he
remembered best holding down her head in love, in some shame,
looking into a book of tears because his words were spoken harder
than the text of any African philosophy. He remembered that
woman and not this woman, well: Marian, his; ploughing the fields
of poverty and a commitment in her barefoot days, dress tangled
amongst the tango of weeds, sticking in the crease of her strength
silken from perspiration, and her dreams cloggy as the soil, and in
her after-days in the northern rich-poor city, her long-fingered
hands again dipping into the soil of soiled sociology Jewished out of
some context, maintained backyards, maintained yardbird poverty,
backward in instruction the smell of soil the soiled smell of the
land in which she was born, the smell of poverty, a new kind of
perfume to freshen her northern ideas, a new kind of perfume

truer than the fragrance of an underarm of ploughing, more telling than the tale in the perspiration of her body, in the fields, in the sociology, in the kitchen, in the bed, in the summer subway sweaty and safe with policemen and black slum dwellers from Dorchester, in the heat, in the bus stations, in the bathtub in Boston; a perfume of sweet sweat that clothed her body with a blessing of pearls, like a birthwrap of wet velvet skin: "Honnn-neee!" the word she always used; honey was the only taste to use; "honey" was the only word she used always; for it was a turbulence of love and time from the lowered eyelids, from the vomiting guts up to the tip of the touch of her skin. She was a woman; she was a woman without woe; she was to be his woman, she should be here in the summerstreet; now in the summerstreet, he watches this alter-native of that woman, he understands that the transparency of this dress, tucked above her knees by the hand of fashion, is really nothing but the vagueness of this doll; he sees now that this transparency is the woman, like the negatives she meddled in for five years' time, like the film on a pond's surface, like white powder, like a glass of water with Eno's in it, like a glass of water in the sun, the water clear and unpolluted, the water the topsoil of the sediments at the sentimental bottom; he wanted to mix this water with that water in the bathtub in Boston, the water and the mud into some heart, into that thick between-the-toes soul of the Georgia woman; he wanted to break the glass that contained that water for the Calgon bath and the sherry and the bathwater; break the vessel, spill and despoil, spill and expel this watering-down of the drink of his long thirst; stir it up and mix the sentiments in the foundation with the upper crust of the water, shake it to the foundation of its scream and yell and turn it to the thickness of chocolate rich in the cup, thick and rich and hot and swimming with pools of fat, so he could drink, so he would have to put his hand into the black avalanche of feeling and emotion and sediment, deep and gurgling as the tenor in her laughter, down the tuning fork of her throat resounding with love and make her say a word, speak a thought, be some witness to the blood in her love. This was his Marian in the vision in the summerstreet. This was

Marian. And the five-year stranger, estranged from her husband's love in a transparency, in the costume of a lover, this woman who used to sit upon the pin of his desires, now on this summerstreet where he thought he saw her, she is nothing more vivacious than a feather worn in her broad-grinned hat: not like the scarf *she* wore, with conch shells and liberty scars and paisley marked into it with water; this negative of Marian passed like the cloud above the roof of the Park Plaza, where one afternoon she sat drinking water, when he was playing he was playing golf in the new democratic diminutive green of the eighteenth-floor bar; and a cloud passed overhead like the loss of lust of a now-dead moment, with the woman; and when the sun was bright again, when the sun was like the sun in Georgia, fierce and full, when the sun was a purpose and passion, when the sun was as bright as the sweat it wrung from the barrels of a black woman's breasts, the laughing beautiful Marian was there, not in his mind only but larger, dispossessing the summerstreet in the buxom jeans of her hips, red accusing blouse belafonted down the ladylike tip of the gorge of sustenance between her breasts, and around her neck, around her throat, a yellow handkerchief and a chain of a star and a moon in some quarter of her sensual religion. He saw her with passion and with greed, he saw her clearer than the truth-serum syrup of a dream, than the germ of love, true as the Guinness in the egg, and the Marian was his stout, this woman. He remembered all this, standing in the summerstreet: when before she climbed the steps to her hospital, she held his hands like a wife going in to die upon a cot, and drew him just a suggestion of new life closer to the relationship and her breasts, and with the sweet saliva of her lips she said in the touch of that kiss, "Take care of yourself." He was young and free again, to live or to travel imprisoned in a memory of freed love, chained to her body and her laughter by the spinal cord of anxious long distance, reminders said before and after, by the long engineering of a drive from Yale to Brandeis to Seaver Street to Brandeis, dull in the winter Zion of brains, dull in the autumn three hours in miles, hoping that the travel won't end like an underground railroad at the door of this nega-tive woman, but continue even through letters and quarrels and long miles down the short street up the long stairs in the marble of her memory, clenched in her absent embrace but rejoicing with his fingers in the velvet feeling of her silken black natural hair . . .

SOMETIMES,
A MOTHERLESS
CHILD

She went back on her knees beside the bed. But the words did not come. "I can't commune with you this morning, Lord." She got up, rubbed the circulation back into her knees, pulled the pyjamas leg from sticking to her body, passed her hands over her hips, promised to eat less food so late at night, touched her breasts for cancer, and said, "Lord, another day, another dollar!" She walked out of the bedroom and into the cold hallway, four paces long, passed through the living room which served also as a dining room and kitchen, and into the tiny bathroom, colder than the short hallway. She looked up at the colour print of a man with a red beard grown into two points, strong piercing eyes, thin face, and sallow complexion. The man's heart was not only bare, but exposed outside of his chest. Something like a diadem, or a crown made of two strands of branches, thick and plaited with thorns sticking into the man's head, was causing drops of blood to fall from his skull. The colour print was above the sink. "Father God," she said. She closed her eyes and continued to pee. The man's hand was raised, the right hand, in a salute like that made by a boy scout, or like a gesture bestowing benediction. It was this gesture which made her say, "Thank you." And with that, she felt better. But the words they were saying, and the words written about the Jamaican, and the sad memories that the snapshot of her husband brought back; and the drying up of her own words so necessary to begin the morning with; and the snoring behind the wall—these three worries passed from her mind, and made her gait and her posture light and carefree as she stepped into the shower. She hated showers. But they were quick. And this morning, in her hurry to be happy, she pulled out the new-fashioned circular shower knob, and the water, pounded against her body, as if it contained small pellets of ice. She shrieked.

And before her scream died down, she was on the telephone to her landlord, who lived on the floor above her head. She hated his walking on her head more than she hated showers.

"*Mister* Petrochuck!"

"Yes, my darlink?"

"Am I paying you rent for this place? Regular as God send? And I can't take a proper bath in peace, without the water turning cold-cold-cold as Niagara Falls, and freezing my blasted body?"

Through the receiver she heard his hearty laugh, and words in some foreign language, which she hated next to having to take showers, which after five years she still did not know the origin of; and when his laughter abated, and her anger died down, she heard Mr. Petrochuck explaining the difficulty.

"I tell you two times now, Mrs. Jones," he was saying, no longer with laughter in his voice, for in a way he both loved and feared her. "Two times I explain it now. You turn knob to left for the cold. And you turn knob to right for the hot. And you turn before you pull out knob."

She felt ashamed to have to be told these explanations again. "So, how the hell am I to know that? Where I come from, you turn to the left for the hot. *To the left!*" She tried to imitate his accent, to diffuse both her frustration and her anger. "And you turn the knob to the right for the cold."

"That's right!"

It was her time now to laugh, and to laugh and talk as she teased him.

"Thanks, Mr. P."

"Thank you, Mrs. J. Thank you, darlink."

"*Sometimes, I feel like a mother-less child!*" She was already in the shower, and the water was warm, and her voice was beautiful and clear above the sound of the water, which came out in jets, as if it were mixed with marbles that had been taken from a furnace, and mixed in cold water. "*Sometimes, I feel like a mother-less child . . .*"

When she was dressed, she started to prepare a sandwich, using Wonder Bread and canned salmon. She put a slice of tomato and a leaf of lettuce between the soft white slices. She wrapped it in a large white napkin, then into greaseproof paper, then into plastic. She dropped it into a brown paper bag. She placed a five-dollar note on the paper bag, and secured it with a paper clip.

She pushed the door of the small room behind the wall where she was standing in the kitchen, and looked at the large body curled in the shape of an embryo, on his left side, breathing heavily through his mouth. She looked down at the sheet and the blanket torn away from his body. And she admired his smooth black body, muscular in the places where men his age are muscular; and with his hair cut in that odd style which she had never liked, with two things that looked like lightning marks shaved deep into his short hair; and after she had taken in all this, as she did every morning during the week, she turned the light on.

"*You!*" she shouted.

This is the way she greeted him every morning, the way she chose to rouse him from his sleep. There was a smile in her shout, as she stood by the door, blocking it, sturdy as if she was a prison guard. "*You!*"

Her voice penetrated the sleep that had been embracing, and it might have penetrated also the nightmare that his sleep had wrapped him into, for with the second call, he sprung upright, and started to tremble in terror. She noticed that he had a hard-on. But she was his mother.

"Don't shoot, don't shoot!" There was terror in his pleading.

"Who shooting you? Boy, who are shooting you?"

"Sorry, Mom."

"Is somebody shooting you? Look, fix yourself in front of me, do!"

He pulled the sheet up, and covered his nakedness.

"School isn't this morning?"

"Yes, Mom."

"Well, get up, you!"

"Thanks, Mom."

And she laughed, and hugged him tight, as if it was a farewell of love. He wrapped his strong black arms round her body, and she could feel his heart and she was sure she could feel his blood. Then, she released him. She turned the light off. She closed the door. She shook her head from side to side in profound satisfaction at the way he was getting along, making plans for him and for herself, but more than anything else, making plans for his future. She was so proud of him. So proud. And he was growing so well. She gathered up her purse. She selected a large bag. She folded it and put it into the leather bag in which she carried her purse and other things. She turned the lights off in the rest of the apartment. She was worried about something. Why would he say, "Don't shoot, don't shoot"? But just as soon, she put it out of her mind. He was such an obedient boy. She began to hum, and before she closed the front door, and before the clock on the mantelpiece chimed seven times, she heard him say, "Bye, Mom. Have a good day."

Her shower this morning was warm and embracing, and the water soaked her body as if she was still bathing in the waves of the sea. She was feeling better. She would manage her work today, and not complain. She would even change her mind about taking showers.

"Life is so good!" she said, turning the key in the lock. When she walked down the short path, covered with snow with ice beneath, her steps went gingerly, and she didn't mind the winter. "*Some-times, I feel, like a, mother-less child . . .*"

"BJ! BJ! Hey, man! It's Marco, man! BJ!" He waited as usual, until he was sure, until the caller had identified himself by name, before he even moved from the chair where he was reading a book, *The Autobiography of Malcolm X*. He wanted to be sure. He had to be sure that he was opening his mother's door to the right person.

"Hey, BJ! It's Marco, man!"

Years ago, when he skipped school on the smallest pretext, and felt he was clever in doing so, his mother got the landlord, Mr. Petrochuck, to check on him; and Mr. Petrochuck asked her how would he check on her son, and she told him how. "He can't fool me, Mr. P, so don't let him fool you. Just look along the alleyway between my place and the house next door, and see if you see if my son left. Make a note of the footprints in the snow, and I sure, Mr. P, that a man with your experience in the Second World War, as you always telling me you was in the Alpine Battalion with skis and a gun on your shoulder, that you would know what time my son passed through the alleyway on his way to school." The landlord's laughter, and hers, and his remark that she was a better spy than any he had faced in the Russian Army, lasted throughout the rest of the conversation that ended with her giving him her number at work, with the instruction to call her back. She spent that morning, with her hands in the rich foamy water in the double sink, washing crystal glasses from the party the night before. But her laughter turned to anger and violence when she heard Mr. P's report; and when she got home at seven o'clock that night, she was tired and blue with fuming, but her energy came back to her, just as she was revived by the morning shower, and she stood over him, ten years old on that cold Monday night, and she counted twenty-one times that the leather slipper was raised and landed on his back; and she stopped counting, and did not hear her words, as she drove the slipper across his back, ripping away one of the thongs, and shouting and muttering and screaming, as she flogged him, "Let me tell you something, you hear me? Let me tell you something, young man. If you don't want to go to school . . . I will take you myself, to the nearest police station . . . and let them lock you up, you hear me?" And it went on that way, the sharp blows from the slipper rising in their unsatisfied anger, and her voice piercing the peace of her basement apartment which she kept clean and in which she made no noise, careful to be decent and respectable, ". . . and, and-and, living in this place with all the things happening to black people, to men and boys like you, and you wanting to turn out like them?" And it stopped only when there was a shortening of her breath, a dip in her energy, and in her anger, and she heard the pounding at the door. At first she thought it was the police. And she got scared. And then she felt grateful that they had come so promptly to take her son away. "Serve you damn right!" And then she was terrified. She saw herself in handcuffs, taken out to the police cruiser, and placed in the back seat, with the road of neighbours watching, and led into the station, the same police station she was going to take him to, and have her fingers placed on the inkpad, and in ten small spaces, printed as a criminal, and the charge of assault, or bodily harm, or violent assault, whichever charge they wanted to lay on her, stamped upon her history as an immigrant of Toronto from the West Indies: branded as another blasted Jamaican, even though she was from Barbados. And then, she recognized Mr. Petrochuck's voice. "Are you going to kill boy?" And in the relief, and the protection his presence brought, as if he was still in the Alpine Battalion and had rescued a detachment of his men ambushed and encircled by their own loss of control and of nerves, she did not lower the broken leather slipper again, but held it in her right hand, as her eyes filled up with tears. And she embraced Mr. Petrochuck, and she asked him to sit with her for a while, and she remained silent and heavy with her grief which shook her body in spasms from time to time. That morning when they had spied on him, as he explained it to Marco on the telephone, hours later, the snow had betrayed him. It had remained firm and pure, clean and like innocence itself, without a blemish, because he had remained in his room all day, listening to music. Marco had supplied the school principal with a note of excuse, with his mother's signature forged on it. But he learned his lesson and deceived the landlord, who continued to report his activities to his mother; and he excelled in class through his brilliance, and because he was bright he had more time to do the things he wanted to do. So, this morning, when he heard her leave, as he has been doing for years, he put his coat, a fur-lined jeans jacket, over his pyjamas, put on his sneakers, and walked from the back door, his private entrance, through the deep snow, right to the alleyway, and through the alleyway to the front of the house. Then carefully, he walked backwards, placing the sneakers exactly into the footprints going away from the back door, retracing his steps, right back into the house. He had been doing this so often that he no longer regarded it as a skill. Or as deceit. It was like brushing his teeth as the first activity after getting out of bed. He took off his sneakers, brushed them off on the mat covered with a copy of yesterday's *Star*; he dusted the snow off his jacket, as he had brushed the low-hanging branches of the tree in the alleyway, and put it back into the cupboard where he kept his stereo and CD player, and his clothes, and which he had covered with a piece of cloth he had bought from the Third World Books & Crafts store on Bathurst Street, just around the corner. The cloth was kente cloth. He had read somewhere in his voracious appetite for books that Malcolm X was married in kente cloth.

"It's Marco, man."

He closed the book, after putting a bookmark between the pages; the bookmark was a six-inch piece of kente cloth, and replaced it into the shelves which took up two complete walls of his small room. The shelves were crammed with books. All the books were paperbacks. All the books dealt with black people, and were written on black subjects, in fiction, philosophy, religion, art, culture, and his favourite, biography. He kept his school texts under the bed, on the floor.

"BJ! Man, it's Marco!"

He was not impressed by the impatience in the voice, and before he went to the door, he rested the Gauloise cigarette in an ashtray, he lit some incense, and he turned down the volume of the CD of John Coltrane playing "A Love Supreme." He put his housecoat on, and went to the door. The ashtray was a square crystal one which his father had bought eight Christmases ago, and had never used. His father did not smoke.

"Fuck, man!" Marco said, stomping one foot after the other on the worn coconut-husk mat. "It's fucking cold out here, man!"

BJ looked at Marco sternly.

"Sorry, man."

A trace of a smile came over his thin lips as Marco remembered BJ's aversion to foul language. His father had drilled that into him, with a few beatings.

So, he opened the door a little wider, and Marco squeezed between the doorpost and him, and went in, and stomped one foot after the other, although his sneakers were already wiped clean on the mat. He hunched his shoulders, and pushed his hands into his jeans side pockets and said, "It's fucking cold, man!" Under his arm were newspapers.

"You should control your emotions better than that."

Marco looked cowed, and said, "Sorry, man. But it's all right for you, man."

They embraced, bodies touching, heads touching the right shoulder, and slapping each other on the back three times, as if they belonged to an old fraternity of rituals and mystery. They let go of each other, and did it a second time, with their heads touching the other's shoulder. It was Italian, and it was African, and it was this that had joined them in their close friendship for the past nine years. They saw each other every day, either at school or here in BJ's room. Their parents had never met. And did not know of their sons' deep friendship. And it never occurred to either of them that they should bring their parents into their strong bond of friendship. BJ's mother went to every school event that required a parent's presence. And Marco's mother and father attended them too. But they never met.

BJ went to the small square table in a corner that had an African print covering it, and on which he kept a large leather-bound copy of the Holy Qur'an. Two glasses and a bottle of vodka were also on the table. Ice was already in the glasses. He had been expecting Marco. The ice was now melting.

"Punctuality," he told Marco, "is also not an Italian characteristic, although *we* are blamed for inventing CPT."

"Fuck, man! Gimme the drink!"

And BJ poured two strong vodkas. He had not forgotten the orange juice, but he could not risk taking it earlier out of his mother's fridge, just in case. He did this now, and when he returned, Marco was sitting in a straight-backed chair, with his drink already at his lips. He poured each of them some orange juice.

Coltrane was at the stage in his song where he was chanting "a love supreme," over and over. Marco joined in the chanting. His voice, similar to a bass, was deep for his age, eighteen.

"*A love su-preme, a love su-preme*," he chanted. "Nineteen times, fuck, you say he does that. Sometimes, you don't know, BJ, but I feel he's gonna sing it maybe twenty times, or eighteen times! Fuck."

"Unless your concentration diminishes, Coltrane won't."

"Fuck!"

BJ went back to the table, brushed a piece of ice from it, and ran his hands over the cover of the Qur'an. It was covered in brown paper, cut from a bag from the Liquor Control Board of Ontario, the LCBO, weeks ago, when he went to pick up his weekly supply of vodka. He was seventeen then. But he looked older. He had always looked older. This did not fool the manager at the LCBO store around the corner from his home, and he knew it; so to save the embarrassment, he used forged identification, including a schoolmate's birth certificate. He felt guilty about doing this, on the first three occasions; but it was the style of the times. Only last week he read in the *Star* that the police had caught five immigrants working illegally under false names and with forged social insurance numbers. It was the way of the times. And he was a born Canadian, so "Fuck!" Marco consoled him, and himself. On the brown paper cover, he had printed HOLY BIBLE. On the bedside table, beside his single bed that had an iron bedstead, he had placed the Bible, just in case. He read the Bible too. His mother had given him the Bible. But he devoted his devotions to the Holy Qur'an. Coltrane was now into the second part of his song. The music came out at them with equal balance, and power, even though BJ had turned down the volume, out of the four speakers. The speakers were four feet tall and more than one foot in width. He had built them himself. The other components in the stereo, he and Marco had reconditioned from spare parts and odds and ends thrown out by neighbours in his district in the Bathurst–Dupont Street area, and in Marco's neighbourhood up in North York. Every piece of equipment, but the CD player, they had reconditioned themselves.

"Did you check out the things for me?"

"Yeah, man," Marco said. He was almost perfect in his imitation of the speech of black people. It came out easily and almost natural. "I got me the *Form*, man."

"Well, let's spend a few moments scrutinizing the entries, and adding to our fortune."

"All these books. Fuck. Man, you's something else! I can't help saying, all these motherfucking books!"

Marco would busy himself by taking out a book, flipping its pages, replacing it, and repeating this until he had touched almost every book in the shelves. And he did this to allow BJ to concentrate on the *Racing Form*. "You're like, like a walking 'cyclopedia, man. And also a genius at the track. Fuck!"

"All it takes is concentration, Marco. I've been telling you this for years. Concentration. *And* dedication."

"I gonna give you something Italian to read. You know anything about Italian classics? Man, I gonna lay some Italian literature on you, one o' these days. Like *Dante*, man."

"Third shelf, sixth book from the right, second bookcase."

The book Marco picked out was *Seven Systems of Dante's Hell*.

"Fuck! I didn't know he wrote this, too!"

"Imamu Baraka wrote that, Marco. That's a different inferno," BJ said. And for no reason apparent to Marco, he added, "My mother is fine. She didn't ask for you this morning."

"Fuck!"

"This morning, she pushed my door and greeted me in her usual way: '*You!*' I pretended I was sleeping, but all the time I could see her face, and the worry in it, and the worry in her body about her work, and I was pretending I was sleeping. I was up all night, reading."

"This Black Power shit?"

"As a matter of fact, Marco, I was reading Shakespeare."

Marco got up from his chair and went to the bookcase. He knew this one. This one was, in a way, his favourite bookcase, for it contained books he too liked. The bookcase was made from unpainted dealboard, sawed and cut by him and BJ; and it occupied the space in the wall between a window and a cupboard. It ran from the floor to the ceiling. BJ liked everything in his room to run from the floor to the ceiling. It had something to do with perspective, he said. Marco did not understand, and said "Fuck!" to show his sentiments. If his room were larger, Marco knew that they would have built the speakers from the floor to the ceiling.

In this shelf in the bookcase were books by Shakespeare which Marco liked, and did well in, in school, preferring *Romeo and Juliet* —"Fuck! Not because I'm Italian, man!"—and *As You Like It*, and *The Merchant of Venice*, which they stopped studying in his school the term before he reached that grade. BJ preferred *Henry IV* and *Othello* —"Because you're black, right? Fuck!" But BJ told him, "Because it contains the best and, perhaps, the most noble of Shakespeare's noble poetry. I don't even like the character Othello. Iago is a more realistic character. I see Iagos every day in class." And to all this, all Marco said, years ago when they had this conversation the first time, was, "Fuck!" They have had this same conversation many times since. And Marco uses the same single word to express his sentiments.

"Today is the last day. I suggest we go out with a bang. But how many classes would you miss if we got there for the first?"

"Lemme see. Biology. Physics. English. And basketball practice."

"I will do *your* biology and physics assignments for you. Or we can do them together at the track."

"Fuck!" Marco said. He rubbed his hands as if he was cold. He poured himself another vodka and orange juice.

For young men, for eighteen-year-old boys, really, they had an enormous "prodigity" for alcohol, which is the term BJ used laughingly, when they would sit in his small room, and consume half of a twenty-six-ounce bottle of imported Absolut vodka, hidden under generous quantities of orange juice; and if his mother had returned home and had seen them, she would shake her head in pleasure at their hearty liking for orange juice: "You two boys don't know how good I feel to see you drinking orange juice, instead of all this damn Coke and Pepsi!" And after these long bouts, their speech was not even slurred.

"Did you remember the *Globe?*"

BJ read the *Globe* every day. He read the racing tips first. He read the sports section second, the editorial third, and the foreign news section fourth. He read nothing else in this newspaper.

"Woodbine, here we come!" Marco said. "*They're at post*! Fuck!"

"Should we invest a hundred each? What is your opinion, Marco?"

"A hundred bucks? Fuck! Why not, man? I deposited yesterday's winnings in my account. Those tellers're *weird*, man. She look at me with all that bread as if I was a drug dealer! Fuck, man."

"Today's the last day," BJ said. Marco noticed the tone of his voice.

"You all right, man?"

"You have to do something with the money in your bank account. Something. *Some* thing. And we have to think about the car too."

"Today is the last day, man. So, if we lose . . ."

"Don't say it!"

"Sorry, man."

BJ went to his dresser, a narrow, tall piece of furniture which his mother had bought at the Goodwill store on Jarvis Street, and he had stained it himself to make it look like mahogany. It looked like a mahogany antique piece of Georgian furniture, although he did not know that. It had five drawers. In the top drawer, under his handkerchiefs which his mother starched and ironed and folded into four, he kept his cash, arranged in denominations in ascending order, inside a box that contained cheques from the bank. He opened this drawer now, and took from it a metal box that had a key. He brought the box to the bed, and unlocked it. There were four boxes that used to contain cheques in the metal box. They were full of banknotes. No note was smaller than a ten. He did not count his money every night, but his memory was good, and he knew that, with the withdrawals and the deposits into his private "safe," he had five thousand, three hundred and five dollars in it. He could not tell his mother about this. He could not offer to lend her money, not even when he saw her moaning and crying and cursing his father for having abandoned them; not even when her rent of four hundred dollars a month was due. And sadly, not even when she had to postpone her registration for one month, in the Practical Nursing course at George Brown College, and never did catch up. She would kill him if she knew that he had so much money, in her house. But he had prepared for her future. At such a young age, it seemed ominous, too adult, too final a thing, this preparation for his mother's life. He had opened a savings account in her name, at a different bank, different from the one she used. Marco put his winnings in a chequing account. But he kept his in cash.

"Here's twenty tens, Marco. I'll take twenty, too. This is the last day, so I'm staking you. What we win we keep. What we lose, well . . ."

"Fifty per cent of our winnings should still go in the kitty, man. Fuck!" It was their business arrangement. And they stuck to this code, like members of a gang. "And look for a long shot, man!"

"There's no such thing, Marco! No such thing. My father went to the races every day. Faking illness from work. And family crises and emergencies. He had to be there. In summer and winter. He even walked there, once. Not to mention the times he *had* to walk home. And he bet on long shots, because he was a gambler. He was a gambler. And was greedy. He was a fool. A damn fool. He thought he could get rich from the track. We are different. We are investors. Don't ever let me see you betting on a long shot! Long shots are for racetrack touts."

"Why can't we use the car?"

"It's not safe for us to drive that kind of car in Toronto. It's safer in Montreal."

"Oh man! What's the point of having the wheels, and not using it? Fuck!"

"Have you told your parents you own a white BMW? Or more correctly, a fifty per cent share in a 1992 white BMW?"

"Well, fuck no, man! For them to put me in cement?"

"Exactly! My mother doesn't even know I can drive. As long as our friend is cool, the car will remain parked in her underground garage up in Scarborough. Now, I have to make my *salats*."

"Make your salads, man. Make your salads. Fuck."

"Respect my religious principles man, or leave."

"I'll respect your salads, man. I'll respect your praying, man."

The Timex watch on BJ's wrist began to buzz. It was the hour for prayer. Marco poured himself a vodka quickly, eager to stop the racket of the ice cubes in his glass, and the sound of the vodka pouring out of the bottle, now almost empty, before BJ began his prayers.

BJ pulled a cheap Persian rug from under his bed, unrolled it, and placed it in front of the table on which were the Absolut vodka, imported, and the Holy Qur'an. He placed the Qur'an on the floor, in front of him, and he placed his hands before his heart in the demeanour of prayer and meditation.

All this time, Marco was looking into the pages of Plutarch's *Lives*, which he had taken from the bottom shelf of the narrow, unpainted bookcase that contained only classical literature. And he sucked on the vodka, straining it through his teeth and the melting pieces of ice cubes, as his friend *ommmmmmm*ed and *ommmmmmmm*ed, and intoned "*alla hack-bar*," which is how Marco understood the pronunciation of the Muslim prayers. *Fuck*, he said to himself, *this motherfucker is real serious. If I didn't know he was serious, fuck!*

It was nine o'clock. The morning was crisp and cold and clean.

The boy flung the newspaper at the house, aiming for a different spot, and it banged against the window where she was with her hands in the thick, white dishwater, foaming like the waves that crashed against the rocks near the Esplanade, and then retreated back into the calm, blue sea. She was thinking of home. She had seen the newspaper boy. "You little bastard!" And the boy jumped back on his bicycle, and sped out of the circular driveway over the crunching snow.

It was ten o'clock. The morning was cold. When she had got off the subway and was walking to this mansion, the wind ripped into her body, and made her think of going back home the moment she had made herself into a woman, meaning when she had money. The ripping wind against her body made her feel as if she was naked. The wind had the same brutal touch as *his* fingers on her backside that day when she was bending over the vacuum cleaner. He had not touched her. She imagined it was his intention. And imagining it, it made it real. The wind swept up her legs, right between her thighs, clawing at her pantyhose with such force that she thought she had left home without putting on her underwear. She felt the shame in the touch of the wind. "I should have been born a man," she said, to the newspaper boy disappearing over the smashed snow, but really not for his ears. Men didn't know how lucky they were, she said, continuing her thoughts; they didn't know how damn lucky they were to be wearing pants to get more greater protection from this damn cold. "And in other things too!" Her thoughts went back to her son. For she had seen the photograph of the Jamaican family on the front pages of the *Star* newspaper many weeks ago, and now this morning, when that damn boy pelted the paper that almost broke the window where she was, here was another short story about Jamaicans and the police. She wiped her hands on her apron, and began to study the newspaper. It said that the young man was seventeen, and it said that he was living with his mother in a big house in the suburbs, in Brampton, and it said he was in the car with another young man about his age, and it said that he was not going very fast and that the traffic policeman didn't have to follow him with the sirens on, and it said he was shot in the back of his head. She felt sad. And wanted to cry. She had just left her own son at home, this morning as always, by himself, before dawn broke, in bed; and she wondered if he was safe. "But praise God, he doesn't have no car. A car is the surest thing to make a police shoot a black man dead. Praise God for that!" And she wanted to take up a cause, and hold a piece of stick with cardboard stapled onto it, and a message written on the cardboard, in thick black letters: THIS COUNTRY RACIST. THE POLICE TOO! "Yes! And put an exclamation mark after it too!" She wanted to cry. She wanted to scream. But who would listen to her? A simple woman like her? That's why, she said to herself, a man has it better; for "I am the least amongst the apostles."

The young man's face, and the face of his mother, wringing her body in tears, filled the space of the double sinks as she returned to her work. Her employers were having a party at five. And when the images of the mother and the son evaporated like the foam of soap from the two sinks, in their place were the faces of her own son, and his father, "that no-good bastard!" She pulled the plug in the second sink, with force, and the face of that "bastard" disappeared. She began to hum, "*Sometimes, I feel like a mother-less . . .*"

BJ got out casually, and with self-assurance, from the taxi, at the front of the tall apartment building near Eglinton and Victoria Park, in Scarborough; and as he walked across the lawn, he passed a blue car in which two men were sitting. The men were watching the same entrance BJ took. They had been there for the past three hours; and they had started watching the door since last Sunday. BJ paid no attention to the blue car. He walked straight to the panel of names, and pressed one of the buzzers. It was a buzzer beside the name G. Harewood. He did not know G. Harewood. He could have pressed any buzzer. It was only two o'clock, and his school friend who allowed him to use the underground parking, without her mother's approval and knowledge, was still in school. This was the only way to retrieve the car.

"Who's it?" a woman's voice, mangled by the magnification and the malfunction in the speaker system, cried out. The voice came through louder then he expected, and he made a start. It stirred him more than usual. "Who's it?" The voice was now irritable. "Is it George?"

"Yeah!" BJ said, trying to change his voice to George's voice, with knowing George's voice.

"Come on up!" the woman's voice screamed. It was less irritable. "Come on up!"

And when BJ entered the lobby, he could still hear the voice saying, "Come on up!" and the buzzer on the door to let him in was still being pressed.

He pressed the button in the elevator to P2, and went down into the bowels of the building. Three women were in the elevator with him. The three women stared at him. When the three women were tired of staring at him, they stared at the floor. Pools of water from melted ice were on the floor. When the three women were tired of staring at the floor, they stared at the illuminated numbers on the panel in the elevator. When it came to P2, the three women stood where they were. It seemed to BJ that they were standing in such a way as to suggest that they had taken the wrong elevator. BJ got out. BJ walked straight to a corner of the large dimly lit underground parking area. Glimmering in the bad light of the dull fluorescent bulbs was the white BMW. He stood beside it. He looked at the front tires. He looked at the hood. He looked at the windshield. The elevator door was still open. The three women were watching him. He went round to the front of the BMW and he looked at the bumper. He looked at the cap which covered the hole to the gas tank. He screwed it tight. It was already tight. It was locked. One of the three women got off the elevator when it reached the main floor, and walked straight to a door marked SUPERINTENDENT. The superintendent answered at the first ring. He was eating a salmon sandwich that had bits of green things it in, which were now between his teeth. The woman started talking to the superintendent.

BJ looked at the licence plate. He passed his hand over it. He was about to brush the dust from the plate onto his trousers, but he remembered in time. He was wearing expensive clothes. His trousers were black. They were full in the leg, and narrow at the ankle. His socks were white. And the shirt and jacket fitted him as if they were three or four sizes larger than his weight and size. He took a handkerchief from his pocket. The handkerchief was white, and folded into quarters. He wiped his hand, and then he passed the handkerchief slowly over each letter of the car licence. When he was done, the licence plate was glimmering almost as much as the BMW itself. The licence plate said BLUE. His beeper was beeping. So, he got into the car, with the doors locked, and the engine still turned off, and he checked the beeper. It was Marco.

He turned the engine on. Gradually, the interior of black leather got warmer and warmer until he felt he was as comfortable, sitting in it, as he was in his room surrounded by all his solid-state stereo and CD equipment and books. In this car, he had installed an equally expensive system. John Coltrane was playing. He had left the cassette in the tape player. "A Love Supreme."

The car was warm. BJ's two large eyes filled up the rear-view mirror, and he could barely see, in periphery, the elevator door open, and a man and three women; and the women were pointing in his direction as they talked to the man; but the BMW was warmed up, and it moved without noise over the caked ice in some parts of the underground parking; and he manoeuvred it through spaces left by bad and careless drivers, past large concrete pillars, and mounted the incline to the exit door, in no hurry, and all the time speaking to Marco on the telephone, and he had to repeat himself two times, for the aerial struck the top of the last exit door, and finally he emerged into the brilliance of the winter afternoon, bright in the sun but still cold. The women had just told the superintendent, "I'm sure he looks like one of those drug dealers, and I feel he is, not because he looks like a Jamaican or anything, but . . ."

The two men in the blue car saw the white BMW emerge from the underground parking. And the two men made a note of it. And they registered BLUE in a notebook. And they made a check on their computer. And they began to talk on the telephone. BJ was heading for Yonge and Steeles, to pick up Marco at the subway station. He was in a good mood. The last racing day was something else: fuck! as Marco put it. They had won and won and won . . .

Facing her now were the most magnificent slender white sculptures of branches on the trees in the backyard. For many years now she had seen these trees change their form, and she still did not know the name of one of them. But this afternoon, around three, with the clear light and the brilliance of the sun which gave no heat, she marvelled at the beauty and thought of men travelling in olden times, over this kind of landscape, walking in shoes made from skins, and following in the tracks of wild animals they had to kill to stay alive. The landscape of this cold winter lay before her as if an artist had applied pearls and other kinds of jewels, with the precision of realism, on the branches of the trees. But she was not happy inside herself. Something was bothering her. And she picked up the telephone and called her landlord.

"Did you really see him?"

"Yes, I tell you, Mrs. J."

"Go out, dressed? In his school clothes? In time for school?"

"Everythink."

"You sure it was my son? You didn't mistake somebody else for him?"

"Sure!"

"Well, thank you, then." And to herself, she said, "I don't know why I am in this mood."

She had selected and laid out on the dining table the crystals and the silvers and the plates; and all she had now to do was choose the serving dishes, and put the placemats on the shining mahogany table. She checked the roast beef in the oven, and shook her head at the amount of food she cooked, with most of it thrown away the next morning, since neither husband nor wife liked to eat leftover food. "And with all this damn food wasting day in and day out, and so many people on the streets of this city starving, with nothing to warm their stomachs with, and that blasted boy I gave birth to, refusing to eat normal like ordinary people, saying he is a Muslim.

What a Muslim is? Is a Muslim a person who doesn't have common sense inside his head, that makes him refuse all this richness?" And she laughed to herself. It was a joyous laugh. A hearty laugh. A laugh from the bottom of her belly. She looked around to see if anyone was close by, to mistake her for a fool, to think that she was going out of her head, laughing and talking to herself like this. "And come telling me that he is fasting. *Fasting*? And all this food, all this food going to waste. I wish I knew somebody on my street, without foolish pride, to leave a plastic container of this food at!" And she began to hum. "*Some-times, I feel . . .*"

As BJ pulled away from the curb in front of the subway station in the East End, with Marco strapped in beside him, and laughing and turning up the volume of the saxophone solo, the BMW was so loud with the music contained within it, that Marco himself felt his head was about to explode; and BJ was becoming nervous that perhaps the BMW would become conspicuous with the two of them in it with so much noise. The windows were rolled up. The BMW took the first entrance on to the 401 West doing eighty. BJ settled behind the wheel, with an unfiltered Gauloise cigarette dangling at the corner of his mouth, one eye closed against the smoke, and he put the car into fourth gear, and the car still had some more power left, and it moved like a jungle animal measuring its prey, and exerting additional power because of the certainty of devouring its prey. The prey in this case was their destination. But they did not have any anxiety of time and distance to reach that destination. It was simply that BJ liked to drive fast. That was why he convinced Marco to buy the BMW instead of the Thunderbird. And that was why he got it with standard transmission. They had won the money at the racetrack, one afternoon when Marco made the mistake of buying the three horses in a triactor race for ten dollars, instead of five, which was their custom. The name of the horse that won, that went off at fifty-to-one odds, was Blue. BJ knew he could not keep all that money in his room; and he knew that he could not open an account, without questions being asked. He knew he could not give it to his mother, even with the explanation that he had won it at the track. What would he be doing at the track? Why was he at the track on a school day? So, he bought a white BMW. He paid a friend of his, a real estate salesman, three hundred dollars to represent him. Real estate was at rock bottom at that time, and the salesman was more than happy to keep his mouth shut, and to pocket this unusual commission. But BJ knew all the time that he had to be careful, and that the time might come when the real estate salesman, still at the bottom of the unsold rocks of houses on the market, would need more help in keeping his mouth closed. He had to be careful.

He turned the music down a little more, and he reduced his speed back to eighty. As these thoughts entered his head, he had been doing one-fifty. He had just spotted a marked police cruiser, with 52 painted on its white side, parked alongside the 401. But he did not know that, as soon as he had pulled away from the subway at Steeles, at that precise moment, a blue sedan, with two men in it, had pulled away too, and had followed him until he entered the 401 going west. The marked police cruiser was expecting him. And as he swooshed by, the traffic policeman was on the radio to another one, somewhere farther west along the 401. Conversation passed between the policemen in the cars. "Drug dealers for sure!" And, through another system, came, "Question of being armed and dangerous." And the two policemen who had been parked in the blue car across the street from the apartment building in Scarborough added their contribution: "We were hoping for a red Camaro, but you never know with these drug dealers; they have the money to change cars . . ." And Coltrane was playing his ass off, as Marco was saying, still fond of the way he thought BJ talked, and should talk. "Trane's playing his ass off!" he said, again. He said it three more times. BJ grunted something. In his rear-view mirror he saw the police cruiser pull into the same lane as his, tailing him. He knew this stretch of the 401 like the palm of his hand. He was west of the Allen Road, approaching on the highway, a little north, the area in the city known as the habitat of drugs and guns and gangs, and called by two names: one the name of a woman, a whore; the other the name of a bird, which may also be a woman and a whore. Jane–Finch. He knew this stretch of road well. He knew he could get into the express lane within twenty kilometres. The cruiser was gaining on him. Marco was oblivious to this. He was listening to Coltrane. The cruiser's red light was still not on. But BJ surmised that any time now, it would be. And the siren would start. The lanes ahead of him were crowded with slow drivers who had themselves seen the cruiser, and had reduced their speed. All four lanes heading west were crowded. But that was what he wanted. He put the BMW into third. He was gearing down to stop; and the car was not so noisy with the music; and that was when Marco commented about Coltrane's mastery of "A Love Supreme," when BJ changed his mind about stopping to face the consequences. For how would he know the cruiser was following *him*? Of the hundreds of cars on the highway, why should a police cruiser pick him out? Because he was a young black man driving an expensive car? He told himself he must not be fooled by the logic of a man, or of a woman, or of a time, a better time than was taking place in this city; he reminded himself that logic had absolutely nothing to do with it. He was intelligent in the ways of the hunter, and in this case, the hunted. He was relying upon his instincts. Somewhere in his vast reading, he had come across something about this. He was not quite sure, nor could he remember the exact quotation; but it had something to do with instinct and emotion and gut feeling. His mother lived by her emotion. He geared up to fourth. The BMW lurched forward. Marco said, "Fuck!" and tightened his seat belt. "Let her ride, baby, let her ride!" It was already in fifth. And in and out of traffic, from the slow lane, to the middle, to the fast lane, and when the fast lane was not fast enough, and the entire width of the four-lane highway seemed to be creeping, the white BMW swerved like a top spinning near the end of its revolutions. "Fuck!" Marco said, when they were safe, for the time being, on a secondary road, somewhere near Dufferin. "What the fuck?"

BJ smiled. He turned Coltrane up. The car was filled once more with the beauty of music, with the pulse of emotion, and with the feeling of the time; and they remained quiet in the waves of this melodious tune they both liked so much, and argued about. BJ insisted, because of his new religion, that it was a religious chant. Marco, equally insistent, said it was a love song.

"*A love supreme*," he began chanting. "*A love supreme*. Nineteen times the brother says *a love supreme*! Nineteen times, BJ!" He never lacked enthusiasm about this aspect of the song. "Fuck!"

"Nineteen times," BJ said. And he turned the music up even louder. They were cruising along Eglinton Avenue, passing record stores from which reggae and dancehall blared out upon them, past barbershops and restaurants and shops which sold curry goat and fish and oxtail and peas and rice, and they felt they could smell and taste the food even in this breathless afternoon, so cold, and so uncertain. Jerk pork. Young men, some younger than either of them, walked, with a patience that came closer to loitering, along the lively street, stopping now and then to place their hands on the parking meters, as if reassuring themselves and the ugly pieces of metal that life was still going on, even in this cold afternoon when it was difficult to breathe; in this heart of West Indian life, when there was no attention paid to the depth of the fall in the coldness and where life remained constant: the laughter and the lightness of dress and manner. "What about lunch?"

"Yeah!"

"Curry goat? Or oxtail?"

"Fuck! Goat *and* oxtail!"

BJ and Marco were driving around. Listening to Coltrane and taking in the sights. It was about four in the afternoon. The white BMW had just been washed at the car wash at the corner of Bathurst and St. Clair. And the music was sounding better, it seemed, now that the car was spotless. As they handed in their chit, the four car washers, who were polishing another car, paused in their work to admire the white BMW. And they looked long at the car and then longer at the two teenagers, and said something with their eyes and said something to themselves, and went back to polishing an old black Pontiac. BJ was accustomed to people looking at him and then at the BMW. And when Marco was with him, they looked at Marco, at him, and at the car. And sometimes, if it was in the parking lot of a supermarket, or in a mall, they would go through the order of looking and staring a second time, in reverse.

They were cruising south along Bathurst now. It was Friday afternoon about five. And the traffic was heavy. And BJ was driving within the speed limit. And as he turned left into the street before Dupont, to tack back on to Dupont because there was no left turn there, from under a low-hanging tree came a police cruiser. BJ and Marco were alone on this stretch of road. And the cruiser came close to them, and BJ understood fast enough, and pulled over and stopped.

"Get out! Get out!"

"Yes, officer."

"You too! Get the fuck out!"

"Yeah, officer."

The policeman was out of the cruiser, and he had his hand on the T-shaped nightstick. His other hand moved to his gun to make sure, it seemed, that it was still there.

"Out!"

They were already out.

"Okay, okay!"

"Who're you talking to like that? Eh? Eh? Who're you fucking talking to, like that? Eh? Eh?"

And with each "eh," he poked his T-shaped stick into Marco's ribs.

"Up against the car! Up against the fucking car! Both o' youse! Both o' youse!"

It seemed that, in his training, his lecturer had had a hearing problem and he had to repeat each answer two times; for he was now saying the same thing two times, as if it was his normal way of speech. Or as if he was also accustomed to talking to fools, or immigrants who didn't understand English, and he had to speak in these short, truncated, repeated sentences.

"Spread your legs! Spread your legs! Come! Open up! Come! Open up!"

And they obeyed him. BJ could feel the dust from the side of the cruiser, which needed a wash, entering his nostrils. He could feel the policeman's stick moving around his legs, around his crotch, up and down, up and down. Touching his penis. He could feel the policeman's hands, tough and personal, strong as ten pieces of bone, feel his thighs, his chest, under his arms, between his legs, and feel his penis and his testicles; and then the ten pieces of bone spun him round, so that he now faced the policeman. BJ stood silent and calm as the policeman did the same thing to Marco. He thought the policeman was treating Marco more severely.

"Where you get this goddamn car?"

Before BJ could answer, the policeman was talking again.

"Where you get this goddamn car?"

BJ was about to say something, when the policeman cut him off.

"You steal this car! You steal this car?"

Marco opened his mouth to speak, and thought better of it.

"Who owns this fucking car? Who owns this fucking car?"

BJ was about to put his hand into the breast pocket of his suede windbreaker, to pull out his driver's licence, when the policeman came at him. His hand was on his gun. His gun was in his hand. The policeman seemed to see red. The policeman seemed to feel his life was being threatened. The policeman was behaving as if BJ had taken out, or was about to take out, a dangerous weapon. The policeman turned red. He came at BJ with great force, as if he was tackling a running fullback, and when he hit him, he had him flat against the side of the cruiser. Dust rose from the side of the cruiser. The cruiser leaned for a short time off its tires. Marco was about to intervene, when BJ raised his hand to stop him.

"Come on, nigger! Come on, nigger!"

And he slammed BJ into the side of the cruiser, a second time.

He put his hand behind his back, and when he brought it from behind his back, he was holding handcuffs. He snapped them on BJ's wrists. He poked the T-shaped stick into Marco's side, and ordered him into the cruiser. And he pushed BJ towards the cruiser, and threw him into the back seat, beside Marco.

"You could put away those! You could put away those!" BJ's licence and ownership papers were still in his hand.

The policeman went to the white BMW, stroked the tires with his T-shaped stick, and was about to smash the front side window, but something made him change his mind. He turned the engine off, put the key into his pocket, and came back to the cruiser.

He drove off. Voices of other policemen and of a dispatcher babbled on the radio. He seemed impervious to the racket of the voices. He drove south on Spadina and turned right at Bloor; and left on Brunswick, and into a few short one-way streets, and then he was back on Spadina going south of College; and then he turned east onto Dundas. BJ recognized the Art Gallery of Ontario; he recognized 52 Division police station. And his heart sank. He had heard about 52 Division. Wasn't it a police officer from 52 who had shot a Jamaican, many years ago? The policeman moved onto University Avenue, turning left, and took them northwards on University. Apart from the crackling of voices from the other, invisible policemen and dispatchers, the cruiser was quiet.

It was six o'clock and the winter light was fading fast and made the afternoon seem like night. And if night should catch them in this cruiser, alone with this policeman, oh my God! The policeman had not spoken in all this time. He had smoked two cigarettes. They came to Queen's Park. BJ could see the Royal Ontario Museum. He visited the ROM twice a month on Saturdays, to study African cultures and art. And Marco went along with him on many occasions. They had been doing this for three years now. The policeman took the roundabout and they were beside Trinity College, and then back on Spadina. Marco had a cousin who was attending Trinity College; and he took BJ there, one Friday night at dinner, and they ate fish that had no pepper sauce. BJ loved the huge oil paintings and the black gowns the students wore. In all this time, BJ had said nothing. And Marco said nothing. Marco had been slapping his trouser legs. BJ sat with his eyes closed, his teeth pressed down tight, and if you were sitting in Marco's place, you would have seen the slight movement in BJ's jaws.

"Get the fuck out! Get the fuck out!"

It took them a while to realize who had spoken to them. It took them a while to recognize where they were. The policeman came around and unlocked the cuffs from BJ's wrists.

"Get-outta-here! Get-outta-here!"

He had let them off beside the white BMW.

His mother remembered it was a big day on Saturday, a wedding she had to go to, and she rushed from work to get to the hairdresser before he closed. There were many women there; some of them had been there since early afternoon. It seemed that every woman in the place had an important church service on Sunday. Or an important dance date. Or a wedding to go to. She was tired, too tired from a long day, and she dozed off as she sat in the chair. She could barely hear pieces of conversation around her.

"I know a Jamaican man that the cops kill."

"But that was five years ago, child!"

"And in Montreal too. Not here. As a matter o' fact, this particular Jamaican had a daughter who went to school with me, in—"

"I mean a particular Jamaican man. The Jamaican who get killed and beaten-up by the police. Those ladies you was having the discussion with, do they know the Jamaican man in question?"

When she opened her eyes, she realized that the hairdresser, Mr. Azan of Azan's, who was rubbing the grease into her hair, had been talking too. He turned now towards the ladies who were still with their heads over the square sinks, and to the others under dryers. But he did not say anything to them.

"How long is this going to take? I have to get home and see that boy."

"How the boy?"

"Bright as anything. Doing well in school. Someday he going-crown my head with pride and glory. Praise God. But apart from that, sir, he's a boy. And that means he has his ways. How long?"

"Well, let's see. It's going on seven now. Comb. Folding. Gimme a few minutes. You'll be done in no time! No problem. Not to worry. Yeah, man. So, the boy's doing well? You'll be out in no time."

And when she left Azan's, a new woman, years taken from her appearance, years taken from her gait, years taken from her attitude to herself; and with her hair a bright mauve, and shining, and smelling of the lotions and the smell of the hairdressing salon, it was eight o'clock the night. But she was beautiful and looking young and feeling sprightly and full of life. And that was what she wanted for the wedding tomorrow, on Saturday afternoon.

The yellow police cruiser was stopped a few yards ahead of her. It was a dark night. She had looked up into the heavens for a few moments, a few yards farther back, and smiled as she wondered and remembered that in this city, you don't see stars as you see stars back home, when you can become dizzy counting more than three hundred in one raised head with spinning eyes. But when she saw the police cruiser, she became tense and the feeling of paranoia, which came to her every time she saw a police cruiser, came to her now. The black-clad police officers always brought a tense, angry tightness into her chest. And the tightness moved swiftly into her guts. And without knowing, she always felt that it was a black man, or a black woman, but more frequently a black man, who had been stopped by the policeman. In all the time she had been living in this city, she had never seen a white man stopped by a policeman. But then, of course, there had to be some white men stopped by the police. All couldn't be so much more better than black people, she said. And she always felt the black man was innocent. She assumed that. He had to be innocent, she figured, because he was black. And she always thought that the policeman had stopped him for no reason at all; that he was not breaking the law; but that the police were merely testing him, to make him break the law, anticipating that he would break the law, to show the black man who had power and pull and a bigger penis. And the way she always saw the policeman hold his truncheon, as if it was, in fact, a long penis, in an everlasting erection, as if he was telling the black man, "Mine is bigger, harder, and longer than yours!" This is the way she felt whenever she saw a police cruiser stop a black man driving a car.

The night was darker now. She was walking on Davenport Road, going towards Bay Street, and the cruiser was still too far from her for her to see clearly. But she was sure that the man inside the cruiser was black. She hurried her steps. And when she drew almost abreast of the cruiser, it was still too dark for her to see the man's face. The roof light inside the cruiser was not on. But she would bet her bottom dollar that it was a black man, a black youth, a black child.

Her stomach became tight. There were two policemen. She remembered the argument in the hairdressing salon. Two? Or three? There were two. And they were standing beside a car. It was a lovely car. She had seen cars like this one all over the ravine where she worked in a mansion. It was a beautiful car. Many times, standing at the cold, large picture window, looking out into the blank, white afternoons, with the rhythm and blues music from WBLK, the Buffalo radio station, behind her, she had admired these beautiful cars coming and going along the street in front of the large house. This was a beautiful car like those. It was gleaming. It was white. And it blended well with the snow that was not falling. And she wondered why the licence plate did not contain numbers like other licence plates. All it said was BLUE. What a strange licence to have! BLUE. And she was feeling so good just a few moments ago. She understood blues. But what was this blue? He must be in a blue mood. What a strange licence to have! BLUE. But she laughed to herself: she herself liked the blues. Rhythm and blues. She stood taller to investigate. She was sure there was someone in the back of the cruiser. She had just passed the show window of Mercedes-Benz, where the bright colour of mauve in her hair was reflected back to her and showed her bathed and professionally coiffeured and tinted. It had startled her. The bright colour did. For the instant of the reflection, she could not move. She stood there. She looked at herself in the reflection. She leaned her head slightly to the right, and then to the left, stood erect before the show window, and could see not only her reflection but also a salesman in the window looking at her, with his right thumb raised in approval. He had smiled and she had smiled. And then she had moved on, after having stolen a last glance at herself. This was before she had seen the police cruiser. And when she saw it, all that gaiety in the reflection in the show window evaporated.

She was beside the cruiser now.

The two policemen were walking away from the cruiser, going to the white BMW; and she caught up with them. She stopped three feet from the policemen.

"Keep moving, ma'am."

She wondered who was in the dark back seat of the cruiser. And she thought of the Jamaican man, the poor man and his two fatherless girl-children. The papers said that when the policemen burst into the house that Sunday afternoon, just before the peas and rice were dished and served, and the shot was fired, his head burst open just like when you drop a ripe watermelon from a certain height onto the sidewalk. They said his head burst open, clean-clean-clean.

"Why you-all always bothering black people? Why you-all don't go and try to catch real criminals walking-'bout Toronto molesting children? And women."

"None o' your business, ma'am."

"Who say it isn't none of my business? I pays taxes. I obey the law. I have a right to ask you this question, young man."

"Move on, lady! Or I arrest you for obstruction."

"Obstruction? Who I obstructing?"

"What did you say?"

She stood her ground. But she was not so stupid as to repeat what she had said.

"Lord, look at this," she said under her breath. She felt she dared not pray, appeal, nor talk to her God aloud, for the policemen to hear. And the policeman who had spoken to her was about to forget about her, when she started up again. "I hope you're not taking advantage of that poor boy you got in the back seat of that cruiser, and I hope you read him his rights, and I hope he has a good lawyer to defend him. Oh God, for if it was a child o' mine I would surely lodge a complaint against the two o' you with the Human Rights Commission and complain and tell this policeman to please kiss my—"

"Lady!"

The policeman knew there was something said, although he did not quite know what was said. And he became uncomfortable, and nervous, and felt threatened, as if somebody, this woman standing in front of him, with nothing in her hands, save her handbag and a plastic bag full of leftover roast beef, was going to take his life from him. And he rested his hand on the side of his waist where he had his gun.

She took a last glance at the beautiful car, and shook her head with some disappointment that she could not see through the heavy tint of the glass to make out the person inside, and satisfy her mind that it had to be a young black man. But she was not going to give up so easily.

She leaned over the hood of the car, being careful not to smear its sheen, almost feeling the cold of the glass, and she peered through the obstructing glass. Inside, on the passenger's side, was a young man. She could see that much easily enough. But she wanted to be sure, to be certain that this tinted glass was not playing tricks as to the young man's colour. Perhaps he was black, and this tint was changing his colour. She could touch the glass now, and feel the coldness of it, and at the same time, the comforting heat from the engine, even though it was turned off. She stared, and saw him. It was a young man. A young white man. And the man inside the car, feeling his own shame for his predicament, held his head aside, as if he thought his profile would hide the identity of his face from this malicious woman whom he had seen only five minutes before. He did not know her, could not remember ever seeing a woman with her hair dyed mauve, and sticking up in the air, as this woman's hair was doing in the tricky changing light caused by the passing cars. He held his face in a profile against her staring eyes. And felt the curiosity in her eyes, and thought he could feel the love and the sadness in her manner. If he were not handcuffed behind his back, he would push the door open, and invite her in. But what would he say to her? Perhaps, he would call out for help. She moved away, walking backwards for the first few steps, and the smallness of his space, and the fit of the manacles, made the car seat large, and it became larger and embraced him in the growing space of his temporary imprisonment. She was walking backwards to get a last glimpse of the licence plate, BLUE, which still made her smile at its eccentricity. And when she walked past the police cruiser, her body flinched, and she flounced at the policeman, and the tightness that she sometimes deliberately put her body into, to prevent the cold from climbing all over her bones, came to her, as she moved beside the cruiser. She could smell no similar smell of polish as she had done standing beside the beautiful car. She could sense no powerful fragrance of leather in the interior, as she had surmised with the white car named BLUE. And she could feel no warmth from the engine of the police cruiser, as she relished in that short moment when her curiosity challenged her wisdom. The police cruiser was cruel, and ugly, and tense, and made her feel guilty. And in this shame, in this surrender of self-control, she walked away, not being able to tell, should she be asked, what was the colour of the cruiser. But she made a note of the writing on its side. 52 DIVISION. She would never forget that number. And she amused herself, heading to the next bus stop—and if no bus came to rescue her from the gnawing cold, the subway station at Bay—with the idea that if she were a gambling woman, she would play combinations of fifty-two in tomorrow's Lotto 6/49.

Time, and not the consequences or the cause of his presence here, this evening, where he was, was heavy upon BJ's nerves. He paced up and down, with various thoughts entering his head, and his panic and isolation made the space much, much larger, so that he was buried in its vastness, and the time and the consequences, what they could be, and the cause became real and he could see his life, his entire life, in three short hours that had passed. All these things passed through his mind, and for each of them, he had no solution. He paced up and down, not having enough length in the square space to make his pacing more dramatic, and less of pathos. And when he again realized the restriction of the square space, his mind bounded backwards to a time, which he had almost wiped from his memory, when he had spent four hours in this same police station, in another cell, alone and not knowing really why he had been locked up, not having had a charge laid against him, not having had a policeman enter the warm cell and interrogate him about the alleged theft of a kid's bicycle that afternoon in August, when he and three other kids were horsing around and pretending to be bagmen—they did not play with girls—near the corner grocery store, trying to beg enough quarters to buy ice cream, when his mother was at work down in the ravine, when this other kid came wobbly on his bicycle, his first, a present *his* mother had given him for Christmas past; and one of the other three kids took the bike playfully from the little kid and the little kid started to cry and ran home with tears in his eyes and told his mother; and his father returned with sunburned arms bristling with black hairs and chest like a barrel covered with the skin of an animal, with the black hairs punching from under a nylon undershirt and with his underpants showing just above the waist of his green trousers, when the kid pointed at "the coloured fella, Dad. The coloured fella is who took my bike"; and all hell broke loose with *mamma mia*s spewn all over the road in white vomit, and as if it was still Christmas and hail was falling, and the cops came screaming down the avenue going against the one-way pointing of the white arrow, two carloads of them, to solve this ghetto delinquency, that began as a small neighbourhood kid's prank—"I didn' mean nothing"—and *slam!* "into the cruiser, nigger; into the goddamn cruiser, you goddamn nigger"; *mamma mia*, Hail Marys, and BJ not understanding the various languages and accents being vomited against him, no explanation in the eyes of the man who owned the peddling grocery store, no explanation from his three friends who did not know Italian or Greek and were no longer within earshot and speaking distance to translate this crime, no understanding from the father with his chest buried in black hairs, ripping the air with gestures which BJ thought at first were karate chops, but later knew their meaning even though he knew no Italian and no Greek, and no understanding from the four cops who descended armed and sunburned like the father, to solve this serious crime: "Git, goddammit, git! Into the goddamn cruiser! No, not in the goddamn front seat, in the fucking back, where youse belong"; and they took him down, and did not book him, and put him in a nice large warm cell, large through his age, bigger, "goddammit nigger, warmer than the piss-small room you and your goddamn mother lives in! You fucking West Indians!"—and they left him there to stew and to mend his thieving ways, and then, hours later when the time for his supper of plain rice and boiled kingfish and boiled green bananas had come and gone, the truth was known and the kind sergeant came with a Styrofoam cup of steaming coffee: "Have a cup, come now, have a cup"; and then said, "A little mistake, if you can understand what I mean, you being such a little fella to know these serious, big things; a little goddamn mistake and you happened to be the goddamn unlucky one. So beat it, kid, and don't let me lay my goddamn eyes on you again! Git!"

Too young to know what he had done; not knowing what he had done; not knowing what the policeman in the cruiser had done; not knowing the exact shape of his fate this time, but wise enough to know that he was going to have some fate, BJ paced and paced. And then, perhaps because of his Black Muslim sense of destiny, he stopped walking up and down. He decided not to worry. "Let the motherfuckers come!" he said, but within his heart. He was calmed by the small square space, and by his history. And then he worked it out, in detail, and with a logic he was capable of, but which in the circumstances of the steel surrounding him in the four smells of impatience and of no restraint, of vomit and old urine, in the circumstances of an unclear head, he had permitted to elude and overwhelm him. But when he had worked out his plan, he lit a cigarette, all that they had left him, and in his mind, for his mind was clean and not touched by his circumstances, he selected the long-playing record, could see his fingers ease it out of its jacket, and put it on his stereo, and remained standing, listening to the words of Malcolm X's speech, "The Ballot or the Bullet." He was asleep, standing, before the introduction of Malcolm X had finished. And he was stirred from his reverie by the opening of the door, and walked out into the dark cold parking lot, to his car now buried and made invisible by the falling snow. Marco was somewhere else: in another cell, held until *his* parents could come down from North York, to sign him out. Two men walked beside him. They were not in uniform. He recognized his car, for the snow had not touched the letters B-L-U-E on the licence plate. And he made the gesture to go to it, even though he did not have the keys. And he was corrected. "We're going for a little drive . . ." And he was put into the back of the cruiser. Left alone, to himself, behind the plastic protector thick as brick, strong as steel, and with his two hands free. The blue unmarked cruiser drove off in the white pouring quiet.

From the top of Wells Avenue, a street that ran west from Bathurst, she could see the red lights. They were whirring. They scared her so much each time, just to see them, that they gave her the impression they were making great noise, and that the red lights were silencers of that noise. She could see the four police cruisers parked in the middle of the road, and one at the side. She could see the large red, ugly vehicle of the fire department. She could see a smaller, but equally ugly, white-painted ambulance. And from the distance where she was on Bathurst, turning into the smaller street, Wells Avenue, where she lived, she could see the road filled with people. People were leaving doors open and running and passing her as she walked, heading in the direction of the spinning red lights on top of the police cruisers and the fire department truck and the ambulance. She had never witnessed a fire of this bigness in this city before, and so she walked as fast as she could, in the deep sliding snow, to reach the scene.

The road became more crowded when another police vehicle, a small panel-type truck marked TACTICAL SQUAD, forced itself into the road, from the other end of the street. She was sure now that someone was holding someone hostage. She had watched many of these scenes every day on the soap opera shows in the mansion down in the ravine where she worked. And tickled by the transformation of a movie into a slice of her real life, she tried to hasten her stride, but without success, for the snow was too deep. She felt the excitement the spinning red lights gave off, the curiosity of staring at these kinds of lights on a highway ahead of you, and she passed each house from one end of Wells to the next, now as long as a block, her blood quickening, and not once through her mind passed the thought "Who's sick?"; and she did not once consider her neighbours nor the landlord in this absent thought of compassion. It was the excitement she was heading to. People—she could see them now—people were being kept back behind a ribbon of yellow plastic, and one policeman stood guarding the yellow plastic ribbon, which measured the area round one house, and disappeared out of sight, perhaps down a lane, or the thin unwalkable space between two houses, and this ribbon reminded her of birthday parties back home, and on Christmas morning, and once when she was no longer a child, taken by her mother to an opening of something where they had a long ribbon like this before the entrance. On that occasion, the vicar of her church had cut the ribbon with scissors. Her excitement was now in her blood, and with her blood hot, she was no longer recognizing things: landmarks and the shape of the uneven concrete steps the landlord had built incorrectly to save money, and that caused her to slip even in the summer. She was forcing herself against these strangers to reach the entrance. And she could see the splotches and the drying small pools, the spots, taking some time to be registered in her excitement as blood. She could see the blood on the steps and blood along the narrow lane, and the lane became difficult to see, as it went beside the house on the left. A dog walked out as if it was drunk. And when it vomited, what came out was like grape juice.

She could see policemen inside the room, collecting things, some of which they were already bringing out. And she could see the attendants from the ambulance arranging something heavy onto a stretcher. She could see the clothes being brought out. She could see the stereo equipment, speakers, CD player, amplifier. And the books. And the small bible. She wondered who lived here. She could see the books. Books always interested him. And then she realized she was thinking of her son. He always had his head inside a book. And one book she saw him read, again and again, was the Bible, covered in brown wrapping paper. "Thank God!" she said.

She wondered if this was the wrong address.

She could see the policemen inside the room, at the back near the door to her kitchen, walking round the small space, nervous and silent. The street outside was silent too. No one was talking. But she could hear their anger and their resentment and their hatred. She was beginning to learn how to listen to this kind of silence.

And then, there was a sound. A sound very similar to surprise, or to shock, or even to the satisfaction that what you are about to see *is* the shock, but that you are not prepared for it.

They were bringing a body out.

Two ambulance attendants were carrying the stretcher, which had wheels like a bier of a coffin, but which had to be lifted for part of the journey, the short journey covered in deep snow, from the back of the house, down the two short cement steps which the landlord had not got around to fixing properly, a little way to the right of the rear door, and to the ambulance, after going through the thin lane, down two more steps, and up the last three steps of the basement apartment's front door. As they lifted it up the steps, the wind, which was cold and strong, blew the cloth off the body of the corpse. A cry went through the people. It was a young man. A boy, still with his mother's features. No more than sixteen or seventeen or eighteen. A black youth, with a close-trimmed haircut, with Zs for patterns and an X for style, dressed in a black woollen sweater, black slacks, white socks, and black shoes that could, if he were alive, help him to jump against gravity, like a basketball star. A Michael Jordan.

And when the wind had taken the blanket on its short wild curtsy to the night, the people made that sound again, like a gigantic taking in of wind.

She could see it too. And she saw the head, and it was out of shape from something that had hit it. Disfigured. And the blood was covering the face. And the stretcher was covered in thick blood. And the black clothes the youth was dressed in were red now, more than black. The blood seemed to have its own unkind and disfiguring disposition, and it seemed to drip and mark the journey from the room at the back of the basement apartment through the apartment itself, through the small backyard, through the lane, over the deep snow, and out into the cold wind. It looked as if a cannon had struck the head, and the head had exploded and had been cut into pieces, like a watermelon that had slipped out of the hand. To her, it seemed as if the brains of the young man were coming through his mouth, as if his eyes were lost against the impact of the bullet. To her, it looked like a watermelon that had been smashed by the wheels of a car.

It was too much. It was too cold. It was too brutal. It was too cruel. And there was too much blood. Worse than the American soap opera she had watched earlier the afternoon of this Friday night, down in the ravine.

"BJ! BJ! Fuck!"

It was somebody screaming. She did not know the voice. She looked around, in this crowd of people, and recognized only one of them, her landlord. And then she saw the owner of the voice. It was a young man. There were tears in his eyes. He was dressed in a black jogging suit, black Adidas, and white athletic socks, and he seemed to have something wrong with his right hand or his right side, for he was doing something with his body which made it shake, as if he had a nervous habit, like a tic: hitting his right hand against his right thigh. He looked Portuguese to her. She did not know him.

"BJ! BJ! Fuck!"

CHOOSING HIS COFFIN

He is still breathing. The room is hot. His face looks like the polished ebony I had looked upon for so many years, in another place, where it is as hot as here, but where there is always a breeze blowing off the sea. Here, in Willingboro in New Jersey, the breeze comes off the melting black tarred face of the parking lot.

"This hotness!" my mother says.

She wipes her face with a gentleman's handkerchief. She uses this same handkerchief afterwards, to wipe his face, her husband's face.

"This hotness could kill a man," she says.

But he is still breathing. He is lying on his back. Dead to the world. Majestic in his coma.

She would remain silent beside him, standing over him, and just as majestic; and she would abuse the rights and privileges that wives whose husbands are dying have, that are given by the hospital; and she would give instructions to the nurses and doctors without deference to their status and to their knowledge of comas and intensive care.

Slow, and uncertain, we set out, my mother and I, and we come to the first intersection. My mother is not sure if we should turn left, or if we should turn right. And I cannot help her, because I do not live in New Jersey; I do not live in America. I am here, on her insistence, from Toronto, Canada, to "see the Old Man before he dead, boy! He in a coma, now three days going 'pon four."

But slowly, the brand new New Yorker car, which she had bought for his birthday, moves over the cleaned, empty streets, and we pass trees and hedges and telephone poles and signs advertising churches of all denominations, and signs for daycare centres, and my mother is still debating with herself the wisdom that "if you are ever loss, it is always more better, in the circumstances, to take the left-hand turn. If possible."

She falls silent for a moment; and then she says, with a declarative confidence, "If there is ever a left to take, take the left, boy."

She turns the radio on, and the voice of a radio evangelist shouts through the speakers at us, ". . . for the whirl is becoming more sinful. Oh Lord! Mankind is become more vilent. He is burned in a mire—oh my God!—in a mire of ungodliness, and sin . . ."

"Praise God, boy!" my mother says, talking to the evangelist and to me. The preacher's sermon is a judgement against all mortal men, spoken in a smooth, thick, syrupy Southern seductiveness. A voice pleasant as molasses.

Cars pass us in the left and in the right lanes, and some come towards us. We drive as if it is yesterday, Sunday, and we are sightseeing in the afternoon after church. In this Monday morning sun, people going to work honk their horns at our indolence. I am following the cadences of the preacher's voice chastising us. We are all lost, he says. I feel I am lost. In this Monday morning traffic, I know I am lost. My mother accepts being lost, and covered in sin, in irredeemable sin from head to foot.

"We're loss, boy," she says.

"And when the day of judgement come, oh my Jesus-God-in-heaven . . ." the preacher screams through the radio.

"First," my mother says, ignoring the preacher, "I want to choose a nice, quiet spot for him."

". . . and on that judgement day, brothers and sisters, I hope there is atonement for some of y'all . . ."

"These Amurcan preachers could turn you into the worst sinner by the words o' their sermons!"

In the slowness of our wandering drive, the morning seems to be no longer morning. Night seems to fall miraculously out of the skies, which a few moments ago were blue and bright. But now, it feels as if we are travelling along streets that are in the South. And it is night.

But immediately, we come out of this dusk and fallen black ashes, and we see women and men walking the streets, the same streets we are now driving on.

"Turn here! Here, boy!" my mother screams.

I slam on the brakes. And she sits in silence, shaken and sullen.

"Jesus Christ, boy! You intend to kill your mother? You don't know your left hand from your right?"

We come to a large, unpainted wooden arch. It spans the entrance.

"Oh my God!" she shouts, "Turn here! Turn! Turn here! Here, boy! This is the place!"

RANCOCAS BURIAL GROUND AND CREMATORIUM is printed in large white letters on the arch, which is now turning brown from the sun and the New Jersey rain.

I drive the New Yorker slowly through the arch. And I stop just outside a small wooden building, painted white. The white paint takes up the sun, and shines it back into my eyes. A very small sign says OFFICE.

It is quiet here. The speeding cars on the street, a few yards behind where we are stopped, seem miles away. A man on my right walks with a long green hose which he pulls along the grass as if he is extracting a worm of interminable length from the bowels of the ground. A second man wearing coveralls walks behind him, carrying a garden tool, a spade.

There is a large map on one wall of the office. The map says "You are standing here." And with difficulty, I find myself, the position I am standing in, among the plots of graves and the numbers given to the plots, marked in red on the directing map. There are no names. There is a fan overhead, like the fan in my mother's kitchen. There is also the sound of laboured breathing, my mother's and the office man's. Inside this office, it is as hot as it is outside on the street. Not like being inside the air-conditioned, loquacious New Yorker car, which had reminded us, just a moment earlier, "Your door is ajar!" And my mother had answered the mechanism, and had told the car, "Why the hell you don't stop talking to we? You don't have no damn manners, yuh know!"

She is standing outside the car now, fanning herself with the makeshift Chinese fan which she has buckled back and shaped from the supermarket advertisement announcing bargains in fruits.

"This hotness! This Amurcan hotness, boy!"

We walk behind the man, from his office, in single file, through the manicured paths lined with graves. I look at the clusters of grass and flowers, some growing in the ground, some in plastic vases, some in soda pop bottles. There are diminutive American flags on many of the graves. The flags do not move. There is no wind. The flags look as if they are washed in starch. But it is quiet here.

"Be prepared, boy," my mother says. And I wonder why she says this to me.

We walk on in the same file, through the avenues of the dead, each spot, each grave, each plot marked by a stiff Stars and Stripes, until we come to the end of the grounds.

The three of us stand under a tree. It spreads its leaves and branches over the three of us. The green leaves do not shake, do not move, and they hover over us like green-painted sculptured figures.

"This is my big-son," my mother tells the man.

"Yeah," the man says, and looks into the lifeless leaves.

"Lives up in Canada," my mother says.

"Yeah," the man says. He is still looking up at the dead leaves.

"A big professor. At Yale. In the Ivy Leagues, boy!" she tells the man. The man is older than my mother by many years. When he looks at her, I feel as if he is looking at a piece of plate glass that has no object in its transparency. "You ever hear about Yale University?"

"Is that right?"

"In the Ivy Leagues, boy!"

"Is that so?" the man says. He stops looking at the unmoving leaves in the tree, and he looks down at the thick reddish soil, checking where we are standing against the grounds plan in his hand, and says, "Here we are!"

My mother looks down at the ground, following the man's indication of it, the ground covered by this thick, strange, healthy grass, smirched in spots by the footprints of the two men nearby, gravediggers, whom I had seen earlier with the green hose and the spade. My mother is intrigued by the strange reddish colour of this earth and ground, in this country of Amurca, that is so different from the dark brown, almost black soil of her own island back there in the West Indies, and she places the makeshift Chinese fan, painted with pictures of fresh fruits shown in detail, with drops of water on those fruits—peaches, pears, plums, apricots, and red grapes—and she raises the fan to her face. And then, without warning, she gives out a cry. A moan. A noise from the bottom of her belly, as if she has been stuck by a deadly blow, delivered at lightning speed, and . . .

I move quickly to her side. And I put my arm around her shoulder. She puts all her weight upon me, and I stumble. She is more than two hundred pounds, heavier than me, heavier than the man.

"Is she gonna be okay?" the man says. Not much concern is in his question.

I do not answer him. I want to push him into the empty grave we are standing beside.

"Happens all the time," he tells me. "People, all kind and colour, choose a spot, and doesn't blink a eye. But the moment I brings them out, and they see the spot they reserve and pay for, wham! I brings them out here, and shows them reality, it hits them like a goddamn whammy!"

"I am all right, son," my mother tells him.

"You all right, lady," he tells my mother.

"Daddy uses to sit under a tree, I remember, the spitting image of this one we now standing underneat', in his cane-bottom chair . . ."

And she laughs. "It was a mango tree, I remember . . . in a cane-bottom chair, reading. And the last colour that he paint this same cane-bottom chair in, just before he emigrade to Amurca, was green. I remember. You remember?"

I do not remember. And I do not answer. I had never seen the Old Man sitting under a tree.

But I can see the colour of the barbecue advertised at bargain price on the rolled-up page of the newspaper ad, and a jumbo-sized box of detergent, as my mother fans herself with the makeshift Chinese fan, passing it back and forth before her face.

"Go-back, and bring that motor car, that always talking to we, up here, boy!" she tells me.

I feel she needs to say something confidential to the man, so I leave promptly, and head down the incline to the office, where the New Yorker stands silent. I hear my mother laugh, a second time, and the last thing I hear her say to the man is, "And I hope you didn't forget that I mention to you that I want to be put 'side o' my husband . . . when the day come . . . if it is your willing . . ." And from my distance, approaching the New Yorker car, I see my mother looking up into the air, into the tree whose leaves do not shake.

I take the path for cars, back to where she is leaning against the tree that shall shade her husband's grave. From the distance where I am, I think I see her shoulders heave, and a large gentleman's handkerchief is held to her mouth, as if she is stifling a deep emotion, or if she expects to cough up something from her chest, and is preventing this thing from erupting through her mouth.

I park the car under the tree, and she gets into the back seat, leaving the door open, ignoring the reprimanding car telling her, "Your door is ajar!"

She fans herself. But now, she obeys the reprimand, and closes the door.

I remain in the front seat, looking through the haze of the windshield, at a large mausoleum that contains the body of Mr. Rueben

Starkman, beseeching him to "Rest in Peace. Beloved Husband of Martha Starkman. Born 30 July 1920. Died 25 December 1992." How did Mr. Starkman die? I try to imagine how he died: collapsed over the dinner table, while carving the turkey? Or in bed, on a full stomach of stuffing and skin, celebrating the holiday season, or yuletide—or even Christmas, and virility, and abandon? And I wonder how many more days, or years, before it will be time for the stonemason, who cut Mr. Starkman's biography into the pol-ished marble, to wait until he shall cut Martha's details into this granite memorial.

"We come a long way, boy," she says. "One more stop. In the mall. The convenience store next."

And she gives me a smile, and the smile breaks out into a giggle. I am back there, in that small island, years and years ago, when she was young and frisky and would throw me up into the air, and giggle, and catch me, on the way down . . . and she would go back to eating the kernels of roasted Indian corn, clean from the cob.

"Wonder if he still breathing? Wonder how the coma . . . ?"

It takes me a while to realize she is speaking about her husband.

There he is, in intensive care, in the Willingboro General Hos-pital, out of sight, on an iron bedstead painted in white enamel, with a rubber sheet to protect the mattress and prevent his pee from rusting the iron frame of the bedstead, a guard against his incontinence, and from becoming too acrid and rising unbearably into the nostrils of the white-uniformed nurses and the white sheets pulled high up over his body.

"Wonder how Daddy breathing?"

I stop the New Yorker at the convenience store in the mall, and wait for her to mention her request.

"What do you want?" I ask her.

"What do I want? You being funny with a question like that? What you mean, what I want? What you think I want?"

"Pringles potato chips?"

"Boy, use your damn head!"

"Chewing gum? Soda pop?"

"Don't be a blasted fool! What would a grieving woman, a widow woman, want at a time like this? You is a professor?"

The wickedness in her smile paints her face with a girlish blush. I can see her, years and years ago back there, smiling as she tears the peel from the sugar cane with her bare teeth.

"Hennessey!"

"You mean brandy?"

"Cognac, boy!"

"And a bottle o' soda to go with it, and . . ."

We are stopped at the farthest end of the parking lot in this shopping plaza where I have bought the bottle of Hennessey. I had entered the liquor store alone, and as I was wandering along the brightly lit aisles, fascinated by the different kinds of brandies and cognacs sold in this small New Jersey town, and marvelling at the cheaper prices of liquor compared with Toronto, my mother had crept up behind me. Just as I was about to lift the half-size nip-bottle of cognac from the shelf, she whispered into my ear, "Not that! What two big people going-do with that nip-bottle? The big one, man, the big one. The forty-ounce. You could take-back some to Canada, by pouring it in a nip-bottle. The biggest one, boy!" She was speaking directly into my ear, in a whisper, although there was no one close to us. She spoke in whispers whenever she had important things to say. And her whispering made me feel that she and I were two teenagers, much below the legal age for buying liquor, later to be drunk in the back seat of a car, or else on a corner of a dark road, parked out of sight, our drink hidden in the brown paper bag in which it was bought. "Get the forty ounces, man!"

Her smile forestalled all comment on her little conspiracy, and I was washed in it, and made to feel I was a conspiring friend, rubbing my hands together in glee, in sweet satisfaction for having broken New Jersey's liquor laws. It was the kind of feeling that went through my mind when I had stood before the man at the cash register, and saw him ring the purchase into the noisy machine.

We were still smiling when we returned to the New Yorker.

"Your door is ajar!" it said to us, just before we closed the doors.

We are sitting in the car, still parked; and with the doors closed, and the motor turned off.

"Keep she running," my mother says. "In case a police. We could drive-off fast, and lose him."

And we sit and sip, and watch men and women enter the plaza to shop; and I sip the brown liquid that scorches my throat, and listen to my mother's voice, as she revels in this illegal drinking. I do not normally drink cognac. My drink is beer. But I am with my mother, in her talking car, and this is America, the land of the free, she tells me all the time, and the occasion is a communion I had never expected to fall upon me. She is talking: ". . . that much he owe me, he owe me that much. After fifty-something years o' marriage, after I bring him here to Amurca, paid for his ticket on Amurcan Airlines, from the money I mek working overtime for the Jewish lady in the brownstone on Columbia Heights . . . I was holding-down three jobs to bring-him-over, with the rest of the family, five boys and the girl, from Barbados to Brooklyn . . ." She takes a sip of Hennessey. ". . . so, he have to now make his peace with me. And with God. The pastor, Revern Doctor James of the Delaware Valley Baptist Church, last Monday, pray for hours and hours over Daddy, that Daddy would come out o' the coma. Daddy start going-church only a few days before the coma hit him. Never once, in Barbados, and seldom here in Amurca, he went-church. He preferred to listen to the church services on the radio, coming from Voice of the Andes and the South. Night after night . . . Yes!" She takes a sip. "I sit on his hospital bed sponging-him-off with a washcloth dip in cool water. But Daddy don't have a chance in hell! . . . Pour li'l more Hennessey in this plastic glass for me, please. Cover it up with a touch o' some more soda water, in case a police . . ."

She is on her third Hennessey. I am still nursing my first.

". . . and so, I sit on his bed, on the right-hand side of his bed, rubbing him down; and waiting. Waiting for a sign. Far's I concerned he gone. He's gone. He is a goner . . . It is so cruel, though, for the man you married to, fifty-something years, to just fall into a coma, without warning, communications between you and that man cut off, punctured like a motor-car tire, all the air gone . . . to just fall into a coma, my God, and dead, without telling you good-bye, thanks, abba-synnia! Nothing? Not a damn word of farewell? Nada. Caput. No leave-taking. Not even a adios?

"And one night. Around three. In the morning. Daddy start gargling words in his throat. Trying to talk. To me. And guess what that man I married said to me? After thirteen nights of me mopping-off his forehead with a cold washcloth? Guess what he said to me."

"I don't know," I say.

"He didn't say nothing. Not. One. Damn. Thing. Not a iota!"

She takes out the large white gentleman's handkerchief, and dabs her lips with it. She crushes the plastic glass with her hands, and wraps it in a large white napkin from Kentucky Fried she found on the floor of the New Yorker. It was from the three barrels of chicken she had ordered in, two nights ago, when her other children, the five boys and the girl, arrived from Brooklyn.

She places the plastic glass in the plastic garbage bag attached to the knob at the bottom of the dashboard. Through the window, she drops the plastic bag on the ground; she changes her mind, opens the door; the engine is running softly all this time, and she bends down, and picks up the plastic garbage bag, and drops it on the floor. The car says, "Your door is ajar." She laughs.

"How can uh door be uh jar?" she says, laughing.

She laughs some more at her humour, and pours herself a fresh plastic glass full of soda water, gargles it about in her mouth, and spits the water on the ground. It splatters with the same sound as vomit, onto the pavement.

"Beg pardon," she says.

I put the New Yorker into first gear.

"Funeral home next! Let we hit there before the sun set . . ."

"But he is still breathing," I tell her.

"Yuh can't wait till he dead, to choose his coffin!"

She is laughing as she says this.

"Yuh can't wait till he gone to buy a box to put-he-in."

She is still laughing as she hands me a bottle of mouth spray.

"Take a sprig," she says, "in case the police . . ."

I squeeze a spray into my mouth, and think immediately of sitting in a dentist's chair. And she takes two more deep sprigs, as she calls them.

"Otherwise, he might find himself in a plain deal-board box, like the ones they buried convicts in, in Amurca."

"You picked out the funeral home?"

"I got one in mind."

"You picked out a church?"

"The one we just pass. With the long white Cadillac park in front."

"Which funeral home?"

"Goes Funeral Home."

"He going by Goes!"

"I don't find that funny. Talking so 'bout your stepfather . . ."

"I do not find it funny either."

"When you come to the next lights, make a slight turn to the right—No! Not the right! The left! No, no, what I saying? Left! Make a slight turn to the left, and you going see the place on your right, staring you in your face. Goes! I know these directions like the back o' my two hands!"

I take her word, make the turn, and find myself climbing a slight hill, bordered by large trees, like the ones on the Rancocas Burial Ground and Crematorium property. These trees hang over to form a canopy over the blacktopped road; and the New Yorker goes into the semicircle of the driveway, as if it is steering itself. We stop at the front door. The canopy of trees is blowing softly, but gaily, just like my mother's voice.

Goes Funeral Home has four white, fat pillars built in the style of Southern colonial mansions. I think of *Gone with the Wind*. And I imagine that I am in the deep South. No ivy clings to these unblemished, white pillars. The trees are blowing gently in the breeze.

On this building there is only the Stars and Stripes. It hangs in languorous slow movement from the pillar, from the flagstaff, nearest the front door. No name is written on this building.

"Press the bell, boy."

And I press the bell. I look at the large trees, and at the three highly polished, black cars that are parked between lines drawn in white luminous paint on the black surface of the tar. Facing the cars are three names, printed on strips of wood: Manager. Assistant Chaplain. Chief Embalmer.

"Press again, man."

While my finger is still on the white dot of a bell, the door opens. Silently, as if there is no hinge. A smell hits my nostrils. It is a smell I have never known. This smell comes out and hits me in the face, like an exhaled bad breath, the very moment the door opens. This smell that has no name. This smell . . .

"Oh, good afternoon, Missis Springer!"

The man is almost singing greetings. His hand is outstretched in a handshake. His voice is sweet. And soft. And deep. And baritone. I think of Billy Eckstine. Of Perry Como . . .

"And good afternoon to you too, sir!" he adds. "This must be the son from Canada, who teaches in the Ivy Leagues!"

My mother remains silent. I am thinking that it must be the atmosphere that dampens her spirit.

"Welcome. Please enter. I am your funeral director . . ."

He offers his hand to my mother; my mother puts all her weight on his much smaller frame; and he loses his balance, just for one second, but he adjusts himself to her weight, while she breaks out in tears. She starts to sob, loudly. And then her sobbing becomes a wail, a moaning, like it was in the burial ground.

Half stumbling, he leads her inside the vast white room, decorated with off-white couches, and white wingback chairs of the same upholstery material, and mahogany chairs painted in off-white. Fresh-cut white lilies are in nine white vases.

In four corners of this vast room are floor lamps. They give off a golden, soft illumination. It is very quiet in this room. And very cold.

My mother turns the neck of her blouse back to form a collar, to keep her body warm. She folds up the newspaper with the advertisements for fruits, and puts it into her purse.

"This coldness, boy," she says. "This coldness. . ."

And she breaks down without warning, and collapses, and cries out, making sounds with her breath: holding her breath, and then exhaling, as if she is choking on her own sadness and sorrow.

"Can I offer you some coffee, Missis Springer?" the man says. "Sugar and cream? Or milk?"

"Li'l Hennessey."

The man raises his eyebrows. His eyebrows are bushy. His eyes become larger.

"Well, if that will help."

"And the coffee, afterwards. Cream, please," she says.

Her tears remain and stain her face, and walk across her white face powder, as she holds the large white starched gentleman's handkerchief in a firm grip, in her left hand. With her right hand, using her three middle fingers, she taps out a tune whose rhythm is different from the one her shoes are tapping on the off-white carpet.

"And for you, sir?" the funeral director says, from a white door built invisibly into the white panelling.

"Sorry?" I say.

"How do you like your coffee?"

"Black," I tell him.

He disappears once more, into the white panelling. My mother looks at me, and says, "Boy, what a thing, eh? This coldness."

"Could kill a man," I tell her.

"We have to choose a nice coffin, for Daddy. With a large enough opening . . . a oval suitable for viewing, that viewers in the church, the brothers and the sisters, could see him good. And dress him in his black suit. What you think?" she asks me. "All I doing, for the whole day, is spenning money on a dead man. What a thing, eh, boy? Let we look at something solid. Like something in greenheart wood, with a lining of red silk. You think they have greenheart wood in Amurca? Something solid I want. *Lignum vitae.* Before I left the first place, I left a cheque with that thiefing bastard, the graves people, for two plots. One for me, and one for Daddy. Boy, if you was living here, instead of in that cold place called Canada, I woulda take the opportunity and buy a plot for you. Yuh can never tell 'bout death, boy. Flourishing today; gone tomorrow . . . Lord-in-Heaven! And God only know what kind o' figure I facing now, with Mr. Goes! But he must be sent-'long nice, in the best manner I can afford, although he don't deserve it. But it is me who would have to face the embarrassment if he didn't send-'long in the best manner I can afford, and nice. What you think?"

I know she does not really expect me to answer. I think she is getting accustomed to the cold, shivering impersonality of this white waiting room.

"These Amurcan undertakers, eh, boy? Back home, we christen them 'duppy agents.' They can take you for a ride, and when they let you off, and you are still able to dismount and get down, when the last tears are shed by the graveside, and they drive off, you are left only for the poorhouse. So, here I am, spending this kind o' money on a man I have no love for, only hate! You know if I can buy one o' these coffins on the layaway plan? Put a li'l something down, and every month when I catch my hand, pay-off the rest, on the first o' the month? You have that up in Canada?"

And just as the funeral director re-emerges, my mother lowers her voice. He holds a silver tray, on which are a white coffee pot, white sugar bowl, and two smaller white bowls, one with cream and one with milk. Hidden by the large coffee pot is a snifter of cognac.

"They does-stock Hennessey in a funeral home? Boy, what a thing!" my mother whispers. She smiles, and pinches me on my leg. "I hope it ain't enbamming fuel they serving we, eh, boy?"

The man is too close for me to comment.

My mother puts the glass to her lips, holds her head back slightly, her eyes closed, and swallows the rich, brown liquid.

"Hennessey!" she says, squinting her eyes.

"Hennessey," the man says.

"Nothing but the best, eh?"

"Nothing but the best for my best custom—clients!"

"Praise God, boy!" my mother tells him. She steals a glance at me, and in that glance, she winks furtively, and says, "For small mercies."

"Coffee, now?"

"Coffee, now."

She sips hers, making slurping sounds as she cools the hot liquid. The little finger of her right hand is cocked out, at an angle of forty-five degrees, from the adjoining finger. I have not touched my coffee.

I am preoccupied trying to find a name to give to this smell that surrounds us. It is now around me, and I feel I can touch it, I can feel it, as if I am submerged in warm salt water in the sea near our house, back there in the island. It is now around me, and I can sense it on my clothes, in this peaceful, white waiting room. Perhaps, I am the one breathing it out. Perhaps, the smell comes out through my pores. Perhaps, it is fear. Perhaps, it is my discomfort at being in a funeral home to choose a coffin. Perhaps, the smell comes from me.

"Take your time, ma'am," the funeral director says. "We have time."

"All the time in the world," she says.

"We have time," he says.

"Time, boy," she says. "Time, and more time."

"I didn't exactly mean it quite that way."

"Still," she says. "But I still have time . . . I will take my time choosing a nice coffin, a proper one."

"That's why we are here, aren't we?" the funeral director says. He puts on a sorrowful and compassionate countenance, with a face matching his words, spoken in a soft baritone. "In this time of deep, sad sorrow . . ." He does not complete the sentiment.

"Ready. I ready now," she says. And to me, she adds, "Come, boy!"

We go down a flight of stairs covered in thick white carpet, in silence, my mother sliding her left hand on the banister, as we go down into a basement.

We come to a large door. It is stained in a dark, mahogany-like colour. Mr. Goes presses something in his hand, and the door opens without a sound. Arrayed before us are coffins.

Coffins according to model, coffins according to manufacturer, coffins according to the material used in their construction; coffins from wood, durable wood, and from wood easy to rot in the earth, coffins from a material that is not wood; coffins according to colour. They reach almost to our necks. Rows and rows of coffins.

And all of them are on stands, as they would rest on biers that sit in the chancel of a church. And from them comes the unidentifiable smell.

My mother stands at the door opened for her to enter. But she does not move. She bursts out into a moan, from the bottom of her belly, a sound of deep, bruising defeat, and pain.

And then she falls.

The coffins, in their number and power, are too strong a force for her composure, and they force her to the ground. In total collapse. I get to her, when she is already fallen. Her weight is now in my arms, heavy and pure and raw. And dead.

"I am all right, boy!"

She brushes my arms away, and passes her hand over the coffins, touching them, and then removing her hand a moment afterwards, and breathing a heavy "Ahhhhh!"

I feel the revulsion she must feel from being here, in this basement, to do this choosing. To touch this wood, and have the wood come alive, take on a personality, perhaps one to match her husband's spirit, to have her entire body shake with the sadness from that touch, and shudder from what that touch really means. Touching wood. One week before the coma buried him in his own powerful introversion, she had said, "Daddy ain't had a day of sickness, in all his years. Touch wood."

The coffins surround her, like lifebuoys in the sea back in that island.

"This coldness, boy! This coldness . . ."

She is writing something. Not with her own ballpoint pen, but with the funeral director's Mont Blanc fountain pen, which he offered her. When she finishes writing, the golden nib flashes, and she gives the pen back to him. A smile of satisfaction comes over his face. It is another day: another dollar. This is the end.

The smell in the basement dissolves, and vanishes.

"We got him a good one, didn't we, sir?" she says.

And the funeral director smiles, but says nothing.

I have been left out of the transaction.

We sit in the visitors' parking area, in the New Yorker, and for a while, I do not turn the ignition key. And she does not speak to me.

My mother is far away, on some journey, perhaps back in the hospital ward; perhaps she is rehearsing what she will say to the nurses and to the doctor, when she takes up her vigil, later tonight. Perhaps, on her watch tonight, he will sense her presence, in some kind of telepathy, and acknowledge and feel the soothing, cold washcloth being rubbed against the bristles on his chin.

I turn the ignition on, and the New Yorker says, "Your door is ajar."

"Shut your blasted mouth!" my mother tells the New Yorker, and laughs, as she was laughing when we were drinking the Hennessey from the brown paper bag, in the parking lot of the shopping mall.

The road disappears before us, in the blazing headlights. It is night. Outside the car, it is black, and soft, and thick, as if we are in the South. I imagine a smell. A different smell from the one in the funeral home. The smell, that comes into the car with us, is the smell of magnolia. In this new glee of perfume, we reach the driveway of my mother's large house; and I park the New Yorker car.

My mother prepares herself for getting out. She touches her face, while she looks into the small mirror in the sunshade, and she presses her lips together, and shows her teeth, and passes a pink Kleenex tissue over her teeth, as if it contains toothpaste. And finally, she squirts a "sprig" of freshener into her mouth.

Music comes bursting loud and with iron in its beat, from deep inside the house, when the door is opened. My five brothers are home.

The door is left unlocked. The windows are wide open. And unlatched. This has never happened before, in the twenty years she has lived in Willingboro. My mother always keeps her house shut, bolted, protected, and safe, from "them," meaning her neighbours.

She is disoriented, and confused.

"Those five brutes bringing Brooklyn up here in Willingboro!" she says, limping out of the New Yorker. "Today cost me a good penny, boy!" She looks tired, and her limbs are cramped. "I argued all I could, to get that man to agree to a refund, in case Daddy emerge from out the coma. But all that duppy agent tell me was, 'Madam, all sales is final. I think you can understand that, Madam.' Christ, Daddy-boy, you cost me a good penny . . ."

And the voice of Bob Marley sweeps over her words, burying them; and she acknowledges the softening of her own disgust in the words of the song:

No, woman, nah cry,

No, woman, nah cry . . .

We are climbing the single step to the front door.

"You looked good today, the way you were dressed," my mother tells me. "You made me proud, boy."

The telephone is ringing.

She leans her weight heavily on me, and I walk with her, slow in this embrace, through the long hallway, with the music of Bob Marley on the stereo in the basement, where my brothers are drinking, pounding into our ears.

"Look how those five brutes have this heathen-music licking-down the house, all day!" she says to the house.

The telephone is still ringing. It is eight o'clock, the hour that she takes up her nightly vigil beside his enamel bedstead.

"He gone," she says. "He's gone. Oh, my-God-in-heaven . . ."

Her face is serene. And there is almost a trace of a smile of relief, moving across her lips.

"Don't answer it," she says. "Let it ring. I know the meaning of these telephone calls, this time o' night. For years and years, I took them when I was a practical nurse at the Brooklyn General Hospital . . ."

And then the expression on her face changes, and the smile becomes a grimace, and it's like tanned leather, tough and old. And her shoulders droop.

She picks up the telephone, and holds the instrument at her side. I can hear the static of a woman's voice: "Is anybody there? Hello? Is anybody there? Anybody home?" I take the telephone from my mother's hand. And put it to my ears. The voice of the woman says, "Missis Springer? Missis Springer? This is the hospital . . ."

And my mother sits now on the stool attached to the small table on which the telephone rests, saying over and over, "After all the money I spend on him, today? After all this money? Is this the gratitude he repay me with?"

My mother takes the telephone, still crackling with the woman's voice, out of my hand.

I look at her sitting on the telephone bench, the receiver in her hand, holding it at her side, and then at her heart, and with her face washed in tears. The large white gentleman's handkerchief covers her face.

"You believe this?" she screams. "You bloody well believe this?"

And there is a pause, and the pause grows into silence, and I can hear her breathing, and then she tells me, "Daddy came outta the coma."

And she remains sitting, and sobbing, into the large white handkerchief she had taken from his chest of drawers, that hides her face.